ALABAMA
DAYS

"*Alabama Days* carries the reader through intrigue, danger, and romance. With writing that sparkles, characters come alive, and relationships develop, both socially and spiritually. Who is to be trusted? What are the consequences of stealing an unknown medication, of finding a flash drive that someone wants destroyed? These mysteries will keep you in Alabama till all is resolved."

~ELEANOR GUSTAFSON,
author of *An Unpresentable Glory* and *Dynamo*

"Daphne takes small-town intrigue, tosses in romance and a strong thread of redemption, and creates a story romantic suspense readers will thoroughly enjoy. A definite heart-warming—and pulse-pounding—read."

~SUSAN L. TUTTLE,
author of *At First Glance*

"A compelling story of small-town corruption and an unstoppable romance, *Alabama Days* entertains while also presenting readers with the hope of the Gospel."

~HEATHER NORMAN SMITH,
author of *Grace & Lavender* and *Where I Was Planted*

"Blockbuster action and a heartwarming story filled with characters who are realistic and well crafted. Recommend Daphne Self for a story that lasts beyond 'The End'."

—LUCY THOMPSON,
author of *Mail Order Surprise*, *A Cowboy's Dare*, and "Waltzing Matilda" of *The Captive Brides* Collection

ALABAMA
DAYS

DAPHNE SELF

Formerly published as D.M. Webb

AMBASSADOR INTERNATIONAL
GREENVILLE, SOUTH CAROLINA & BELFAST, NORTHERN IRELAND

www.ambassador-international.com

Alabama Days

ISBN: 978-1-62020-712-3
eISBN: 978-1-62020-736-9
Library of Congress Control Number: 2020938608

Cover Design and Interior Typesetting by Hannah Nichols

Scripture taken from the New King James Version®. Copyright © 1982 by Thomas Nelson. Used by permission. All rights reserved.

Elliott, Charlotte. (1789-1871). "Just As I Am." Public Domain.
Stead, Louisa M.R. (1850-1917). "Tis So Sweet to Trust in Jesus." Public Domain.
Van Deventer, Judson W. (1835-1939). "I Surrender All." Public Domain.

AMBASSADOR INTERNATIONAL
Emerald House
411 University Ridge, Suite B14
Greenville, SC 29601, USA
www.ambassador-international.com

AMBASSADOR BOOKS
The Mount
2 Woodstock Link
Belfast, BT6 8DD, Northern Ireland, UK
www.ambassadormedia.co.uk

The colophon is a trademark of Ambassador, a Christian publishing house.

My thanks is given to my Lord Jesus Christ, first and foremost. Without Him, I am nothing.

To my husband, Nathan, you journeyed with me throughout the years it took to write this novel and never stopped encouraging me. I love you forever and a day.

To my sons, Caleb and Blake, you made all this worthwhile. Follow your dreams because you can make them come true.

To my mom, you listened and offered advice as I wrote Scott and Angela's story. You were there at the beginning, and you will always be there at the end. You helped make this possible.

To my cousin, Jason, thanks for taking me to the "deepest jungles of Alabama" all in the name of research.

To my family at Ambassador International, God put you in my life for a reason, and I am blessed to have you by my side. To my editor, Katie Cruice Smith, thank you for helping me strengthen this novel.

PROLOGUE

The ambulance's sirens grated against Scott Wilson's ears. He grimaced and flung out his hand to catch the sliding clipboard as the vehicle careened around the sharp curve.

Scott glared at his partner. "Douglas! There's gonna be need of a second ambulance if you don't slow down."

Douglas Tomlin shot a suave grin in his direction and turned his eyes back to the road.

"Relax, Scott. Not going as fast as you think." He snatched the mic from the dashboard and chucked it in Scott's lap. "We're here."

Scott grimaced again as he took in the scene ahead of them. Five-car pile-up. Some victims were mobile. Garrettville Fire Department on hand. Emergency responders triaging.

He pressed the button. "Dispatch, show Medic Two on scene."

He kicked the door open and grabbed his red field bag as he leapt to the ground. Douglas veered to the right toward a group huddled around a black Ford pick-up. Scott took the left.

"Scott!" A firefighter waved him over to a smashed-in Chevy Cobalt.

The familiar little blue car sparkled in the bright sunlight. A little sapphire glinting against the coal black asphalt. The firefighter half-submerged himself inside the shattered back driver side window.

"Chief, whatcha got?" Scott pushed the older man out of the way with his shoulder as he slipped on his green nitrile gloves. They snapped against his wrist, sending a sharp sting down his hand.

He leaned in and swallowed the lump that crawled up his throat. Not good. Not good at all.

"He looks to be about three or four years old. We've managed to stabilize his head, but we don't have a child's collar. Used rolled towels instead. None of us can get an accurate reading on his vitals, but he's falling fast. Boys are bringing Jaws to extract him . . . "

The chief's voice faded away as Scott leaned into the cramped space. The towels provided little stability to the child's head, but it would do until they got him out. He wormed his way further in and pressed his fingers against the white, soft skin of the little boy's neck.

A thready, slow beat tapped against the pads of his fingers. He ran his hands down the small body still encased in the car seat. A pained moan, more of a whimper, issued from the unconscious child as Scott's hand brushed against his legs.

"Scott! Hey, Scott!"

Hands pulled at his belt loops, hauling him out of the small space.

"Jaws is here, man."

Scott stood back as a burly firefighter rammed the monster of a tool between the car door and its frame.

A screech fought against the symphony of sirens, yells, and sobs. Traumatic musical in B flat. Scott's hand beat out a tempo against his thigh as the screeching came to a crescendo. Then silence descended upon him.

Mouths moved. Hands grabbed. Scott leapt forward. Another firefighter, smelling of burnt rubber, assisted him.

Scott grunted as they lowered the car seat to the asphalt. His scissors sliced through the belts of the seat. Blood pooled underneath his knees.

Pooled? Urgency hit him in the chest. His heart slammed heavily against his rib cage. "Give me the pads and tape!"

A gloved hand with a fistful of gauze and a roll of tape reached over his shoulder. He grabbed the materials, ripped the packet open, pressed the gauze tight against the open wound on the boy's leg, and stripped a piece of tape off the roll.

One pass. Two.

He pressed it tight, staunching the flow.

He slid his hand behind the little neck, cradled the head, supporting it as he and a firefighter lifted and lowered the little boy to the backboard.

Scott ripped his stethoscope from his neck and pressed it against the boy's chest. No heartbeat. No respiration.

The firefighter had the portable defibrillator out and prepped. Scott tore the child's shirt in two. He slapped the pads against the pale skin.

One. Two.

"Charging."

Another firefighter positioned an air bag over the child's mouth and nose. One puff. Two puffs. Blood trickled from the child's mouth.

A high-pitched beep shattered the silence.

"Clear!" Scott held out his hand; the air bag disappeared; and he pressed the button. The electric jolt caused the body to spasm. No beat.

"Again!"

The air bag resumed its rhythm. Scott pressed his fingers against the little chest and beat his own rhythm. Another high-pitched beep.

"Clear!"

Zap. Nothing. No beat. No count.

"Again!"

The air bag resumed. Scott pressed. A beep split the air.

"Clear!"

The little body issued a spasm. Scott looked at the machine. Flat line. No beat. He ripped the leads off and pressed the chest again. "Bag him!"

The firefighter hesitated with the air bag. Scott shoved him away.

He bent down. Blood slicked his lips as he covered the little boy's mouth and nose with his own mouth.

One. Two. Three. Back to the chest. Press. Press. Press.

Again.

One. Two. Three.

Press. Press. Press.

A hand landed on his arm and pulled him away.

Scott hurled a curse and lashed out. His hand slammed against the heavy material of the fire chief's turnout jacket. One of the men lowered a thin sheet over the boy.

They had no right to make him stop. He would make this child live again. Just watch.

Scott threw the sheet aside and resumed his duty.

One. Two. Three.

He lowered his head to the chest. No beat. No rhythm.

One. Two. Three. Air inside the little lungs. One. Two. Three. Again. No beat. No rhythm.

The vaguest hint of a voice penetrated his head. "Scott! Stop. He's gone."

This time, gentle hands pulled him away.

Sounds rushed back to Scott.

Sirens wailed. Cries drifted across the hot, summer air. Yells from the firefighters clashed against the soft murmurs of the police officers taking statements.

Scott stood and stared at the surreal scene.

The little boy lay at his feet, blood beneath his small body. The sheet, slowly sopping up the blood and bunched around his shoulders, looked like little, battered wings. An angel on a Christmas tree highlighted by the red Christmas lights.

He turned away as he wiped the blood from his lips. Inside the car sat Julie Bergmann. Dead. He glanced back at the little body of Billy Bergmann. Dead. Now the house down his street would be just as silent, just as dead.

If there was a Heaven, then maybe he was there with his momma. He snarled. Heaven was a fairytale for the weak.

Scott pushed all thoughts away from him.

He snatched his bag off the ground and moved to the next victim. Again, silence descended upon him as he worked the next patient, assessing the wounds. His mind played his mantra. Quick. Precise. By the numbers.

One. Two. Three.

His hand trembled as he applied splints to the leg of the man before him. He cocked his head. In his silence, in his little bubble, a soft, childlike laughter echoed. Billy's laughter during yesterday's daycare field trip at the ER.

CHAPTER ONE

A ngela Mabry glanced in the rearview mirror. She pushed a wayward curl back under its band. The red lock sprung out again and tickled her forehead. She grimaced and then shrugged. Oh, well, couldn't be helped. Nothing ever tamed her hair, so why even bother with it now?

Her car door squeaked as she pushed it open. She slammed it close and slumped in defeat as her purse pulled at her. Great. Perfect. Absolutely spectacular.

She fumbled with the lock, opened the door, freed the bag, and slammed the door close again.

Angela took a deep breath as she stared down the brown brick building. The squat, one-story *Garrettville Gazette* occupied the corner of the eastside of downtown. The only one-story building on the square.

It had been quite a few years, but apparently Garrettville changed nothing. The dinky, downtown square was still narrow and ramshackle. A gust of autumn wind whipped at her light cardigan and fluttered the green and black canvas awning.

She huffed a sigh. Time's a-wastin'. She crossed under the tattered awning and pulled open the double glass doors.

Cool air greeted her, and goosebumps traveled up her arm. The reception area was empty. Faint clacking sounds of a keyboard tap danced up the gray-hued hall to her right. A phone trilled in an office to her left. Muffled opera music filtered past the closed door. Beyond that, she spotted a small, brown paneled hall. Angela walked to the entrance of the hallway.

"Hello?" Her voice echoed to the back, where the whirr of machinery murmured behind a set of swinging doors. She ventured further down the hall. "Hello!"

The doors burst open. Angela cocked her eyebrow at the skinny blonde with red-tipped spiked hair and more metal on her face than in her mouth. She apparently had a side job as a burglar. Black liner generously encircled her eyes, which sported glittering blue massacre.

She smiled and popped her gum. "Hi. Sorry, we didn't hear you come in."

Angela caught the fragrance of roses as the girl breezed by. She followed the camouflage-garbed girl back to the front of the building. "You work here I take it?"

"Yes, ma'am. Receptionist, copygirl, delivery driver, gopher—you name it, and that's me. Rochelle's the name. And how may I help you?" The girl settled in her chair, nudging the mouse to wake up the computer.

Angela placed her purse on the tall reception desk. "I'm Angela Mabry. Mr. Tom Echols is expecting me."

Rochelle nodded. "Oh, yeah. He said the new investigative reporter was coming in Wednesday. That's today! Hold on while I get him." The girl swiveled the chair around and ignored the phone. "POPS! Your appointment is here."

Angela jumped as the shout bounced off the walls and ceiling.

The left office door opened. "Gracious girl, didn't I tell you to use the phone? I'm trying to run a professional newspaper here, not some fish market."

"Sorry, Pops. I'll write a Post-it note so I'll remember next time." Rochelle jumped up and sailed down the hall, yelling over her shoulder, "Gotta finish the run! Machine two is jamming, Pops. Need to call Jackson to fix it—"

The double doors swung closed behind her, shutting off the rest of her sentence.

Angela turned to face Tom Echols. The man grinned and held out his hand. "Angela Mabry. Goodness, it's been a long time. Come on into my office."

She grabbed her purse and followed him. Tom Echols hadn't changed much. Still balding. Still wearing black pants, white shirt. She half-expected to see a chalk smear on the back of his slacks.

Walking into his office, music assaulted her ears before he twisted the knob to lower the volume. Papers fluttered on his desk as he settled in his leather chair. It squeaked beneath his weight. "I'm sorry I didn't hear you come in. I always have the music turned up. It helps me write when I have to do the editorials. So, how was the drive up?"

Angela sat in the hard-back chair across from the desk and lowered her purse to the floor. "It was tiresome. Long. But we made good time from the coast to here. Thanks for asking, Mr. Echols."

"Tom." He smiled. "I don't teach anymore since I took over the *Gazette* ten years ago."

"Tom, then. We got settled in yesterday."

Tom leaned forward, his left elbow bumping a bronze paperweight to the side. "You moved into the old Bergmann house on Johnson Street?"

Angela nodded. "Yes. It's small, but in a quaint way. Max, my five-year-old, loves it. Nice yard. Even has the white picket fence."

Tom smiled. "It is a nice place. If there is anything that needs fixing, let me know. I know of a few guys who are handy with a tool, and it wouldn't cost you much. Speaking of money, I posted it in my email to you. The pay here isn't the same—not even close—to what you were making in Mobile."

Angela nodded. "I know. And that's fine. I knew it would be a reduction. But I really wanted to move back to my hometown."

She accepted the forms Tom handed across the desk to her.

"Take these home. Fill them out, and I'll get you started on the payroll. There is one hitch to your position."

A truckload of lead dropped into her stomach. "And that would be?"

"You'll not only have the investigative reporter position, but you'll also cover the social function position, too."

"I see. But no pay increase for the second position."

Tom laughed. "No. Actually, we just call y'all reporters and tell you what kind of reporting you will be doing. There really aren't any positions, but I like to make my *Gazette* sound professional, you know."

Why was she not surprised? Angela stood when he did. "I see. Well, then, first thing in the morning?"

"Bright and early, Ms. Mabry."

"Angela. If I'm to call you Tom, then please, call me Angela."

"Okay." He held the office door open for her. "I'll see you in the morning, Angie. Have a good rest of the afternoon."

Angela cringed at the hated nickname as the door slammed shut behind her. Music resumed its thumping against the wall.

She stood there and stared at her surroundings. Rochelle was nowhere to be seen. More than likely still in the printing room. That ghostly keyboard still clacked away somewhere down the other hallway. Framed front-page editions hung on the walls. Pinned directly across from her, dominating the wall, was a large map of Garrettville.

Two potted bamboo plants stood sentry at the door as she turned to leave. Yes, she'd accepted the job; but no, she didn't expect this. A complete and utter one-eighty from Mobile.

She let the door bump close behind her and heaved a sigh. The afternoon sun glared across the sidewalk. Traffic filled the area. She frowned. Traffic clogging downtown in a rinky-dink town? Oh, yeah. The shortcut to the high school led through the square. She glanced at her watch. Yup. Three o'clock. School's out.

Well, if she could handle Mobile traffic, then this would be a piece of that clichéd cake. Angela stalked to her car and hoped that it would be coconut cake. Then it would fit right in with her nutcase of a job, her nutcase of a workplace, and her nutcase of a brain for accepting the position in the first place.

"Mom!" Max's voice greeted her as she pulled open the screen door to Ms. Dottie Berryhill's house.

Angela swept him into her arms. "Hey, munchkin. How was your visit with Ms. Dottie?"

Max wrapped his arms around her neck and leaned back. His hazel eyes sparkled as he looked at her. "She made me some 'oconut cookies. They tasted just like yours, Mom. But they was a little brown on the bottom. But I didn't tell her I didn't like the brown because that would be rude, and you told me to never be rude, so I ate it anyhow."

Angela hugged him. "Thank you, Max. That was big boy of you." She set him down and trailed behind him into the living room.

Dottie sat on the living room couch, another older woman next to her, sharing a cup of tea. Angela's mouth watered at the sight of Dottie's *English Breakfast* tea. Crumbs littered the platter beside Dottie's periwinkle teapot. Teatime was coming to an end.

"Angela, come sit down for a moment and have tea with us, dear. Max, you can go out back and play with Frolic. Just be gentle; he's an old, tired doggy."

"Yes, ma'am!" Max raced from the room, and the back door slammed shut.

Angela stifled her groan as she sank into the soft cushion of the white wicker chair. Heaven. Dottie poured tea into another delicate cup and handed it to her. She took the cup, sighed at the warmth that seeped into her palms, and sipped. Ah, another piece of Heaven.

"Angela, this is Mrs. Debbie Wilson, who lives three doors down from me."

Angela held out her hand to the tall, white-haired woman. Her aquiline nose dominated her soft features while sharp, blue eyes peered at her. Full lips curved into a welcoming smile.

Slender, cool hands slid into Angela's hands. "I'm so glad to meet you, Angela. And welcome back home. Dottie tells me that you used to live here."

Angela nodded and settled back into her chair. "Yes, ma'am. Fifteen years ago. Lived in Mobile, but I wanted Max to grow up in a small town instead of a big city."

Ms. Wilson cocked her head to the side. Angela hid her smile behind another sip of tea. The woman resembled an eagle. A mamma eagle, watchful, intent.

She hesitated slightly. "You moved into the Bergmann house?"

"Yes, ma'am. I knew Jake Bergmann growing up. I was sorry to hear about his wife and son. Actually, he wanted to move to Mobile. So, we practically traded houses. Worked to both of our advantages." She set her cup onto the saucer. The warmth of the tea settled into her bones, inducing a drowsy state.

Ms. Wilson tsked behind her teeth. "Yes, yes. My grandson, Scott, was heavily affected by the death of them. The Bergmanns were good friends of his." She set her cup and saucer down on the coffee table. "I'm glad to have met you, Angela. Your little boy, Max, is a precious child."

"Thank you, Mrs. Wilson."

The woman leaned over and patted her knee. "Oh, child. You're Dottie's friend, so you can call me Debbie. None of that Mrs. Wilson stuff. I'm an old lady and don't need to feel any older."

Angela laughed. "Yes, ma'am. I'll remember that. It was very nice to meet you, too."

Debbie turned to Dottie. "Well, I need to leave. Scott gets off work in a while, and I want to make him a good supper tonight. I declare that the man is skinnier than a string bean."

Dottie laughed and rose from the couch. She followed Debbie to the door. "You and Scott will come for supper Friday night?"

Debbie nodded as she pushed the screen door open. "I told him. He said he will try and make it, but he might be a little late. Fridays are very hectic for him." She waved to Angela. "Make sure you come visit soon, Angela."

"I'll try, Ms. Debbie."

The two ladies filed out the door and onto the porch. Angela raised her cup and drank another sip as she replayed the woman's conversation in her head. She'd have to look up the story on Julie and Billy Bergmann again. She didn't remember Jake mentioning a Scott before. Curious. She shook her head. Enough. It was teatime, not investigating time.

Still, a part of her wondered. Who was this Scott? Why did Debbie Wilson hesitate before mentioning the Bergmann House? And why in the world did Tom Echols hire a girl like Rochelle?

Scott pushed open the door and sighed as the aroma of pot roast greeted him. He pulled off his uniform jacket and hung it on the stand in the corner of the foyer. The pocket rattled. Scott grimaced. He had forgotten about that.

He dug the orange container of pills out of the pocket and slipped them inside his cargo pants. He'd put them in the room soon. No need to worry Nana Debbie.

"Scott?"

"In the foyer, Nana Debbie!" He emptied his other pockets onto the side table. Wallet. Keys. Lip balm. Parking ticket.

Yeah, need to pay that soon, or Dan would hunt him down.

"Go wash up, honey. Supper's ready."

Scott rounded the corner and greeted his grandmother as she set the platter of pot roast on the table. "Why in here, Nana?"

She cocked her head, and he dropped a small peck onto her papery, soft cheek. "Thought it would be a nice change. Don't you get tired of eating in front of the telly?"

He shook his head. "Not really. And why do you insist on calling it *telly* instead of television or TV?"

"Because telly has such a nice ring to it." She smacked his hand as he reached to pluck a piece of the meat. "Go wash up."

"Yes, ma'am." He filched a piece as she turned her back before leaving the dining room.

Nana Debbie's Siamese cat barred his way into the hall.

"Not in the mood for you tonight, Judas. Go find your mouse; or better yet, go jump in Dixie's mouth." He nudged the cat out of the way with his foot and hissed as Judas' claws sank into his ankle. Scott bent and picked it up, cradling the fat female in his arms. "Infernal cat. You win . . . this time."

Her purr rumbled as he toted her into his room. A small Boston Terrier raised his head. "Dixie, dinner time."

Judas jumped down from his arms and raced out of the room with Dixie hot on her heels.

A crash echoed from the living room. Hisses and barks followed, along with his grandmother's shout. "Scott Weatherby Wilson!"

He grinned and closed his door as Nana Debbie scolded the animals. Scott chuckled to himself as he entered his bathroom. He and Jake had spent long hours training them to chase each other on the command of "Dixie, dinner time." It was all harmless fun. Someday, she'd realize that they were only playing.

He turned the water on. Half-turn for cold. Full-turn for hot. The pills in the container rattled as he slipped them beside the toilet paper rolls on the shelf near his sink. He frowned. The items had been moved. Nana cleaned today.

He front-faced the rolls, lining them evenly with the edge. That was better.

Scott unbuttoned and stripped off the smelly blue uniform shirt. Tomorrow, he needed to remember to take his uniforms in to the cleaners. The raunchy smell of dried sweat and other body oils assaulted his nose as he threw it in the hamper. Yeah, definitely tomorrow.

He tugged his undershirt over his head and threw it into a separate hamper. A shower called, but the smell of dinner tantalized him even more. He ducked his face down to the sink and scrubbed at the grimy film, rinsing it off his skin. Stubble scratched at his palms.

He turned off the water and dried his face and hands. With a critical eye, he pulled the towel over the bar until its edges were even and separated the hand towel from the bath towel. He pushed the bath towel down another inch until there was an even amount on both sides. There. Better. He grabbed the pill containers and walked into his room.

Dixie pawed at the closed door as he walked to his closet. He turned the knob as he passed by; and the dog, tongue hanging out in a goofy dog grin, bounded on his sleeping pad.

"Dixie a good boy? Yeah?" Scott pulled open the nightstand drawer and dropped the orange medication bottles inside. They rolled around until they nestled against the black, frayed Bible that had belonged to his grandfather.

He closed the drawer and padded to his closet. Dixie thumped his tail as he spoke to him. "You get the kitty? He's a good doggy." He pulled a brown, long-sleeved t-shirt from the brown hanger.

"Scott!"

He pulled the shirt over his head, leaned down and rubbed the dog's head, and left the room.

"Smells good, Nana." Scott settled into his seat and straightened the placemat as his grandmother set his plate in front of him.

"Thank you. I made you a pitcher of unsweet tea." She sat beside him and lowered her napkin into her lap. "And I need a favor from you, dear."

Nana's bribe of unsweet tea was duly noted. The vague memory of his father liking the same came to mind as he held out his plate, which dipped when she dropped a large helping of mashed potatoes onto it.

"And that would be?" He spooned some carrots and celery from the pot roast broth and added two slices of roast on top.

"Dottie's new neighbor moved in yesterday. I was wondering if you can do a few handyman jobs on the house for her."

Scott shrugged. "She doesn't have anyone to do it for her? Unmarried?"

His grandmother nodded as she filled his glass with unsweet tea. The ice clinked as it settled. "Yes. You know I don't gossip, but Dottie said her husband killed himself a few years ago."

"Horrible." Scott twirled his glass around. "So, that's the woman who traded houses with Jake? I knew he had two people interested, but he didn't tell me who it was." He sipped his tea. "He stopped telling me anything."

Nana Debbie placed her hand over his. "I know it was hard to lose your best friend, Scott. It was equally hard on Jake to lose his wife and child."

Scott forced a smile and pulled his hand out from under hers. "Six months ago. That's over and done with, Nana." He cleared his throat and pushed his potatoes to the side, away from his carrots. No touching. "What's needing done over there?"

"Loose boards on the porch, and I think Dottie said something about the back room's light fixture. And I can't remember the other. Something with the pantry."

"I'll see if I can fit it in, but only if it's okay with the woman. What's her name?"

"Angela. Angela Mabry." Nana stabbed at her pot roast. "I also have another request."

"Hmph." Scott shoveled the potatoes into his mouth. "Let me answer that before you ask." He cleared his throat. "No."

"You don't even know what I was going to say."

"If it's about the animals, you say it every other evening. And my answer is no."

Nana Debbie huffed and chewed her roast for a moment. "Then at least train them to go out the back door and not around my knick knacks."

Scott smiled. "They go wherever Judas takes them. Serves you right. Judas for a female? Dixie for a male? You're going to give them a complex."

"Oh, pooh. They don't know that. You should see what he does when I call him 'cupcake.'"

"Whatever, Nana." He grinned as the dog waddled through the dining room and into the kitchen. "The poor animals. To have to live with such a stigma."

Judas padded into the dining room and jumped up onto an over-stuffed corner chair by the bay window. His mouth twitched.

"Dixie, dinner time!"

Judas leapt off the chair and tore off after the dog. Dixie yelped and scampered down the hall. The sound of books falling off the hall bookcase echoed.

Scott mouthed along with his grandmother's shout. "Scott Weatherby Wilson!"

He chuckled and continued eating. Oh, how he loved baiting his grandmother like that.

CHAPTER TWO

Angela threw the last of her folders into her thin briefcase and then turned to the hall mirror to check her clothes one last time. She shouldn't give a rat's bumper about how she looked, but it was a Monday. She didn't need to *look* like it was a Monday.

She smoothed her jacket's lapel. A small, red strand flipped out of her headband and curled itself against her forehead. Stupid hair! She tucked it back one last time just as a tiny body hurled itself into her legs.

"Mom!" Max clung to her legs.

Angela smiled and brushed at the small tears that clung to his lashes. "Max. It'll be fine. Remember Sammy and Mr. Johnny from church? They're going to make sure you're okay."

"But, Mom, can't I just stay home? I can go next year. I promise!"

She sighed and knelt down to Max's level. Her little man. "Kindergarten is fun, sweetcakes. You'll have a grand time. We met Mrs. Allison last night, remember? She's going to be your teacher. You had no problem back in Mobile. What's wrong now?"

Max stuck out his bottom lip. "I don't know no one."

A horn honked outside. Angela scooped up her briefcase and Max's backpack. "Come on, big guy." She ushered her reluctant son out the door, locked it, and turned to the yellow bus waiting at the end of the walkway.

Max's feet dragged as they approached the bus.

"It'll be fine. It'll be fun." Angela smiled at the driver as he opened the folding doors. "Johnny, good morning!"

"Morning, Angela. Max all ready for his first day?"

Angela slipped the backpack onto Max's shoulders and gave him a nudge. "Not quite."

"Max!" The owner of the squeaky voice poked her head out the window of her seat. The girl pushed her tangle of blonde hair out of her eyes. "You gotta see this. Bubba found this cool bug!"

"Sammy! Really?" Max flew up the steps and then halted. He looked over his shoulder at Angela. "Bye, Mom! Have a good day!"

She smiled as his little form bounced into the front seat and huddled with two others, their heads bent peering into their companion's hand. Angela glanced at Johnny. "Well, I take that back."

Johnny laughed. "See ya, Angela. Drop him off at Dottie's?"

"Please. She's keeping him in the afternoons until I get off work."

The bus's doors hissed closed. With a grind and a belch of putrid smoke, it slowly pulled away from the curb. Angela waved goodbye to the three pairs of hands. She sighed and turned to her ratty Grand Am.

She shook her head as she slid onto the cold seat. Maybe she should've warmed up the car first. This morning offered little time to worry with pleasures. Her nerves jumped around until they threatened to escape her skin. Even her stomach flipped at such a pace that she had barely touched her food. Max had enjoyed the second helping instead.

Angela pressed her hand to her stomach as she cranked the car. Oh, it had to be still. Stupid jackrabbits were determined to make her lose the coffee she had drunk. This wasn't her first day, for crying out loud.

She backed out of the driveway and wrinkled her nose. It had to be the stupid schedule. Tom just had to move things around on her. After her two days in last week, this was what she got. Mondays and Tuesdays on ambulance chasing. Wednesdays and Thursdays on editorials. And Fridays on investigative. Order, order, order.

She jammed on the brakes at the one red light on her road.

"Order. Not for this lady. Reporting is all about spontaneity." Angela reached over and turned up the radio. "Someone's going to think you flipped your wig if they see you talking to yourself, Angela dear."

The light turned green, and she drove straight for another two miles before turning into the main part of town. She relaxed slightly.

A thin line of traffic moved both ways on the main road.

"Far cry from Mobile." She turned her car onto the small street that led into downtown. Buses filled one of the lanes. She frowned.

Now *there* was a piece she needed to research. Why was the school so determined not to use the side streets? Yeah, they were bumpy and potholed. Why couldn't the town repair them properly? What was Garrettville's budget like?

Angela slowed to a stop behind a bus and grabbed a small notebook out of her console. She glanced around and then jotted her questions down on the paper. Now she had a story to investigate on Friday, if she survived today.

She followed the bus through the light and then pulled into the small parking area in front of her building. Time for work.

She hopped out of her car, the door barely missing her jacket as it closed, and she hurried to the doors. Chaos greeted her.

Rochelle yapped on the phone, her hand flying across the pad in front of her. With the other hand, she threw a notebook at Michael, the typing ghost from down the hall. He pushed his long bangs out of his eyes before he grabbed the notebook and disappeared to his office.

The clacking of his keyboard mingled with the crashes, beeps, and yells. Tom rushed out of his office as Angela passed by. He barreled across the reception area and down Michael's hall.

"Rochelle, what's going on?" Angela picked up a stack of messages from her inbox on the reception desk.

Rochelle replaced the receiver in its cradle and grinned. "What do you mean?" Her ever-present gum smacked in her mouth.

"All the running around. We get a big lead on something?"

The girl laughed and fluffed her vibrant red-tipped strands. "I wish. This paper is becoming a bore. Nah. This is a typical Monday. Pops has to get Michael on the ball, so we can have the stories by Wednesday's publication. Michael takes his own sweet time doing those political bits. And—"

"Angie!"

Angela cringed. How many times did she have to tell him? "Tom?"

"I've got a story for you. Come to my office."

He barreled back past her. The whirlwind that followed him buffeted against her. Good gracious!

She followed him and slid into the hard chair. "So, what's up? Thought I was working on ambulance chas—I mean, personal interest stories today."

Tom grunted. "You are. Came over the scanner. You missed the car accident at Follows and Turnpike; but I bet if you went to the hospital, you can grab some info. Take the digital camera with you and take some pictures of the accident or the scene. Whatever is left." He pushed the small Canon Powershot toward her.

Angela scooped it up and dropped it into her handbag. Tom handed her a sheet torn from his notepad.

"Time is—"

"Of the essence." Angela flashed Tom a bright smile—or at least as bright as she could on this Monday. "Heading out now. Hear of anything else, give me a call."

She glanced back at Rochelle as she padded out of Tom's office. The girl had the phone plastered to her head again, her voice barraging the poor soul on the other end with questions. Michael yelled for Rochelle from his cave. Angela shook her head and walked out.

The morning sun pierced her eyes. No gray Monday today. She read the address from the slip of paper. Follows and Turnpike. Intersection accident. Probably boring, but she'd see if there was anything there that might spice up the report.

Doubtful. She threw her handbag and briefcase onto the passenger seat and scowled as she backed the car into the road. What did Garrettville offer other than Farmer Joe's lost cow standing in the middle of Little Deer Road?

Two black smears stared at Angela. She toed the burnt rubber pattern with her boot. Pieces of glass sparkled in the morning sun, and she squatted and moved the pieces of tempered glass around with her fingers.

With a huff, she stood and surveyed the rest of the accident scene. The metal guard rail lay crumpled along the edge of the curve. The tracks led to it and then veered sharply before abruptly ending. She narrowed her eyes and followed the tracks.

There was nothing. She turned and overlooked the scene from her new vantage point. Again, nothing. Wasted trip. She raised the camera and shot a few frames of the accident—or whatever remained of it.

She pulled the small notepad from her jacket pocket as she walked back to her car. Her list ran only half the page. She clicked her pen and checked off *accident scene*. Now only five more things left on the list.

Her phone issued its customary bubble-pop sound as a text came through. She tapped the icon and read the latest from Tom:

Check w/ PO for report before returning.

"Great. Another on the list." She reopened her notepad and squeezed in that order between *hospital* and *city hall*.

Her car protested with a grinding groan as she started it. Time for a tune-up apparently. She pulled away from the side of the road and dialed her phone.

"Garrettville General Hospital, how may I direct your call?" The chirpy voice grated her nerves.

"Emergency room please. EMS director." Angela turned left onto Springs Run Road. She rolled her eyes at the road sign bearing the name. There wasn't a spring, creek, or body of water along this road.

"One moment."

She sighed and waited. And waited. The next turn came up, and Angela took the left onto Jamison Avenue. The hospital loomed ahead.

"Assistant EMS Jonathan Trickle."

"Jonathan Trickle? Is Grace Harrison available?" She drove her Grand Am into the parking area near the emergency entrance.

"Today's her day off. May I help you with something?"

"Yes. My name is Angela Mabry with the *Garrettville Gazette*. I need some answers, please." She slammed the car into park and pushed open the door. "Will you be available?"

She slammed the door shut as silence answered her for a few seconds. "I'm not sure. I have a pretty hectic schedule. I can see about fitting you in sometime tomorrow or the day after."

Angela smiled as she approached the automatic doors. They swished open, and cool air rushed past her.

"Oh, I only need a few moments, Mr. Trickle." She hurried inside the lobby. Amber-lit lights greeted her as she strode across the green diamond patch carpet.

"Well, I have only a few moments right now, but the rest of my afternoon is crammed. Let me put you down—"

"That's great, Mr. Trickle. I'm in the lobby now. I'll tell the receptionist that you are expecting me. Thank you for taking this time to see me." Angela disconnected and pocketed her cell phone. Her boots clicked as she strode from carpet to tile on her way to the desk.

The receptionist looked up from the computer as she approached. "May I help you?"

Angela shot the white-haired lady a smile. "I'm here to see Mr. Jonathan Trickle. He's expecting me. Angela Mabry."

The woman pursed her lips as she picked up the phone. She turned away and spoke into the receiver in a hushed tone. Her hair wiggled dangerously atop her head as she nodded. She turned to Angela and nodded at the double doors to the left of the desk.

"Go right through there, honey. Take the first right and follow the bend to the ER desk. Mr. Trickle will see you as soon as he can."

"Thank you so much, uh—" Angela peered at the woman's shirt. "Mrs. Connie."

A bright grin lit the woman's face. "You're welcome." She pressed a button on the wall behind her. At the buzz, she waved Angela through.

Brightly polished corridors gleamed under the harsh fluorescent lights above. A couple of blue-garbed nurses walked past. Angela turned to her right and ventured down the hall. Most of the rooms were empty. She approached a curtained off area and fought down a smile at the old man griping about being there.

She peeked through the crack in the curtains as she passed. A nurse placated him in hushed tones as she hooked monitors to him. He leaned over the edge trying to swing his feet to the floor. Angela raised an eyebrow and continued straight.

The hallway curved to the left. Angela rounded the corner. She slowed to a stop and absorbed her surroundings. A door labeled *Restroom* occupied the end of the small hall behind her. Bright sunlight poured into the ER from the emergency doors to her right. Ahead was a smaller hall with a swing door.

She turned to her left. Trays and stacks of paper jumbled the high counter of the dark blue desk. For an ER, it was quiet. A nurse in maroon scrubs came from behind the area. She skidded to a stop when she saw Angela.

"I'll be with you in just a moment." She hurried down the hall and around the corner. Her voice echoed back, "Now, Mr. Donaldson . . ."

Angela pulled out her notebook as two EMTs came through the small door behind the desk. She studied them as they pulled out the chairs in the corner. The youngest looking one, his blond hair falling into his eyes, kicked back and propped his booted feet onto the desk. His partner, burly and balding, swiveled his chair around and straddled it. He started peeling an orange as he spoke.

"Where's he at right now?" He chucked a portion of the peeling in the trash can by his feet.

"He was right behind me. Remember, it's veggie day. Make it good." The blond one smiled and popped his soda can open.

Another man with close-cropped dark hair pushed through the door and dropped a digital tablet on the desk near the EMTs. Angela arched a brow at him. Blood splattered his shirt in odd places, and he held his watch between his teeth as he flipped through some files in his hand.

"So, dude, I told you . . . " the blond one said with a smile. "The secret service squash saw it happen."

The dark-haired man paused and dropped the files on the desk. He quirked an eyebrow at the younger one and shook his head as he rounded the corner of the desk.

Angela moved out of the way slightly. She peered at his uniform. A splotch of blood covered the name, but "paramedic" stood out in blue thread.

He slowed down and glanced at her, his lanky form towering over her. He removed his watch from his mouth and fastened it around his wrist. "Help you any?"

The balding EMT's voice boomed. "Yeah, well, haven't you heard that the Peas Police already labeled them as untrustworthy?"

"Seriously? You're trusting peas? Everyone knows all the reliable information goes through Baker Beanstrom," the blond EMT retorted.

The paramedic rubbed at his jaw. Stubble rasped against his hands. "Ignore them, miss. I'm heading to pharmacy now for their psychotic meds." He shouted over his shoulder, "You are idiots!"

"Oh, come on! Beanstrom? He's only saying that stuff to impress that sweet potato of his . . . " the balding EMT continued.

Angela shook her head. What had she walked into? "I see . . . "

The dark-haired man smiled. Laugh lines crinkled at the corner of his eyes. Extremely white teeth—so white she suddenly felt the need to brush her own—peeked out. "Seriously, ignore them. I try to. So, you here for someone?"

The maroon-scrubbed nurse returned just then and pointed to his uniform. "That's my job. Now, you're violating policy. Go get cleaned up before I label you a health hazard."

"Was heading that way, Arlene. You're as bad as Nana Debbie." He winked at Angela and sauntered to the end of the hallway. His lanky body disappeared into the small washroom.

"I'm Arlene Nesbit. You must be Angela Mabry. Connie rung and said you were heading this way. Jonathan just went to the south wing, but he'll be back in a moment." Arlene sat down at the desk and pulled a few files toward her. "You here about the wreck?"

Angela clicked her pen. "I am. Anything you can tell me?"

"Not really. I haven't been cleared to say anything, but it wasn't as bad as it seemed. Although, how the boy wrecked there is beyond me. That spot is not normally a hazard."

Angela scribbled Arlene's statement in her hybrid shorthand and grinned. She mentally noted to check on the location and see if any other wrecks had happened there.

The blond EMT walked over and leaned over Arlene's head. He moved one of the trays until it sat at an angle to the others, and then he pushed one of the stacks of paper until it teetered dangerously.

"Mercy, Douglas, do you have to torment the poor man like that?" Arlene shook her head and turned back to Angela. "I'll ring Jonathan and see if he's back."

Angela nodded. "I appreciate that."

Douglas glanced up from the desk and hurried back to his chair. "Mack, dude, we've been over this. It happened. If you want to know for sure, just ask Count Carrot."

Arlene rolled her eyes and reached for the phone. "Don't pay any attention to them. Every day, they lose brain cells."

Talk about lack of professionalism.

Angela opened her mouth, but the dark-haired man's deep voice spoke behind her. "Arlene." He reached out and straightened the tray and stack of papers. "Jonathan just texted. He's back in the office. Said he had a visitor."

Angela turned to him. A dark blue t-shirt with Garrettville General Hospital's logo on the breast had replaced his uniform. "I'm the visitor."

"Oh, okay. Well, follow me." He glared at the two others.

"—not talking to crummy Count Carrot. I'll go to Granny Green Bean instead."

Angela stuffed her notebook into her bag, "Arlene also said to ignore them."

"Good advice." He motioned to the small hall ahead. "This way."

He pushed open the swing door.

One of the medic's voices followed her through the door. "Oy vey! I hate going to Granny Green . . . " The rest of the sentence stopped abruptly as the door closed behind them.

"There's not much to say about the wreck, by the way." His coffee-brown eyes glanced over his shoulder at her.

"What makes you think I'm here about the wreck? I haven't even introduced who I am."

"No need. Snazzy clothes, big bag, notebook, pen. You're the new reporter for the *Gazette*." He gave her another razor-sharp smile as he tapped on an office door. "Small town. No secrets."

Angela slid past his paper-thin form. Bet no one could hug that man without getting a paper cut. "Well, we'll see about that. Every town has secrets, and it's my job to discover them."

Again, his eyes twinkled. "Interesting." He gave the paunchy man behind the desk a half-salute. "Jonathan, here's your visitor. And Dr. Melbourne's looking for you. Glad to meet ya, miss."

Then he was gone. Angela blinked. Such a strange morning.

She turned to the man seated and held out her hand. "Angela Mabry with *Garrettville Gazette*. Appreciate the time you are taking to answer some questions for me. First, I would like to know about the procedures followed at the scenes of wrecks before we get to the specifics."

His deer-in-headlights look rooted him in place. She gave a bright smile. Oh, an easy target. One up for her.

Scott paused before the swing door. He glanced back at Jonathan's office. Bet the pretty redhead was bowling him over with questions.

She looked like a tough chick. He grinned. Bet she was like those hard candies. Tough outside, but sweet goo on the inside.

Trouble waited there. He had enough to deal with. No need to look for more.

Douglas glanced up as Scott walked back in the room and took a seat in Arlene's now-empty seat. "The food is good but her long stemmed sprouts kept attacking me."

Mack laughed and nodded. "Well, duh, man. You should never have called them squeamish sweet peppers. They're way sensitive."

Scott dropped into the comfy chair across from them. "You two have way too much time on your hands." He leaned forward and straightened the trays. People never kept things straight around here.

"Yeah. Slow day. What do you expect us to do?" Douglas flipped through a *Southern Homes* magazine.

"Well, for one . . ." Scott turned Arlene's chair around to face the boys. " . . . you and Mack can go do a count of supplies in number three. Plus, swab it."

"Now?" Mack frowned as he picked at his fingernails with a pocketknife.

Scott threw a clipboard at Douglas. The young man caught it against his chest. "Yeah, now. Privileges of being higher rank. I call the shots with you two."

Mack thumped his shoulder as he walked by. "Yeah, until Jonathan finds you something to do. Better get out of Arlene's chair before she gets back."

The two disappeared down the short hall and out the emergency doors, their strange conversation about vegetables becoming an argument about the merits of asparagus versus beets.

Scott pulled another folder to him and browsed the charts. Only three patients. Mr. Donaldson—a long-time visitor. Shelby Pierce—the young teenager he and Douglas brought in from the wreck. Gina Portsmith—in for severe abdominal pains.

Scott ran his finger down the chart. Maybe one of these days, the hospital would get with the times and use computers. Probably wishful thinking.

The teen sat in radiology at the moment. Kid was lucky. Unlike Gina, who would never learn to stay away from the shellfish.

"Out of my chair."

He about jumped out of his skin when Arlene's voice sounded in his ear.

She pushed at his shoulder.

He leapt up and bowed, sweeping his arm toward the comfy chair. "I was keeping it warm for you, milady."

"And you're full of it, Scott Wilson." She opened the chart for Mr. Donaldson and scribbled in it. "And too nosy. Better not let Edna catch you reading these files."

He dipped down and wrapped his arms around the older woman. His cheek pressed against the soft skin of her face. "Edna loves me. Everyone loves me; you know that."

Arlene chuckled and patted his face. "And that is why you get away with everything." She looked up and jutted her chin at the hallway. "Here comes that woman. Who is she? Connie only said someone was here about the wreck. I figured it may have been insurance related."

"The new reporter." He stood and bounded toward the tall, shapely redhead, giving his best mega-watt smile. "How did it go?"

The woman grinned, with small dimples forming in her cheeks. Her blue eyes gleamed. Mischief and mayhem danced in those deep-colored orbs. "Oh, he was quite cooperative actually. He wasn't sure about answering anything at first, but eventually he came around."

She slowed to a more sedate pace as she passed the desk and waved to Arlene. "Thank you, Arlene. You have a good day."

"You, too, darling." Arlene beamed, and then she returned to her reading.

Scott followed the reporter around the corner. "How did you manage that? Last reporter who tried to interview Jonathan left in tears; and here you are, all cat in the cream."

She paused and rested her hand on a lobby door. "I told you, I have my ways. I learned a long time ago to bulldoze with a smile and plenty of flattery." She pushed the doors open and then grabbed one, halting it from closing. Her other hand landed lightly on Scott's bare forearm. Her long fingers tickled the hair along his arm. "I do thank you for showing me to Jonathan's office."

A grin spread across his face. He let his gaze roam over her freckled face, from her mouth to a little freckle above her brow before settling on her eyes. "No problem."

"But tell me something."

"Yeah." He reached out and held the door open as she dug in her purse. Her blue eyes twinkled back at him. If he had to choose, he would say her smile outshone her eyes. "What's that?"

"The curve where the accident happened. The boy, is he okay?" She tapped the pen against her teeth, her tongue barely touching the end.

Scott's breath left him as he stared at her soft, pink lips. "Yeah. Shelby's going to be fine. Maybe a few broken ribs if anything."

"That's good to know." She pursed her lips and turned. "Thank you very much."

She left a rose-and-peach-scented whirlwind in her wake as she breezed out and through the lobby. Scott heaved a sigh and shook his head. He was right. Mischief and mayhem.

He slapped his palm against his forehead. He had just divulged a patient's name. He squeezed one eye shut and screwed up his face as he let the door swing close.

"Looks like you ate a rotten, sour lemon, Scott," Arlene said as she pushed through the doors. "Do you have the file up here, Connie dear?"

Scott held the door open for Arlene after Connie handed her a folder. "I was just hoodwinked."

Arlene shook her head. "And I bet you never even got her name, either."

"Um . . . no, I didn't." He laughed as he followed Arlene back to the ER desk. "That's a first for me."

"Well, I know it." She grinned as she sat down. "If you want to know it, you have to do me a favor. And you can't ask Jonathan because he already left."

"No doing, Arlene." Scott backpedaled from the desk. "I don't do your minions' jobs. I'll find out on my own who she is." He retreated out the doors and headed for the ambulances in the bay. Better to help clean the vehicles than empty bedpans.

The boys' voices echoed loudly from the bay, arguing about last night's baseball game. Scott looked up just as a battered Grand Am whizzed by the ER entrance and down the small entrance road. Thick red hair bounced around as the driver checked both ways before pulling out into the street.

He bit his lip. He knew where he had seen that car before.

CHAPTER THREE

Rochelle pushed open the glass doors to Garrettville courthouse. The aroma of musty tomes, floor wax, and heated air worked a sneeze out of her. Her gig-a-frog-sounding sneeze echoed down the dim hallway.

She rubbed at her nose as she pulled out a notebook and jotted down "look into budget for remodeling court." If Angela took notes and dished out great stories, then she could, too. Her phone beeped.

"Pops! What's up?" She retreated into the small foyer and sat on one of the hard, plastic chairs.

"Are you at the courthouse with Angela?" Her grandfather's voice sounded muffled over the phone. She pictured his head half-buried in his desk drawer, as usual.

"Just got here. Why?" She nodded and smiled at two ladies from her church as they passed by her.

"Good. Tell her that the packet from Mobile came in. I think she was looking for it earlier. And . . . " A crash, sounding a lot like his mail tray hitting the floor, rattled the speaker of her phone.

She waited until the huffing and puffing was over. "And?"

"Oh, and I have a new angle on the story about the wreck she was investigating. Tell her I want her to run with it instead of the budget story."

"Why don't you call her?" She stood and stared at her reflection in the window. A tall, dark-haired guy sauntered by. Her eyes followed him as she fluffed at her red-tipped strands. Brent Sanders could not look any better in his flannel and jeans.

" . . . and she always turns it off by this time. I don't know why."

Rochelle rolled her eyes and popped her gum. "Because you bother her all the time, Pops." She laughed and headed toward the hallway again. "I'll tell her, and I'll see you at dinnertime. Love ya."

She closed her phone without waiting for his reply. Her grandfather could outtalk a teenage girl on the phone. She paused by the trashcan and spat her gum into it. Her fingernails raked the wax off her braces, and the nasty wad followed the gum.

Dr. Thomas would kill her if she got gum stuck in her braces again. She ran her tongue over the metal as she pulled open the door to the chancery clerk's office.

"Hey, Judy!" She threw a wave toward the dark-haired lady who wore too much make-up. Heat worked its way up her neck at that thought. Like she could talk.

"Afternoon, Rochelle. She's back there in with the plats and minutes." The woman returned to her computer and Solitaire game.

Rochelle peered around the corner of the doorway to her left and scanned the rolling shelves. One of them rolled to the right and gently bumped against another. Mr. Elwes, his balding head gleaming under the fluorescent lights, walked through the narrow space and pulled a manila folder from the shelf.

He barely looked up as she walked by.

Red deed books, the large black index book, and a few manila folders littered the long, chest-high table that occupied the middle of the room. Angela's red hair bounced as she turned and pulled a large, metal plat holder from its rack. It clanged as she set it on the table.

"Angela." Rochelle picked up a red book and peeked inside. Deed to a Dwayne Melbourne.

Angela looked up, pen in mouth, and tried to smile around it. "What's up?"

Rochelle gave her a grin, and hoped it was bright enough. "Came to help. Pops also sent a message your way."

An eye roll was Angela's reply. She returned to the plat and flipped a large sheet over.

"He said your package from Mobile arrived—"

"Spectacular!"

"And . . . " Rochelle pulled out her notebook and jotted down the deed's number. "He also wanted you to follow up on some new info about the Pierce wreck."

Angela nodded with a grunt. "See if you can find the previous owner to that deed. I'm not finding it on this plat at all. Northwest corner, right?"

Rochelle ran her finger across the paper. "Yup. Section three, Township nine." She frowned. "That's strange. Township nine is commercial and industry, isn't it?"

"That's what it seems. Hmmm . . . " Angela replaced the plat and pulled another out.

Rochelle watched for a few seconds and then quickly read the deed. Bought ten years ago from a Mr. McOwen. McOwen? That sounded familiar. Rochelle noted the book number and walked to the back wall. She pulled the black binder from the shelf.

A small plume of dust spiraled up as she set it on the table beside Angela's plat. Rochelle flipped open the book, looking for page sixteen. She turned page fourteen and landed on twenty. Weird.

She flipped back to the beginning and started checking page by page. The last page fell against the others. No sixteen. "Angela?"

"Hmmm?"

"I think something's wrong." Rochelle picked up the black deed book and the more recent red book and carried them over to Angela, who had moved further down the table to compare two plats. "Look at this."

She plopped the books on top of the plats. "This deed shows the original owner as a McOwen; but when I checked the book against the deed book listed on this one, there's no page. Page sixteen doesn't exist in this book."

Angela looked at her for a moment, a frown creasing her brow. Rochelle swallowed. She had done it right, hadn't she? She pushed the books toward Angela.

With a quick grab, Angela held the book up and scanned its contents. She huffed, picked up the other, and then placed it on the table. Her pen tapped against her teeth.

Rochelle pointed to the black index at the end of the table. "Should I check the index? See if I can find a McOwen?"

"Yeah, do that. Go back at least twelve years, allowing for some leeway."

Rochelle nodded and hurried over to the black tome. She opened it to the pages, yellowed with age, and ran her finger down the lines. Her eyes crossed numerous times trying to decipher some of the handwriting.

"McOwen. McOwen. There's a McGhee. McSomething-or-other. Man, these people have horrible handwriting." Rochelle blew out a breath, turned the page, and checked the year. Five years ago. "Angela, there's no McOwen."

Angela wrote in her notebook and sighed. "Okay. Did you make a note of it?"

"Oh yeah, wait." Rochelle pulled out the notebook and scribbled in it: *No deed found for McOwen, no deed from twelve years up, who did D. Melbourne buy land from?*

She closed the book. "What's next?"

Angela replaced the plats and stacked the deed books together. "You know how to look up minutes?"

"As in board minutes?"

Angela smiled. "Yeah."

Rochelle pursed her lips. "No. Will you show me?"

Angela waved her over, and she followed Angela to the corner in the back. Alternating colors of red and black books—did the courthouse not have other colors?—lay in single slats on the shelf. Angela pulled on the top book.

"This is the book, much like the deed index, that tells you which book contains which meeting according to month and date. We are looking for . . . "

As Angela pulled out her notebook, Rochelle smiled. She knew that one. "July of this year. Budget committee met. I wanted to do the story, but Pops let Michael cover it."

"Yeah. So, we look here. And . . . hmm . . . "

She turned the book around for Rochelle to read. "There's nothing there for July. No minutes, no meeting. But we know they met."

Rochelle turned at the rustling sound behind them. Mr. Elwes replaced his handful of folders and cast them a look. He gave a small smile that turned Rochelle's stomach. For a balding man, he sure seemed oily. She sniffed at the imaginary body odor that wafted from him.

"Afternoon, Mr. Elwes." Angela cast him a smile that would've scared sharks away.

Rochelle smothered a giggle. Weren't all lawyers considered sharks?

He nodded and slipped out of the room.

"Irritating man. He's in here every time I come here." Angela returned back to the book. "I don't get it, Rochelle."

She slid the book back.

"Wait, I got an idea, Angela." Her mentor—or at least she hoped someday Angela would be—turned to her, eyebrow raised. "I can search the archives at work. Michael is particular and makes sure every story, whether published or not, is saved on the archive file."

Angela smiled. "That'll work."

Heat touched her cheeks. "It'll be a snap." Rochelle smiled back at Angela, and then gasped as her lip caught on her braces. Stupid metal tracks!

"You okay?" Angela scooped up a stack of the books.

"Yeah. Lips keep getting caught on my braces. I am so ready to have them off." She grabbed a couple of the books.

"When's that?"

"Next week, hopefully." She helped Angela replace the deed books and then followed her out of the room. Their footsteps echoed in the hallway. Rochelle bit at her inner cheek. Should she ask? It would be awesome if Angela agreed.

Rochelle slipped under Angela's arm as the woman held the front glass door open. "Angela?"

"Yeah?" Angela paused on the court steps and turned on her phone.

"Can I ask you something?" Rochelle's breath hitched. She bit her bottom lip.

"Like what?" Angela looked up and pierced her with those blue eyes.

The wind picked up. October air swirled around them. Rochelle hunched her shoulders and took a deep breath. "Do you think I could help you with this story? It'll look good on my resumé when I apply for a scholarship come spring. I mean, I really want to learn, and you are great at it. I read a lot of your articles when you worked in Mobile. They were totally awesome."

Angela leaned closer, her brows practically into her hairline. "Did you even take a breath during that?"

A laugh burst out of her. She shook her head. "No. I had to get it all out, in case you tried to stop me from finishing. So?"

Angela smiled. Her hand landed on Rochelle's shoulder and squeezed. "Yes, you may. But there is one thing you need to do."

Rochelle grimaced. "Look more professional?" Talk about total image make-over.

"Yes." Angela reached into her bag and pulled out a small book. "Here. I like to carry this around. A small etiquette book. If you want to keep your hair, then fine; but lighten up on the make-up, sweetie, or the police may arrest you as a burglar instead of a reporter . . . hmm."

Rochelle grinned. "There's a story there, isn't it?"

Angela laughed and started walking toward her car. "Yeah, but I'll tell you another time."

Angela opened her car door and turned to Rochelle. "Want your first assignment?"

Rochelle fought the impulse to bounce up and down like a hyperbirthday party kid. "Look up the meetings?"

"You got it." Angela slid into the seat. "Text me with the info, okay? I've got to get my packet and head to Dottie's for dinner tonight. Oh, Rochelle, be careful."

"I will." Rochelle stepped back and watched as Angela pulled out of the parking lot. She grinned and looked at the book in her hand. Yes! This was better than she imagined. Her first truly official assignment. No more just a gopher for the *Gazette*.

She hugged the book to her chest and ambled toward her moped. The only other way for the day to get any better would be if Brent asked her out. She sighed, slipped the book into her side bag, and started the small engine. That was a dream world, though.

One step at a time. She pulled out of the lot and headed back to the newspaper.

###

"Dottie, I got the forks, but where did you put the spoons?" Angela closed the long drawer to the antique William and Mary china cabinet.

"I've already placed them, dear." Dottie's voice drifted out of the kitchen and into the small dining room. "You did get the Regency design, didn't you?"

"Yes, ma'am." Angela padded back to the table and placed the forks by the plates. Semi-formal Friday dinner. She smiled at the three-tier platter filled with delicate chocolate bonbons for dessert.

Max climbed upon a chair and propped his elbows on the pale-yellow linen tablecloth. "Just one, Mommy? Please!"

What did this make? The tenth time or the millionth? "No. The bonbons are for dessert. After you eat your chicken and sprouts, then you can have a couple." Angela swatted at his little hand as it reached for the dessert. "Max! You touch one, you don't get one."

He plopped back and pouted. "But I don't like chicken."

"Yes, you do." Angela smoothed his hair as she passed by. "And you like sprouts. Ms. Dottie made a cheese sauce for it." She grabbed a handful of linen napkins from the cabinet's drawer.

"The yummy kind?" His face lit into a bright smile as he turned in his chair to watch her fold the napkins.

"Yes, the yummy kind." She pointed at his hands. "Go wash your hands again. You've been playing with Frolic."

Max picked at the dog hairs that clung to his fingers. "Only a little bit. But I go wash them. Don't want doggy fur on my sprouts." He slid off the high-back chair and ran down the hall to the bathroom.

Angela shook her head. At least he didn't complain about washing up this time. She laid the napkins on the plates as Dottie brought in a steaming dish of maple bacon-wrapped chicken breasts. The delectable aroma teased Angela's nose, and her mouth watered. Dottie sure knew how to whip up a dish.

"When's Debbie coming by?" Angela turned to the door as the bell chimed. The chords of "Blue Danube" reverberated off the walls.

Dottie grinned. "About now, sweetie. She told me that Scott was able to come tonight."

The woman untied her apron and chucked it over a quilt rack as she hurried toward the front door. Angela shook her head. Dottie and Debbie may think they were clever, but their little schemes were crystal clear. Maybe she should give this Scott a heads-up on them.

Max barreled down the hall and skidded to a stop outside the dining room's doorway. Angela didn't blame him. Debbie chattered with Dottie as they rounded the corner, but it was those chocolate-brown eyes that suddenly skewered her. Scott was the paramedic? Her eyes traveled down his tall, skinny form and took in the black sweater and dark denims. The man certainly knew how to make her feel underdressed. Well, maybe not. She smoothed a wrinkle out of her baby blue button-down and plucked a thread off her camel brown skirt.

The corners of his eyes crinkled as he smiled. Those seriously white teeth flashed her way. "Well, hello again. Did you ever finish your story?"

He paused at one of the chairs across from her as Debbie flowed further into the room. "Angela, dear. It's so good to see you again. Have you met Scott?"

Angela smiled and nodded. The man's eyes glimmered as his grin widened. "I have actually. It's nice to see you again, Scott." She held out her hand across the table. His warm hand slid into hers, long fingers entangling with hers. "As for the story, you should see it in Saturday's edition. And don't worry about your HIPAA slip. I didn't use any names, since they had not been released."

A touch of red highlighted his sharp cheekbones as he removed his hand. "Ah, yes. I was hoping you hadn't. Sorry to say that was the only time I have ever made that mistake."

She softened her smile. The red on his cheeks rose higher. How cute. "Well, I'm surprised that I have such an effect on you, Mister . . . uh, I didn't catch your last name."

His eyes deepened and twinkled. "I didn't give it, Miss Mabry."

"Scott Wilson." Debbie shook her head and waved him into his seat. "He'll string you along, Angela, just for fun."

She laughed and settled into her chair. "Never worry, Miss Debbie. I can keep up with the best."

Scott unfolded his napkin, placed it in his lap, and turned his plate. "Oh, I'm the best, am I? That's good to know."

Angela rolled her eyes. "Best? Wouldn't know, but it might be fun to find out if you are in my league."

Dottie cleared her throat, ending their bantering. Killjoy. "Scott, I'm glad to see you here. How's your job?"

Angela served Max's food as Scott answered Dottie, telling her about some new measures the hospital was thinking of implementing. Hmm, new plans? She made a mental note. Max grinned as she scooped up the sprouts and then smothered them with cheese sauce.

Her ears pricked at the mention of the EMS. She handed the serving bowl of melted cheese to Debbie and turned to Scott. "You mean the EMS is still part of the hospital? I thought they had a buy-out a few years back. I remember Jake mentioning it."

Scott's face clouded slightly at the mention of her old college classmate. Now *there* was a story. She made another mental note. "They turned down the offer. I would have loved it if they had accepted it. Fewer hours, more pay, plus better benefits."

"Why stay then? Surely Sheffield or Florence would offer a better deal." She smiled her thanks to Dottie as she poured a glass of tea for her.

Scott shook his head and accepted his glass of tea. "I could have, but my heart is here. I'll stick it out for a little while." He waited until his grandmother and Dottie picked up their forks before he speared a sprout. "Why did you leave Mobile for this rinky-dink newspaper?"

Angela jutted out her chin. Hmph. Touché. "I was asked by Tom. And I decided big city life wasn't for me. Too noisy." She speared her own sprout.

"Well, I'm sure Tom's paper is the better for it." He popped his small, green morsel into his mouth and looked at Dottie. "Tell me, Dottie, how's old Frolic nowadays?"

"Too old for your shenanigans, Scott Weath—"

Scott tsked behind his teeth. "Oh, no. No using the middle name. I was just asking."

Angela grabbed her tea. "What shenanigans?"

Debbie shook her head and passed a saltshaker to Scott. "He and Jake trained the animals to respond to certain commands. He can make my sweet Dixie and Judas chase each other by saying, 'Dixie, dinnertime.' Frolic will sit there and beg at the command of 'mashed potatoes.'" She sighed. "It's quite irritating."

Scott chuckled. "But all in good fun, Nana Debbie."

Padding paws and the click of toenails echoed down the small hallway. Frolic, with his big, old basset hound eyes, ambled into the dining room. Angela hid her grin behind a bite of chicken as Scott's eyes gleamed.

She listened as Dottie and Debbie chatted about the upcoming political rally at the square next weekend. Frolic lowered himself next to Dottie's chair with a huff.

Scott cleared his throat. "Dottie, question for you." The man was mischief. Angela watched his eyes crinkle again at the corners. "When are you going to make your special mashed potatoes?"

Frolic's ears perked up, and he sprung up on his hind legs. His doleful eyes gazed at Dottie, paws on her legs, as he whimpered.

Dottie gritted her teeth. "Scott Weatherby Wilson!"

Weatherby. How cute.

A spot of red shot across his cheekbones as a big grin etched itself across his face. Angela laughed as Dottie gave the old dog a small slice of chicken.

Debbie and Dottie scolded Scott, who placed his hand innocently over his heart. His gleaming eyes met hers, and he threw a wink her way. Innocent nothing. The man was pure mayhem.

"Can I say it?" Max bounced in his seat, giggling.

The two women whirled. "Absolutely not!"

Scott's chuckle rolled across the air, and Angela smiled. Max would be relentless now. Heaven help Dottie in the afternoons. Poor old Frolic.

Scott shrugged into his jacket. His stomach pressed against his waistband. He had eaten way too much food, but Dottie's cooking was absolutely superb. He looked up as Angela, with Max asleep on her shoulder, rounded the corner of the small foyer. Dottie followed behind.

"Oh, Scott. You're leaving already?" Dottie pulled Angela's coat from the hook and helped her slip into it.

"Yes, ma'am. Nana Debbie, as usual, will stay a while, but I have an early shift in the morning." He grabbed Max's little blue coat and passed it to Dottie.

Angela smiled her thank you. "Just place it over him, Dottie. He's so sound asleep, I don't want to wake him."

Dottie draped Max's coat over him. Angela used her free arm to tuck the sleeves under the sleeping boy, effectively cocooning him. Scott smiled and opened the door.

"Shall I walk you home?"

Angela shook her head. "No, that's okay. We live just across the street and two doors down." She turned to Dottie. "I'll see you Sunday, Dottie."

"Good night, sweetie. Good night, Scott. Don't let her say no; you walk her home. Be a gentleman."

Scott tipped a non-existent hat. "I'm always the gentleman." He dipped down and placed a kiss on her soft cheek. "Tell Nana Debbie to call before she comes home. I love walking beautiful women to their doorsteps."

He caught Angela's eye roll. Was that at his statement or because he thought her beautiful? Dottie bade them good night one more time and gently closed the door behind them.

He bounded down the steps and opened the small, white gate. Angela breezed past, her back arched as she carried her son. Rose and peaches once again lingered in the air behind her.

"Thank you, Scott. But there's really no need to walk me home."

Scott jammed his hands in his pockets and ambled along beside her. "Oh, there might be no reason; but if you would look back at Dottie's house, you will see two white-haired ladies peering out the window at us." Her red hair flew out as she whipped her head around. He followed her gaze. The red curtains in Dottie's dining room window fell quickly back into place. "I fear Nana Debbie's tongue lashing, so I might as well walk you."

"You make it sound like I'm a poodle or something. Walk me?" She snickered and turned her gaze up at him. "I can't imagine you being afraid of anything."

Scott shrugged. Wouldn't she be surprised. "Everyone's afraid of something."

"True." She shifted her son a little further onto her shoulder and crossed the road. "But only if we really allow it to scare us."

"So, you're this fearless reporter? Able to take down men with a single pen? Can you leap tall buildings at a single word?" He chuckled at another of her eye rolls.

She snorted. "Hardly."

He closed his hand over hers as she reached to unlatch her fence gate. "I got it." He flicked the stubborn latch open and swung the gate inward. "Where's the key? I'll open the door for you."

She nodded at the windowsill to the right as she clambered up the rickety steps. "There, under the bird."

Scott lifted the ceramic robin. The key nestled in the twigs of the nest. He retrieved it, unlocked the door, and replaced the key.

The old oak door squeaked on bad hinges as he pushed it forward. "Nana Debbie said that there were a few things needing repair. If you want, I can swing by Wednesday and fix them for you. Jake wasn't much of a handyman, and I had to do most of the work for him."

She squeezed by him and leaned against the jamb. "There's not really that much to do, Scott, and I appreciate the offer. But I've learned to do a lot of it myself."

Her smile disappeared. A closed book. He held the door open and shrugged. "Well, if you need me, just call Nana Debbie. I don't mind."

She nodded. "Thank you, Scott. And I think you should know something about your grandmother and Dottie."

His chuckle brought a rise to her left eyebrow. "I know . . . the Double D's are trying to hook us up. Those two are easy to read and predictable."

Angela's body relaxed. "Then since you know, you need to understand that I'm not looking for a relationship, Mr. Wilson. So, if I ever sound . . . clipped, believe me, it's not you. I don't want wagging tongues sticking their faces where they don't belong. Not that I'm calling Dottie and Debbie wagging tongues."

A cold wind whipped around the corner of her house. Scott nodded. "I understand completely, Miss Mabry. Friends only."

"Friends only." Her face lit into a smile. "And I'll see you Sunday at church?"

Scott shook his head. Women and their churches. "I don't do church."

"Really?" She shifted Max again.

Guilt ate at him. Here he was chatting her up with the door wide open and her struggling to hold her sleeping child. "Let me leave now, so you can put Max to bed. I'll see you around, Angela."

Her serious gaze followed him as he backed out of the door. The old weathered slab slowly closed and clicked into place. He hunched his shoulders. Her eyes had held so many questions.

Fool. She's a reporter. Give a morsel, and she'd take the whole plate. He trudged down her little sidewalk that was practically hidden in the brown grass. Jake never did try to keep the grass from growing up over the walkway Julie built. Billy had used the tall grass as a jungle for his G.I. Joes.

His breath hitched as he passed through the gate and let it close gently behind him. Well, he'd done it. He had visited Julie's home. Her home that housed a new woman inside, a new child.

He survived, didn't he?

His feet led him across the street and one house down. Home. His hands shook as he opened the door.

He paused at the foyer. Coat on the hook. Empty the pockets. The shaking increased. Wallet. Keys. Another parking ticket. Man, Dan really hated him. Either that or the man hated Mercedes Benz C300s. More than likely, Dan hated him.

Scott heaved a sigh and leaned against his forearm as he propped himself against the wall. He fisted a hand over his heart. The erratic beats slammed against his ribcage.

Tremors ate him.

He pushed off the wall and hurried down the hallway. Dixie looked up from his spot on the floor. Judas gazed at him as she lay at the foot of his bed. She meowed as he sank down on the mattress, turned on his lamp, and ripped open his nightstand drawer.

The bottles rolled toward the front. He lifted one. Empty. He grabbed the other. The medication rolled and plinked around inside. The shaking increased as he pried off the stubborn top.

He shook the small pill out into his hand, paused, and shook out another. His throat tightened. He shouldn't, but he really needed it this time.

The water glass at the side still held a small amount from last night. He swallowed the pills down with that little bit. It wouldn't take too long. Calm would come. It always did. Should happen sooner since these were stronger than the last.

He held up the pill container. Only three more left. He would have to somehow find a new supply. Dr. Morrison would not renew any more for him.

Scott sighed and fell back onto his pillows. Alprazolam was good but hard stuff. He threw an arm over his eyes and drew in a breath. Tomorrow, he'd figure something out. He had enough for two days if he stretched it.

A buttery feeling seeped into his muscles. Judas climbed onto his chest and started happy-pawing his sweater.

"Tomorrow, Judas. I'll figure it all out tomorrow." He closed his eyes.

Darkness descended upon him. Somewhere in the black void that greeted him, a faint buzzing called to him. His eyes popped open. His phone.

He grabbed at it and hit the icon. "Nana?"

Maybe he shouldn't have taken two this time. His words fell out like cold molasses.

"Scott? Were you asleep, dear?"

"Um, yeah. I'll be right over to walk you home, Nana." He swiped Judas off his chest and swung his feet over the side.

"Oh, sweet boy, don't worry. I only called to tell you that Dottie and I are heading into town to the bakery. She'll drop me off on the way back."

"Hmm. Grab some orange danishes for me?" Her reply was lost as his eyelids betrayed him and lowered. "See ya, Nana."

His arm fell to the side, and the phone slid over the comforter to Judas.

Scott used the last of his strength to push off his shoes. Their *thunk* against the floor echoed. He curled up and rolled over, bringing the edge of the comforter with him. Just a little while. Then he'd get under the covers. Darkness greeted him again. Scott welcomed the void. No more shaking. No more thoughts. No more memories.

CHAPTER FOUR

Angela rose with the rest of the congregation and stood with her head bowed as the pastor led them in closing prayers. She forced herself to listen, to pay attention. Good gracious, she was in church. She needed to keep her mind off work.

"As we go out in the world, dear Father, be with each of us . . . " The pastor's voice faded.

World? Wasn't there an article in that little magazine Garrettville printed about the death of a man and that the world had lost a great soul? She'd spied Dottie's magazine stash last week. Angela mentally added that to her check list. Maybe Dottie had that edition. If she was correct, that man's name was McOwen.

Nerves jumped around inside her. Oh, she needed her pen and notebook. A sharp pinch on her arm brought her head up.

"Did you fall asleep on your feet, Angela dear?" Dottie's eyes twinkled as she stared up at her. "I know he gets a little long-winded."

Heat flamed the side of her neck, but she mustered a grin. "Almost, Dottie. My mind actually wandered off again."

"You and your work." Dottie filed into the aisle, and Angela followed, baby stepping as they merged with the rest of the congregation. "Want to try the side door?"

"Sure. Debbie goes out that side, anyway." Angela squeezed past a tall gentleman in a dark, blue tweed. She did a double take. Retro clothes, for sure. The scent of tobacco and mothballs drifted to her. Yup, the man definitely pulled that suit out recently. She shook her head and followed Dottie through the two pews.

Bright sunlight shot through the golden, stained glass windows. She walked through the dancing dust motes as she and Dottie moved into the far side aisle where there was less traffic.

"Mom!" A little form hurled itself at her.

Angela spread open her arms and swept Max into her embrace. "How was children's church?"

"It was awesome. We learned about Shad's rack, my shack, and a billy goat." His big blues grew wider. "And guess what, Mom?"

She set him back on the floor and pushed through the side door. "What?"

Debbie and Dottie followed, grinning as Max danced around, his worksheets flying from his hands. "And we learned about how Daniel ate the lions."

Angela collected the papers from the grass and raised a brow. "Ate the lions? Are you sure?"

"No, Max. How did we explain it?" Debbie smoothed the top of his hair as he pursed his lips in concentration. "The lions were going to eat Daniel, but he . . . "

"Yeah, he knelt and prayed. The lions shut their mouths." He grinned and looked back at Angela. Max leaned forward and whispered, "Then he ate them."

Angela chuckled as Debbie shook her head. They walked across the paved parking lot to the car. "Never fear, Debbie. The end of all his stories is that something eats something."

"Well, if Daniel was anything like me, then he was hungry, too. Right, Max?" Dottie held out her hand.

Max's little paw slid into hers as they walked. "Yup. I'm so hungry I could ate a lion."

"Right about that, Max." Angela turned to Dottie. "Do I need to bring anything over to your house for lunch, Dottie?"

"Oh, no, sweetie. Debbie and I have got this covered." She waved Angela away as she weaved her way between cars toward Debbie's blue Taurus. Dottie glanced back over her shoulder. "And don't be late!"

Angela snickered. As if she was ever late. She opened the back door and ushered Max inside. "Buckle in." She bent and collected more of Max's fallen papers from the ground as Max buckled himself into his booster seat.

She flipped the paper over and frowned. "Max, who's this?" Angela ran her finger over the blue stick figure holding a circle-shaped object.

Max pulled the paper from her hand. His eyes lit up as he set the paper in his lap. "That man from dinner. You know the parry-medic. He's holding a shield, keeping the lions from attacking. See? And that's his spear. But there's no blood because he doesn't hafta stab them. One word. Boom. They stop."

Angela smiled and smoothed his hair. "That's sweet. It's a nice picture."

She shut the door and rounded the car. As she slid into her seat, Max's voice floated toward her.

"Will you frame it, Mom?"

"Of course. When we get through eating at Dottie's, I'll find the perfect frame. Okay?" Angela turned the ignition. The motor ground for a second before it caught and turned over. She sighed. It needed a tune-up or a complete overhaul. Next week. When her money wasn't so tight.

She pulled out onto the street and headed home, listening to Max chatter about the kind of frame needed for his masterpiece. She interjected with a few "uh-huhs" and "yeahs," but her mind strayed to that magazine at Dottie's.

"Wait . . . no. This isn't it." Dottie stacked the magazine to the side.

Angela, her legs splayed to the side, bent over and pulled a magazine from the bottom of the stack. The precariously piled structure wobbled and then stilled.

Max popped his head over the side of the chair. "Wouldn't it be cool, Mom, if the mags toppled? Be like dominoes, you know."

Debbie laughed from the chair by the fireplace. She replaced her cup of tea on the side table and motioned for Max. "Come sit in my lap, munchkin. Let Dottie and your momma find the magazine."

"But I wanna read one, too."

"Here." She held up a thick, glossy magazine. "This one has stuff about movies. You want to read with me?"

Max hopped off the chair and climbed into Debbie's lap. Angela smiled her thanks and returned to the pile as Debbie read a review on the latest Hollywood release.

Dottie leaned down from her perch on the ottoman and pulled a wayward periodical from behind the pile. "Oh, here is one, Angela.

Yeah, *World of Garrettville*. Mercy, I didn't think I was that bad of a packrat. This thing was printed eight years ago."

Angela accepted the magazine. "That's it and right now, I am glad you are." She restacked the others and pushed them back to their corner.

"What's in it that you need?" Dottie grunted as she rose from the ottoman and shuffled over to the chair across from Debbie.

Angela pulled the ottoman over to the fire that crackled in the fireplace and sat down. The wind whipped around the corner of the house. Her October Sunday decided to be blustery this afternoon. She glanced outside as she replied to Dottie, "There was an article, if I remember correctly, about the death of a man named McOwen."

"I remember him. Don't you, Debbie?"

Debbie looked up from the magazine that Max had commandeered. "Casper McOwen. Don't remember much. Just that he was in cahoots with—oh, what's that doctor's name? Melbourne?"

Angela glanced up. "Dwayne Melbourne?"

"Yeah, that was him." Dottie picked up her teacup and took a sip. "And you remembered that article?"

Angela smiled as she flipped through the magazine. She folded back the cover and scanned the page. "Yes, ma'am. And here it is."

"Scott's that way."

"What? Like a folded-back magazine?" Angela laughed at Dottie's snort.

Debbie chuckled. "No. Like you, he can remember anything that is said to him. Repeat it verbatim."

Angela perused the article. It would definitely help in tracking down that deed. Hmm . . . no family. "So, whatever is said, he remembers? I'll learn to keep my mouth shut around him then."

"Really?" Dottie laughed and handed an afghan across the space to Angela. "Give that to Debbie for Max, Angela dear."

She stood and placed the red and blue afghan over Max. His body curled up in Debbie's lap, his head pillowed on her chest. "Let me go lay him down, Debbie."

"Oh, no, honey. He's fine. It's been so long since I held a little one like this." She tucked the afghan a little tighter around Max.

Angela resettled back on the ottoman. She glanced up at Dottie and continued. "And yes, back to our conversation, I can keep my mouth shut. Most of the time." She fought the smile that teased her lips. "Fine. Sometimes."

Dottie snickered and picked up a word find booklet. She perched her reading glasses on her nose. "That's what makes you, you."

"So, he's really like that? Really good at remembering?" Angela dog-eared the magazine and lay it on top of her bag on the coffee table behind her.

Debbie nodded. She sipped another swallow of tea. "He refuses to go to church, so every morning I read passages from the Bible out loud. He won't say anything, but I can tell the words are branding themselves into his brain. I told him, 'Scott, you have a sharp mind. You remember everything you hear, dear boy, so I know that you can remember things I've read to you.' He just grunts, finishes his break-fast, and heads to work."

Angela hugged her knees. In the words of Alice in Wonderland, curiouser and curiouser. She spoke before she gauged her words. "Why won't he attend church? I asked him Friday when he walked me home, but he didn't answer."

Debbie plucked at a stray thread on the afghan. "Julie. And Billy."

Dottie nodded and spoke from behind her booklet. "He blames God for what happened."

Angela rose from the ottoman and grabbed the fireplace poker. She stoked the fire some more, sending red sparks up into the flue. "He was close to Jake?"

"No. Julie. Julie was his best friend. They grew up together in Florence. Their mommas were best friends."

"People thought . . . " Dottie paused, lowered her booklet, and looked at Angela. " . . . well, people thought that they would get together, but it was Scott who introduced Julie to Jake right before they finished college. From then on out, those three were always together."

Angela rubbed her hands over her upper arms and erased the goosebumps that had rose upon them. "But why would he blame God? I don't understand. I mean, when Mike killed himself . . . " She glanced over at Max's sleeping form. His breathing rose and fell in a soft rhythm. "I didn't blame God. I blamed Mike, for being stupid and for being a coward."

"Do you still blame him?" Dottie's brows rose above her eyes, stirring the loose strands of white hair that fell across her forehead.

Angela paused. Did she? She pulled her knees to her chest and dropped her chin onto them. "No. Not now. Mike was clinically depressed. The doctors tried every conceivable variation of meds to help him; but in the end, nothing worked. I *almost* blamed God. Why would He allow a man to fall so far? I really don't know if Mike knew what he was doing or if he thought taking so many would help him; but either way, I almost blamed God for Mike's overdose." She heaved a deep sigh. "I just wish he knew that he was about to have a son. I always believed that knowing Max was on the way would have changed things."

"Then again, it may not have." Debbie brushed at her eye and hugged Max. "And you have a fine son, dear. You felt a lot of sadness then; well, Scott feels that now."

"Tell me what happened." The fire's heat beat against her back. If she didn't move, she would become a melted puddle of goo. She slid back onto the ottoman. "I knew Jake during my first two years in college before I transferred. We lost contact, but I knew he had married and was running a successful construction business up here. When I heard about him losing his wife and son, I sent my condolences. We emailed for a while, and that's how we came up with the plan to trade houses. He and I both wanted a new start."

Debbie gave her a small smile. "There's much I can't say. Julie was returning home from picking up Billy at daycare. A truck sideswiped them. Julie was killed instantly. Scott tried to save Billy, but the poor baby died. Since then, Scott refuses to set foot into the church, refuses to talk about it; but more importantly, he refuses to slow down."

"Outrunning the hurt." Angela nodded. She could relate. How many times did she send herself to the doctor from total exhaustion? Only when her doctor explained the danger she was putting her son in did she try to slow down. Once Max was born, she drove herself. If she didn't pause long enough to think, then she didn't have to fear thinking about Mike. And how lonely life had become without him.

"Still with us?" Dottie nudged her shoulder.

Angela blinked. "Yeah. I was just thinking. I did the same after Mike. My guess is Scott's afraid, but he'll never admit it."

"Well, speaking of the man, I think I forgot to take out the steaks to thaw. I wonder if he'll be satisfied with frozen pizza."

Angela sat up straight. Maybe the two wouldn't take it the wrong way, but she just had to help the guy. She understood how it felt to feel such utter torment alone. "What if I invite him to dinner tonight, Debbie? I still have some leftover vegetable soup. Wouldn't take much to make some garlic bread and a nice salad to go with it." She smiled at the gleam in their eyes. "Don't go getting any ideas now, ladies. I figured I might be able to weasel him back into church. Plus . . ." she glanced at Max. "I have a secret weapon."

Debbie kissed Max's dark head. "This little guy would melt anyone's heart." She smiled and picked up her magazine. "I think it's a fine idea. But beware; the man's as sharp as a razor. If you're going to invite him, you had better do it soon. Need his number?"

Angela popped up off the ottoman. "Well, if you don't mind, I wanted to do it in person. Mind babysitting for a little bit, Dottie?"

Dottie grinned and waved her away. "Go. Max is never a problem."

Angela swooped down and kissed her son's temple. "I won't be gone long."

She ignored the two women's calculating smiles and grabbed her bag off the table. With a last look at their happy faces, she opened the door and ventured out into the bitter wind.

She hurried down the sidewalk and across the road to her driveway.

Stirring up loads of trouble she was, but this would be beneficial to him and to her. If Scott could remember things he heard only once, then maybe, just maybe, he might know something about the deeds and McOwen. Not only that . . .

The car door creaked as she opened it.

Angela slid into the seat, started the car, and pulled away from her house. Not only that, but Scott seemed truly interesting. And she really could use a friend around here.

###

"EMS, ETA two minutes . . . "

Scott filtered out Douglas' voice. He ripped the paper from the gauze with his teeth. One hand pressed against the IV entrance. Even with the pressure applied, blood seeped between his fingers. He slapped the gauze against the man's forearm and applied pressure once more.

The ambulance bounced over a pothole and practically slung Scott into the upper cabinets above the patient.

He whispered a hard oath. The clotting agent wasn't working. Gauze didn't work. Pressure didn't work. He wound the tape over and over the IV opening.

The ambulance bounced again.

"Douglas, for the love—" He bit off his curse and tore the tape with his teeth. "Tell the ER the bleeding won't stop. Need two bags, O neg."

"Already on it." Douglas shut off the siren. "We're here. How's he doing?"

"Not good." Scott's curse echoed off the inside walls as the monitor flatlined. "He's crashing!"

"Don't have time for the defib, Scott. Jump him!" The ambulance rocked to a stop, and Douglas shoved open the door.

Scott raked the used supplies and soiled gauzes to the floor and hopped up on the gurney. He straddled the man.

White noise filled Scott's head, and then silence descended. His hands compressed the patient's bare chest. One. Two. Three . . . his hands pumped against the man . . . fourteen. Fifteen.

He bent his head down. No breath.

The Plexiglas cracked as he opened the door of the cabinet above him and snatched the ambu-mask. He slapped it over the man's face.

One. Two.

Back to the chest. One. Two. Three . . .

The back doors swung open. Bright afternoon sunlight shot into the gloomy compartment. Hands reached in and pulled the gurney out. Supplies were dumped next to his knee.

. . . fourteen. Fifteen.

Scott listened for the man's breath. Still nothing.

One. Two.

"Argh! Useless!" He cast the mask away. Supplies tumbled around him when he snatched an oral airway in the pile beside his knee. His teeth ripped the package, and Scott quickly eased the man's head back and jaw down. The airway slid in easily, and he covered the opening with his mouth and breathed. There was no time for the bag.

One. Two. A bump rammed the airway's edge into his lower lip.

Back to the chest. One. Two. Three . . .

Douglas's mouth shouted words to the ER doctor on call.

The gurney bounced across the rough asphalt and onto the sidewalk.

Warm air hissed around them as the emergency doors opened.

Scott pressed the man's chest as the gurney roller-coastered down the hall.

. . . thirteen, fourteen, fifteen.

The man's body shuddered.

"Come on!" He breathed into the man again, tasting blood. He raised his head, and Arlene slipped an air bag over the man's mouth.

Scott pressed and pressed.

One. Two. Three—

Douglas grabbed him. "Scott, crash cart."

Scott hopped off the man and stood back as a nurse slapped the defibrillator pads onto the man's chest.

"Charging!"

The sounds bombarded him as Douglas pulled him out into the hallway. Monitors, with their incessant whine, grated his nerves. Scott flinched at the doctor's yell as he applied the charge—"Clear!"

The body jerked.

"Three fifty!"

The nurses rushed around.

Scott shook off Douglas's hands and stalked down the hall and then back. He glared at the doctor and nurses futilely working on the man. He was dead. A sigh escaped Scott. He had felt the life leave the man, felt that small shudder underneath his hands.

Scott rubbed at his lips and peered at the reddened tips of his fingers. Great. Might as well moonlight as a vampire.

"Is that yours or his?"

"Mine." He unbuttoned his shirt. "Again, it didn't matter."

Douglas shook his head. "What happened to that guy? You rip a vein?"

Scott threw Douglas a hard look and scowled. "No. As soon as I pricked him, he wouldn't stop bleeding. Hemophiliac?"

"The clotting agent should have worked then. Another mystery, I guess."

They both glanced back as the flatlining monitor ceased. Quiet pervaded the hallway. The doctor looked at the clock on the wall, and a nurse jotted down his response as another pulled up a sheet to cover the man's face.

A hot lump settled inside Scott's heart.

"What does this make? The third? You and Mack had one seven months ago. Then there was the lady last year that Trammel had before he left. And then this one."

Douglas pushed him toward the washroom and away from the trauma room. "Stop worrying about it. You did your part. They did theirs. Let the medical examiner worry about it now."

"Wilson!" Jonathan Trickle's voice reached them before he appeared around the corner. "Just heard. How you doing?"

Scott shrugged out of his shirt. Just let him get to the washroom and get the stink of death off him. "Just peachy. Lost another one."

"See me in my office once you get cleaned up. Another death on your watch. You know the procedures." Jonathan turned on his heel and disappeared around the bend.

Scott hung his head and sighed. Death and paperwork. He rolled his shoulders. Now would have been a great time for his meds.

Douglas slapped his shoulder. "You didn't do anything wrong, Scott. You know that."

But it didn't matter. Scott leaned against the wall to quell the shaking. Another death. Another report. Another mark against his record. Jonathan was just looking for an excuse—he was sure of it. "Go on. I'll catch up."

"Okay." Douglas backed away, started around the corner, and skidded to a stop. "Oh, hi. Scott!"

Scott glanced up as Douglas called his name and cocked his head as Angela rounded the corner. Her white jacket flared out as she approached him. Now what? Another story.

"I don't have time for an interview, Angela."

She waved him off as she shook her head. "I'm not here about whatever just happened. Are you okay? I was at the desk when they rolled y'all in."

He narrowed his eyes at her. "You were? I didn't see you."

"I wouldn't imagine." She laid her hand softly against his arm. One lone silver ring flashed in the harsh fluorescent lighting. "I'm sorry."

"For what?" Her fingers, long and soft, tightened slightly around his arm.

"You couldn't save him. I saw you trying." A weak smile flitted across her lips.

He shrugged and peered past her. His eyes followed the grooves of the white-painted, cinder-brick wall. "Part of the job. A hated part, but I guess you can't outrun death."

A soft current of air swept down the hallway and fluffed out her red hair. A single lock curled against her forehead. "Is that what you try to do, Scott? Outrun death?"

"Sometimes, I try." He reached to push back the lock but paused.

Blood stained his hands. He held them up. No time for this—this visit. "I need to wash up and then head to the lab for the blood work. Gloves broke during the ride; and not to mention, I split my lip. I don't know where his blood ended and mine began. Protocol demands a hepatitis screening."

She nodded and stepped back. "Okay, but before you disappear, I came to invite you to dinner."

"Dinner?" Scott furrowed his brow. What part of Friday night had she not understood? Friends meant friends only. "I thought . . . "

"I know, and this is only a friendly dinner. But I thought it would be a welcomed change and plus . . . "

Scott smiled, and a laugh shook his body. Once a reporter, always a reporter. "You want to pick my brain on something."

"Exactly. My place at seven?"

The woman wasn't shy. "No church tonight?"

"Not tonight. The preacher had a family thing to attend." She took another step backward. "Get cleaned. Do your paperwork. I'll see you at seven."

Her scent of roses and peaches followed her as she breezed back around the corner. He shook his head to clear the cobwebs.

Death. Blood work. Paperwork. Then dinner. He peered down at his blood-spotted undershirt. First, clean-up.

He balled his shaking hand into a fist and shouldered open the washroom door. What he really needed more than a washing was his alprazolam, which he finished off last night.

He turned on the water. Half-turn cold. Full-turn hot.

He ducked his face into the stream. His body shook as he rose and propped his forearm against the mirror. Stubble rasped against his skin as he lowered his head onto his arm. His breath fogged the surface.

Deep breaths. He inhaled deeply and let it out slowly. One. Two. Three.

He pushed away from the mirror and turned to the soap dispenser. The shaking diminished a little as he pumped a handful of foam cleanser into his hand. He really needed those meds, but it'd have to wait. Later. He'd figure out how to obtain his meds later.

First clean-up. Then blood work. Then paperwork. Then dinner.

Scott sighed. He never did actually agree to dinner. How did she do that?

He would call in a while and reschedule. Tell her some other time.

CHAPTER FIVE

Rochelle moved the cursor to the next file and clicked. It had to be this one. She scrolled down the archived headlines. Name after name blurred in front of her. This type of researching sure was hard on the eyes.

She glanced around. So quiet with no one here. Pops left earlier for the supervisor's meeting, and Michael had tagged along. The electric heater by her feet emitted its customary buzzing sound. At least it didn't have to compete with Michael's clacking keyboard.

The furnace kicked in, and the vents overhead poured out semi-heated air, stirring the potted plants. Pops had added another one. Sooner or later, the building would be a jungle.

She cupped her hands around her mouth. "Ooh, ooh, ooh, ahh!" Well, Pops could do a better monkey impression than she could, anyway.

She frowned. Angela should've been here by now.

The phone trilled beside her, and she jumped. Rochelle placed one hand over her heart to calm its erratic beat as she picked up the receiver. "*Garrettville Gazette*, Rochelle speaking. How may I help you?"

She returned to her computer screen.

"Rochelle, I'm running late. Ran into Tom at City Hall." Angela's breathless voice crackled over the line.

"City Hall? I thought Michael and Pops were taking that story this time." She exited out of the article and chose the next in line.

"Oh, they are. I was here on the budget information. I'll tell you about it when I get there. Should be there in about ten minutes. I took a quick side trip to the police department to see if there was any more information about the wreck."

"What did they—"

"Tell you when I get there."

The line clicked. Silence. Rochelle stared at the receiver for a second before replacing it in its cradle. Must be extremely important information if Angela wouldn't tell her over the phone.

She scanned the lines of information and sighed. This wasn't it.

Only three more to go.

The door chimed, and she looked up as Brent Sanders wandered into the building. Oh, be still her beating heart.

He pulled his cap off and brushed his hand through his shaggy, brown hair. She ran her tongue over her braces. Please, let there not be any food attached to the tracks.

"Hey, Brent. Here to see Michael?" She leaned her elbows on the desk and stretched forward. Warmth heated her cheeks when he smiled.

His green eyes gleamed as he swaggered toward the desk. A watery, citrus scent washed over to her. Goodness, he smelled good. He propped his own elbows on the counter.

"Nah. I was looking for Mr. Echols. Is he here?"

"Pops is at a meeting this morning." She tugged one of her spiked strands and tried to twirl it. "Anything I can do for you?"

He shook his head. "No. That's okay. I just had a message to deliver to him from Dr. Melbourne."

Her breath hitched as he reached out and flicked at her hair. A small piece of lint drifted to the counter's surface. Warmth turned to fiery heat.

"Looks like you've been dusting the building with your hair." His eyes narrowed as his smile widened.

Rochelle cleared her throat and ran a hand over her head. Lint and miniature dust bunnies floated down. She sagged. "I've been in the archive rooms. Very dusty back there."

His laugh boomed. He swiped some of the dust to the floor. "Researching? You were always doing that in school."

She fought the smile. He remembered. "Yeah. Looking at old budget articles for a piece Angela and I are working on."

His fingers crept closer to hers as they tapped against the dark surface. "Budget articles? That has to be boring. Angela's the new reporter?"

"Yeah. Didn't you read last week's newspaper? We printed a nice interview and introduction. I typed it all up and everything." Her heart fluttered against her ribs as his finger accidentally brushed against hers.

"I was too busy in Florence last week and didn't get a chance to read it." He shifted his stance, and his cologne drifted across the air to her again.

She could get used to that wonderful surfer smell. Got to get some distance before the guy bowled her over with his delectable self. A copy—that was what he needed.

She ducked down and snagged a copy of last week's edition from the bottom shelf behind the counter.

Her hair dust scattered in a puff of air as she plopped the newspaper on the counter. "Here. Complimentary back issue."

He gathered the paper and folded it. The newspaper touched his brow in mock salute. "Thank you, Ro."

She grinned as he started to walk away and then turned back.

"You'll tell Mr. Echols that I dropped by?" He replaced his cap. The bill shaded his eyes and gave him a rebellious look.

"I will." She held out her hand as he turned away. "Oh, I forgot."

"Yeah?" His eyes opened wide in expectation.

"Congratulations on the new job. Medical courier, right?"

"Yeah. And thanks." His grin pierced her and fluttered her heart again. "See ya around, Ro."

The door chimed as he strode out, and Rochelle let out a big sigh. Oh, boy. She pressed her hands to her chest.

"Be still my fluttering heart." She resumed her seat and stared at her computer.

Brent had spoken to her. He'd called her by her nickname. He'd spoken to her. Really, really spoken to her.

Angela whipped her car into the parking space a second before it sputtered to a shuddering death. She turned the key, and the engine ground in a highly grating noise.

Spectacular. She twisted the key one more time and slapped the dash with her other hand. "Start, you worthless piece of metal!"

The engine turned and belched.

Angela sighed, turned off the engine, and leaned back. "Thank you!" She pressed her fingers to her lips. "Please give me just a few more days, Lord. Just a few."

Hopefully with no other pressing matters that would take away her savings, she could finally get that tune-up before her poor little Grand Am collapsed into a heap of nonfunctioning metal scraps.

The door creaked as she pushed it open. WD-40. She pulled out her phone and tapped the notepad icon. Milk, eggs, bread, pens, notebook. She added "small can of WD-40" to the list. Every day, it grew. Strike that, every hour.

She ran her hand over the hood of the car Mike had bought her. "Looks like it might actually be longer than I would like for you to be fixed. Poor thing." She shook her head as she stepped upon the sidewalk. "Poor me for talking to a car. You are losing it, Angela dear."

Warm air blasted her as she pulled open the door. The plants fluttered in the air current. A pop station blared from the desk as Rochelle sat hunched over the computer. She looked up and flashed her shiny smile.

"Angela!" She reached over and lowered the volume as Angela dumped her purse on the chair in the corner. "I found two obits that you might be interested in, and I was right about Michael. He had an old article written on McOwen, but it was never printed."

Angela rounded the desk, stepped up on the raised platform, and leaned over Rochelle's shoulder, careful to avoid a short, red spike. "Show me, please."

"What'd you find about the budget?"

"That not only are July's minutes missing, but I have three more. July 2010; July 2013; and September 2016. Nice little pattern."

"Yup. Seems so. What about the police report?" Rochelle turned from the computer.

"There wasn't anything more. Just a basic vehicle accident. I just find it odd Tom didn't want to run an article about the son of city hall member Donald Pierce being involved in an accident."

The girl shrugged. "Mr. Pierce called Pops and asked him to keep it quiet. He said Shelby was embarrassed enough over the fact he was speeding and wrecked the car."

Interesting. Angela made a mental note to follow up on the city hall members later tonight. She pointed to the screen. "Show me, please."

"Oh, right." Rochelle twirled the chair around, reached for the mouse, and dragged the cursor over to the corner and clicked a file. She ran her finger down the screen and tapped it, the liquid crystal blossoming under her nail from the pressure. "Here. Casper McOwen, 56, died July 17, 2010, from injuries sustained from a vehicle accident located at Follows and Turnpike. Services will be held at Foster Mortuary, Tuesday, July 20, 2010, followed by graveside services at First Methodist Church." She closed that file and pulled up another. "I found this one. See anything interesting?"

Angela scanned the short obituary. "Seymour Whitecloud, 77, and long-standing advocate for Garrettville Native American Foundation, died from injuries sustained from a hit-and-run on Turnpike Road. Services and burial for Whitecloud will be held in Florence at Free Assembly Church. More details forthcoming."

Angela frowned. "Who wrote that article? That's terrible."

Rochelle blushed and cleared her throat. "Um, I did. It was my first attempt."

If only the earth would open up below her now. Angela's shoulders drooped, and she sighed. "I'm sorry, Rochelle. That was very rude of me."

The girl looked up with a hint of amusement in her eyes. She smiled and then laughed. "No, that's okay. I was, like, fifteen then, and I wanted to play reporter. So, Pops got Mr. Denning, who used to own this paper, to let me work here part-time." She turned back to the article. "But it is horrible. I didn't even put in the date, and Mr. Denning let it go through that way. I think that's why the paper declined so drastically. Mr. Denning didn't really care about what was printed, as long as the society pages were top-notch. You know, country club and cotillions, and who went to Europe or shook the senator's hand—"

"I get it." Angela straightened and placed her hands on her lower back. Her fingers worked at a knot. "Do you remember the date?"

"It was summer, the beginning of vacation." Rochelle tapped at her braces with a fingernail. "May 2013? No, early June."

Angela snagged the other office chair, rolled it beside Rochelle, and collapsed into it. "Okay. Let's do this then. Turnpike is the common element between these two. Let's see what we can find on Whitecloud and the Foundation. I take it the Foundation didn't survive?"

"I kind of remember a court case about something concerning it, but I didn't pay attention. I'll search the archives again and see. I do know that there were a few articles printed. Here." Rochelle typed in some search words. A long list of articles filtered through. "These are some of the printed and unprinted files. Let me run to the back and check the microfiche."

"Y'all still have the archives on microfiche?" Angela raised her brow and scooted closer as Rochelle vacated her spot.

"Unfortunately. Pops had planned to hire someone this summer to convert the microfiche to discs. But he kept procrastinating." Rochelle's voice echoed down the hallway as she breezed out of the reception area. "I'll be back in a jiff. Doesn't take long. I know exactly where to look and . . ."

Angela glanced over her shoulder as Rochelle's voice faded and a door slammed. One of these days, that girl would make a good reporter. She turned to the computer in front of her.

An article about the closing down of the foundation. Interesting. She quickly scanned the article that Michael had written.

> With the death of Seymour Whitecloud, the Garrettville Native American Foundation will permanently close its doors. Whitecloud's unfortunate death left no heirs, and there were no board of directors appointed in the Foundation's charter.
>
> Speculation and rumors abound around the true design of the Foundation, but no one can deny the wonderful works that the GNAF provided for the community . . .

Angela skipped past the praises about scholarships to local students, donations to local businesses, and numerous speaking engagements. Her gaze settled on the part about the donation of land to the hospital. She hopped up and retrieved her bag from the chair. The notebook had fallen to the bottom. She pulled it out, and the contents of her bag scattered along the floor.

Spectacular.

She scooped up her pens, wallet, and business card holder and stuffed them back into her bag. It clunked against the hard back of the chair as she cast it back onto the seat and hurried to the computer.

The chair spun as she plopped down, and she caught herself mid-spin and halted its rotation. Her fingers quickly scribbled down a list: *Check deeds for Whitecloud and Foundation, Check for court cases involving GNAF.*

Rochelle rushed back into the room, flapping an old newspaper in the air. Angela waved at the flying dust bunnies. "Check it out! I found an article about the closing of the Garrettville Native American Foundation."

She slapped the yellowed paper onto the desk and jabbed her finger on the bottom half of the front page.

Angela cocked her head. "It says that city hall bought out the Foundation's building. Where is it located?"

Rochelle opened the paper and turned to the third page. "Here. At Jamison Avenue. Next to the hospital. Hey, I remember now. It became part of the new addition. The north wing, I think."

Hospital, hmm? "I know someone who might know more." She opened a drawer and searched inside it. "Is there a flash drive in here?"

"Wait, I know where some are." Rochelle rounded the desk and bounded down the hallway toward Michael's office. Minutes later, she came back with a bright pink casing. "He wouldn't use it because it was pink. I had ordered flash drives a few months back and thought it would be cool to have the colored ones."

She pushed it across the desk toward Angela.

"Well, it'll work, regardless of what color it is." Angela stuck it into the port. "Which file did you find it on?"

Rochelle rounded the desk and pushed her aside. "Here, let me." Within a few quick clicks, Rochelle pulled the drive from its port, pushed the cover up, and handed it to Angela. "Downloaded and ready for your reading pleasure."

Angela grinned and held the little pink item in between her thumb and finger. "Perfect. And now . . . "

"Yeah?" Rochelle's eyes gleamed.

"I have an assignment for you." Angela ripped the page from her notebook. "Do you know how to search for court cases?"

"Yes, ma'am. Judy can help me."

"Then here. When Tom and Michael return, I want you to head to the courthouse and find the deeds on Whitecloud and the Foundation; plus, see if there are any cases—and I mean *any*—that deal with the Foundation or with Whitecloud."

"You think there might be a connection somewhere?"

"I really don't know." Angela jumped up and hurried to her bag. "But we must cover all aspects, whether farfetched or not. I'm heading to the hospital. There's someone who might shed a little bit of an insight about the new addition."

CHAPTER SIX

Scott secured the straps across the patient. Douglas cast him a quick glance as he spoke into the mike. "Could you say again, EMS?"

The radio razzed as dispatch came across. "All ER arrivals are to use the south wing entrance."

"Copy, EMS."

Scott leaned forward between the seats as Douglas replaced the mic. "Sounds like the door must have broken again."

"I keep telling them, man, that those doors need to be replaced. But does Trickle listen? Oh, no. Even Grace is never around long enough to tell her. By the way . . . "

Scott gripped the seats as Douglas swerved around the corner of Jamison Avenue. "Slow it, Douglas. This isn't a trauma, so there's no rush." He glanced back at their patient, who quietly laid on the gurney, staring at the ceiling of the van.

"Yeah, I know. But these fools in charge make me mad. As I was saying, by the way, have you seen Grace lately?"

Scott shrugged as the ambulance rocked to a stop outside the outer door to the south wing. "No. Thought she went on vacation."

He returned to his patient, resettled her bag of medicines beside her, and unlocked the wheels on the gurney. "Were these all your meds, Mrs. J?" The back door flew open, and Douglas hopped inside.

"Yes. I always keep them in that there bag." She blinked against the bright afternoon sunlight.

Douglas grinned down at her. "Mrs. Johnson, how you feeling so far?"

Scott grabbed the head of the stretcher and steadied it as Douglas stepped backward out into the open. The wheels clicked and locked in position as the lady spoke.

She patted her chest. "I'm feeling slightly better. Not as tight."

Scott reached behind him and slammed the doors shut. "That's good. We'll get you inside soon, and Dr. Morrison can have a look at you."

The gurney bounced over the rough sidewalk, and Mrs. Johnson's voice bounced along with it. "She's a sweet doctor."

"That she is." He eyed the bag of medicine as it bobbed up and down beside her. The label mocked him. "How long have you been on alprazolam, Mrs. J?"

"Oh, not long. Dr. Melbourne prescribed it a month ago."

Not long.

He bit at his lip and sniffed, looking away from the bottle that called to him. He slowed the bed as they came to the south wing's door. Douglas swiped his card through the security lock, and then swiped it again.

"Trouble?"

"Yeah. Card's not working. Hand me yours."

Scott pulled his tag off his shirt and handed it over. The door's lock beeped green, and Douglas pushed it open. He handed back Scott's tag. "That's the third time this month."

The slightly warmer air of the hospital washed over them as they pushed inside. "Third time you left your card in your pocket when they went to the cleaners?"

Douglas laughed. "That happened only twice, dude. No, third time the door refused to open with my card."

Mrs. Johnson patted Douglas's hand that rested on the gurney's rail as they pushed her down the hall. "I ended up washing my daughter's bank card. It was a wonder it still worked after it went through the dryer."

Scott laughed. "I think we've all done that before, Mrs. J." His smile died when her face paled. "Are you feeling strangely again?"

Her breath gasped in short heaves. "A little, Scott. There's a slight pain in my chest now."

Douglas angled his head toward the small hallway ahead. "Let's cut through the med hall."

Scott nodded and increased his pace, guiding the gurney to the small door. He swiped his card and pushed through. "This will get you there quicker, Mrs. J. Nice little shortcut."

She responded with a weak wave of her hand.

Scott let Douglas take the lead and pushed the door close. It clicked into place. He whirled from the door and hurried to catch up with Douglas. The bed rolled around the slight bend. A crash echoed back to Scott.

He rounded the small corner. The pharmacy nurse on duty glared at Douglas, who scurried about on the floor where medicine bottles littered the tile along with files and charts.

The nurse dropped to her knees. "Idiots! You can't use the med hall to transport a patient."

"It was faster, Pammy. Mrs. Johnson needs attention." Douglas dumped a handful of files into her hands and placed two bottles on the gurney's bed.

Scott frowned. It was a mess, but his opportunity. He cleared his clogged throat. "Douglas, take Mrs. J on. I'll help clean up."

Pammy looked up. "Thank you." And then glared at his partner.

Douglas huffed and wheeled the gurney through the door and into the ER wing. Scott knelt and helped collect the folders and Mrs. Johnson's bottles.

"Here." She traded a bottle for a file. "That woman sure has a lot of meds."

He accepted the small bottle and reached for another. His finger brushed against one and sent it skittering toward another bottle. His eyes locked onto the label: alprazolam. There wouldn't be much in there, but it would be enough. Just enough . . .

He jerked his head back to the nurse. "I'm sorry, what did you say?"

"I asked, what were y'all doing taking this route?" She reached behind her, collected a few papers, and then turned around to pick up another folder.

Now.

He fought against the sudden rise of guilt as he grabbed the bottle and pocketed it, stuffing it deep down into his cargo pocket, and then grabbed the other bottle as she turned back around and faced him. "We were rerouted to the south wing. Mrs. Johnson started having chest pains again, so we decided to cut through."

Scott rose to his feet and held out a hand. Pammy accepted it, and he pulled her to her feet. She shook her head. "When are they going to fix that?"

"Wish I knew." He swallowed. Maybe it wasn't such a good idea. He touched his pocket. "Did you get everything?"

"I think so." She turned away as he started for the door and paused. "Hey . . ."

Scott froze. His breath hitched. "Yeah?"

"There's one of the bottles."

Scott looked down at his feet and spied a small, orange bottle by the door jamb. He scooped it up. "Thanks."

"No, problem. Tell Douglas I expect a coffee as an apology."

She turned and flounced away. Scott released an unsteady breath. He shouldn't, he really shouldn't, but he needed the sleep. He needed that drug-induced void tonight.

He pushed through the door and into the ER wing. Dr. Morrison's voice reached him from the triage room. He couldn't do this, but he had to do this.

They wouldn't know.

The bottles threatened to spill out of his hands.

Dr. Morrison looked up as he entered. Her gray brow furrowed. "You got the medicines?"

Scott nodded. "Yeah." He dumped the bottles onto the tray and reached into his right pocket. The overhead light glinted on the orange plastic. The small bottle of blood pressure medicine rolled against the metal surface. The alprazolam burned through his pants. He reached into his left cargo pocket, ran a finger over the bottle, and pulled out his empty hand. "That's all. I'll go back and check to make sure nothing was missed."

"Mrs. Johnson, do you remember how many bottles you brought with you?" Dr. Melbourne leaned over her and smiled gently.

"Oh, no. I take so many that I can never keep count. They were all in the bag." Her eyes widened. "Should I start keeping count?"

The doctor patted her hand. "No. Don't worry. I will pull your medical history and see what's been prescribed. I will call Dr. Melbourne's office."

Scott patted Mrs. Johnson's foot. "Take care, Mrs. J. I'll come by and check on you, okay?"

"Thank you, Scott." Her voice followed him out into the hallway, along with Dr. Morrison.

"Scott!"

He slowed and took a deep breath before turning around. Could she see the bulge in his pocket? Surely, everyone could see it. Someone had to know he swiped it.

He cocked his head, not trusting his voice.

"Are you okay?" Her wizened eyes studied him.

Scott shrugged and fought the urge to look away. "I'm okay. Why do you ask?"

She studied him a little longer and then smiled. "You haven't been to the office for a check-up. No withdrawal symptoms?"

He looked away and shook his head. "Nothing more than what was expected. Still having a hard time sleeping; that's all."

"I can prescribe some Ambien, but nothing stronger." Her eyes stared at him for a moment longer. A slight air current whipped down from the vents overhead and stirred her gray hair. "Why don't you schedule an appointment for tomorrow?"

"No. I'm fine." He was just a thief; that was all. His throat threatened to close on him again. He cleared it and offered his trademark smile. "I'll deal; don't worry. Time to get back."

He left her standing in the hall. His hand itched to caress the bottle, to remove one and ease the pain inside.

Tonight. Tonight would be soon enough.

He arched his head to the side. Muscles and cartilage popped.

Now he was a liar and a thief. Oh, how the mighty had fallen.

Douglas looked up as he eased down into the chair. "Here's the report. You want to fill it out or restock the ambulance?"

Scott took the form. "I'll fill it out."

"You okay, Scott?" His eyes narrowed.

He avoided Douglas' gaze. "Just peachy. Go on. Get it restocked before life decides to call us out again." He watched as Douglas ambled down the hallway and toward the south wing. His gaze drifted to the emergency doors where the maintenance crew worked on the tracks.

A shuddering sigh left him.

If it weren't for those doors, he never would have received his chance to get his hands on some more medicine. He absently touched his pocket. Would Nana Debbie's God allow such a thing, or was it that devil?

He snarled, ducked his head, and started filling out the form. Maybe it was a good thing he believed in neither. Again, he reached down and touched his pocket.

Angela frowned at the ER doors. Two maintenance men on ladders struggled to replace the sliding door back into the track. She sighed and reversed direction. Her booted feet clicked across the concrete sidewalk.

A harsh wind nearly rocked her back as she rounded the corner. She glanced up at the sky. Storm was a'coming. The air seemed charged with electric currents as the dark clouds rolled in.

She ducked her head against the wind. Maybe the storm would blow through this time. Probably not, though, since the weatherman predicted storms until Thursday. She shook her head. Those poor little trick-o-treaters. Wednesday night was going to be awful if it stormed.

The entranceway yawned before her. Beautiful, potted trees lined the archway, obscuring the tall, sand-filled ashtrays, or whatever they were called.

Warm air gushed past as she pulled open the doors and stepped inside the softly lit lounge area. To her right, a long, tiled hall gleamed. A lady at the reception desk talked into the phone. Commercial-grade couches sat in a pleasant semi-circle around a muted TV. She turned to her left. A pale green, rounded Formica counter guarded the entryway to the emergency hall and triage center.

She crossed the lounge and approached the counter. "Excuse me."

The girl looked up with a bored expression. "Yes?"

She shot a smile to the girl. "I'm here to see Scott Wilson. Could you let him know that Angela is here?"

"Sure. No problem." The girl picked up the phone and pressed a button. "Hey, Scott back there, Arlene? . . . Scott, Angela is here to see you." She replaced the receiver and smiled up at Angela. "He said he'll be here in a moment."

"Great. I appreciate it . . . uh?"

"Stephanie."

"Thank you, Stephanie." Angela leaned against the counter. "You've known Scott for very long?"

Stephanie shrugged. "Only here at work. But all the nurses here love him." Her eyes twinkled, and her grin grew wider. "He's, like, the ladies' man here."

Angela shook her head. Why was she not surprised?

The door behind the girl swung open, and Scott slid through. His gaze landed on Angela, and a small gleam filled his eyes. "Stephy, I'm stepping out for a while. And thanks." He lightly touched her shoulder as he passed.

"Sure, Scott." Her face flushed a bright pink.

Angela raised a brow and regarded the man as he rounded the counter. His uniform hung loosely on his frame. She frowned. The man was already a sack of bones, so how could he get any skinnier? Thick stubble covered his jaw, deepening the shadows under his eyes.

"You look tired."

Scott pursed his lips as he stopped in front of her. "A little. Not sleeping well. Had lunch yet?"

He waved toward the front entrance and started walking. Angela furrowed her brow and followed. "Not yet. Why?"

"I'm famished and want to eat something." He ambled down the long hall and turned to the immediate right.

Angela hurried to catch up with his long strides. The tinking sounds of coins dropping into a vending machine reached her ears before she rounded the corner.

He punched a few buttons, and then looked over at her as a bag of chips fell from the rack. "Want anything?"

"No." She spied the cola machine. "Well, a Dr. Pepper probably. But I'll get it."

Scott shook his head. "No. Let me. There's a trick to it." He dropped his coins in, hit the Dr. Pepper button, and banged the side of the machine. A metallic clang issued two cans into the slot. "Here."

She laughed and closed her hand around the cold, wet cola can. Her fingers brushed against his. "You do this all the time? Stealing two drinks?"

He shrugged. "I usually give one to Stephy, or Arlene. If you don't bang it, the drink gets hung up inside, and you'll have to pay double. Hit it, and you receive a double blessing."

He collected his chips. "Mind sitting outside?"

She sighed. "Yes. It's windy."

His eyes bored into her, gauging her. "Put on a hat, then. I would prefer to, please. Been cooped up inside all morning. One patient and nothing since."

Angela popped the top to the can. "Fine, then. Feeling antsy?"

"In a way." He stepped past her, his arm brushing against her sleeve. "Thank you for the sacrifice of mussed-up hair to allow me a breath of fresh air."

She laughed and fell into step beside him. "You are most welcome then. You missed a good dinner last night."

"I was too tired. Sorry I had to cancel." He held open the door. A wooden bench stood against the side of the building by some holly bushes. He pointed to it.

Angela settled on the surface and swigged a drink of cola. "That's okay."

The chip bag rustled as he opened it. The cheesy smell of the chips reached her, and her stomach growled a response. He chuckled and held out the bag. "Have a few."

Her face heated as she pulled out a few of the nacho tidbits. "Yeah. I was trying to hold off on eating."

"Dieting? You don't need it, you know."

"No. Not dieting. I was hoping to have lunch with Dottie and Debbie later at Cooter's Diner."

Scott grimaced. "Ack. I hate that place. Too . . . " He waved his hand in the air. " . . . disorderly."

And that summed him up. She popped a chip into her mouth. She had a feeling that he was the orderly type. A place for everything, and everything in its place.

"So, what'd you come by for? Unless it's my good looks you can't get enough of." His eyes gleamed, and a small smile formed at the corners of his mouth.

"Ah, wouldn't you be so lucky." She laughed as he sputtered in his cola. His laugh choked out of him. She slapped his back. "You okay?"

"Yeah. Wrong pipe." He wiped at his mouth and ate another chip. "So, would that be lucky on good looks or that you wanted to see me?"

Angela shook her head. "You can't banter words with me, Mr. Wilson." She pulled out her notebook and turned to the page about the hospital's buy. "I wanted answers and thought you might have some."

"And here I was hoping it was more than business-related." He leaned back and crossed his ankle over his knee and continued snacking away on his chips. "So, tell me. What's fearless reporter Angela Mabry chasing down today?"

He held out the bag to her again. She grabbed two more chips and read from her notebook. "This fearless reporter is chasing down information on the hospital's purchase of Whitecloud's property."

Scott frowned. "Wow. That's old news. They bought it. The north wing was built. The hospital faced bankruptcy over the lien. Not to mention federals citations, which are still ongoing, for not being up to federal code. Melbourne and Associates stepped in to the rescue. End of story." He took a sip and regarded the approaching clouds. "You know, I do remember a little of it. I wasn't on duty when Whitecloud died. Douglas had that shift with one of our former paramedics. Let me ask him what he remembers—"

Scott's cell phone beeped. He sighed and pulled it from its holster. His shoulders sagged slightly before he straightened. "I've got to go. Meeting."

Angela stood when he did. He wadded up his chip bag and dropped it into the trashcan next to the bench.

"Okay, but will you accept my offer to dinner tonight? Friendly dinner and—"

"To pick my brain." He smiled. "Sure. About what time?"

Angela followed him into the lounge. "About six-thirty?"

"That'll do. Give me time to clean up before then." He threw her another smile and a wink. "Until then, my fearless reporter."

She watched his long legs eat up the floor as he rounded the counter, whispered something to Stephanie to make her laugh, and disappeared through the door. Such a flirt.

The sky darkened even more as she stepped back outside and paused under the overhang.

Bankruptcy, huh? She jotted that down on her notepad before hurrying to her car. There had to be something about that at the office. She unlocked the door and slid inside.

Angela pressed a fingertip against her temple. So many things crisscrossing each other, but not adding up at all. She breathed a quick prayer. Oh, Lord, what was she unearthing?

Rochelle placed the sheet of paper on the floor next to the others. Already half of Angela's small living room floor displayed an array of deeds, articles, and files. She swapped two deeds.

"I think I've got the timeline right." She touched each sheet in progression. "Casper McOwen dies at Follows and Turnpike, July 2010. The budget minutes should be here, but they are missing." She placed a yellow Post-it note labeled "missing BM" in the empty space. She glanced up as Angela walked into the living room from the kitchen.

Angela sat down on the worn couch and handed her a can of cola. "Scott texted and said he'll be here in a few short minutes." She waved at the line of papers. "Continue."

Rochelle popped open her cola and took a quick swig. She pressed her fist to her mouth and squelched the burp that threatened to rise. "Well, nothing until June 2010. Whitecloud is killed at Turnpike Road. Again, no budget minutes for July 2013." She attached a yellow note to that paper and then a blue note on the next papers. "I labeled the articles about the land buys in blue. The hospital bought McOwen's land. We got that article from the magazine. The article about Whitecloud's GNAF property mentions city hall buying it, but I can't find an article about the hospital getting it. Again, I tagged it in blue."

"Scott said he is bringing Douglas to tell us what he remembered. Maybe we will be able to narrow it down some more." Angela bent and scooted one of the papers closer to the others. "Another gap until September 2016. No articles in the archives about a special meeting?"

Rochelle shook her head. Oh, she hated failure, but the reports just weren't there. "I can't figure it out. There were no reports, no articles, no minutes. I couldn't even find any court cases about it. Should there have been something in probate?"

"Should, but only if there was a dispute about it. And we know there had to be, since there were no inheritors for the property."

Rochelle touched the next sheet. "Then the missing minutes from last year. And this is your article on Shelby Pierce's accident at Follows and Turnpike."

"Can you see the pattern, Rochelle?"

Rochelle stood and stared down at the white sheets with yellow and blue notes attached. "The accidents all happened around Follows and Turnpike. The land is by the hospital, which is not too far from Follows and Turnpike."

Angela smiled. "Don't deduce. We're not looking at the land yet."

"Oh." She slumped slightly and heaved a sigh. "Hold on then. Let me stare at it for a while longer."

The doorbell rang, and Angela stood and disappeared to the front. Male voices drifted through the small house as Rochelle pulled off some bright pink Post-it notes and labeled them. She looked up.

Scott grinned at her. "Rochelle, been a long time, girl. How are you?"

She offered a grin back at him, but her eyes seemed glued to the blond and buffed man behind him. "Doing good. Pops upgraded me to receptionist now."

"Still working the print room?"

"Yup. Double the job duties, but not the pay."

Scott's laughter boomed. "Sounds about right. Welcome to the world of slaves."

She snorted.

Heat ran up her neck as the blond man smiled at her. Kill her now for snorting in front of such a hunk. She cleared her throat. "Angela, I tagged McOwen and Whitecloud with pink for the land. McOwen's land bought by the hospital, which borders the hospital to the east. And then Whitecloud's land, which was bought by city hall and bordered the hospital to the north. Pattern?"

The blond man settled on the chair near the couch and leaned forward, his hands draped over his knees. "That's impressive. If I didn't know better, I would say you were plotting some suspense novel or something."

Heat flooded her cheeks at the compliment. "Um, thanks. But unfortunately, this is actually true-to-life stuff."

The man leaned down and started to pick up one of her yellow notes. "Missing bowel movement?"

She slapped her hand down on the yellow square. Her face flamed even hotter as he chuckled. "No. That stands for 'budget minutes.'"

Scott motioned toward the guy. "Rochelle, this is Douglas, my partner in blood and guts." He turned to Angela as Douglas smiled a greeting at Rochelle. "Like I said, he knows more about Whitecloud's accident than I do."

Angela cast a look at the floor and then back at Scott. "I ordered pizza earlier. Let me bring it in here." She disappeared to the kitchen. Scott followed her.

Rochelle turned to Douglas. Couldn't let silence reign. "So, you were at the accident? There wasn't much written about it. No article or anything."

His brow furrowed. "Really? I remember it quite clearly. It was my first hit-and-run." He slid off the chair and knelt across from her. His finger tapped the pink note. "I know there was an article on it. I was interviewed. Green as I was, I ended up telling more about it than I should have."

His blue-eyed stare pierced her. She swallowed. He seemed the total opposite of Brent. Shame on her. Brent was taking her out to-night, and here she was salivating over a man with surfer dude looks. She ducked her head and straightened the papers. "It's all a jumble, hard to keep straight, but there are missing minutes." She tapped the yellow papers. "Then there's the obits and accidents that happened at Follows and Turnpike." A quick jab at the white printouts. "And then the land buys." She thumped the pink notes.

"Which shows that there is more to the story than we realized." Scott's voice sounded behind her.

Rochelle whipped around. "Yeah. But what is it all about?"

Douglas accepted a plate piled high with pizza and a can of cola from Angela. "My guess, probably something shady. You sure you really want to delve into this, Angela?"

Angela nodded and perched on the edge of the chair Douglas had vacated. She handed Rochelle a plate and then turned to Douglas. "I just follow the story, Douglas. Tell me what you know."

Rochelle picked up a slice and bit into the cheesy pepperoni concoction. She couldn't eat too much, since Brent was taking her to Burger Joint outside of town.

Douglas wiped at his mouth. He poked the white sheet about Whitecloud. "You've got the location. I was called out about eight that night. It was strange because Whitecloud never walked that part of the highway. In fact, he never walked any highway. Always drove that beat-up Volvo of his. By the time I arrived, he was already in cardiac arrest. Loss of blood. Trauma to the head, legs, and abdomen. DOA by the time we got to the ER." He set his plate to the side and regarded Rochelle. "I find it odd that it happened shortly after the heated debate about his foundation's land. Something about taxes and re-zoning."

Rochelle shook her head. "No way. There wasn't anything at the courthouse about that. And nothing in the paper's archives. Are you sure?"

"As sure as I am sitting here eating pizza and staring at a pretty girl." His eyes flashed a deep blue.

Rochelle nearly choked on her bite. "Um. Yeah. Okay." She hid her blush behind a sip of cola.

Angela passed Douglas the pizza carton. "Another slice?"

Rochelle shot her a relieved smile. She had a date, for crying out loud. She didn't need a man flirting with her. "I'll search the archives again, Angela, to see if I can find anything about the rezoning. Looking at the dates and then look at the obits, I know there has to be a connection."

Three heads bent closer. Scott shuffled her timeline, swapping two pages. He tapped them in order. "McOwen in July. No minutes in July. Same year. Whitecloud in June. No minutes in July. Again, same year."

Angela scooted down to the floor and sat cross-legged by Douglas. "Then, no minutes for the emergency board meeting in September of 2013. And then there's July."

"You know," Douglas said before taking a sip of his cola and swallowing his bite, "I remember Melbourne meeting with some of the city honchos back then. I think you were on vacation, Scott."

Rochelle leaned forward. "Do you know what it was about? Did it have anything to do with the land buys?"

Douglas shook his head. "I don't think so. I think you are just chasing a white rabbit. There might be a story about kickbacks or something concerning the minutes, but how in the world would missing minutes and two old coots' deaths be related to the hospital's buys?"

Scott shrugged. "There's always a story."

Rochelle nodded. "And leave it to Angela to find that story." She ducked her friend's swipe and grinned. "Anyway, I'll search the archives later this evening."

"That'll be great." Angela offered the pizza box to Scott, who grabbed two more slices. "What time were you leaving, Rochelle?"

"Eight." Rochelle glanced at her watch. Five after seven. "I guess I should head back home and at least freshen up, huh?"

Angela reached over and rubbed at her cheek. She held up a black-inked finger. "Yeah. You've got newsprint smeared on your face."

Once again, heat tormented her neck. She slapped her palm against her cheek and scrubbed. "Yeah. Pops likes the cheap ink." She jumped up. Scott and Douglas stood while Angela took her used plate. "I better head out. Got most of the timeline done for you."

Angela smiled. "And I thank you. Be careful tonight, okay?"

Rochelle nodded and collected her bag from the end of the couch. "I will. See you around, Scott. Nice meeting you, Douglas."

The man smiled and threw her a wink.

She spun around and hurried for the door. Get a grip! The man was just flirting. Besides, she had a date with an extremely handsome guy. She gently closed the door behind her and hurried to her moped. As she settled onto the seat, she glanced back at Angela's door.

There was something about that man. After her date with Brent, she'd look up the Douglas dude. Surely, that interview about Whitecloud had to be in the paper's archives. She revved the motor and pulled away.

What was the proper length for a first date? An hour? Two hours? She bit her lip. Brent or the research?

It was a no-brainer, indeed. The idea of a true-life mystery won. She'd give Brent two hours max, and then to the office.

Scott leaned back against the couch and rubbed at his eyes. "So, what you are saying, Douglas, is that the hospital is knocking off people to gain their lands?"

"I ain't saying that!" He scratched his head and stretched out his legs. "I just remember that when Whitecloud died, there was a heated argument about his land. You were too wrapped up in your studies to pay attention. Pammy talked about it all the time. You know, she worked in Melbourne's office for a while, until she got the job at the hospital."

"Studies?" Angela stopped her scribbling in her notebook and glanced at Scott. "What were you studying?"

Scott shrugged his shoulders. He rubbed at his eyes again and stifled a yawn. "Paramedic. I was an EMT back then. Been trying to certify myself in everything I can."

Douglas crossed his arms across his chest. "Yeah. Because you want Grace's job. You gotta knock Trickle out of his first, though."

A yawn escaped Scott. "Yeah, well, I'll give it time. The man is bound to screw up sooner or later. If he doesn't fire me first."

"Fire you?" Angela's eyebrow quirked. "What for?"

"Oh, anything. I swear up and down that the little—" Scott cleared his throat and started again. "That the weasel is trying to find something on me so he can discharge me."

"Chalk it up to jealousy." She smiled at him, her eyes deepening into a dusky midnight.

His chest tightened.

How could she stay just friends if she kept looking at him like that? "Maybe."

"Mommy?" The owner of the little voice rounded the corner of the hall. Max slithered over the side of the couch and into Angela's lap. "I can't go back to sleep."

Scott reached over and ruffled the little boy's hair. "Hey, little man. Did we wake you?"

Max nodded. "A little."

Angela wrapped her arms around her son. "Want some pizza? There's a couple of slices left in the box. On the table."

The boy's eyes brightened. "Yes!" He slid off her lap and stumbled to a halt when his gaze landed on Douglas. "Mom? There's a surfer man in our house."

Douglas laughed and held out his hand. "Hey, Max. I'm Douglas. Scott's friend."

Scott watched the hesitation before Max reached for Douglas' hand. The little boy turned his gaze to him.

"Is he a parry-medic like you?"

Scott furrowed his brow. "A parry what?"

"Paramedic." Angela stood and guided Max to the kitchen. "And yeah, he's a paramedic, too."

Douglas smiled. "Well, actually, EMT, but I'll take the promotion."

"We'll let it slide, then." Angela's voice sounded from the kitchen. "Scott, Douglas, you guys need another drink?"

"No, ma'am," Douglas regarded Scott for a moment. "Thank you, though. I think we've overstayed our welcome. Looks like you need to put a sleepy tyke back to bed."

She returned from the kitchen with Max and began settling him at the table in her small dining room. Max climbed into the chair, accepted his glass of milk, and pulled the pizza box to him.

"That's okay. I've enjoyed the company." Angela eased onto the couch beside Scott. The cushion sank slightly as she tucked a leg beneath her. Scott covered another yawn with his hand. "But I better let you two head on. I think Scott is tuckered out."

"You got that right." He rolled his head. Muscles popped in his neck. "And I think we gave you plenty of information to digest."

Scott stood, and Douglas followed his lead. Douglas paused and looked at Angela for a couple of seconds. "I have to ask again, Angela. You sure you really want to investigate this? I mean, something is fishy about all this now that you have it laid out."

Angela pushed off the couch and toed the papers on her floor. "I do. I need to follow this through. Maybe it's nothing. But when you follow the crumbs, it all leads right back to city hall and the hospital. Wouldn't be the first time city officials took kickbacks from a large corporation."

"Well, I know there should be something on the hospital buy-out by Melbourne and Associates. You almost lost your job, didn't you, Scott, when the hospital went bankrupt?"

Scott shrugged. "Almost. Wished it was Baptist or Methodist that bought the hospital and not these boneheads. But that's another story for another time." He bent down to help Angela stack the papers.

"Oh, don't worry about those, Scott." She waved his hand away. "Leave them. I will probably look over them one last time."

He grinned. The woman wouldn't stop until she got her answers. Relentless chick. "Okay." He followed Douglas to the door. As his friend pulled open the door, his gaze fell onto a framed child's drawing that stood on the small table. "What's this? Max draw it?"

"I did!" The little boy padded to Scott's side, a pizza slice drooping in his hand, and pointed at the drawing with his free hand. "That's you with a shield. One word and all the bad lions fall dead."

Scott smiled. "Cool. I have awesome powers, then?"

Max beamed. "Yup. Parry-medics are superheroes."

He had been called a hero once. By another little man.

A lump lodged midway up his esophagus. Scott cleared his throat, but his voice still croaked. "Wow. Superhero, huh?" He placed his hands on his hips and puffed out his chest. "How's this? Scott Wilson, paramedic, to the rescue."

Max giggled and almost dropped his pizza. "Totally cool!"

Angela rolled her eyes. "Don't encourage him, Scott Wilson Paramedic."

"You tell him, Angela. He's going to be horrible all week. Superhero indeed." Douglas snorted and skipped down the steps. "Thank you for the pizza!"

"You're welcome, Douglas." She shooed Max back to the dining room and held the screen door open as Scott passed the threshold. "I'm glad you came, Scott."

He grinned and slipped his hands into his pockets. "Glad to have the chance to pick my brain again?"

Her eyes held his for a brief moment before a dimpled smile spread across her face. "That and I enjoyed your company. I'd forgotten how it felt to have friends over."

A cold wind whipped through the trees and through his long-sleeve shirt. It cooled off the warm feeling that surrounded his chest. He offered a small smile. "It was nice." He glanced back at Douglas, who waited at the gate. "I better head on. We've all got work tomorrow, and Max has school."

"I hate school!"

Scott threw his head back and laughed as Angela heaved a sigh at her son's shout. "He's a handful, isn't he?"

"Pretty much. But I wouldn't have it any other way."

He took a small step toward her. His hand landed on the screen door frame next to hers. "A lot like his mother, yeah?"

What was he doing? She said friends only, but her soft expression pulled at him. There was so much more to this woman. His smile faded from his lips as his gaze landed on her mouth.

Her lips parted. Then she spoke. "Yeah, a lot like me. Good night."

He tore his gaze away from her and sucked in a deep breath. "Night, Angela."

The screen door closed, followed by the weathered wooden door. It creaked and clicked into place. He backpedaled across the small porch until his heels touched the lip. Scott sighed and turned around and bounded down the steps.

Douglas looked up from his fingernail cleaning and pocketed his knife. "You really got a thing for her, don't you?"

Scott glared. "Shut it. Only friends." He shoved his hands into his pockets and headed home. Douglas followed him.

"Yeah. Well, that's how it all starts."

"And this from a guy who dates a girl for only what? Two weeks tops?" Scott shook his head. "Nah. She's a great woman, but she only wants to pick my brain for information."

"Maybe that's her excuse. I mean, she's been to the hospital, what, three times already?" Douglas stopped at his truck and opened the door. "I did mean it when I asked Angela if she really wanted to follow that rabbit trail."

Scott paused. "You think it will be trouble?"

"I always think things are trouble." Douglas bit at his lip. "I just have a feeling, man. You and I both know that this town is kinda crooked. Hate to see the pretty redhead get into trouble."

Scott tapped the hood of Douglas' truck. "I'll keep an eye on her. You piqued her curiosity even more when you told her about Whitecloud. Guarantee she will be up all night researching the internet on whatever."

"Or that sweet little assistant of hers?" Douglas waggled his brows. "Now there's a hot chick. Like those little red spikes of hers."

Scott narrowed his eyes. "You lay off Rochelle."

Douglas touched his chest. "Hey. She's my age limit."

"Not that. She's not the type for one of your plays."

"I won't hurt her, man. I'll just admire." Douglas pulled his door shut. "See ya at work tomorrow."

Scott stepped away and watched his friend pull out of the driveway. The truck revved once and then sped out of the little cul-de-sac. He heaved another sigh. Man, he was tired tonight.

The aroma of tomato soup poured over him when he opened the door. "I'm home, Nana Debbie." He touched his jacket that hung on the hook, then emptied his pockets.

Wallet. Keys. Yea, no parking ticket this time. He smiled. Dan was off duty today.

Nana Debbie entered the foyer, drying her hands with a dish towel. "Have a good time?"

She offered her cheek, and Scott dropped a peck onto it.

"Actually, yeah." He nudged Dixie out of the way with his foot. "Despite the woman picking my brain for information."

"She must be working on some big story." Scott followed Nana Debbie into the kitchen. She hung the towel over the edge of the sink. "Just hope she knows what's she's doing."

Scott pulled open a cabinet door and chose his Crimson Tide glass. "She's from Mobile. I think she'll be fine." He filled the glass with cold water. "I'm beat. Good night, Nana."

She patted his arm. "Night. Want anything special for breakfast?"

He shook his head. "No, ma'am. Just whatever. Sweet dreams."

Her slippers scuffed against the wooden floor as she shuffled to the living room. The soft sounds of the late-night news filtered down the hall and into his room. Scott eased the door slightly closed, leaving enough room for the pets to squeeze through. The lamp lit up the room with a soft glow when he turned its little knob.

He opened his closet and chose the empty black hanger. His black pullover mussed his hair as he pulled it over his head. There was probably one more good day left to the shirt. He brought it to his nose and sniffed. Maybe not. He replaced the black hanger and ventured to his bathroom. The shirt sailed into the hamper.

Half-turn, cold. Full-turn, hot. He ducked his head under the stream and scrubbed at his face. Working quickly, he brushed his teeth and turned off the water. He replaced his towel, pushing it down until it was evenly spaced. His gaze traveled over the items on his shelf. Everything seemed straight.

He unbuckled his pants as he walked to the bed. The mattress dipped when he sat down. He paused in unlacing his boots. Did he put that hanger back?

Scott pushed off his boots, set them at the foot of the bed, and hurried to the closet. Yeah. The hanger hung after the aqua-colored one, but before the blue one.

He pulled off his socks, hung them over the chair arm by his nightstand, and then stepped out of his pants. With quick movements, he folded them and laid them in the chair.

The comforter soared to the foot of the bed with one quick flick of his wrist.

The house was too hot for the thick cover tonight. Scott eased down on the bed and pulled open the nightstand drawer. He held the orange medicine bottle up to the lamp light.

He pursed his lips. Interesting. No need for the medicine tonight.

The bottle landed back into the drawer.

Scott sipped the cool water and then slid between the sheets. He snapped his fingers. Judas leapt upon the bed and happy-pawed his chest.

He stroked the feline's head.

One. Two. Three.

Judas purred as Scott reached over and turned off the lamp.

He folded his hands behind his head.

Maybe Wednesday, his day off, he'd go cut that grass of hers. Maybe. Or maybe ask her out.

"No way, Scott. Remember, she said friends only." Judas paused in her purring at his words. He touched Judas' head as a yawned escaped him. "Whaddaya think, Judas? Think I should risk it?"

The cat poked her nose into his hand, and he absently scratched at her ears.

He'd just wait and see what Wednesday held for him. Scott yawned again and rolled over, tucking his hand under the pillow. His brain replayed the evening's conversation. The images of the papers on the floor fluttered through his mind's eye.

There was something there. It screamed at him. Scott sighed. His thoughts dove deeper into the images, running over the pages and the notes. It was there. Somewhere. Oh-seven, oh-ten. Thirteen. Sixteen. June, July, September. Follows. Turnpike.

Darkness filtered through, and the pages disappeared.

CHAPTER SEVEN

"Okay, Tom. Here's the article you wanted." Angela placed the print-out on his desk. "And here're the AP stories."

Tom looked up from the book in his hand. "Which ones did you choose?"

Angela flopped into the chair next to his desk and crossed her legs. "Let's see. AP bulletin about a new drug awareness program in Jasper City, Mississippi. It's received statewide attention. Then there's the one about the upcoming senate candidate in Carsontown, Tennessee. Memphis had a riot on Beale Street. Protest about the upcoming elections." She flipped to the next page. "For entertainment, here's one about the Zion Music Fest. You know, that big festival that travels from Savannah, Georgia, to Springfield, Missouri. And a country music concert at the Grand Ole Opry."

Tom set his novel to the side. "Okay. Let's go with the Jasper City story. And for the entertainment, go with the concert in Nashville."

Angela marked the pages. "Oh, a robbery in Birmingham. Looks like there was a barge spill at Pick Wick. Plus, a few more international stories centered on France and Italy—financial situations and weather. Do you want to run a few Mid-East stories for the 'World Outside Garrettville' section?"

Tom accepted her pile of printouts. "No. I think a change of pace would be good. Go with the France story for international and the extreme weather in Europe. Add the robbery in Birmingham. What do you think for the political piece? Memphis or Carsontown?"

"I would choose Memphis."

Tom handed her the sheets and smiled. "I like this idea of running a new section in the paper. Good thinking."

Angela smiled. "Don't compliment me. Rochelle and Michael came up with it. It should help with sales."

"And what about your piece?" Tom leaned back and folded his hands across his middle. "You sure you really want to run with it?"

Angela smiled. "You're the second person to ask me that. And yeah, I do. Missing budget minutes. It's all coming together, but it's posing more questions than answers."

Tom huffed. "Don't they always."

"Well, the stories you wanted about the road repairs and the school's new building are already in the queue and ready for layout." The lobby door chimed, and Rochelle's voice yelled out.

"Pops!" Rochelle rushed into the room and gave them both a wide grin. She spoke past her toothy smile and waved her chip bag-laden hands toward her face. "See anything different?"

Tom picked up his spy novel and turned the page. "You got spotted teeth?"

Rochelle's smile died, and she threw a small bag of chips at her grandfather. "Funny, Pops. Dr. Thomas said that they will even out eventually. Gave me a whitening paste to use." She twirled into the office and then plopped down on Tom's lap, knocking his book aside. "No more metal tracks."

"What about the metal on your face?"

Rochelle wrapped her arms around her grandfather's neck and dropped a kiss on his forehead. "One track at a time, Pops. At least I'm toning down the red."

Angela laughed. "Your hair does look better without the spikes. I didn't know you actually had curls."

"Yeah, well. Can't go drastically changing my looks, now can I?" She hopped up and flounced out of the office. "Enjoy your chips! I'm heading to the print room, Pops."

Angela shook her head. "I heard she put you on a diet."

The bag of potato chips puffed when he tore the bag open. "Unfortunately. The girl was listening in when Dr. Morrison's office called with the menu list. I have to limit my sodium intake. So, Rochelle took it upon herself to make sure I am allowed only two bags a week. Today is my mid-week allotment."

"She does it only because she loves you."

"I know. And I put up with it only because I love her. She's all I've got." He pointed a finger at Angela. "Now, go get the next story started. Take your pick—the high school FFA's upcoming trip or the Waterloo-Garrettville scenic byway proposal?"

"I'll take the proposal, thank you." Angela collected her papers. "I'll send the AP stories to Rochelle. Don't forget the mayor's meeting later this afternoon."

Tom huffed and turned his attention to his computer screen.

Angela walked down the small hall and peeked into Michael's office. Again, the man was gone. And always on a Wednesday. She shook her head and continued to her little cave. The brown, paneled walls loomed over her as she sat at her desk.

She moved the mouse to wake up the screen and pursed her lips. The Post-it note on her monitor stared back at her. She removed it and read over the list. The story on the proposal wouldn't take long, so she should have time to find information on Julie and Billy Bergman's death.

Should she even venture into that part of Scott's life? She read the next to-do: *Look for anything on hospital bankruptcy and anything on Melbourne & Associates.*

Well, time to get busy.

Scott flicked the medicine bottle, and it rolled across the bed. It stopped near the pillow. He reached out and rolled it back to him. Over and over. Back and forth.

The light glinted against the plastic, flashing in erratic patterns. Pills inside clinked against each other. A strange melody of organic compounds and plastic. Over. Rattle. Over. Rattle.

Judas struck out with a paw and sent the bottle sliding toward the pillow. Scott nudged the cat out of the way and picked up the medicine. He eyed it. Not even a full bottle. Only fifteen—and he had counted them—rolled around in there.

Once again, he popped off the top and fished out a pill. The thin, oblong, yellow pill lay against the palm of his hand.

No brand.

No scoring across its smooth, chalky surface.

No markings of any kind. He glanced at his pill identification book lying next to him.

Not alprazolam. Not even diazepam.

Nothing in the book.

He rolled the pill between his finger and thumb.

Almost. He almost took this last night.

The front door squeaked open. Scott dropped the pill back into the bottle and recapped it. His hand shook as he slipped the bottle into his slack's front pocket. Somehow, he had to figure out how to make this right.

He rubbed at his jaw. The beginnings of whiskers scratched against his skin. He steepled his fingers and held them to his lips.

To make it right, he risked too much. To not do so might be more than he could bear. What-ifs played through his mind. What if the pharmacy unknowingly gave the wrong pills? What if they didn't? What if the pills were not legal? What if he had taken one last night without looking at it first? His mind turned them over and over.

He turned the situation from every angle, viewed it from every perspective.

No matter. He lost either way.

Somehow, there had to be a way out of this.

"Scott?" Nana Debbie's sweet voice called out to him.

He sighed and levered himself off his bed. The what-ifs and how-to's could wait. The nightstand drawer gaped open. He frowned.

Scott reached in and pulled out his grandfather's Bible. He slowly ran his hand over the worn, hardback cover. The gilt edging had begun to dull. His finger glided over the smooth edges.

Scott held it in his hands and let it open. The black and red print peppered the pages. He glanced at the top. *Gospel According to Matthew.*

Whatever.

He chucked it onto his bed and closed his eyes. No matter how the book called to him to read it, he didn't have the time. He had to figure out what he had in his pocket. What was Mrs. Johnson taking if it was not alprazolam?

"Scott?" Nana Debbie poked her head into his room. "You hungry? I thought I would reheat the leftover tomato soup and make some grilled cheese."

His stomach rumbled. He turned his back on the black book laying on his bed. It remained open to the same page he had glanced at. Not happening. "Sure. I'll come help."

Her gaze fell to the Bible. "You've been reading?"

Scott eased past her and continued down the hall. "No. That's your department. I was just cleaning out the drawer."

Her sigh followed him.

Why was she so insistent that he read those archaic words? He stalked down the hall and into the kitchen.

The refrigerator door stuck slightly. Scott held back his snarl and yanked it. Bottles on the door's shelves clattered against each other. Nana Debbie stood in the doorway watching.

He pulled out the cheese and container of soup and walked to the stove. His anger threatened to spill over. His nostrils flared as he dumped the soup into the pot on the stove. He turned to retrieve the flat skillet, but Nana Debbie had it held out to him.

"You okay, Scott?" Her blue eyes searched him.

He swallowed against the lump in his throat. "Yeah. Just something came up suddenly, and I can't figure out the solution."

Her hand patted his arm. "I'm sure you can figure it out. You always do."

Scott took the skillet away from her and banged it on the stove. His mind cursed the pills and whoever gave the wrong ones. He needed them last night. Now he was suffering from not having what he needed.

No. That was partially what was wrong. There wasn't a snowball's chance he was going to go visit the other reason.

He started when Nana Debbie took the tub of butter from his hands. Scott shook his head. "No. I've got it, Nana. You just relax."

"You sure? You keep staring off into space."

"I said I've got it." Scott smacked a small spoonful of butter onto the hot skillet. With jerky movements, he sandwiched the cheese slices between the bread and set them on the skillet.

Nana Debbie had moved off and sat at the table. Scott glanced at her and fought down a sigh. She turned a page and started reading. "Not everyone who says to Me, 'Lord, Lord,' shall enter the kingdom of heaven, but he who does the will of My Father in heaven. Many will say to Me in that day, 'Lord, Lord, have we not prophesied in Your name, cast out demons in Your name, and done many wonders in Your name? And then I will declare to them, 'I never knew you; depart from Me, you who practice lawlessness!'"

"Which part is that?" Scott paused in his stirring of the soup. Her words still echoed in his head.

"Matthew. Chapter seven. Verses twenty-one to twenty-three." Her brows lifted. "Why?"

Scott shrugged. She just had to read from the same book that he had looked at moments ago. "Just wondered."

As she continued reading, he pulled down two small plates and slid the toasted sandwiches onto them and then ladled the soup into two bowls. The silverware drawer rattled when he pulled it open.

Nana Debbie's voice wrapped around him as he brought her plate and bowl to her. " . . . and the rain descended, the floods came, and the winds blew and beat on that house; and it did not fall, for it was founded on the rock. But everyone who hears these sayings of Mine, and does not do them, will be like a foolish man . . . "

Scott tuned out her words and retrieved his plate and bowl. He pulled out his chair and sat. Nana Debbie set her Bible aside and bowed her head.

Again, irrational anger beat at him. He waited for her to raise her head and then started eating.

"Do you want to talk about it, Scott?" She dipped her spoon into the soup.

"No." After a few seconds of silence and a couple of bites of food, Scott leaned back in his chair. His appetite had disappeared. Just like his options. "I did something, Nana. And it's going to cost me to rectify it."

She set her spoon to the side. Compassionate eyes gazed at him. "What exactly did you do?"

Scott turned his bowl. How could he tell her? What would he tell her? That he was going to lose his job? And how would he support her then? Yeah, he could just blurt out, "I stole some pills, Nana, and it turned out those pills were not what I thought I stole. You see, I'm a drug addict."

He snarled. Yeah, that would go over well. Disappointment would probably kill sweet, dear Nana.

"Scott?"

His hands itched to hurl his soup bowl against the wall. He clenched his hands. He'd never kept secrets from her before. A deep breath fortified him. "I stole, Nana Debbie."

"Stole? What did you steal?" Her soft, papery hand laid over his.

Scott ripped his hand out from under hers. "Alprazolam. Or what I thought was alprazolam."

She leaned back into the chair and regarded him. A deep furrow formed between her regal brows. "I thought you were off them."

"I was." He pushed back his chair and took his dishes to the counter. They clattered as he dropped them onto the surface. "But I . . . Last month, I forged a different strength onto the prescription. Then when I ended my allotted amount, I found that I needed more."

He leaned his hands against the counter and stared at the floor. She was making this difficult. He would have preferred if she had ranted and raved about his crime. Instead, she sat there at the table, gazing at him, waiting. As always. Always patient with him.

"Monday, when we took Mrs. J. to the ER, her meds fell. I pocketed her alprazolam." He pushed away and paced the floor of the kitchen.

Walk. Turn. Walk. Turn.

"Did you think you needed them because of Julie and Billy? You lied when you told me that you had been sleeping okay?"

Scott sped up his pacing. Oh, yeah, he had lied. "You are missing the point, Nana. I stole from an old lady to supplement an addiction. And now that I know the medicine isn't really alprazolam, I have to let Grace know. Which means, I lose my job. But if I keep my—" He bit off his curse and blew out his breath. Calm was needed. He set his hands on his hips. "I can't *not* tell, Nana Debbie. And that's the problem."

She rose from her chair and approached him. "But you have always done the right thing, Scott. You've never backed down, no matter the consequences."

"Well, there's always the first time for everything." He propped his back against the cool door of the refrigerator and crossed his ankles.

"Not in this instance."

He scratched at his jaw. There had to be a way. "Well, I could always say that I found the pills in the van. I've lied before. I can do it again."

"Scott Weatherby! You will not compound this sin with another!" Her eyes flashed at him.

He looked away from her and crossed his arms. "Sin? Only you Christians spout out that word. There is no sin. Right and wrong, yes; but there are variations of right and wrong. The world is gray, Nana. Not black and white."

She huffed. The heels of her shoes clicked sharply against the floor as she hurried to the table. Her hands shook. The pages of her Bible rustled. "Blessed are those who are persecuted for righteousness' sake, For theirs is the kingdom of heaven."

"Stop!" Scott balled his fists. Fairytale words again. "Always with the reading. Every morning. Every night. I tolerate it, Nana. But that archaic fairytale isn't going to help me one iota!"

Her hand feathered against her chest. Her eyes widened. "It will if you would only believe, Scott. Your father and mother were believers. You were raised in church. You used to believe." She set the Bible down and fell into her chair. "What happened?"

He snarled. What happened? What did she want to hear? Well, her precious Bible always talked about the truth. Might as well give it to her. "The truth? How about, God isn't real! No loving God would ever let a child die like that. I see it all the time. Children beaten and battered. Children raped. Killed. No God would do that! And this God who you so lovingly speak about allowed it. If that's what your God does, then I want no part of it!"

Tears formed in her eyes. "Things do happen, Scott, but there's always a reason."

"Yeah? What reason?" He tapped his chest. "What reason did God have for taking away my best friend and her child? Tell me, what reason for that?"

Her face grew pale. "When it's time, it's time. Have you ever thought that God wants you to be part of His family? Julie and Billy were. Even Jake. He didn't rile and curse their deaths. He drew closer to God."

A bitter, harsh laugh escaped him. "Closer? If that's how He wants us to get closer, then I ain't a part of it. And never will be."

"Scott?" She held her hand out to him.

He kicked the refrigerator and backed away. "Stop. Just drop it, Nana. I should have never told you. Should have known you were going to drop that holy God mumbo jumbo on me." He stalked back to his room. The nerve of his grandmother.

He slammed open the door to his bedroom. The Bible still lay on his bed. Judas looked up at him as he approached. She jumped off the bed and dove under it. Scott picked up the book.

Light from the window danced across its black, leather surface.

Stupid words! He pulled his arm back. The dart board on the far side offered the tempting target. A flash caught his eye. He paused.

He turned his head and gazed at the man who looked back at him from the mirror. Rage distorted his face. Muscles bunched along his forearm as he held the Bible in the air. A parody of a pulpit pastor.

The Bible fell out of his hand and bounced on the bed. This wasn't him. Rage wasn't him. He wasn't one to scream at his grandmother. Scott slumped and sank down onto the mattress beside the Bible.

She was right, though. Sometimes, doing the right thing gave a person the short end, but he had always done the right thing before. Why stop now?

He hung his head and heaved another sigh. A chuckle escaped. He'd been doing a lot of sighing lately. He scooped up the Bible and dropped it back into the drawer. Grace would be on staff today. He glanced at his watch. Yeah, she was still on shift.

He stood. Might as well add an apology to his righteous list.

"Judas?" He bent down and checked on the cat. She raised her head and gave him a squinty glare. "Bed's all yours, girl."

Scott pulled his door open. "Nana?" He ventured into the kitchen. "I'm sorry, Nana. I shouldn't have yelled at you like that. I shouldn't have—"

His gaze fell to her slumped form on the floor by the table. He rushed to her and rolled her over. "Oh, God, please, no!"

A faint pulse beat against his fingertips. He thumbed back her lids and checked her pupils. His fingers fumbled as he ripped his phone out of his pocket and dialed.

"Nine-one-one emergency."

"Jean. Nana Debbie's unconscious. Suspected heart attack or stroke. I need an ambulance. Patch me through to EMS." A tear ran down his nose and splashed down onto his Nana Debbie's cheek.

Scott's heart clutched into a knot inside his chest as the nine-one-one operator patched him through to EMS.

He had killed his nana.

CHAPTER EIGHT

Angela set her third cup of coffee to the side. Fatigue battered her, winning the war against caffeinated energy. She rubbed at her eyes to erase the blurriness. Thankfully, the article on the bypass proposal was short and sweet. That gave her enough time to research. She fought a yawn. Although, this time, her research had nothing to do with Follows and Turnpike, nor with the hospital. Well, not exactly anyway.

She leaned back and stared at the articles from one of the spring editions. Pandora's Box. That little fable ran through her mind. She'd opened it, and now she couldn't stuff the knowledge back into that dratted box.

Her finger tapped the down arrow, and she continued reading.

Julie Bergmann was an outstanding citizen of Garrettville. Garrettville Middle School will mourn the loss of their beloved teacher and drama team director.

"Julie was an amazing woman," stated Principal Mallory. "I don't think we will ever truly replace her. Her spunk and spirit broke through even the toughest of shells when it came to the students."

Julie leaves behind a husband, Jake Bergmann, owner and operator of Bergmann Construction. Bergmann Construction won the bid for Garrettville General Hospital's east wing expansion.

She scrolled back to the top and reread the beginning. Her eyes zeroed in on Scott's name.

> Julie and Billy Bergmann were pronounced dead on the scene. Victims of a five-car crash, the Bergmanns were the only fatalities, despite, as onlookers reported, the heroic attempts by Garrettville General Hospital's EMS medics, Scott Wilson and Douglas Tomlin; and Garrettville Fire Department rescue crews, Chief Jerald Downey, Captain John Nelson, Timothy McDonald, and Fred Dunnaway.

She scrolled up one more time and peered at the photo that was printed along with the story. Her fingernail traveled the small print of the caption as she read aloud. "Scott Wilson, Douglas Tomlin, and Chief Downey on the scene."

A candid shot, its objects unaware. Douglas and Chief Downey stood near a shell-shocked, blood-covered Scott. His eyes gazed into the distance. So much hurt, anger, and disbelief poured from her friend's eyes.

Now she understood what Debbie and Dottie were talking about that afternoon. She swallowed against her closed throat. She was right about him running. But she was wrong about the direction. He was running *toward* death. Ready to fight it for all he was worth. Didn't she see that when that poor devil died the other day?

She paused.

Another death? Wonder if it was at Follows and Turnpike.

She hopped up from the desk and hurried to Tom's office. Opera music bellowed out from the half-opened door. "Tom!"

Her hands splayed against the doorframe and halted her flight.

He jerked his head up and then reached over to lower the volume. His eyebrow quirked. "Yeah? Got another lead on something?"

"A question. Sunday, the person who died at the hospital. Have we run the obit yet?" Her heart hammered. Was that on Sunday? Seemed like eons ago to her.

"Not yet. Family doesn't want it published until the arrangements are finalized. I think they dropped off the information today." He leaned forward and fished through his in-box tray. "Yeah, here it is."

Angela accepted it. "James P. Turnstile. Just basic stuff. Do we know where it happened?"

Tom shrugged. "Michael said it was a call from his home. He went into diabetic shock or something from what EMS chatter stated. I nixed the story. Regular ambulance run."

Angela handed Tom the sheet and sank into the chair. She blew out a sigh and leaned her head back and stared at the ceiling.

"You thought we may have been on to something?" He replaced the sheet in the tray.

"Sort of. The accidents either happened at Follows and Turnpike or nearby. This guy died. I wondered if it might have been connected. But I guess not. He was the second accident that I've seen Scott work. The first was Shelby Pierce at—"

Angela jerked her head forward. Tom met her gaze. "Tom, I didn't think about that. I was so intent on the Whitecloud and McOwen information I completely overlooked a major key."

Tom shook his head and rose from his desk. "Angela . . . "

She jumped up. Her hands waved wildly in the air as she ranted. "I can't believe it. Shelby at Follows and Turnpike. You sent me there, Tom. Think!"

"I am, girl. And I don't like where you think it's going." He rounded the desk and pushed his door shut. "Shelby is the son of Donald Pierce, who is on the board. That's a hornet nest you're poking."

"And we know that city hall had bought the land that belonged to Whitecloud and McOwen. Plus, the missing minutes. The missing land deeds." She tapped her fingernail against her front teeth and started pacing Tom's small confine. "We were just joking about it last night, Tom. But what if it's true?"

"What?"

Her eyes widened. "That city hall is killing off people to gain their lands."

Tom stared back and then burst out laughing. His hearty booms echoed in the small room. After a few seconds, he wiped at tears. "You have watched too many episodes of crime shows."

Angela plopped down in the chair and smiled. "Maybe read too many murder mysteries." She propped her chin in her hand. "But what if I am on to something? Maybe not so dire, but what if I really am uncovering some land scheme of city hall's or the hospital's?"

Tom sobered. He sat back down in his chair and steepled his fingers. The tips pressed against his lips. "Then tread lightly, Angela. Keep it under the table."

Angela nodded. "I will. Quiet as a dormouse."

Rochelle's voice penetrated the closed door. "Pops! Angela in there with you? She's got a caller on line two!"

Tom turned his desk phone around and handed her the receiver. His finger hit the line button.

"This is Angela Mabry. May I help you?" Her finger played with the coiled cord.

"Angela!" Dottie's voice rushed over the phone. "I need to get to Florence. Max's bus will be here in about an hour, but I can't stay. You need to leave early."

"Okay." Angela frowned. Dread ate at her, but there was no source for it. "Why? What's happening?"

"It's Debbie. Scott called. They're on their way to Florence by ambulance. She collapsed, and the hospital rerouted her to Eliza Coffee Memorial in Florence."

Angela fell back into the chair, nearly bringing the clutter on Tom's desk with her as the cord caught. "You leaving now?"

"Yes. She'll need me. And Scott will be a nervous wreck, I'm sure. He . . . he could barely talk when he rang me."

"Go." Angela jumped up again and leaned over the desk, the receiver plastered to her ear. "I'll get Max and will arrive as soon as I can. Be careful, Dottie."

The receiver clattered into its cradle. Angela twirled and practically ran back to her office. Tom's huffing followed her.

She breezed into her office; raked the files, notebooks, and flash drives into her bag; and then turned to find Tom blocking her way.

"Something happen?" He stepped aside.

"Debbie is on her way to the hospital in Florence. Dottie is leaving. I've got to get home to be there when Max gets off the bus. And then I'll be in Florence. If I don't come in tomorrow, that means I'm still in Florence."

Tom waved her explanation away. "Don't have to be here in the office to work a story. Let me know how Debbie fares."

She threw him a wave and hurried out the doors. The cold wind whipped at her. Trick-or-treaters were going to freeze tonight; that was a given. She slid into her car and slammed the door, and a quick prayer for Debbie and for her car to behave long enough to reach Florence shot up toward Heaven.

###

Rochelle looked up as Angela rushed out of the building. Pops rounded the corner of the desk. "What's going on, Pops?"

His eyes held a weary look. "She said Debbie Wilson was taken to Florence hospital. Angela's heading home to wait for Max while Dottie goes to Florence."

Rochelle pressed her hand against her breastbone. "Oh, I hope everything will be okay. Need me to help with anything while Angela is gone?"

Pops shook his head. Wisps of hair danced around his ears. "She can handle it. Although," he said as he leaned against the counter, "what have y'all collected so far on the budget minutes? Angela seems to think she may have another lead."

Rochelle twirled in her chair and brought up a file on the computer screen. "Just a pattern. McOwen, land to hospital. Whitecloud, land to hospital. Follows and Turnpike."

A loud harrumph billowed from his lips. "That's what Angela is about to run with. Follows and Turnpike has had a few accidents in the last few years." He thumbed his lower lip. "When's the delivery guy come by to pick up the route papers?"

"About eight."

"You staying here until then?" At her nod, he continued. "Then I want you to do a little more digging for Angela. Run through the PD reports we have on file from January oh-seven to this month. See what you can find on Follows and Turnpike."

Rochelle grinned. "No problem, Pops. I'll get started on it right away."

Pops moved off toward his office. Rochelle propped her chin in her hand and pulled up the archives on the police accident reports. With a few clicks, she broadened the search parameters and started scrolling.

Line after line blurred. In between the cascade of letters, *F* and *P* popped out. She backed up a page, hit print for two copies, and then continued.

She paused and read a report. No. A fender bender at Turnpike. Again, she scrolled. The shadows in the office lengthened even further, until eventually Pops walked out of the office.

"Heading to the courthouse, then home. Make sure you lock up."

Rochelle gave an absent nod and waved him on. Silence descended into the office. More and more fender benders. A broken-down derelict. Nothing major. Shelby Pierce was the most recent major accident. She leaned back and rubbed at her eyes.

Only one printout. She reached behind her and grabbed the two sheets of paper from the printer's tray. Jonathan Hopskins. One vehicular accident. Minor injuries sustained at Follows and Little Deer Road.

She pulled open her desk drawer and extracted the county map. "Let's see . . . Follows. Little Deer Road." Her finger ran down the list of names in the index. "Map six, E, three." A little voice shouted in her head, "Bingo!" as she flipped to the page.

The E-Three grid put Little Deer Road as the first major road before Turnpike.

She tapped her teeth with a fingernail. Interesting.

Suddenly, the door chimed. Her breath caught in her throat as Brent sauntered across the floor.

"Hey, pretty thing." His eyes traveled to her hair and then downward before coming to a rest at her eye-level.

"Hey, Brent. What's up?" She tried to give him a genuine grin. Hard to do when the guy had insulted her the other night.

"Wanted to say that I'm sorry." He leaned against the desk surface. His citrus scent wafted over her. "Can you forgive me?"

Instead of responding, Rochelle huffed at her hair. She grimaced as the lock fell back across her face and stuck to her mascara-coated lashes. There was a reason why she wore spikes. "It was pretty harsh, Brent. I'm not sure what kind of girls you are used to dating, but I ain't one of those."

He reached out and pushed the frustrating lock away and tucked it behind her ear. His touch sent a wave of heat across her face. "I know. And no, you're not. You are absolutely great. That is why I am asking for a second chance. Let me take you to dinner this Friday?"

Rochelle started to shake her head, but stopped as his hand covered hers. Strong, callused hands gently squeezed her fingers. Oh, what would it hurt? She opened her mouth to speak again, but the back door buzzed.

She glanced at the wall clock. Only six-thirty.

"Hold that thought, Brent. Let me let Tommy in to collect the papers." And for her to collect her thoughts.

"Sure." He let go of her hand.

Rochelle hurried down the hallway and through the double doors of the small print room. Hopefully, one day their budget would allow them to send the paper to a larger printing company. For now, and maybe for a while, she was stuck with the printing.

She turned the deadbolt lock and pulled open the heavy warehouse door.

Tommy, his dark hair tucked under a ball cap, grinned down at her. "Rochelle, hope you don't mind if I'm early. Teresa is expecting company tonight and wanted me home in time for dinner."

She gasped. "Company, as in, the soon-to-be in-laws?"

A sheepish smile spread across his red face. "Yeah. Tonight, we break the news to them that we are getting married."

"Oh, Tommy! Don't worry. They are gonna love you! What's not to love?" She wrapped her arms around his broad chest in a quick hug. "I can't wait until Tuesday for you to tell me how it went."

He squeezed past her and stood just inside the doorway. "Don't worry. I'll let you know."

Rochelle propped the door open with a cinder block. "You better. Well, I'll let you get to it. Just close the door. I'll lock up later."

"You bet. Tell Pops I'll catch up with him tomorrow for my paycheck."

Rochelle left the broad-shouldered man as he lifted the boxes of papers and started loading the bed of his truck. A faint smile drifted across her lips. Teresa was so lucky to have a guy like Tommy. Wonder if Brent would be as great as Tommy? No matter how hard she tried to think of Brent loading boxes of newspaper or driving an old pickup truck, her mind kept trying to make her picture a tall, blond, surfer-looking EMT instead.

She slowed to a stop and leaned against the wall. Maybe going out with Brent wasn't such a good idea. Was there a way out of this? No matter what, it seemed like she couldn't say no to the guy.

A deep breath fortified her. Rochelle rounded the corner and stepped back up to her chair behind the receptionist desk. Brent lounged against the counter, playing with the paperclip holder.

"Everything ship-shape?" His lips shifted into a sly smile.

"Yeah. Tommy's loading now." She straightened the mail trays. "About Friday, Brent—"

"I really would like it, but I just got a call from my boss. I'm heading out to Nashville that morning. Won't be back until much later. Think we can go out another time?" He leaned further over the desk and captured her chin in his hand. "I might make it back in time for coffee or a shake? Think about it. I'll call Friday."

Her breath hitched. She turned her head at the last moment and his lips stole a quick kiss to her cheek. Fire smoldered in his eyes. He winked and sauntered out the door. She bit her lip. He never waited for her reply. Dratted man.

She rubbed her lips, safe once again from Brent's kiss, and then sat back down at the computer. Her finger paused over the mouse. She hadn't minimized the window. Or had she? She could have sworn she didn't. Man, she really needed to get her act together. With a click on the *x*, she closed the program, and then placed the computer in sleep mode.

A sigh escaped her. It wasn't really a long day, but it sure felt like one. A pounding tapped against her skull with a vengeance. Her stomach growled, reminding her that suppertime approached. She collected her bag from under the desk, kicked the chair back into its place, and turned to pick up the printouts.

Only one lay on the desk's surface.

Argh.

She ducked under the desk. No paper there.

When she rounded the desk, she glanced under the chairs in the lobby and around the room. No paper.

Maybe it became mixed in with the other papers when she straightened the mail trays. Oh, well. She'd check it in the morning.

Her boot heels echoed down the hall as she hurried to the back. Tommy had closed the door. She quickly locked the deadbolt and slid the overhead bolt into its slot.

As she walked past the machines, she checked to make sure the power was off. Good. With a flick across the switch, darkness bathed the room. She hit the switch as she exited the hall. Darkness followed her, eating at her heels as she passed through the lobby.

She exited the building and locked it. Pops would be home. Her thoughts drifted to what he would burn for supper tonight. She started her moped and paused.

That missing printout was going to bother her. She peeked into her bag. Nope. Only one sheet. She glanced around. No streetlamps. No cars. The sun barely peered past the horizon. She rubbed at the goosebumps on her arms. For some reason, it all seemed darker.

CHAPTER NINE

Scott hung his head and wrapped his hands around the back of his neck. Tension rolled through him. Knots bunched in his neck and shoulders.

It was the waiting. The waiting was going to kill him.

He checked his watch for the umpteenth time and returned his hand back to his neck. Two hours. From the ER to Radiology for Nana Debbie. From the ER to waiting room for him.

He lifted his gaze to Dottie, who sat across from him. Her nimble fingers flipped through a fashion magazine. Her eyes ran the length of both pages and then turned to the next. She cast the one in her hands to the side and picked up her fourth magazine, a home and gardening issue.

Scott stood.

This was going to kill him.

He needed some news. Something. Something to tell him he wasn't the reason for Nana's collapse.

His hands clenched. He stalked to the window and peered out across the parking lot. Light reflected from the overhead lamps and onto the black surface of the lot. Few people dotted the world below.

He turned and stalked away from the spy hole to the outside world.

One. Two. Three.

Turn.

Back to the window. The same people down there. Turn.

One. Two. Three.

Turn.

And back again. Oh, someone new. The figure, carrying a small bundle, hurried across the asphalt. Turn.

One. Two. Three.

Turn.

"Scott."

He paused by Dottie. "Yeah?"

"You need to talk?" Her soft gaze peered up at him. She patted the chair next to her. "You're so tense. Come sit beside me, son."

Scott shook his head and continued wearing down the threads of the carpet. He clenched his fists and peered out the window. All the people were gone. Only light peppered the parking lot.

The heel of his boot snagged the carpet, as he stalked back to Dottie.

Her thin, white hand captured his arm as he passed by. "Dear boy, sit down. Debbie will be okay. Gotta trust the Lord on this one."

Scott gently removed her hand. "That's your department. Yours and Nana Debbie's." And the same department that practically killed Nana.

The elevator dinged, and the metal doors swished open.

"Dottie!" Max flung his little form into the old woman's lap.

Angela followed Max and leaned down to hug Dottie. "We came as soon as I fed Max." She turned to Scott. Her hand gripped his upper arm.

He placed his hand over hers. Warmth radiated underneath his palm. The sorrow and empathy that poured from her threatened to do him in. He cleared his throat and found himself wrapped in her hug. He couldn't handle this, not right now. He needed distance.

His arms didn't listen to his brain and encircled her back, holding her near. He buried his face in her wild, red strands. Roses and peaches drowned his brain cells.

"Oh, Scott!" She rocked a little in his arms, and then stepped away, her hands still on his arms. "Have you eaten?"

He sniffed and shook his head. "No. I didn't want to miss the doctor when he came out. Nana is still in Radiology at the moment. No one is allowed in right now."

Her hand traveled up and down, sending miniature goose bumps down his arm. "It will be like that for a while. Come on, you have to eat." She turned to Dottie. "I'm taking this walking rail of a man down to the cafeteria before they close for the night. Call when you hear anything?"

Dottie shook her head. "I left my phone at home."

Angela pulled her cellphone out of her bag. "Here. Come on, Max. Do you need me to bring you anything, Dottie?"

Dottie smiled and placed the phone near her purse in the seat next to her. "I ate earlier. And let Max stay, and don't worry about us. We'll be okay. Now, go feed the man. I will call if I hear anything."

Scott and Angela started for the elevator but Scott stopped. "Not just anything, Dottie. If the doctor even steps into the lobby, you call me. On second thought, I'm not really hungry. I'll just stay."

"No, you won't, Scott Wilson." Angela snagged his arm and pulled. "You need to eat; otherwise, what good will you be if you drop from low blood sugar because of the lack of food? Won't be there for Nana Debbie then, will you?" She tugged him into the opening elevator.

"Fine." He called out to Dottie as the elevator started closing. "But you better call me, Dottie!"

The doors shut with a whisper. Angela hit the first-floor button, and motors whirred to life. The descent pulled at his stomach, reminding him of how empty it was. So much like his heart.

He practically killed his nana, and now he was going to eat. As if he didn't feel bad enough.

"Scott?"

He slanted his gaze toward her. She returned his stare. "What?"

"She's going to be okay." The elevator lugged to a stop. Angela slipped past the opened doors. Scott followed. "You know that, don't you?"

Scott shrugged. Sure, he knew that. Logic dictated that. But his mind kept telling him that he'd killed her; he'd hurt her.

"What happened?" She followed the signs pointing the way to the cafeteria.

He followed his nose. The scent of fried foods and bread wafted down the hallway. "She collapsed. At first, I thought heart attack. Or stroke. But I'm not sure now."

The clanking of silverware and plates announced that they had arrived at their destination. Angela stepped through the doors. The aromas from various foods elicited a deep gurgle from his belly. Scott placed a hand over his flat stomach and let his shoulders slump. The woman was right. He would need something to eat if he was going to be any good for Nana Debbie.

He accepted the plate and tray from Angela and followed her down the line. Fried chicken, wing and thigh; mashed potatoes loaded with thick gravy; corn; and two hot, buttery rolls quickly filled his plate, courtesy of Angela. He nodded as she motioned toward the green beans. The server spooned a generous helping onto his plate.

No conversation. Angela just pulled him along the line.

A small dish of apple pie landed on his tray, once again courtesy of Angela, along with a can of cola. Condensation trailed down the aluminum side. He placed his tray down for the cashier to total.

His hand met emptiness when he reached into his pocket to pay. He frowned and checked his other pockets. All empty.

Scott sighed and closed his eyes. Great.

"I got it, Scott." She smiled that understanding smile of hers and handed the cashier her debit card. She accepted her receipt, picked up her tray, and nodded toward the windows overlooking the outside. "Come on."

He followed her. His feet dragged against the tiled flooring. His legs refused to operate as they should. Fatigue leeched into him and pulled at his body. Maybe this wasn't such a good idea.

Her warm hands pushed him down into the chair. The pop-hiss of his drink brought him around and out of his muddled thoughts. She set his silverware in front of him.

"Here. Eat. You'll feel so much better once you get some food into you." She spread her napkin onto her lap and started eating her own mashed potatoes. A small roll and small helping of green beans accompanied her potatoes.

He picked up his chicken and took a tentative bite. She was right, of course. Food would help him cope. To deal with the guilt. Give him energy to face what he did.

Scott blinked in surprise. He dropped the stripped chicken bone back to the plate.

"I was like that when Mike died. Never realized how hungry I truly was and then was surprised that I actually ate." She took a drink of her tea. "I take it you have never been in this particular situation before?"

Scott picked up the next chicken piece. "No. Doctor's visits, but not this. Nana Debbie has always been in good health." He chewed and chewed before forcing the swallow down. Wonder if she would hate him if he told her? "I had a fight, an argument with Nana."

Angela dropped her hands to her lap. "Before she collapsed?"

"Yeah." He shoveled potatoes into his mouth. Fill it, and it wouldn't pour out his wrong-doings. The potatoes disappeared. Angela sat silently, picking at her green beans. He moved on to his own. Down the gullet, bury the guilt, silence the urge to confess.

He swallowed and gulped at his cola, washing it all down. If only he could wash it away.

"You feel responsible."

How did the woman know that?

Scott dropped his fork onto the tray. He clutched his hands under his chin. "Yes. I did something at work. I argued with Nana Debbie about it. Yelled and insulted her God. When I came back into the kitchen, she had collapsed."

Angela reached out, gripped his hands, and pulled them down. "What did you do, Scott? Whatever it was, I am sure it wasn't the cause of Debbie's collapse. You'll see."

"I hope you're right about that, Angela. I couldn't bear the thought that I killed Nana."

She opened her mouth, but his phone bellowed out "Earth Angel." Heat flushed his face as she smiled faintly at the ringtone.

He fumbled with his phone. "Dottie? News? . . . Okay, we're on our way."

Angela collected the trays as he pocketed his phone. "What's the news?"

"They moved Nana Debbie into a private room. She's being transported now, and the doctor will be up there shortly."

He helped Angela shove the trays and plates onto the conveyor belt that led to the kitchen. They hurried out of the dining area and back to the third floor's waiting room. Finally, some news, and hopefully, news that he could handle.

Angela sat back in the hard chair as Scott was led away from the waiting room and down to Debbie's room. Relief flooded through her at the doctor's announcement that it wasn't a stroke or heart attack as previously thought. Respiratory infection and a viral infection, coupled with low blood sugar, caused her collapse.

Dottie stroked a sleeping Max's hair. His small body curled in her lap. "At least Scott can relax enough. The poor man was stretched to his limit."

Angela nodded and gazed down the hall. Scott said he would return shortly after he saw to Debbie's comfort in the room. The staff allowed them only a short few minutes to visit for the night. She glanced at her watch. A little past ten. She'd call in tomorrow and let Max stay home from school. He could draw Debbie a picture. She would need to get a get-well gift for her.

"I'm sorry, Dottie. What did you say?" Angela brought her attention back around to the woman.

"I asked if you were planning to come back tomorrow to visit."

"I plan to. I'm sure Scott will spend the night here." She shifted in her seat. "He feels guilty about her collapse."

"Well, I'm sure he knows now that it wasn't his fault. That man carries the weight of the world on his shoulders." Dottie nodded her head toward the hallway. "Here he comes now."

Scott's booted feet echoed down the hallway. His pockets bulged from where he had shoved his clenched hands deep inside them. She had to agree with Dottie. From his hunched shoulders and tight expression, you could tell Scott carried more burdens than any man should.

His teeth flashed briefly as he gave a quick grin. The cushion of the seat sighed when he lowered himself down. She half-expected his bones to groan.

"Nana is doing fine. They are planning to keep her tomorrow. They started an infusion of antibiotics; and even though she showed no signs, they ran an MRI and EKG on her. Should have the results of the MRI tomorrow. To be safe." He leaned his head back. "She ran herself into exhaustion. Doing too much, apparently. She's sleeping now."

Angela placed her hand over his. The roughness of his fingers and knuckles contrasted with her own lotion-softened skin. Strong fingers laced with hers. "I will come by tomorrow. Do you need anything?"

Scott nodded and looked over at her and Dottie. "Think you could grab my wallet off the foyer table? I feel naked without it."

"I can." She stood. She watched Scott jump up and collect Max from Dottie's lap so she could stand. "But you will call us if anything changes? And tell her we will be back?"

She reached for Max. Scott helped settle the sleeping child in her arms, and his hands lingered briefly over her arms. "Thank you. For being here."

"Anything I can do to help, Scott." She quickly reached out and stroked his dark-stubbled cheek. "You get as much rest as you can, okay? We don't need you collapsing, too."

He pressed his cheek against her hand and then stepped back. A wall re-erected itself between them. "I will."

Scott turned to Dottie and gave her a hug and kiss.

Dottie placed a kiss on his chin and patted his cheek. "I'll call in the morning."

Angela followed her to the elevator. The urge to say something more slapped at her, but what would she say? There was nothing else to do but go home. And pray. Not only for Debbie, but for Scott. Somewhere deep within him was his cry for help, for understanding, for . . . for something she couldn't name.

The doors slid together, closing off Scott's sorrowful face. The image of his coffee-brown eyes, pain and guilt glazing them, burnt into her mind. Definitely pray for Scott.

"Dottie?"

"Hmmm?" She straightened her bag on her shoulder.

Angela opened her mouth, and then shut it. No. She'd keep it to herself for a while. What Scott confessed, although not in its entirety, was for her and no one else.

"Never mind." She stepped out into the lobby once the doors hissed open. "It'll wait."

Dottie walked with her to her car. "I'll pray. Things will work out."

Angela nodded. Yeah, eventually they would, if only she knew what "things" Dottie was talking about.

CHAPTER TEN

Scott peered back at Nana Debbie as his hand rested gently on the edge of the opened door. Her soft, white hair fanned out along the pillow. Soft light bathed her face, erasing the lines and hollows on her face.

She was old, so old. His nostrils flared. When had she become an old lady—his nana?

He turned away and slipped into the quiet hallway on the fifth floor. A couple of nurses looked up from their stations and gave him a brief smile before returning to their tasks.

They had flirted some, but mostly, they had seen to his comfort and Nana Debbie's. Good nurses. Sweet and attentive.

He paused at the desk. "I'm slipping downstairs to stretch my legs. Call me if Nana needs me, please?"

Trina, the head RN, smiled. "I will, Scott. She should sleep the rest of the night with no problems."

Scott nodded, stuffed his hands into his pockets, and ventured to the elevators. No destination but down. His heart seemed to slam against his ribs, and blood pulsed in great, heavy waves. Sleep refused to come. And again, he craved the drug. What was he going to do?

The metal doors slid open. Scott stepped inside the tight box and jabbed the first-floor button. Ground-level sounded nice. Flat and level. No more feeling the hum of a hospital floor beneath his feet. No more looking out the window at a world below him.

Hydraulics creaked, and the square box jerked downward. When the doors opened, he hurried into the brightly-lit corridor. No one roamed the hallway. A trickle of sound filtered down the lonesome tunnel.

Scott frowned. Piano chords.

He followed the invisible trail of sound. His sleep-deprived mind watched as his hand pushed open the chapel's door. Sweet-smelling air—a soft, resin smell—enveloped him. The piano's soft notes flooded his ears.

The unfamiliar song eased around him like a soft, warm blanket. Tense muscles melted. The other occupants never noticed his entrance. Scott scooted along the back bench and into the far corner, letting the shadows obscure him.

Scott watched as the small group stood at the front near an altar. The older man had his arms raised above his head, swaying to the music, while a younger man with his hand over his heart sang. His other hand gripped the hand of a young, dark-haired woman. His wife? She clutched at him as though she might be.

She sang with him, her free hand half-raised as if reaching for something unknown.

An older woman played the piano. Wisps of gray-streaked, dark hair fluttered about her face, escaping from the harsh confines of her clip. Her voice mingled with the crisp sounds of the keys. He had heard that song before. Reach out? Sounded like begging to him. Touch the Lord? How was that possible?

A few more chords played before she repeated the chorus. Apparently, that was all she knew, or maybe that was all there was. Didn't matter either way. Scott leaned back and listened.

Such nonsense, but her voice sure was soothing.

Her fingers slowed and blended into a new song. The melodic notes whirled toward him. "'Tis so sweet to trust in Jesus, Just to take Him at His word; Just to rest upon His promise, Just to know, "Thus saith the Lord.'"

Scott's breath caught. Goosebumps prickled his skin.

"Jesus, Jesus, how I trust Him! How I've proved Him o'er and o'er! Jesus, Jesus precious Jesus! O for grace to trust Him more!"

The people stood there, singing and praising, but it wasn't them. It was Julie and Jake, his nana, and, so many years ago, his mom and dad. Somehow, he had forgotten that song, a memory of his past, of his childhood, of just a few months ago.

No way!

He wasn't going to believe what they wanted him to believe.

How could they sing of a Lord and his promises when that same Lord allowed such horrible happenings?

His hands gripped the edge of the wooden bench. He started to push up from his position and ease out, but an old man sank down onto the pew and barred his way. A huff of heavy breathing escaped the man.

Of all the seats in the chapel, the old Santa-looking man just had to choose his bench.

"I've always found that song soothing, no matter what." He leaned back and propped his cane along the bench beside him. "What about you?"

Scott sank back down and crossed his ankle over his knee. His hands latched themselves across the knee, quelling the shaking.

"Never gave it much thought. Just an old hymn from childhood."

The group had stopped singing and now stood side by side, hands raised, as the older man prayed. His voice rose and fell. Heartache and joy, a paradox, ran through his words. Again, why praise a deity who gave hand-in-hand heartache and joy. Talk about a stressful life, never knowing what was coming.

The man beside him spoke in quieter tones. "Name's McDaniel." He pointed a gnarled finger toward the floors above him. "My wife is up there. Stage four cancer. Started out as ovarian and moved into her kidneys."

"I'm sorry." Scott continued watching the praise display. How many times had he experienced this at Garrettville's hospital? They just needed someone to talk to as they waited. "How long?"

"They're giving her a few more weeks." He ran a finger under his nose and sniffed. "We'll probably ride it out at home. She would prefer to die around her plants and books and family instead of a cold, antiseptic hospital room."

Scott shook his head. "I couldn't imagine wanting to stay here either. I work in a hospital. ER. Once my shift is up, I'm out of there."

McDaniel snorted. "But then, that's life, isn't it?" He shifted position, hooking his arm over the back of the bench, and then regarded Scott from underneath his bushy, gray eyebrows. "What about you? Why you here?"

"Grandmother collapsed. Nothing too serious, but it scared me. She's all I got left in this world." Scott frowned. Now why would he say that to a complete stranger?

"Nah. I don't believe that. There's always more in this world than most people realize." He pointed at the group. "Take them, for instance. Just a small family. Mom and Dad. Son and daughter-in-law. The son and his wife lost a baby and another through a miscarriage, but yet they still find good in their life. The dad lost his job last week. Cutbacks. The mom is still trying to find a job; but with this economy, work is hard to come by. So, the son and his wife moved in with them to help."

Scott shrugged. "Lots of people go through hard times like that."

"Sure, they do. But you see, they have only each other left. Mom and Dad. Son and wife. Granddad and Grandma. No little ones. No luxuries in life. Hardly any money to put food on the table but look at them." Again, their voices lifted in song, the same unfamiliar song as before. "Would you think they had difficulties?"

Scott shook his head. "No. Figured they were praising their God for someone's recovery."

"Their God?" The man laughed softly. "No. They are praising God for life. The dad's mother is dying."

"And they are praising God for that?" Scott scoffed and stretched out his legs. "I think I would curse and yell at a God who demands praise for someone's death."

McDaniel turned his head toward him. Dark eyes pierced through Scott. "God doesn't demand our praise. He wants our love; and when you love with all your heart, you can't help but praise, even through the bad times." A smile softened his features. "I used to believe the same thing. But once I truly believed, I couldn't stop praising."

The group turned and started up the small aisle. McDaniel stood and picked up his cane. "The thing is . . . no one deserves it. But God still loves us."

The dad wrapped McDaniel in a hug. "How's Mom?"

Scott's teeth clacked hard as he clamped his mouth shut.

"Weaker. Dr. Fletcher will release her in the morning. She's going home." McDaniel smiled down at Scott. "We'll pray for your grand-mother, young man. Take care."

McDaniel shuffled out of the chapel with his little family.

Scott shook his head. He propped his elbows on his knees and bur-ied his face in his hands. He'd wake up soon. A strange dream because of a strange place. Just a weird coincidence. The man just had the com-pelling urge to talk to someone. Doesn't a chapel bring out confessions?

The first song's line danced through his mind. Could he really touch the Lord? He would have to research what that song was. It seemed so familiar, however vague in his memories.

And trust in Jesus? They called it sweet to do so, but how could they? Why should he take Jesus at His word?

Why? Why him? And why would God even think he would care?

Scott pushed up from his position. It was a mistake coming here. He stomped to the door and paused. He gazed over his shoulder at the simple altar. Nana Debbie's voice echoed, "You used to believe."

Not anymore. Never again.

Scott turned his back to the altar. The door closed behind him, and he hurried to the elevators. Time to be back by Nana Debbie's side.

Angela pushed aside the notes and paperwork. Concentration on the budget story was shot. Her mind kept wandering back to Scott and Debbie.

She sighed and rubbed at her eyes. She really needed sleep. A shiver coursed through her. Sleep and more blankets.

The old house provided more and more hidden drafts every day. She threw her covers down and slipped into her black, fuzzy house shoes. Her bedroom door creaked. The coldness leeched further into the hallway.

She shuffled down the short passage to the thermostat and bumped it up a notch. A heavy, handmade quilt hung over the chair around the corner. Angela scooped it up and padded down to Max's room.

His deep breathing filled the small room. She reached down and moved some of the covers away, and then smothered a giggle. The kiddo had somehow burrito-ed himself in the quilts and sheet.

Quickly, she rearranged the covers and left his sleeping and warm form to dreams of superheroes and adventures.

Angela closed her bedroom door with a soft click and threw the heavy quilt across her bed. Soon, she'd be toasty.

She scooted down in her bed and propped up on her hand, gazing at her phone lying beside her glass of water. Scott's worried faced hovered in front of her. Might as well see if he was still up and doing okay. Then she'd be able to sleep.

She punched in the text and waited.

The siren notification sounded loud in her small bedroom.

Still up. Nana doing ok.

Angela smiled. That was good to "hear."

What about you?

Ok.

Going to sleep any?

Yup.

She shook her head. Poor man.

Anytime soon?

Nope.

Typical. Did the man ever sleep?

Well, make sure you get some sleep.

Now know why people can't sleep in a hospital.

Angela laughed. Didn't she just know it? All those sounds, nurses in and out, and so cold, no matter the many blankets.

Yup.

She waited for the tell-tale siren. After a minute, it sounded.

Ask you a question?

She poised her finger over the keyboard. Hesitation feathered against her, fear of what the question might be.

Sure.

Dottie will probably stay. Ride back with you?

Angela sighed. That wasn't too bad a request.

Sure. I'll see you tomorrow.

Thx.

Welcome. Get some sleep.

K.

Nite Scott.

Nite.

She closed her phone and placed it back on the charger. Somehow, this "just friends" thing was starting to seem more than that. But it was only a ride back home. Just a ride.

"Get some sleep, Angela girl. Just your imagination." She rolled over and buried her head under the pillow. Tomorrow started a brand-new day and a brand-new month. Somehow, it seemed as though a brand-new life was cropping up in there, too.

CHAPTER ELEVEN

Rochelle leaned back in her chair and sighed. Angela had called in to say she was heading to Florence and would arrive later that afternoon. She would give her king-size Three Musketeers bar to have Angela here right this minute. If she had to field one more call from his lordship the mayor—

The phone blared.

Rochelle snatched the receiver. "*Garrettville Gaz—*"

"Let me speak with Tom." The anger in the gruff voice practically strangled her through the phone.

"Tom's not here at the moment, Mayor—"

"Then, where's that new reporter of his? I won't be put off any longer. You let them know that."

Rochelle clenched her hands around the handheld. "I will. As soon as they come back into the office, I will make sure that they know you have called for them six times this morning."

The dead silence of the line echoed back into the ear. Wasted words apparently.

She slammed the receiver down, grabbed up a stack of papers, and marched to Michael's office. He barely peeked over his monitor when she threw the stack in his inbox. "There's your printouts. How's the article coming along?"

"Fine." His precise, clipped voice wove through the clutter on his desk.

The man never looked up from his computer. Rochelle left him alone with his computer and tech playthings that littered the desk. She rounded her desk and glanced at the itinerary for Friday's paper. Ah, so that made sense. Michael was doing an article on identity theft and the internet. A little behind the times, but not so for Garrettville. This town moved at a dead snail's pace when keeping up with technology.

Rochelle sighed. Might as well pull up some more on the Follows and Turnpike lead. There was nothing else to do on this slow Thursday morning. Page after page blurred in front of her. Nothing about the roads. Not that she expected anything. She'd searched pretty well last time.

She tapped a finger against her front tooth. Maybe there was something else. A search through her bag produced her notebook. The hearts and skulls glittered under the bright lights of the lobby.

Rochelle flipped to the fourth page. There. That would do. Now to see if she could find anything on Whitecloud's Garrettville Native American Foundation.

She entered the search parameters for the archives. The screen brought up two articles. One written by the former reporter and the other by Pops. Rochelle pulled up the most recent one, the one written by Pops.

Nothing much leapt out at her. Basic info about the charitable donations and Whitecloud's vision for the future of the foundation. No matter, she printed it just in case there might by a tie to it all, anyway.

She closed out that article and pulled up the other one. Maybe this would be pay dirt.

Monday will be the deciding factor in the case of the re-zoning of the area from Follows to Jamison Ave. The re-zoning will affect many businesses, including the newly created Garrettville Native American Foundation. Seymour Whitecloud commented that he has high hopes for an out-come in his favor . . .

Rochelle scrolled through the rest of the article. No more about GNAF. But what rezoning was proposed, and did it ever go through?

She hastily scribbled the info in her notebook. The bell above the door chimed.

"Hey, Pops. Did you get what you needed?" She hit print, closed the article, and set her notebook to the side.

"Yes and no. I placed a few calls, but it doesn't seem good." He shuffled his way into his office. A huge sigh escaped as he allowed himself to plop down into the leather chair. "Looks like Angela is onto something. There isn't much listed at the courthouse. The neighboring towns didn't have much either. Are you sure about the deeds?"

Rochelle nodded. "I'm sure, Pops. Angela and I searched the courthouse. I've been checking the archives for anything mentioned. There's not much there. But I am sure there's got to be a connection. I've printed out the articles."

"Bring them here then."

"Okay." She hurried out the office, grabbed the papers off the desk, and rushed back to Tom.

"There's not much. Angela has copies. Most were still on mi-crofiche, but I did find a few older newspapers. I've got them in my backpack."

Tom scanned the articles. "I'm not sure about all this, though, my girl." He flipped the pages and frowned. "I remember the case between Seymour and the rezoning commission. They were to settle out of court, but he died before then."

"Do you really think that this town is like those suspense novels and movies? Knocking off the competition in order to get what they want?" Rochelle perched on the edge of her chair. "You know, Pops, there is one angle we haven't followed."

"What's that?" He handed her the printouts and woke up his laptop.

"The one thing that has been at the center of the whole thing. The hospital. Think about it. The accidents happened only a short distance from the hospital. The hospital gains the land for their addition of the north wing. Even had land donated to them. Each time, it was the hospital somewhere within there. Even Angela has learned a few things from Scott." She pulled out her phone and sent a text to Angela. "I asked her when she would be in because we found another angle for her."

Pops nodded and then frowned. "Keep this quiet, okay? If the hospital is involved, then this goes beyond just a land grab and into something more heinous."

Rochelle scoffed. "Pops, people don't use the word *heinous* anymore."

"Yeah? Then what is used?" He grinned and shooed her out the door. "Let Angela know to take the rest of the day off. We can go over everything tomorrow before you gals go off investigating."

"Okay, Pops. And nowadays, people use *odious* or *despicable* because *wicked* means cool or good." Rochelle sailed out of the room laughing at her grandfather's bemused and confused expression. The man really needed to get with the times.

###

Angela pulled into Scott's driveway and slid the gear into park. "Are you sure, Scott? I don't mind the company."

Scott shook his head and fought back a yawn. "I'm sure. Nana is coming home tomorrow, and I really didn't get any sleep last night." He raised his hand and aimed it at the door. "I'm walking in, heading straight to my room, and collapsing onto the bed. Sleep will be my companion for a little while."

He watched her smile stretch a little further. This is why he was heading straight into the house and not spending any more time with her. She was everything he ever wanted. Kind. Considerate. Generous. Spunky. And beautiful. But she'd said it, and he'd agreed: just friends. *Just friends.*

"Well, call me if you need anything, okay? Food. To talk. To visit. Whatever." She glanced at the backseat, where Max was curled up in his booster seat asleep. "Max will sleep for a while, too."

Scott lightly thumped his fist against the console. "Well, I'm heading in. Thank you, Ang. For everything."

Her hand caught his and gently squeezed. "Not a problem, Scott. And I mean it—call if you need anything."

"I will." The door creaked as he pushed it open, and his bones answered the same as he unfolded from the low-sitting car. "Again, thanks."

He gave her a small wave, shut the door, and shuffled inside. The Grand Am slowly backed out of the driveway, and she drove the small distance to her house. Scott unlocked the door and stepped inside. The smell of Nana's cinnamon candles enveloped him. How he missed that smell, compared to the sterile and astringent hospital. He caught the door with his foot and gazed down the road toward Angela's house.

She had scooped the little bundle from the back and was fighting with the front door. A small chuckle escaped him when she angrily kicked at the heavy oak door, forcing it open. He'd need to oil those hinges for her sometime. It always became stuck during the colder months. Julie had always had a hard time with it, too.

His smile faded at the thought of his best friend. With a shake, he pushed the door closed and emptied his pockets onto the small table. Only a wallet and cafeteria receipt this time. Dixie, with his food bowl in his mouth, met Scott at the kitchen's door. Poor poochie.

"Hey, boy. Hold on." Scott leaned down and opened the door under the kitchen sink. He shook the nearly empty bag. At least there was another bag in the pantry.

He grabbed Dixie's bowl. "Gotta let go if you want your food." Dixie shook his head, relishing in the tug-of-war game before hunger won.

Scott set the plastic bowl on the floor and emptied the bag contents into it. He balled the bag and threw it away before dumping a couple of cups of cat food into Judas' bowl. At least it would be there whenever the cat decided she was hungry.

He washed his hands under the kitchen faucet. No turns this time. Who cared?

Cold water splashed over his hands, and then he splashed his face. But no matter the frigidness of the water, it wouldn't erase what he knew had to be done. Scott shook his head and grabbed a hand towel to scrub his face dry. Whiskers rasped against the cotton material.

Judas sauntered into the kitchen. Scott chuckled at the haughtiness of the cat. Guess Judas was determined to make them pay for ignoring her for so long. Scott returned her attitude and sidestepped around her. His footsteps echoed hollowly down the hall. Amazing how empty it seemed without Nana Debbie around.

He pushed open his door, shrugged out of his jacket, and dropped it on the chair by his bed. His grandfather's Bible still laid on the bedcovers where he had dropped it. Or had he? He could've sworn he'd placed it in his drawer. Oh, well.

Scott sat down next to it and gazed at the worn leather. A faint hint of sawdust filtered through his memories. The man had died when he was young, but yet the memories of peppermint and sawdust still reminded him of the grizzly man. How his debonair grandmother had ended up with a roughneck man was beyond him. Nana Debbie always said that love had no boundaries.

He picked up the book, caressed the leather, and then slid it into the still-opened nightstand drawer. He then slid it quietly closed. Scott sighed and lay back on the bed.

Tomorrow, Nana Debbie would come home. Tomorrow, he would talk to Grace. Nana Debbie was right. He always did the right thing, no matter the consequences. He'd tell Grace he stole the meds, but also stress that they were not alprazolam. At least, that may help lessen the outcome. One thing he did know—tomorrow, he wouldn't have a job. No income.

He slid his hands behind his head and stared at the ceiling. There was one positive aspect of being single. With no one to spend money on but himself, his savings account had racked up a good bit of money. He'd splurged on himself only once, and that was because he couldn't pass up that sweet deal on the Mercedes sitting in the driveway. That was one sweet ride.

The quiet of the house seeped into his tired mind. He should have taken Angela up on the offer of tea. He could really use some at the moment. First thing in the morning, at work, he would tell Grace, confess what he did, and come home to Nana Debbie. Tomorrow, his world would end.

CHAPTER TWELVE

Scott stood right outside Grace's office and stared down the one thing that stood in his way of admitting his wrongdoing and being terminated. The single sheet of printer paper glared back with its black ink message, "Be Back in One Hour."

Again, Grace was gone. Did the woman never stay in her office?

He turned from the door, stuffed his hands into his pockets, and eased away.

Maybe it wasn't such a good idea to come back to work so soon. Maybe he should have stayed with Nana, even though Dottie claimed that it wouldn't be much trouble to transport Nana home. He pushed the urge to sigh back down his gullet. Nana probably wanted to rid herself of him. Who would want a troublesome, thieving grandson?

No. Self-pity wasn't the answer, no matter how easy it seemed. Nana probably couldn't handle his pacing in and out of the hospital room. He barely handled it himself.

Nana's voice filtered through his head. "Depart from evil, and do good; Seek peace . . . " What was that verse? Psalm thirty-four or was it thirty-five? He shook his head and cast Nana's voice into the wild.

Scott shouldered the double doors open and stepped into the quiet ER hall.

What did it say about a hospital that was too quiet? He leaned against the wall and crossed his arms. His head thumped gently against the white-painted blocks.

"And the peace of God, which surpasses all understanding, will guard your hearts and minds . . . " Scott almost jumped, so loud was it in his head, at the memory of Nana's voice as she read the passage from Philippians chapter four yesterday morning.

Scott ground his fists against his closed eyes.

What surpassed understanding was why he had not taken that job in Florence instead of staying in Garrettville and riding out the storm. The hospital should have accepted Baptist's offer and sold to them, instead of allowing a new medical group to take over. Pay reductions, longer hours, missing EMS director, understaffed departments, a budget drowning in red—and he just had to stay. Things would have been so much different.

Scott dropped his hand and touched his cargo pocket. The stolen meds still burned their way into his skin.

"All in your head, boy." His whisper floated back to him in the quiet hall.

Everything would have been so much different. And in an hour . . . he would lose his job. Lose everything.

At least, he didn't lose Nana.

He pushed away from the wall and headed for the ER desk. The doors behind the desk swung out, and Arlene gave him a smile.

"How's Debbie doing?"

Scott shrugged. "Dottie is bringing her home."

"Surprised you didn't take another day off to do that." Arlene patted his hand that rested against the surface of the desk. "You look like you could use another day of rest."

"I don't think one day could give me the rest I need." Scott stepped past her and sank down into the other chair. "Give me a thousand years, and I might feel rested."

Arlene laughed and turned to her computer. Her fingers flew across the keyboard. "I hear you, Van Winkle. Even I wish I could have a thousand days—at this rate, I would jump at the chance for a thousand minutes." She paused, her head cocked to the side, and then grabbed at an orange calculator in the cubbyhole of the desk. "How long is a thousand minutes, anyway? Let's see . . . "

"Sixteen hours, forty minutes." Scott picked up a home and garden magazine.

She let the small calculator drop. "How do you do that?"

He looked up from the page advertising Carnival Cruise Lines. "Do what?"

"How did you do that in your head so fast?" She turned back to her computer.

"Easy. Sixty times sixteen equals nine sixty. Forty left to reach a thousand." He flung the magazine to the side and picked up a local trade magazine. Ad after ad filed through his brain. His eyes stopped at an ad for puppies. "Do you know anything about puppies, Arlene?"

"Huh?" She gave him a quick glance. "What kind? Thinking of getting one?"

"I don't know yet." He read the ad aloud. "Toy schnauzers for sale. Three females, two males. AKC registered. Eight hundred dollars."

"Those are expensive pups. I don't cater to expensive dogs. I tend to have mutts."

Scott circled the ad and dog-eared the page. He didn't know why the urge to buy a pet suddenly invaded his thinking, but it did. Diversion. Escape from the real world.

Emergency tones pierced the quiet. "Dispatch, EMS. Respond to a one-vehicle MVC at Follows and Turnpike. Caller states at least one person, unknown entrapment. PD on scene, and scene is secure."

The doors behind him flew open, and Douglas barreled through. Scott grabbed the mic. "Medic Two copies. MVC one car, PD on scene. Go ahead and roll an engine to be en route. Show Medic Two en route at this time."

The mic clattered onto the counter as Scott hurried away.

The automatic doors hissed open. Scott ran through and snatched at the passenger door. Douglas maneuvered the van out of the parking lot as Scott slammed the door closed.

Follows and Turnpike. He and Douglas glanced at each other. Angela's research. She'd be there.

Scott turned on the sirens.

Angela practically buried her head into her bag. It was in there. It had to be. Pens, cards, and notebooks moved aside as her hand dug deeper and deeper. She huffed.

Now where was it? She growled and pushed her chair backward. Everything scattered along her desk as she upended the bag. And no little notebook.

She sighed and threw everything back inside the large purse: pens, business cards, the too-full business card holder, wallet, keys, checkbook, and notebooks. But not the black notebook. The notebook that had the addresses listed.

Angela sat back down and lowered her head into her hands. It must have been left at home. The last couple of days were hectic enough to make anyone forget anything. She peered through her fingers and glanced at the clock. Did she turn on the crockpot? Too late to worry about it now. If she didn't, tonight would have to be a quick fix.

She reached down and opened a side drawer. A stack of little black notebooks sat in the corner. Guess she would just have to redo it all.

The new notebook's slap against the wooden desk barely competed with the ghostly clacking of Michael's keyboard. She stood and pushed her door closed. It clicked softly against the latch but didn't catch. It was enough to bar the irritating clacks down the hall.

Angela flipped open the notebook, opened the file on her computer, and copied everything down . . . again: McOwens at Follows and Turnpike. July 20, 2010. Land bought by hospital. Whitecloud at Turnpike Road. June 2013. Land donated to hospital by city. Shelby Pierce at Follows and Turnpike. Father Donald city official.

She scrolled down to the missing dates and frowned. Two years the same as two deaths. July 2010 and July 2013 were missing. Coincidences were something in which she had no faith.

A knock hammered her door a second before Rochelle burst through. She held up her grandfather's digital camera. "Ambulance call!"

"Where?" Angela sent her chair spinning when she leapt up and grabbed her jacket from its backrest. "Just now?"

Rochelle's eyes gleamed. "Yeah. Follows and Turnpike."

Angela paused, zipping her bag. "What?"

"I know, right?" Rochelle hurried toward the door. "Come on. No coincidences, right?"

Angela rushed toward the front door, trying to catch up with the girl. She fumbled for her keys. Tom met her in the foyer.

"Make sure you take good photos. I don't need the council after me this time to suppress. Keep the victim out of the frame but concentrate on the wreck."

Rochelle waved away her grandfather's statement. "Got it, Pops."

Angela gripped the keys until the sharp edges dug into her palms. This was it. Had to be. The tide was turning. Apprehension flowed from head to toe and back up again.

"And don't worry about Dan, girlie. I'll take—" The front door slammed closed on the rest of Tom's statement.

"Come on, Angela. Hurry!" Rochelle danced from foot to foot by the Grand Am. "This is it! I mean, no way could three wrecks be at the same place. No way!"

Angela hurried to the car and unlocked it. She hit the auto unlock and slid inside, but not as fast as Rochelle. The girl grinned from one single-pierced ear to the other single-pierced ear.

"Calm down. Remember professionalism. It's a wreck, so that means the likelihood of someone being hurt. We don't get excited about that." Angela cranked the car. The engine turned over once and roared. She breathed a quick prayer of thanks. Just please, a few more paychecks more, and she'd get the thing fixed. Just please keep it going.

Rochelle's face flamed, and she sank into her seat. "I'm sorry. I just meant it as in we would be one step closer. I didn't think about the victim."

Angela turned left onto the main road. "It's understandable. Don't let it worry you." She risked a glance over at the girl. The black headband barely held back the short, blonde strands. Faint traces of red dye still tinted the tips.

All morning, Angela had kept staring at the girl, trying to piece together what was missing. The bright sunlight shot through the trees and hit Rochelle across the face as Angela shot another glance at her. "Yes! I got it! I have been trying all morning to figure out what was different. You removed your hardware."

Rochelle grinned and smoothed her hand across her brow and then over her ears. "Yeah. I took a look in the mirror the other day and realized that, maybe, that was why Brent acted like he did with me."

"Do what?" Angela slowed around the curve and took the next right. If not for the winding roads, she would have shot a shocked look at the girl. "What did he do?"

"Tried to force me to kiss him." Rochelle screwed her face up. "I mean, I don't kiss on first dates, nor second dates. Don't get me wrong, Angela. I have nothing against kissing." Rochelle wrapped the strings of her pullover around her finger. "I just want my first kiss to be something special, with a special man. I watched a Moriah Peters video that talked about that. Is that so wrong?"

Was that so wrong? Tears pricked Angela's eyelids. If only half the kids thought like Rochelle. She turned left onto Turnpike before answering.

"No. Nothing is wrong with that at all, Rochelle." She reached over and gave the girl's hand a gentle squeeze. "I find it admirable. And so would Jesus."

Rochelle sighed. She stared at the passing trees for a moment before turning back around. "You never mention much about your faith, but I just knew you believed. Pops believes, too, and I think that is why sometimes he gets into trouble with the city. Lots of liberals with their socialist agendas."

Angela laughed and then gasped as the car narrowly missed the shoulder of the road. "You sound like Tom."

"Well, that's what he says all the time." Rochelle pursed her lips and stared ahead.

"Like grandfather, like granddaughter?"

"Something like that . . ." Rochelle leaned forward. "Oh, my. Look."

Angela slowed the car and pulled to the side.

The yellow tape stretched across the road. Two officers guarded the tape. An ambulance sat angled across the street. The red strobes flashed, competing with the nearby rescue truck. The blue lights from the police cars danced with them, a red-blue waltz of lights.

She eased her door open, dipped down, and fished the notebook out of her bag. Rochelle stood by the car mesmerized by the scene, the camera dangling by its strap around her neck.

Angela didn't blame her.

A luxury sedan—maybe a Bentley or a Jaguar—and the guardrail meshed together to the point she couldn't tell where the car's metal started and the rail ended. Yells and shouts issued from the rescue workers. Yellow helmets dipped and bobbed. Metal screeches pierced the air.

More shouts. More curses. Officers rushed around, yelling into their radios.

Rochelle looked to her. "Are we going up there?"

Angela nodded. "Just stay behind the yellow tape. Listen to the officers. Don't argue."

She forced herself to take a step. Apprehension didn't describe what she felt now. Fear . . . and something else, something elusive.

She and Rochelle reached the tape. The camera in Rochelle's hand blurred as she whipped it up to her face. Angela pulled out her notebook and jotted down the scene description.

Three officers rushed around, shouting into the squashed car. Firefighters heaved chunks of metal out of the way. Skinny legs clad in black cargos hung out the shattered window. They kicked once, and Scott slid from the opening. He turned to the rescue crew and shouted. The din around him swallowed his voice.

The car door popped off, and the metal screeching ceased. As a firefighter hauled away the large extraction tool, Scott and Douglas jumped back into action.

Angela reached out and blocked the camera's view. "No victim pics."

Rochelle lowered the camera and pressed her lips together so hard white lines appeared.

"Grab the gurney!" Scott's voice sliced the air. It was a needless shout. A firefighter and police officer already had the stretcher extended and ready.

Scott's cheeks puffed out; and from a distance, Angela barely made out the veins popping up along his neck as he worked. He angled his body and pulled on the man's upper torso. Douglas reached in and grabbed the driver's legs, and together they eased the man out of the crushed cab.

She watched as they lifted the man, his body covered in blood, onto the stretcher. Straps flew as they secured the patient. Without a glance around him, he and Douglas rushed back to the ambulance and loaded their passenger.

Angela reached for the camera. "Go back to the car if you feel sick."

Rochelle shook her head. "I don't." She pulled the camera back from Angela's grasp.

The ambulance siren split the air. It sped away into the distance. Angela watched it go and turned to the scene. A firefighter moved from the front of the car, and the leaping jaguar hood ornament gleamed in the sunlight. Angela frowned. Only two people she knew of drove late model Jags.

Rochelle sniffed. Angela turned her gaze to her as the girl ran a finger under her nose. "I saw his face. All that blood."

"There's always blood at wrecks."

"But, Angela. It's not the blood. It was him." Rochelle turned. Tears threatened to spill from her eyes. "That was Donald Pierce, Shelby's father. He was dead, wasn't he? I mean, who can survive with all that blood everywhere?"

Angela watched as the officers made their notes and firefighters loaded their equipment. Donald Pierce. "He may still be alive. They used sirens, Rochelle. They won't use sirens if the patient was dead."

Let the girl believe the lie if it helped. She wished she could believe that lie. But the look on Scott's face, the defeat . . .

CHAPTER THIRTEEN

Scott hung his head until his chin pressed against his breastbone. The muscles in his neck stretched, and vertebras popped. Just let it end. It needed to end.

His body shook slightly. Oh, how he needed those pills. He touched his pocket. If only . . .

Voices penetrated his bubble.

Scott raised his head and peered from his darkened corner across the lobby where two women sat. Their voices raised and lowered like an incoming tide. He leaned his head back, gazing at them through his lashes, and listened. Amazing how soothing it seemed, the ebb and flow of their conversation.

"It's like the Good Book said; there be only one way out of this world and into the next." She shifted in her seat and regarded her fellow black companion. "The preacher don't mince words."

"I know it. It amazes me how little these young folks pay attention to what is said and what it means. You take the book of Revelation. All talk about fire and suffering. But are we going to be here to experience that? I say, no, I ain't. But they don't listen one bit."

"Hallelujah, you got that right." She waved her hand around like she was lassoing in a herd. "They just think to themselves, 'Oh, I have time.' But they don't. It's like car insurance . . ."

Scott huffed. Now this was something he wanted to hear. Comparing religion to car insurance.

" . . . I'll get it tomorrow or when my next paycheck comes in. But that afternoon, they get in a wreck or get caught speeding. Big ol' fine for no insurance these days. And they say the same: 'I'll get Jesus tomorrow or Sunday. I got time.' Then they get killed the next day. Too late to say they was meaning to get saved. Too late."

Cold crawled up Scott's neck. Too late? His whole life he had always been too late. Too late for his parents. Too late for Julie. Too late for Billy. Too late for Donald.

Her companion leaned back and adjusted the multi-colored dress to cover her knees. "You believe that, don't you, Iris? I believe it, too. We need our insurance. We need our Jesus. But what I want to know of Revelation is the suffering people will endure if they don't get saved. You believe we won't be here? I see the news and all that is happening, and I can't but believe that Jesus is on His way."

The big woman patted the other's hand. "Honey, He already said He was on His way. God's timing. Each day, we get closer to Him, either through the rapture or through our death."

The conversation was interrupted by Dr. Morrison. Her white coat floated around her tiny frame as she approached the two women.

"Iris Hamilton?"

The black woman rose from her seat and leaned heavily upon her dark, oak cane. "That's me." Her friend rose with her and steadied her with a hand on her arm.

"Good news. His test came back negative. Not a heart attack or stroke. We want to keep him under observation tonight . . . " Dr.

Morrison's voice faded away as she led them through the double doors and into the ICU area.

Silence once again reigned through the small ICU lobby. His place of solace once again his own. He stretched out his legs and closed his eyes, hands folded over his belly. The two women's conversation repeated over and over in his mind. Jesus as insurance. What a concept.

"There you are." Angela's soft voice drifted to him.

He sighed but kept his eyes closed. A soft rustle sounded beside him, and then the scent of roses and peaches drifted in his nose. Scott inhaled deeply. Even her scent complemented the ambience of the room.

The hum of the water fountain, the buzz of the overhead lighting, and the bubbling of the nearby fish tank swirled together with her scent. He pictured her staring at him with those bright, blue eyes, patiently waiting for him to acknowledge her.

A soft touch on his hand was the only warning before her fingers interlaced with his. "I understand if you need time alone. Stop by if you need to talk."

He squeezed her hand in reply. Not right now. Talking would come later. Maybe Grace would be here soon.

"Rochelle left not too long ago. Headed back to the office with the story. We plan to print it tomorrow." A slight sigh escaped her. Scott kept his eyes closed but tightened his grip on her hand. "I can imagine the heartache the Pierces are going through right now. Tom agreed with me that we will keep the story just the basic elements, nothing flamboyant."

Scott peeked over at her. Her red hair swirled in heavy waves around her face. Sorrow pinched at her eyes, adding more wrinkles to her fine laugh lines. Even sorrow couldn't erase her beauty.

He reached out and pushed an errant strand away and tucked it behind her ear. "I still have clean-up on the van to do before I leave for the day. Thought I would swing by your place. Fix that stepping-stone, the pantry door, and whatever else there is."

Angela shook her head. "No, Scott. You don't have to do that."

Her words were meant to be empathic; but they grated against him, rubbing him raw. He sat up and grabbed her face in his hands. Her skin cooled his hot brow as he pressed their foreheads together and closed his eyes.

"Please." His plea hissed from between clenched teeth. "I need to do something. Stay busy."

A heartbeat. Then another before she moved.

Her hands covered his. She turned her head and pressed a kiss into his palm. "Okay, Scott."

"Thank you." He pulled away, keeping his hands on her face, his thumb absently stroking her smooth cheek. His gaze traveled over her freckle-peppered face. "I just can't deal with everything right now."

She pulled his hands down from her face. Instead of letting go, she clutched at them. "It's not your fault, Scott. You tried. I know you well enough to know that you did everything conceivable to save Donald."

He eased his hands from her and rubbed at his eyes. So tired. Tired of death. Tired of fighting. Tired of not sleeping. Tired of life.

He didn't realize he had closed his eyes until he felt Angela's hand rub up and down his back.

"Come by when you need to." Her lips pressed against the side of his head. Then she was gone. The faint aroma of roses and peaches the only evidence she had ever been beside him.

Scott forced his eyes open and heaved himself to his feet. Might as well get through with the last portion of his shift. He slid his card through the lock and pushed through the swing door. The ICU stood as quiet as the lobby—or at least quieter than the rest of the hospital.

His soft-soled boots thudded against the gleaming commercial tile. Under his breath, he counted his steps. One. Two. Three . . . Fifteen. Sixteen.

The faint beeps of the monitors kept time with him. The hushed voices of the nurses at the station he passed by added to the accompaniment. Soft sighs, murmurs of voices, and muffled moans wove in and out through the beats of his footsteps.

His hand touched the door just as it opened from the other side.

"There you are, man." Douglas stood aside and allowed him to pass. "Grace called earlier. She's heading in. Donald Pierce's death has the whole hospital on edge. The mayor just came in to speak with Dr. Melbourne. Jonathan disappeared up to Melbourne's office. Hey . . . " Douglas' hand landed on his arm, stopping his continued trekking toward the ER doors. "Where you heading?"

"The van." Scott shrugged off Douglas' hand and slowed to a slug's pace. "Need to get it cleaned before next shift."

Douglas nodded. "Need help? I've finished the report and filed it with Jonathan."

Scott stopped and leaned his back against the wall next to one of the triage rooms. "No. Prefer to do it alone."

"Speak to me, man. This isn't the first time someone died on our watch. What's eating at you?" Douglas crossed his arms across his chest. His gaze pierced Scott. "Is it because it's Donald Pierce who died?"

"No." Scott shoved his hands deep into his pockets. Fingers stroked the pill bottle. "It isn't that. This was just more or less the topping of my cupcake from Hades. I've got other things to figure out, to speak to Grace about, to do."

Douglas pursed his lips and nodded. "Understandable. Jonathan asked me to run a double tonight. I said yes. Teaming with Mack."

Scott chuckled. An odd sound to his ears, considering today. "More conversations about vegetables?"

"Are you kidding? We have all new material to drive you and Arlene crazy with, but that's for another time." Douglas slapped Scott's shoulder. "See you around. I promised Jennifer a dinner in the cafeteria."

Scott watched his friend disappear around the corner and listened as Douglas' voice greeted the nighttime ER nurse. He heaved one more sigh and headed out the door. Might as well get the job done before the blood dried up too much.

The night air greeted him. Birds tweeted as he quickly strode to the ambulance bay. The distant sounds of a whippoorwill. Life went on.

He opened the passenger door and grabbed the clipboard from its rack. Time for cleaning, inventory, and replenishment. Busy work.

Fresh gloves snapped against his skin. Scott opened the back doors and stepped up into the darkened interior. The cast-offs of the run littered the floor and side bench—bloody gauze, used lines, and wadded tape. He knelt and brushed at the pile near the back of the seats. A silver watch gleamed back at him.

Must have fallen off during the transport. Scott snatched a red biohazard bag from the dispenser and placed the watch inside. An onyx cufflink and bits of change joined the watch. Donald's widow would receive the bag later after he turned it in to Grace. He checked once more. Nothing else, so he laid the bag to the side.

He raked the used materials into a pile. A bubble of silence fell around him. Sweep. Scoop. Dump. He stepped outside and grabbed the antiseptic rinse. His own concoction to battle the hidden drops of bodily fluids on the floor. Around and around the mop went, scraping and scouring. Scott gritted his teeth. If only his troubles could be as thoroughly scoured as this floor. He set the bucket back into the ambulance bay and then returned with a spray bottle.

The liquid rained down on the bench's vinyl cushions. Scott scrubbed it even harder with a sponge. His hand hit the gap between the two cushions. The sponge flew from his hand and sailed to the floor behind the seats.

Scott held back his curse. No reason to get mad at a square piece of polyester material. He bent down to retrieve it.

His gaze fell on a small, black object under the edge of the passenger seat. Interesting. How had he missed that?

He plucked it from the floor and held it up to the light. A flash drive. He turned it over in his fingers. Strange item to find. He glanced back at the ER doors. They swooshed open as Douglas came out with a fresh stretcher to load.

Scott pocketed the drive. He touched one cargo pocket. It held the stolen pills. He touched the other. Now it held a flash drive that didn't belong to him.

Douglas approached with the stretcher.

"Thought you were having dinner with Jennifer." Scott grabbed the bio bag and jumped down.

"Yeah. I am. But I looked at the clock and realized that your shift is up, dude." Douglas pushed the stretcher into the ambulance. "Go home."

Scott shook his head. "I'm waiting for Grace."

"She ain't back yet. Just head home. Whatever it is that you need to talk to her about can wait." Douglas slammed the doors shut. "Those personal effects?"

Scott passed the bag to him. "Yeah."

He stuffed his hands into his pockets and looked across the parking lot to his Mercedes C300. Yeah. He needed to head on home. Maybe Nana Debbie would be there by now. He'd go home. Clean up. Change. Go to Angela's.

Hmm, wonder what Angela would say about the flash drive. Would she consider it coincidence that he found it after a patient died at Follows and Turnpike, just like the others?

"You heading home?"

Scott glanced over at Douglas. "Yeah. I'm heading home. If you see Grace, tell her I need to speak with her in the morning."

"Will do, man . . . "

Douglas' voice faded as Scott hurried away.

Angela turned the dial on the dishwasher. With a swoosh, it clicked on. She heaved a sigh and leaned heavily against the counter.

Max was in bed. Dinner dishes were washing. The sky was darkening.

She reached out and pulled the kitchen curtain to the side. Clouds swirled. Leaves danced through the air. Another storm brewed.

Her phone vibrated on the kitchen table. She let the curtain fall back into place and hurried to pick up her phone.

Rochelle.

"Hi, Rochelle. You okay?" Angela pulled out a chair and sank down onto its cushioned seat.

"Yeah. I was trying to get in touch with Pops. Have you seen him?"

"No. Last I saw him was when I dropped off the accident notes. He isn't home?" Angela fought back a yawn.

"Don't know. I'm still at the office. Thought I would do a little more digging. I sent him a text, but he hadn't responded. If you see or hear from him, will you let him know I am still at the office?" A puff of breath came across the connection. "I have the doors locked, so he doesn't need to worry."

"I'll let him know if he calls. He probably just hasn't read his messages yet. After Pierce's death, he's going to be busy with phone calls." Movement outside her bay window captured her attention. "Just stay safe. Text me when you leave and get home."

"Sure thing, Mama."

Angela laughed. "Can't help but worry."

"I know. And will do. Bye."

Angela hit END and set her phone back on the table. The shadow outside moved to her gate. It stood there a moment before reaching over and unlatching the panel.

She rubbed her temples. Poor Scott. He carried so much on his shoulders.

No knock on the door came. Angela frowned and hurried to the door. She flipped the porch light on. The hinges creaked as she pulled open the heavy, oak door. She pushed at the screen door, and the springs squeaked.

Scott sat on the steps. He barely turned his head when he spoke. "You need some WD-40 on those hinges. If you have some, I'll spray it on there."

Angela let the screen fall closed behind her. "I have some. But I don't mind the squeak." She settled down beside him. "But you didn't come here to play with WD-40."

"Hmm." Scott stared straight ahead with his mouth pressed into a grim line.

Her gaze traveled along his short-cropped hair, down his darkly whiskered jaw, over his hard mouth, and up his thin, angular nose. Not exactly the most handsome of men, but his eyes sparkled when he smiled. Although, he hadn't smiled in days. His mouth, usually bright and animated, flexed every few seconds in a hard frown.

He had showered. The spicy scent of his soap drifted over to her.

His jacket rustled as he shifted on the steps.

She pulled her sweater tighter around her. "Scott?"

Her voice drifted along the wind and away from them. What was she supposed to say? Silly woman, the house used to belong to his best friend. He would feel at home here, a place where he probably came whenever he needed company.

"I've got some tea. Would you like any?"

She started to get up, but his hand lashed out and grabbed hers, holding her in place. "Not yet. I'll fix everything in a bit. I just need to sit here."

His voice barely rose above a hoarse whisper. He sighed once and turned to face her. Words died in her throat. Sadness permeated his eyes. Sadness and defeat. Creases formed all over his face. He was barely holding it together, ready to crumple. Ready to give in.

This wasn't Scott. Not the Scott she had come to know.

"Let's leave off fixing stuff until later." She squeezed his hand. "Talk to me. What's happening?"

Scott took a shaky breath. "I need . . . " He yanked his hands away and stood abruptly. "No. Never mind."

Anger filtered through her compassion. She snatched at his jacket when he tried to stand. "I will *not* never mind. You came here for something, to talk. And I ain't letting you go until you do so."

Scott's nostrils flared. "Why? What business is it of yours?" He shook his head and stumbled down the steps. "I shouldn't have come. I thought . . . I used to . . . It's that . . . "

He looked at her, his eyes pleading, his mouth wordlessly moving.

She skipped the last step and rushed to him. Her fingers wound around the material of his black Columbia jacket. She wasn't going to let him go. Not until he talked. Not until he realized she was here for him . . . as his friend.

"Look, I understand that this used to be Julie's house. You used to come here, talk with her and Jacob. But they aren't here. I am, though. You've talked to me before, and you will talk to me now." She gave his jacket a little tug for extra emphasis.

"I will?" He clamped his jaw, tension hardening his jaw even more. "I thought I could. But I can't. I can't tell you."

"Oh, my—" Angela bit off her words. Just like the man to make her fall back into her old habits. "That does it. You will come inside, have some coffee, eat a slice of peach cobbler, and tell me what's going on." She yanked at him.

His feet stumbled, his body hunched over, as she roughly pulled him back up her steps. She wasn't giving him time to gain his footing, or he would bolt. "I don't care if you think it's too much for me to hear; but I will tell you right now, I will think less of you if you don't tell me compared to whatever it is you have done or not done."

His hands splayed out against the door frame. "Okay. Okay. Just let go of my jacket."

She let go and stood face-to-face with him. The porch light haloed his head, and the short strands glistened in the light. He let the screen door fall against his back and straightened his jacket.

"You'll come in, then?"

A brief smile played across his lips. "I would be too afraid of being tackled if I didn't."

He eased past her and into the dining room.

"And I would, Scott Wilson. You came here to talk, and I wouldn't have allowed you to leave until you did." His eyes followed her as she walked into the kitchen to pour him a cup of coffee. "Do you honestly believe that you have done something that I would hate you for?"

Scott shook his head. "I didn't say that."

Angela poured another cup of coffee. "You didn't have to. I saw it in you." She picked up the brimming cups and settled at the table with them. "You like your coffee black, right?"

He smiled. "Yeah, I do. A morsel of info from Nana?"

"And Dottie." She took a sip of her hot liquid, and then looked at him. "Might as well just blurt it out. Like a Band-Aid. Nice and quick."

"I stole meds and a flash drive, and I'm about to be fired." His eyes about popped out of his head as soon as the words left his mouth.

"Well, that was quick." She regarded him for a moment. His gaze fell away, and he twirled the cup around and around on the table. "Let's start with the first confession. What meds?"

"It's complicated."

"It always is." She hopped up. "You talk, and I will dish out the cobbler. Food. The Southern answer to every dilemma."

He shrugged off his jacket and hung it on the chair behind him. Angela pulled two small plates down as Scott pressed his hands against the table, apparently organizing his thoughts.

She pulled the white casserole dish that sat beside the coffee pot closer. The peachy aroma rose as she removed the foil. Two big spoonfuls for him, one for her. Small gestures to give him time. She replaced the foil, grabbed two forks, and picked up the plates.

The tightness in his voice pulled at her heartstrings. "When Julie and Billy died, I couldn't sleep. So, Dr. Morrison put me on alprazolam. When she decreased the dose, I changed the prescription back to the original." He picked up the fork and stabbed a peach. She sat down beside him and toyed with her cobbler. "Then the prescription ended. I needed more. I needed to sleep."

Angela took a bite. She swallowed and took a sip of coffee. He needed time again. She took another bite and one more sip of coffee. He continued, his voice strained and hoarse. "When we were transporting a patient, her meds fell. Melbourne had her on alprazolam, too. It wasn't much and a low dose, but I pocketed them."

He reached behind him and pulled an orange bottle from his jacket. It fell to its side when Scott placed it on the table. The pills clacked against each other as the bottle rolled toward her.

She set the bottle upright. "I—"

"No. Let me finish." He gulped the coffee and winced. "It wasn't alprazolam. I found that out the other day when Nana collapsed. It's something else. But I stole, Ang, stole medication because I thought I needed it." He hung his head. "And then tonight, while I was cleaning the ambulance, I found this."

His hand disappeared into the back pocket of his jeans and removed a black, oblong object. He placed it on the table and slid it toward her. "A flash drive that must have belonged to Donald Pierce. I don't know why I didn't turn it in."

Angela held it in front of her. Light bounced against the black plastic, highlighting the etched letters. Initials. D.P.

Heat and adrenaline rushed through her. Donald Pierce.

But first, Scott. He needed her first.

She reached out and covered his hand with hers. His fingers interlaced with hers. "What are you going to do now?"

He looked up at her. "You didn't hear me? I stole. I'm a thief."

"You're an addict. Okay?" She used her free hand to push her plate away. "You aren't the first person to be addicted to medication. I was after Mike killed himself. Thought I needed the medicine to sleep, to function. The only thing that stopped me was Max. I couldn't risk losing him."

"And I almost lost Nana Debbie."

Angela shook her head. "Let me get this through your hard head. You didn't cause Debbie's collapse. She was ill. And now she's better and coming home." Angela collected the plates.

Scott pushed his chair back and followed her into the kitchen. "But I argued with her. About the medicine. About . . . everything." He leaned against the counter while she rinsed the dishes.

"Scott, you know that didn't cause her to collapse. Debbie is a lot stronger than a heated argument with you." She turned off the water and dried her hands. "What else?"

"What do you mean, what else?" He shrugged and glanced away from her. "I committed a federal crime. I will have to admit what I did to Grace. I will be fired and probably jailed."

Angela sighed. The man was right. It was a risk he took. "And your good conscience will not allow you to just turn in the medicine anonymously, right?"

"Oh, no. If it was that simple, I would have." He crossed his ankles. "The medicine isn't alprazolam. I don't know what it is."

"What?" Angela hurried back to the table and opened the bottle. She shook out a small oblong pill. Yellow. No markings. "When you said they weren't alprazolam earlier, I thought you meant you grabbed the wrong one. Aren't there supposed to be markings on medicines, like stamped letters or scorings or something?"

"There is." His presence loomed behind her. "But not on this one. I almost took one the other night. I don't know what these are, Angela."

She dropped the pill back into the bottle. "You try to look it up?"

"In a pill book, online. Nothing." He sank back down in the chair. "That's why I have to tell Grace. If this isn't alprazolam, then what was Mrs. J. taking? And when I tell Grace how I came across the medicine, I won't be able to keep my job."

Angela pulled her chair closer to his. "Would you do what's right, even though it would cost you a high price?"

He didn't miss a heartbeat. "Yes." She opened her mouth, but his hand stopped her. "And it has nothing to do with your God. Don't go down that road with me."

She smiled against his hand and kissed his palm. He quickly removed it. "I won't for right now. Only because I think He is already working on you."

"Oh, I doubt that. What kind of God would want a thieving, lying, addicted paramedic?" A harsh laugh poured from his mouth, his teeth flashing briefly in the sneer. "I won't pretend that there is a God for me."

"Oh, Scott. God is there for everyone." He opened his mouth, and anger flared within her again. She held up a hand. "Just stop right there. You may curse God and spout hateful things about Him in your own time, Scott, but not in my presence. I ask for that consideration, okay?"

He bit his lower lip and looked away. Seconds passed before he nodded. "Okay. But answer me this, would you?"

"Sure."

He turned his gaze back to her. Anger, pain, sorrow, and hopelessness swirled across his face. "If your God is so loving, why did He allow my parents, Julie, Billy, and even your husband to die? If they were such believers, why allow them to suffer like that?"

His eyes penetrated her, eager to cast doubts into her mind. Angela pressed her hands together. She had to compose the right words, the right things to say. No. Not her. Lord, give her the ability to tell him.

The clock on the wall ticked off the seconds. Its sound echoed loudly in her ears. She looked up into his face. His eyes searched her own, boring into her, pleading for answers.

Matthew chapter seven came to mind.

"Seek, and you will find." She took a deep breath, mirroring Scott's own sharp inhalation. "That's all I can tell you, Scott. The search for answers is always different for each person. Some find the answers in a sudden rush, some in a long study of His Word. I asked myself that when Mike died.

"How could God allow Mike's illness to overtake him, cause his depression to worsen to the point that Mike overdosed? Did Mike know what he was doing? Or did he forget how many he took or when he took the medicine? I don't know. All I do know, and what I eventually received peace about, is that Mike believed in Jesus; and as surely as the thief on the cross, Mike is in paradise today. No more suffering."

She leaned her elbows on the table and fought against the tremors in her voice. "We all suffer here on Earth. All in different forms. But it's how we live our life that determines where we are in the eternal scheme of things. And there's only two destinations. I take solace in that Mike no longer suffers. Neither do Julie or Billy. Or your parents.

"God doesn't cause the evil in this world. The fall of Adam and Eve did that. What God granted us was free will. He doesn't want automatons worshipping Him. He wants true love and devotion, so He gave us choice. It is His will that we make the right choice."

Scott's stare fell away. He turned his head toward the window. His gaze had softened. Debbie said he remembered all that was said to him. Please, Lord, let him remember this.

"I cannot tell you why anyone dies, and others don't. I cannot tell you why some things happen, and others don't. But I can tell you that God is consistent, always there. He never breaks His promises."

He chuckled softly. "I've never known anyone who was able to keep a promise. Even through good intentions, I inevitably break a promise—never by choice, but usually through work or happenstances."

Angela smiled. "God isn't just anyone. He's God. He's everything. Beyond comprehension."

His fingers tapped out a slow rhythm. "I thought I said no God-talk."

He turned his head in her direction, and his eyes bored back into her again. She smiled and covered his hand with hers. "Yeah, well, when God wants to speak, He speaks." She gave his hand a squeeze. "Tell you what. I won't speak again about God if you promise one thing."

His eyes narrowed. "What's that?"

"You promise you will try to come to church on Sunday. I said *try*, make an effort. Okay? Just one visit, and all this God-talk will be dropped."

More seconds ticked by. Longer this time as he considered her request.

Did she go too far? Surely not. Once again, her mouth outran her brain.

"Fine."

Angela jerked her gaze back to him. His eyes were narrowed, his gaze thoughtful. "Really?"

"Yeah. I'll make an effort; better yet, I'll show up. Like you said, if I visit, no more God-talk."

Angela smiled. That's all that was needed, one step. Now Scott was served in God's court. Time to completely sit back and watch the match between Scott and God. Good thing she always cheered for the victor of the game.

He leaned against the back of his chair and pointed toward the flash drive on the table. "Well, before I have to lose my career, let's see what's on that drive."

CHAPTER FOURTEEN

Rochelle closed down the computer and sighed. After looking through article after article in the archives, still nothing. Until she expanded her search onto the internet and into some of the nearby Tennessee newspapers. Only two stories, and each one about the imminent hospital bankruptcy. Each one lauded how Melbourne and Associates stepped in to save a dying hospital. On a whim, she googled the good doctor and associates.

There were quite a few articles and publications in the *American Journal,* and all were about how his team aggressively and diligently researched diabetes and the cure of the disease. She pursed her lips. Sounded pretty good on the outside, but she frowned at the mention of stem cell research. Just where did he obtain those stem cells?

Sounded like the doctor was determined to find his cure. She had printed out what she could and copied to her email, but she still couldn't find much information. Only more questions. Why would such a successful doctor come down and save such a rinky-dink hospital in a two-bit town? And his name was attached to the land deed, too. What was that "good doctor" up to?

She swiveled around in her chair and stuffed the printouts in her bag. She would just drop these off for Angela to go over. Maybe together they could string together some of the clues and find out if this town was actually part of some diabolic plot worthy of an Agatha Christie or Terri Blackstock novel. She smiled at the thought. How cool would it be if there was a future novel written about her town? Then Garrettville would become famous, and the paper would be the first with the story.

Rochelle could see it now. Her name in the byline. Headlines reading, "Reporter Uncovers Hospital's Diabolic Plot."

The phone rang, and she squawked, almost toppling out of her chair.

She grabbed the receiver. "*Gazette*, Rochelle speaking." Her heart thudded heavily against her ribcage.

"Hey, Ro. I thought you may be at the office still." Brent's voice carried over the line.

The guy didn't get it, did he? She shook her head. How did she ever think he was so cool and good-looking? "I'm just leaving to head to Angela's. Whatcha need?"

"Asking for one more chance, that's all." His voice sounded hopeful.

Rochelle rolled her eyes as she cradled the receiver between her ear and shoulder. She rummaged in her bag for some gum. Just talking to him gave her a bad taste. "I said *no* the other day, Brent. I just don't think it will work between us. You and I are too different."

His sigh echoed across the line. "Come on, Ro. It won't hurt. Just a burger or coffee."

She unwrapped the gum, popped it into her mouth, and shook her head. Then rolled her eyes at herself. Like he could see over the phone line. "No. Not this time. I gave you two chances already."

"Third time's the charm?"

"Third time is the one where I will maim you." She stood and slipped her bag onto her shoulder. "I'll see you around, Brent, just not as in dating or going out. I gotta go now. Bye." She dropped the receiver onto its cradle and effectively muted whatever objection he started to spout.

Dim lights shone through the newspaper's hall as she walked to the back and checked the locks. Locked. Locked. And she peeked into Pops' office and checked the windows. Locked.

She pulled out her phone and dialed Angela's number. It rang a couple of times as she waited by the front door, swatting at the plants that drooped into her face.

"Hey, Rochelle. You're home?"

"No. Just leaving the office. Look, can I head over there for a bit?"

"Sure. Hold on." Angela's voice sounded faint as she talked. "It's Rochelle. She's coming over." A male's voice rumbled in the background. "I'll ask. Hey, Rochelle, Scott wants to know if by any chance you may have found anything else. I told him you were still poking around on older articles."

Hmm, Scott was there. Interesting. "Yeah. I actually found some things that were printed in Carsontown's paper about Melbourne and Associates and his publications in the *American Journal*. That was what I was planning to show you."

"Great. We'll be waiting for you."

"Okay, Angela. See you in a bit. I'm locking up now." She ended the conversation, pocketed her phone, and fished out the keys. She paused, pulled out her phone, and opened the memo app. With quick motions, she entered the addresses where she had found the information. Just in case she forgot. Or lost the papers.

She slipped the phone back in her pocket and pushed open the door. Wind whipped at her as she exited the building and then fought with the lock. It stuck a couple of times before she could get the lock turned all the way. Why, oh why, did things have to be so old and broken down?

Her boots clicked across the uneven sidewalk as she walked to her moped that was parked around the corner. Soon, she would have to start hitching a ride with Pops. Riding a moped in winter invited pneumonia, and she wasn't making that mistake again.

She secured her bag to the back, climbed on, and brushed dust off her helmet. Little, pink Jolly Roger skulls glittered under the streetlight. She rammed the helmet down on her head and started the motor. A quick glance ensured that she was alone, but that eerie feeling that followed out of the office stuck to her.

Rochelle shook her head and pulled away from the curb. Angela's house wasn't that far away. Maybe it was just the cold November air that chilled her. She pulled up to the traffic light and stopped. As she waited for the green, she looked around. Only a truck was pulling up behind her. Other than that, no one else was around.

The light turned green, and Rochelle turned right onto the road that led toward Angela's house. The next road was always scary to her. A dark street before she reached the next well-lit road. Rochelle bit at her lip. Maybe she should have taken the long way. But with this shortcut, she would be there sooner. And the sooner, the better, especially since the truck behind her wouldn't get off her tail.

She sped up a little, and then slowed as a car pulled onto the road ahead. It swerved slightly, inching into her lane. Rochelle's heart fell further into her gut. She scooted her moped over a little further to the right, but the car still aimed at her.

Rochelle braked hard and started to turn. Better the long way.

She gasped as the truck blocked her way. Now what? What did they want? This town may have been crooked, but crime was always low. Didn't they know who her Pops was? She held back her fear and started to turn around to drive along her original course, but a hand violently clamped over her hand.

She opened her mouth to scream, but a fist connected with her jaw. Pain lanced through her skull, but she fought against it. No way was she going down without a fight. Hands grabbed at her legs; her helmet was ripped off, scraping against her chin; something foul slammed against her mouth, and then she was whipped up into the air.

Rochelle arched her back, or at least tried to, but whoever held her had squeezed so tight, air barely reached her lungs. Fear claimed her. What was happening? What did they want?

She banged her head back and connected with bone. A horrible curse yelled in her ear telling her to stop. Hands grabbed and twisted. Fabric ripped. Pain coursed through her. Then she landed on the cold metal of the truck bed, but she wasn't alone. Something was slipped over her head as the truck sped down the road.

One of the voices whispered in her ear, and she knew that gravelly voice. No amount of disguising would mask it. "Tell me where the flash drive is. I saw you there."

What?

She tried to speak past the gag. Couldn't the stupid idiots realize she couldn't speak with her mouth stuffed with a rag? She shook her head. What was special about the flash drive? It had only copies of articles.

"Did you think you could really go up against him?"

Him? Who was him? She tried to scramble away from his hands, but her knees found no purchase against the bumpy metal as the truck bounced around. His hand slammed against her lower back and pinned her against the truck bed. The gag fell away from her mouth.

"I don't know what you're talking about." Sobs fell from her mouth. Why couldn't she be strong? Strong women didn't cry when in danger. "It only has articles on it, and I don't have it anymore. I left it at the office."

"You really think I'm that stupid? We saw the papers you printed." Movement came from beside her. "And I've got what you had tonight. We're going to find what you were hiding."

Rochelle whimpered as another hand grabbed her arm. "We can't let her go, dude. She'll tell."

She started shaking her head. Her cries were whipped away by the wind. "No. No, I won't tell. I promise. Please, I promise not to tell."

The truck slowed. Rocks crunched underneath as it came to a stop. It had been driving at a high speed, which meant it must be beyond city limits by now.

Brent's voice sounded in her ear again, but he wasn't talking to her. "Then we fix it. I told you we shouldn't have grabbed her. I could have gotten the information another way."

"This was best. Take care of it, okay? We have the papers and the keys. If it's at the office, we'll find it. Dan's got your car. Catch up once you finish here."

The truck bounced twice, and then rough hands grabbed her ankles, yanking her from the truck. She kicked and pushed and fought against hands and arms. A strong hand clamped around her wrist and twisted it. Rochelle cried out and fought against the pain of being dragged. Sharp rocks dug into her legs as she slid to the ground and tried to pull away. A spray of rocks hit her in the face as the truck apparently sped away.

She grabbed for her blindfold, but her arm was captured and forced up behind her back. The muscles in her shoulder tore. She cried out and suddenly tumbled down an embankment. Cold and sharp blades of grass cut into her.

Water seeped into her skin. Pain paralyzed her right arm, and her left seemed to barely operate as she tried to pry the blindfold off.

"Not so fast." Brent's hard hands grabbed her hair. "I told you to give me another chance. So maybe now, I'll just take this chance."

Rochelle ignored the agony of her wrist and shoulder as she fought against Brent. His hands grasped and pulled. She kicked and screamed, which only made him laugh. He cheered her on.

She raised a leg and kicked out with as much force as she could. It met yielding flesh and kept going. His strangled and garbled moan was all she needed to locate his position. Rochelle kicked and kicked in his direction, connecting with each strike.

Suddenly, both ankles were grabbed, jerking her around, flipping her over, and then a sudden pain flashed against her head. Red light blossomed behind her eyes, and then she fell into a cool blackness. Finally, safe from the pain.

Scott held the flash drive in his hand. He turned it over and over, rubbing at the cool and smooth surface with his thumb.

The overhead light glinted against the plastic. He reinserted the drive into the port and watched as the window on the screen filled up with file after file. To think all those missing budget minutes, missing deeds, and missing cases sat on this drive. Donald had it all. Scott shook his head and looked over at Angela, who gazed out the window waiting for Rochelle.

"Do you think he was a part of it?" Surely not. Donald Pierce had always seemed a decent man. A politician, sure, but for a politician, he always seemed trustworthy and honest.

"I don't think so. There were memos. Emails from Melbourne and Tribble, not to mention the mayor. Kickbacks. Extortion. Donald seemed to be collecting the information for a reason. Think he may have been an informant or about to turn them in to the authorities?"

Scott shrugged. "I don't know what to think anymore. This has a lot of information. Not just what you were looking for, but drug trials and controlled experiments. I think it goes beyond a simple land grab."

Angela left her vigil by the window and sat in the chair beside him. "You don't know what that medication you have actually is. With those drug trials, you think that may be it?"

Scott shrugged again.

"What was the north wing built for?"

"It's part of the lab and radiology. There're admin offices there. The hospital has been trying to be more self-sustaining. We have to send most of our trauma cases to Sheffield or Florence. I don't see how they can do it. We are already over-budgeted and under-staffed."

Angela ran her fingertip over the table's wood grain. "Would Douglas know anything about it?"

"Probably no more than me, but I'll ask tomorrow." Worry etched itself further into her face. Scott leaned forward and gazed into her eyes. "What's wrong? It can't be just the flash drive."

Her brow furrowed even deeper. "I do not know what to do with the drive. We can't keep it. But knowing that there is a memo from the mayor on there, there is no telling how far this goes. Who do we trust?" Her hands started twisting her sweater hem into knots.

Scott captured her hands and held them. "Listen. We can trust Douglas and Grace. We can trust Tom. We'll start there, okay?"

Angela nodded. She held his hands even tighter as she glanced at the door. "Rochelle should have been here by now. I'll try calling her and see if she was delayed somewhere."

He agreed. The girl always took the shortcut here and everywhere she went. How many times had he seen her and that moped zipping in and out of side streets? He stood and gently squeezed Angela's shoulder as she dialed and listened to the phone ring. "She's not answering, I'm going to try Tom," she said as he walked to the door and peered out the window. No one moved along the street. Dottie's car glistened underneath the streetlight. He needed to check on Nana soon.

Angela's voice drifted over to him as she spoke on her phone. "I know, Tom. I'll keep trying. It's not like her to not call. Her phone probably died; but if she doesn't show up in a little bit, call me. Okay? Scott and I'll start looking, too."

He smiled at how she automatically included him. Interesting how that happened. She set her phone on the table and resumed her worrisome look. "Trouble?"

"Rochelle hasn't been answering her phone. Very unlike her. Tom is heading to the office to check on her. He said he'll call if she's not there. Her moped has been acting up lately, but she would have called if something happened."

She stood near him. Too near.

He cleared his throat. "I need to run over and check on Nana. You don't need to come, you can stay here so Max can sleep."

Angela pointed to her laptop where the flash drive poked out by the wireless mouse's drive. "Don't forget the drive." Then she collapsed onto a dining room chair.

He retracted the flash drive and slid the item into his front pocket. He'd hold on to it until they could figure out what to do with it. "Did you copy the drive?"

"No. Even though I ran a virus check on it, I didn't want something like that in my computer. It may not be safe." She rose and strode to the door, looking out the side window. "Go check on Debbie. Let her know that I'll see her in a bit after Max wakes up."

Scott stood next to her. Roses and peaches, so faint he could barely smell it, drifted to him as she moved the curtain aside. He propped his hand next to hers and placed his other hand on her lower back. "She'll call, Angela. She'll be here soon."

She stared up at him, her expression closed off and her eyes distant. "I keep praying. But it doesn't feel right. Rochelle has consistently been dependable."

Scott nodded. "I will be back in a little while." He reached up and pushed her hair behind her ear. Just this short time with her this evening seemed to deepen their friendship. Her breath caught as he dipped his head down, and her body relaxed as he pressed a kiss on her forehead.

As he left her standing at the window and skipped down the steps, his mind replayed the light that flared in her eyes as he'd bent toward her. He had almost kissed those lips but remembered at the last moment . . . friends only. The feel of her soft skin still lingered on his lips. He smiled as he wondered if she'd realized he pressed a kiss on that nice, little freckle right above her left eyebrow.

He hustled across the road and down to his house. The door opened on silent hinges. The television cast its blue light around the darkened living room. But no Nana. Scott paused at the table and placed his wallet on the surface, and then he ventured into the kitchen. Still no Nana.

A slight cough came from the end of the hallway. Scott trailed his fingertips over the stucco surface of the wall as he walked to his grandmother's room. "Nana?"

"In here, Scott."

He entered Nana's cinnamon-scented room. Victorian style décor assaulted his senses, but he ignored the frilly frippery as he searched for his grandmother. She stood at her opened closet, pulling down a shoebox from the shelf above.

Her regal profile glanced his way. Such beauty in that face. "How are you, dear boy?" She held out her hand, but Scott rushed into her arms.

He wanted to crush her against him, hold her, and never let her go. Her slight build melted into his, and he shook as he buried his face in her soft hair. "I'm sorry, Nana. I'm so sorry."

Nana Debbie rubbed the back of his head and leaned away from him. "Whatever for, Scott? It wasn't your fault. I'm okay now. Still a little weak, but the doctor said as long as I stick to the medicine schedule, I should start feeling better in a few days."

Scott let her pull away and joined her as she sat on the bed with the shoebox in her lap. "I never meant the hurtful things I said. I don't know what came over me. I should have told you long ago about the medicine."

"Yes, you should have, but that is the past, Scott. It's done and over with. You are still my dear grandson." She patted his cheek and then clucked at his whiskers. "Didn't you shave this morning?"

Scott chuckled. "No, not this morning. It's going to really hurt when I finally shave all this off." He plucked a photo out of the box. A picture of him when he was eighteen, right before he left for college. Julie stood next to him. His thumb rubbed the face of his best friend. Funny how it no longer hurt to look at her photo.

"Remember how excited you two were?" She took the photo, replaced it, and then pulled out another one. The man in the photo looked a lot like him, only the military garb and the sepia tones hinted at a much older photo. "This is your grandfather when he was younger. We had been married for just about two months. About ten months later, I lost our first child."

Scott whipped his gaze to his grandmother. He never knew that. "You lost a child?"

"Stillborn. We named him Clarence Donovan Wilson. Your Grandfather Weatherby was dead set against naming a son after him." She smiled. "He was such a handsome man, and you look a lot like him." She slid the photo back inside and pulled out another one. "This is your father when he was one."

"I don't see Granddad in this one."

"You wouldn't. He wasn't around then. In fact, he had left me." She handed the photo to Scott. "He fell into a dark time when Clarence died. After I found out I was expecting another, Weatherby started drinking. Eventually, he found the allure of opium. It was easy to obtain back then. His life spiraled down until he was a shell of a man."

"What happened?" Scott reached in and found another photo of his grandfather sitting in a lawn chair next to his dad. "I don't remember him being a small man. He always seemed larger than life. Bold. And happy."

Nana Debbie set the box to the side. A heavy sigh escaped her. Apparently, the past was not an easy subject nor a happy one. "Your grandfather almost killed someone one night. In a drunken rage, he attacked a man who was abusing his wife and daughter outside the hardware store. Spent three days in jail, and that was when he said he found himself. Or when God found him. He confessed his assault and his addiction. Spent months in a rehab facility. By the time he came home, Peter was almost three. It took a while before I could find it in myself to love him again. But I realized that Weatherby had risked everything dear to him by telling the truth and coming clean."

Scott set the photo beside him on the bedspread. How strange that not only did he share his grandfather's name but also his demeanor. "Yet you loved him."

"Yes. I loved him. And still do, regardless that he's been with our Lord for ten years." She gripped his hand. Her gaze bored into his. "You always do what is right, Scott. And even though you have done wrong, it is never too late. Things may not turn out the way you want, but you will always have a life here and with me." Her palm cupped his cheek. "You are very much like your grandfather, but the most important thing you inherited from both your father and your grandfather is your integrity."

He pressed his cheek into her hand and covered it with his own. "I love you, Nana."

"I love you, Scott." She pulled him down into a hug, rocking him gently. "Now, tell me what else is bothering you."

He sniffed and leaned back against the bedpost, twirling the photo between his fingers. Never could he hide anything from his grandmother. "There's a lot. I'm afraid it goes beyond stolen medication."

She slid the box across the bed and turned to him. Judas crept into the room and jumped on the bed to settle in the crook of his knee. His grandmother waited patiently, but he really didn't know where to start. *Like a Band-Aid, Scott.* Angela's voice rode through his mind.

Well, here he went.

"When I stole the meds off Mrs. J, I thought it was alprazolam; but I discovered the other day, it wasn't. I have no idea what it is. And I can't tell Grace because she hasn't been around when I'm on shift. Plus, I found a flash drive in the van after our run involving Donald Pierce. I didn't turn it in. Instead, I showed Angela. It had memos about the hospital, the buyouts, the land deals, drug trials, experiments, city budgets, and meeting minutes. Now I think that what I have in my jacket pocket isn't just a simple medication, but something more. And to top it off, no one can get in touch with Rochelle."

He paused for breath and looked up at his grandmother. When had he started staring at the floor? Probably midway through his monologue.

His nana patted his hand. "First things first. Find Rochelle. She's more important than some city or hospital or your job." She stood and plucked the photo from the bed. "What does Angela say about it all?"

"She's just as confused. We don't know where to go with this information."

His grandmother frowned. "Tom. Or go to Grace. What's wrong with the police?"

"Because of city hall. What if the cops are corrupt?"

"Not all of them can be."

"Sure. But who do I trust?" He shook his head, pushed Judas aside, and started pacing. "I thought I would just turn it all in to Grace in the morning."

"And that is a start. Let's take this first step and then worry about what comes after."

Scott smiled and stopped before his grandmother. "You are a very wise woman, Nana."

She wrapped her arms around his chest and squeezed. "Only because life made me so."

His phone buzzed before he could respond. He looked at the display. "It's Angela."

And for some reason dread ate at his gut.

CHAPTER FIFTEEN

Angela held Max even closer as she hurried across the street. The wind picked up, threatening to rip away the quilt she had bundled around him. Even with the heavy coat over pajamas, a fleece blanket, and the quilt, Max's cheek seemed frozen to hers.

She nudged Dottie's gate open with her hip. It banged against the inside panels and then slammed shut behind her. Her shoes slid a little on the wet pavers. Warm light poured from Dottie's house as the woman held the door open for her.

"Thank you so much, Dottie. I didn't want to have to lug Max all the way to Sheffield." She deposited Max on the couch and started unwrapping his sleepy form. Layers fell away, and he watched from dream-hazed eyes while Dottie plumped a pillow for him.

Dottie patted the blue, embroidered pillow, and Max sleepily laid his head against it, drifting off once again into his sleep. Angela tucked the quilt around him and turned to her neighbor. "I need to call Scott."

"Of course. Max will be fine with me. He always is. And don't worry about anything. Just make sure that Rochelle is okay, that poor sweet child." She headed for her kitchen. "I'll fix a to-go cup for you and Scott."

Angela nodded her thanks and dialed Scott's number on her phone.

It rang a couple of times before his deep voice answered. "Angela."

"Scott. Tom called. Highway patrol found Rochelle in Colbert County along Highway 21 by the Natchez Trace. They had her transported to Sheffield to the Helen Keller Hospital—"

"The Natchez Trace! I don't understand."

"Her moped was off the embankment. She was found a few yards from it. She's in rough shape, Tom said. Still unconscious." Angela collected her purse that had fallen to the floor and started stuffing its contents back in. "I don't have enough gas in my car to make it to Sheffield, and I want to know how in the world the girl ended up over twenty miles away from us. You think—"

He interrupted again. "You don't even have to ask, Ang. Hold on . . . " There was a rustling sound, and then his voice calling out to his nana. "Nana Debbie, did you move my stuff? The black shirts are on brown, and my blue is with the greens . . . that's weird." His voice came back full strength. "I'm heading over there right now—"

"I'm at Dottie's." Somehow in the middle of this mayhem, she found perverse pleasure at interrupting him.

"Okay." His voice drifted away. "She's at Dottie's, Nana." Then he was back. "Nana is going to come stay with Dottie, too." There was a small grunt, a squeak, and then a jangle of metal. "I'm heading there now."

"Okay." She disconnected and collapsed on the couch beside her son. The softness of the well-worn couch promised a plushy rest, but she couldn't succumb to its promise and temptation. Not yet.

Dottie peeked around the corner of the dining room and held up the Kangaroo Express convenience store travel mug. "I hope you don't mind sharing with Scott. I had only one mug." She paused in the middle of her trek to the living room when the doorbell rang and turned to open it. "Scott, come on in."

He dropped a small peck on Dottie's cheek before turning to Angela. "Ready to go?"

Angela hopped up and slid her purse over her shoulder.

"Yeah." Angela leaned down, smoothed Max's hair to the side, and placed a small kiss on his temple. "Sleep well, sweetie. Mom will be back soon."

She stood and gave her son one last look. Dottie pushed the mug into her hands. Heat radiated from the mug and warmed her still frozen fingers. "Thank you, Dottie."

Her neighbor waved her off and herded them out the door. "Give us regular updates and don't worry about Max. He's in good hands."

They met Nana Debbie coming up the sidewalk. The regal woman enveloped Angela into a hug. "You two be careful and keep us updated. Do you want us to take Max to school tomorrow?"

Angela shook her head. "No. Let him have the day off. No need to try and trouble yourself with getting him prepared. He's not an easy child to deal with in the mornings."

"Okay, dear." Debbie rubbed Scott's cheek, and then shooed them on. "Drive safe, Scott."

"I will, Nana." He opened the passenger door for Angela. She slid onto the soft leather seats, and the door shut gently. Within seconds, he was around the car and inside. He reached in between them and slid a bracket from a hidden enclosure and locked it in place. "Cup holder."

"Thank you." Angela set the mug into the snug opening and glanced around the car. Not a spot of dirt or lint marred the dark brown interior. Even that new car smell hung around. Give Max five minutes in here, and it would look like a minivan carrying a herd of wild cats. She looked at her shoes and grimaced. A trace of mud had fallen from her boots.

Scott glanced at her as he pulled away from the house. "Don't worry about the mud, Angela. It's just a car. There is such a thing as a vacuum." His smile took the bite out of his words.

"It's a nice car. I can't imagine driving anything so nice. Or expensive."

"Well, with it being just me, this was one of those splurges that I bought for myself. Although, Nana Debbie uses it more than I do."

"I thought she had a car."

Scott chuckled. "She does. A Taurus. But she will find any excuse to use my car. I don't mind. I'll do anything for Nana Debbie . . . Well, just about anything. I won't use those wire hangers she keeps trying to get me to use."

Angela laughed. "Hangers? Really."

"They bend and put puckers in my shirts. Then I have to rewash, re-iron, and rehang. Plastic, and only if they are the coordinating color, or the wooden hangers." He turned onto Highway 14 and sped up a notch. The engine increased its hum. "It's just one of those things."

She shook her head. "I pretty well pegged you for OCD. Don't ever look into my closet then. Pink shirts on yellow plastic. Reds and blues on wires. No purple, though. My hair clashes with purple."

His laughter faded after a few seconds, and quiet resumed to dominate. She looked out the window. The tree line flew out of the headlights' beams and into the darkened world behind. Underneath them, the road beat out a pattern beneath the tires. Her mind thumped along with it. For once, there was no thought. Only fear and worry for Rochelle.

"Was that all that Tom said?" His quiet voice drifted over to her.

Angela gripped the hem of her coat and nodded. "I didn't ask much. Just told him we were on the way and would be there as soon as we could. He sounded . . . I don't know. Worried? Fearful? He was barely coherent."

Scott's hand slid over hers, and his long fingers interlaced with her cold ones. "Rochelle is his only grandchild. I can't imagine his pain at the moment. But I'll find out what is going on once I'm there. And don't worry." A slight squeeze, but he didn't pull away from her. "At least, try not to worry, okay?"

She cupped his hand between hers and held on. Friends did this, right? Holding on to each other? "I'll try not to, Scott."

"You can pray, right? That's what you do?" He seemed hesitant about asking that.

She looked over at him. No emotion at all showed on that chiseled face. "I've been continually praying. Always. In the back of my mind. Right now, but there's no thought. I can't seem to form the words." And that was the first for her. Words were her life.

Silence hung heavily around them. Scott bit at his lip for a second. He glanced her way. "How does that work? If you don't talk or think, how can you call it prayer?"

Angela returned to stare out the window. "You want to have a God-talk now?"

"It's not God-talk, per se. I'm curious how anyone can call it prayer if they don't speak the words."

She pulled her hand away from his and reached for her bag on the floorboard. Somewhere in its depth was her small Bible. Her fingers dug around a moment while Scott's gaze traveled from her movements to the road and back to her.

Apparently, curiosity won. "What are you doing?"

"You want to know the answer. So, I'm trying to find my little Bible. Oh, here it is." She pulled the little red Book from the darkened interior. Scott reached above them and pressed on one of the interior lights.

The soft glow illuminated the deep scratches and small tears along the edges of the cover. The thin pages rustled as she flipped through the pages. "This is the one I like; listen.

"O Lord, You have searched me and known me. You know my sitting down and my rising up; You understand my thought afar off. You comprehend my path and my lying down, And are acquainted with all my ways. For there is not a word on my tongue, But behold, O Lord, You know it altogether."

"I've heard Nana Debbie read that. Psalm one thirty-nine, verses one through three?"

"Four." She glanced at him. "You can remember all that?"

He shrugged. "I don't always remember the verses, but I can remember what is said and read."

"Debbie did tell me that." She flipped to another book. "Here is another that helps." She ran her finger under the lines. "So, God, who knows—"

Scott's voice was barely a whisper. "The heart, acknowledged them by giving them the Holy Spirit, just as He did to us." His fingers tapped against the steering wheel.

Angela closed the Bible and slid it into her bag. "There's a lot more, I'm sure. I would probably need a concordance to look them up. But in essence, God is saying that He knows us because He formed us. So when we can't speak, He still knows our hearts and knows how we feel." She let her bag fall to the floor again and shifted in her seat. "How do you remember so much?"

He shrugged. "I don't know. Made school easy, that's for sure." Scott removed his right hand from the wheel and rested it palm up on the console between them.

She hesitated. Such strong hands. Long fingers. She envisioned those long fingers curling around her waist or trailing down her arm. Those same fingers that played with her hair not too long ago. She slid her hand into his. His grip tightened.

"So, if I can't form the words or even know what to say, you are telling me that God already knows?"

"Do you really want an answer to that? Because I think you already know." She picked up the coffee mug with her free hand and drank a small sip. Hot, sweetened brew coursed down her throat and immediately started warming her insides.

Scott let go of her hand and reached for the travel mug as she tried to set it in the holder. He grimaced when he swallowed. "Ugh. Sugar." He took another sip and shuddered. "Ugh." Then he took one more sip.

"Why are you still sipping it if you don't like it?" She laughed as he replaced the mug.

"Because I needed the caffeine jolt." He shuddered one more time. "We're almost there. Call Tom and tell him we will arrive in about ten minutes."

Angela slipped her phone from her pocket and dialed Tom's number. A part of her lamented the loss of feeling his hand in hers, and the other part reminded her that "friends only" meant limited hand-holding. And somewhere in the back of her mind, while the phone rang on Tom's end, a little part of her acknowledged the idea that maybe she was starting to wish for something more than "just friends" with Scott.

Scott looked across the hospital room where Angela stood next to the head of Rochelle's bed. She held the girl's limp hand and periodically stroked the dirty, red-tipped strands of blonde hair. Braces adorned Rochelle's wrist and ankle. Contusions and abrasions marred the girl's light skin. He unclenched his fists and forced down the hatred at whoever had hurt Rochelle.

The door opened behind him; and Tom entered, his face a maze of fatigue, worry, grief, and lack of sleep.

Scott accepted the coffee and took a sip. Anything to busy his hands. "Tastes like nurse's station coffee."

"Marianne—she'll be the RN for Rochelle during the day—said that I could help myself to the coffee and drinks in the break room." He sank into the squeaky vinyl chair. The television mounted on the wall above him flickered with its muted conversation. "They said it's not a coma. She has a mild concussion, broken right wrist, fractured ankle, but should wake up eventually. Sleep is the best thing for her right now."

Scott leaned against the wall next to Tom and reached down to squeeze the man's shoulder. "And they're right. She'll wake when the swelling subsides. And you will be here for her."

Tom looked up at him. Beyond the worry, a flicker of fear flashed in his eyes. "I've answered all I could to the police, but Scott, there's more. And I think it ties in with you and Angela."

Angela looked up from her hovering and mother-henning. "What do you mean? The budget minutes?"

Tom shook his head. "Not just that. Rochelle was bringing something to y'all. She left me a text message, but I had left my phone in the car when I went to talk to the Rotary Club about next month's scholarship dinner." He reached up and set his coffee on the rolling food tray. "She had been slowly finding articles about GNAF and the hospital."

"But that's not all, is it?" Scott settled on the visitor's couch under the window. "A few articles here and there isn't enough for someone to rough up our girl."

Tom sighed. A heavy, soul-wrenching sigh. "I have to protect my granddaughter, Scott. I was at the office when I received the call about Rochelle. It was trashed. Papers everywhere. The computer had well over twenty files pulled up on the screen. Drawers were opened. Those colored flash drives were scattered everywhere. They were looking for something. I was about to report it when I got the call about Rochelle."

Angela's gaze burned into him. Scratch Tom off the list of people to talk to. No need to worry him more or place him in danger any further. That left only Grace, and he would have to wait until he made it home. Right now, he planned to stay with Tom and Rochelle.

"Tom?" Angela brought Rochelle's hand to her cheek and rubbed it against her own. A motherly gesture. A big sister gesture. "I'm sorry. But they probably thought that we found something. I didn't think about it until you mentioned the office. When I got home this after-noon, I noticed a few things misplaced. I thought I had done it. But if they went through the office, then they may have pilfered through my things. My house doesn't have the best of locks or windows."

Scott bit his lip. His clothes. Jumbled up. His nightstand opened. The Bible on the bed. He knew he put it back, but what if . . . He frowned and forced his memory back to the nightstand. The empty medicine bottles. His name. But they were pushed to the back.

"I think, Tom, they have been to all our houses." Scott looked up at Angela. "My clothes. Things moved. I was too worried about Nana and what I needed to do that I really didn't notice at the time."

Anger clouded Tom's face. "You mean that you are involved in this, too, Scott?"

"Angela came to me about some things the hospital did. Remember the buyout?"

Tom nodded. A thoughtful look swam across his face as his gaze traveled from Rochelle to Scott to Angela and back to Rochelle. "Then what Angela unearthed goes beyond what anyone thought."

Scott ran his hands over his face. Stubble scratched against his palm. Regardless of what Tom was enduring, he had to know. Scott dug into his pocket and fished out the flash drive. "I think this is what they were trying to find."

Light from the wall lamps reflected off the plastic. Tom looked from it to Scott.

"Donald Pierce? You were at the scene."

Scott had to hand it to the man. He was sharp and could fit pieces together in no time. "Yes. Everything about the budget, minutes, memos, land buy, and drug trials."

"Drug trials?" Tom's brow furrowed, and he glanced at Angela, who had resumed her stroking across Rochelle's hair.

She nodded. "From what we could tell, it was disguised as alprazolam. But what the results were showing was a human drug trial for a diabetes medication. The hospital must have been cutting corners or were denied testing. That's my guess."

Tom shook his head. "And the only thing Rochelle knew was the articles she pulled up?"

Scott nodded. "We just found out ourselves about the drug trial. They don't know we have the flash drive. At least, I hope not. I found it in the van after Donald was taken to the hospital."

He rose and knelt in front of Tom. "I swear, Tom, we didn't know. We didn't know how dangerous this was until earlier when we looked at the drive. We never meant for anything to happen to Rochelle."

Tom raised his head. There was anger there, but not directed at him. A hard gleam flashed behind the hazy gaze. Tom slapped a hand onto Scott's shoulder and squeezed.

"And I don't blame you." He shot a glance at Angela. "Neither of you. If anything, I am thankful for your influence in Ro's life and being her friends."

He rose and took Angela's place. Scott quickly scooted the hardback chair toward Tom, and the older man collapsed onto it. His hands engulfed his granddaughter's. "Will you turn over the flash drive? Keep my Rochelle safe from harm?"

Scott nodded. "We will. As soon as we know whom to trust."

"Then trust me."

All three turned to the new visitor. Douglas stood outside the opened door.

CHAPTER SIXTEEN

Scott waved the man inside and met him halfway. Angela glanced at Douglas. If the man had a hat, it would be in his hands by now, so contrite was his attitude. And that was puzzling. Why would he feel contrite? He barely knew Rochelle.

The blond EMT reached past her and shook Tom's hand. "I'm sorry to hear about Rochelle, Tom. I came to see how you were holding up and how she was doing."

Tom nodded his thanks. "Concussion. A few broken bones, wrist and ankle. Bruised ribs."

Douglas cleared his throat and glanced at Scott. "SAE?"

"Negative."

Angela felt more than saw the relief come from Douglas. His face contorted with raw emotions as he gazed down at Rochelle and her grandfather. The flirtation between the two was evident from that night, but Rochelle never mentioned anything further between the two.

"May I stay with you, Tom? You need rest, and it would be nice, I know, to have an extra set of eyes on Rochelle."

Tom nodded. "I would welcome it."

Angela rose, caught Scott's attention, and nodded toward the door. "Tom, the breakroom is down the hall and to the right?"

He absently nodded and returned to his vigil.

Scott followed her out the door. "What is it?" His whisper hissed in the quiet.

"Can we tell Douglas?" She frowned. Her hand landed on Scott's arm. "How did he know about Rochelle?"

"Probably Nana Debbie. He had mentioned catching up with me later." Scott's face hardened, and he turned toward the room. "But let's find out. I do not want to think that my friend could be a part of all this."

"No." Angela grabbed his arm and stopped him. "Let's wait it out first. See what he does." She pulled him down the hall. "We said we were getting coffee, so let's get the coffee and one for Douglas."

Scott stumbled behind her and chuckled. "You know, you really don't have to haul me around."

Heat flushed her neck.

She let go and hurried to the breakroom. His heavy footfalls followed. "If it was Nana Debbie who told him, should we include him on the flash drive? He knows we were looking into the budget minutes." Her mind flashed back to the night. Douglas playfully teasing Rochelle about the sticky notes on the pages.

"He was also the one who tried to warn you away." Scott picked up a cup and dumped some French Vanilla creamer into it, stirred, and then grabbed the next cup she filled.

Angela stirred two packets of sugar into two cups and then followed Scott back into the hallway. "And that probably meant that he knew something?"

Scott shrugged. "Who knows? Let's ask him how he found out first."

She fell quiet as they walked the rest of the way back to the room. Scott pushed the door open with his shoulder. Hushed voices greeted them. Douglas and Tom sat at Rochelle's side talking in undertones. Tom looked up as she passed him his cup of coffee. Douglas nodded his thanks to Scott.

Tom expelled a quick chuckle. "I'm probably going to be living off this stuff for the next few days." He downed a large gulp.

Angela perched on the edge of the vinyl chair. "Then allow Douglas to spell you for a while. I know for a fact that those hospital sofas aren't that bad to sleep on."

A fleeting smile passed over his face. "That's what Douglas was just saying to me."

Douglas glanced up at Scott. "I stopped at your house, man. No one answered, but Debbie called out to me from your neighbor's house. Told me that you were here and then what she knew about Rochelle."

Scott scooted back onto the sofa and crossed an ankle over his knee. "Thanks for coming."

"No problem." He looked over at Angela. "Do you think it was the stuff you two were looking into?"

That feeling that he knew more than he was letting on niggled at the back of her mind. "I'm starting to think that way."

Tom shot her a glance. "You can tell him, Angela. I already told him some of it." He ran a hand over his head and left a slight Mohawk in his hair.

She glanced at Scott, who just regarded her with impassive eyes. She would keep the flash drive secret for now. Just for a little while. "Yeah. We were digging up quite a lot about the budget, city hall, the hospital, and GNAF. Just little stuff. Rochelle was bringing some printouts to us before . . . "

Silence reigned in the room. All heads turned to the still form of Rochelle.

Tom picked up a bag and handed it back to Scott. "That was all that was found with her. Just her purse. Empty. Her little notebook. Written in some code of hers with lots of numbers. And that's it. No printouts. No files."

Angela reached for Rochelle's heart and skulls notebook. "Let me see that, Scott."

He passed her the book, and she thumbed it open. Rochelle's barely legible handwriting had columns of letters and numbers. Each one corresponding with the plats and deeds they had both been researching. And the missing dates. "These are the deeds, plats, and land titles. Plus, the dates where the meeting minutes were missing. There's also some that I don't recognize. Tom? Right here."

She stood, leaned past Douglas, and pointed to a group of letters and numbers at the bottom. "Is that a file on the computer?"

Tom took the book and held it from him as he peered at the writing. "I recognize some, but not all." He pointed to a small list to the side. "Those are her research files. RG. Rochelle Gwen. That's the file folder. B11-a would be a file, I assume. She's always had a certain way of filing her notes since school."

He handed it back to Angela.

Angela closed the book. "Mind if I hold onto this? I can check the computer tomorrow morning."

Tom fished around in his pocket and pulled out a key. "Here's the key to the office."

She righted her purse and slipped the key inside it. As Douglas and Scott entertained Tom with highlights from the last football game, Angela leaned back and watched. Rochelle's breathing rose in a rhythm—in, out, in, out. Tom's voice wove with the cadence. Douglas' mellow speech contrasted with Scott's deep voice.

Tom would be here with Douglas to keep Rochelle safe, but would they be safe? If it was the research and flash drive they were after, would Max be safe? Or Debbie? The poor woman didn't need another hospital stay.

Scott met her gaze. His dark eyes questioned her. And she didn't have to guess. He was thinking the same thing.

CHAPTER SEVENTEEN

A ngela turned the lock and opened the door to the *Gazette*. Tom was right. It was trashed.

Papers, flash drives, and folders littered the floor. Rochelle's chair laid upturned at the end of her receptionist station. Angela strode across the floor and peered into her office.

Her chair was tipped on its side against the wall. Papers littered the floor and crinkled as she stepped onto them. She pulled the drawer to her desk further out. She couldn't tell if the stuff inside had been tampered with, but it was a mess. The other drawers showed more disarray with folders half-standing up.

Nothing in those, anyway. Nothing of importance. She left her office and ventured further down the hall.

Michael's office sported the same chaos.

Angela walked to Tom's office and turned the knob. It was locked. And she didn't have the key for his office, just the main building. She turned back to Rochelle's station.

She righted the chair and sat down at the desk. With a nudge of the mouse, the computer screen blossomed to life. Tom wasn't kidding. Dozens and dozens of files were pulled up on the screen.

Angela glanced at them and quickly closed them out.

She opened the printer file. Maybe there was a way to see what was the last thing printed. Well, that idea was shot down. She clicked through all the options, but nothing showed anything in queue nor an option that showed any information on the last file printed.

Rochelle wouldn't have the files on the desktop. She pulled up the file explorer and searched under each PC file. In downloads, Angela spied a file titled *JobStuff.* She opened it and scanned the files listed, noting one particular file: B-11a.

She clicked it open and grinned. The girl was exceptional. B-11a contained a timeline of the missing budgets. Angela printed it out and opened the other sub-files. All of Rochelle's research was quickly printed. Didn't she say the girl was exceptional?

If the people looking for stuff really knew how to search, they would have found it. Apparently, they underestimated the girl. Although, these printouts alone wouldn't make a case against anyone, added to Donald Pierce's flash drive, it all made for a compelling argument.

She grabbed the stack of printouts and stuffed them in her bag. After closing out the files, her phone rang. Angela pulled it out of her jacket pocket. "Hey, Scott. Thought you were at work."

"I am. Had planned on talking to Grace today, but she's in Florence at some day-long conference. I'm about ready to give up on meeting with her."

Angela shut down the computer and leaned back in the chair. "What were you planning to say to her?"

A heavy sigh huffed through the phone. "I was going to tell her about the medicine I stole. But maybe it is for the best. Did you find anything?"

She shook her head. "Not really. She had a lot of research filed away, so I printed them out. All about GNAF, the hospital, Whitecloud, and rezoning articles. By themselves, it means hardly anything."

"But add them with the flash drive . . . " His voice drifted away. "Yeah, I can see that. Listen; head over here to the hospital, please. I want to run an idea by you."

"Okay. I'll be there shortly." Angela ended the call and pocketed her phone. Pretty sure what Scott wanted to speak about had her quickly locking the door to the *Gazette*.

She shuddered as she turned away from the door. What was that old saying her grandmother always said? Someone just walked over her grave.

Yeah. That was it. She fought down a shudder again and slid into her car. Something just wasn't right.

Scott paced the outside the emergency doors. If he were a smoker, he would have cigarette after cigarette between his lips. If he wasn't so allergic to the smoke, he would start now. Anything to calm his nerves.

He turned and paced the other way. One, two, three . . .

When he reached the corner of the building, Scott paused. Pacing wasn't helping. Maybe he shouldn't have had those four cups of espresso. Between worry over Rochelle and Angela's investigation, sleep hid from him. Without his meds, he couldn't coax himself into any form of nighttime rest.

Scott shoved his fists into his pockets, nodded a hello to Mack and Arlene as they passed by, and fought the urge to pace.

He looked around the parking area. Angela would be here soon. The woman was always either early or right on time. Probably one of the features that attracted him. That and her freckles. Her red hair. Her bright eyes.

Stop it! He shook his head. They agreed, friends only.

He checked his watch and then shoved his hand back into his pocket. Only ten minutes had passed. It took at least fifteen from downtown to the hospital.

Scott pivoted on his heel and strode back to the double doors. A little pitter-patter hit the metal top of the walkway. Another light drizzle. And it matched his mood. Forecast called for rain again in the near future. Storms, actually.

Douglas stepped out the doors and grinned. "Scott. Hey, man, you heading to the hospital after shift?"

Scott leaned against the building's side and nodded. "Yeah. Going to go with Angela. Why? Are you going there?"

"Later." He pulled a pack of gum from his side pocket and offered Scott a piece. When Scott shook his head, he shrugged and unwrapped a piece. "Tom asked if I would come by. The man is ragged. Poor guy." He popped the strip of gum into his mouth.

"Can't say I blame him. Barely slept myself last night. Racking my brain over who would do something like that to Rochelle." He glanced at his partner. "Doesn't make sense, unless it's about what she and Angela were researching."

"Budget minutes?" Douglas shook his head. "I don't see how just budget minutes would threaten her life."

"Not just budget minutes." Scott pushed away from the wall and stood in front of Douglas. The man's eyes widened slightly at Scott's proximity. "What do you know about the buyout of the hospital? The extension of the north wing?"

Douglas' eyes narrowed. "Not much. Probably the same as you. Melbourne and Associates stepped in and bought the hospital. City hall sold them land for the extension." He pursed his lips and shrugged. "Never paid much attention to what was going on at the time. Other than Gracie had to fight for her job and promotion, almost to the point it was about to go to court. They were going to bypass her and give it to Jonathan."

"I forgot about that." A rumble from the road reached him, and Scott turned to watch a ratty, red Grand Am pull into the parking lot and play musical spots. After the fifth lane, it whipped into a space. The wind picked up and tossed red hair all about her face when she climbed out of the driver's seat.

Douglas smiled and nudged Scott's shoulder. "I see that Angela's here. I'll let you talk to her. Catch ya later, man."

A whoosh of warm air surrounded Scott as Douglas disappeared inside.

Scott stepped to the edge of the sidewalk. Angela hurried across the lot and stepped under the walkway seconds before the bottom let loose. Heavy raindrops pounded against the metal overhang above them.

"Made it." She pulled her jacket tighter and looked up at him.

No make-up today. Nothing to hide those freckles. Especially that little freckle over her left eyebrow.

He gestured to the metal bench at the end of the sidewalk. She followed him. Scott settled on the cold metal and waited until she situated herself beside him.

"So." She thumped her fist on his knee. "What do you need to talk about? Speaking to Douglas?"

Scott shook his head. How did the woman guess correctly? "I'm starting to wonder if fearless reporter Angela has hidden superpowers."

She snorted at his statement. "Hardly. I just know you. So, I'm right?"

He slid back, pulled a knee upon the bench, and propped his arm along the back, his fingers brushing ever so lightly against her curls. "He can be trusted. And we need someone on our side."

Angela nodded. "What about Dottie and Nana Debbie? Tom wasn't kidding about the office being trashed. And we suspect them already being at our houses. I don't want them, or Max, involved."

He sighed and captured a curl. "Let's wait until Rochelle is awake and see what it was that she found. You can stay at Dottie's if it makes you more comfortable. I'll be with Nana. I already put in for a couple of days off."

"How did you get that approved so soon?"

Scott smiled. "Took some sick days. Had so many stored up that no one complained. Mack jumped at the chance to have some over-time." The silken strand pulled away from his fingers as she twisted around to face him.

"Do you think Douglas knows more than he's letting on?" She bit her lip.

His gaze fell to her mouth.

Lack of sleep. That was why he was tempted to kiss her. He was just too tired to think clearly.

"I don't know. Sometimes, I think so." He glanced back down the sidewalk at the double doors where the object of their conversation was flirting with one of the ER nurses while she took a smoke break. The wind blew their way, and the stench of the smoke tickled his throat.

He cleared it and turned his gaze back to Angela. "I was thinking of inviting him over tomorrow after church. Maybe show him the flash drive?"

"Why not tonight?"

Scott coughed against the smoke-induced irritation. "He's going to be at the hospital tonight."

"Then, let's tell him then." She reached for his hand. "We need help with this. Don't you trust Douglas?"

Scott caught the man's gaze. Douglas nodded at him and returned to his conversation. Yeah, he trusted his partner. Had to. "Yeah, I do. Then we tell him when he shows up at the hospital?"

Angela nodded, and then looked at her watch. "Max will be home soon. I need to be there when he gets off the bus. Come to the house when you finish showering, and we'll head down there."

"Wait." He pulled the flash drive from his pocket. "You keep this with you, okay? Until tonight."

Her fingers closed around it and stayed pressed to his for a moment before sliding the memory device into a small compartment in her purse.

Scott stood and followed her to the edge of the sidewalk. He reached out and stopped her before she stepped out into the rain. "Please be careful, Ang. I don't want anything to happen to you."

"I will, Scott." She paused and looked up at him. A moment of indecision played across her face before she reached up and cupped his jaw. Her lips placed a soft kiss on his cheek, her finger running a small line down his jawline as she withdrew. "And you be careful. We can't let anyone know that we suspect anything."

Then she was running across the pavement to her car.

Scott leaned against the metal support pole. Her car pulled away and raced through the rain toward home.

He wasn't expecting that kiss. She was definitely making it hard to keep it as "just friends."

He shoved his fists inside his pockets and trudged back to the ER doors. Two more hours left of his shift. And then he'd figure out what to do about all this.

The doors swooshed open, and the emergency tone vibrated through the air. His heartbeat accelerated as Douglas met him at the door.

"Giddy-up, man. Rain is bringing them in."

Scott jogged to keep up with Douglas, rounded the front of the ambulance, and pulled open the passenger door. His mind clicked into the familiar cadence of work as he settled in the seat and called in their ETA.

CHAPTER EIGHTEEN

Angela sat on Dottie's porch swing, watching Max play with Frolic at the other end of the porch. She pulled a small cushion onto her lap and hugged it to her chest as she sent the swing back into motion with a kick of her foot.

To say that worry ate at her would be an understatement. Tom said that Rochelle was still asleep. The doctor decreased the medication, so she would wake sooner. The police had arrived again to check on her condition. No evidence to who had done that to her. At least not yet, Tom had said. She clicked a fingernail against her front teeth. Hopefully, DNA evidence would have something, but that would take a long while. Rochelle wasn't exactly a high-profile case. Angela sighed and leaned her head back.

She closed her eyes and prayed. Prayed harder than she ever had before. Let Rochelle be healed. Let her remember. Help bring justice. Help them all. Show Scott the way.

Words in her head drifted away like water across Max's fingerpaint. It swirled, blended, and then disappeared down the drain. A dark drain full of nothing.

A gentle touch to her shoulder, and Angela jerked back up. She scowled and straightened in the swing as Dottie handed her a cup and saucer.

"I didn't think I was so tired, Dottie." She held the cup steady and glanced at Max. How long was she out of it? "Max? You okay, sweetie?"

He waved at her and held up an army figurine. "I think my lu-in-it is done for. Frolic bit him."

Angela shook her head as her son returned to setting up a line of defense against the plastic dinosaurs.

Dottie smiled. "He's fine. You weren't asleep but for a couple of minutes."

"I didn't think I was so tired. And now I'm repeating myself." She sipped the English Breakfast tea and set the cup back onto the saucer. "Are you sure you don't mind watching Max while we go to Sheffield? I feel as if I am abusing your generosity."

"Oh, Angela, dear." Dottie shook her head. "I enjoy having Max here with me. He is simply a delight. Such a soft-hearted little boy."

"He's a lot like Mike. Even that dark hair of his. Glad he didn't inherit my wild mane." She swallowed another sip of the smooth drink. "Thank you, though."

"And you are welcome." Dottie leaned forward and set her saucer and cup on the side table at the porch's corner. "Debbie is coming by again tonight. I think she loves being around Max, too."

"Really?" Angela shook her head. A loose strand of hair fell across her brow, and she huffed at it, blowing it to the side. What a blessing it seemed to have two sweet women willing to look after her son. Her extremely active son.

A black car whipped into the driveway down from Dottie's. The door flew open, and Scott unfolded from it. A scowl stretched across his face while he talked on the phone. Long, hurried strides had him inside the door, which closed with a bang.

She frowned. Something had him upset.

The siren notification startled her enough that she jumped. She pulled the phone from her jacket pocket and opened Scott's message to her.

Looks like I'm off longer than I asked. HR forcing me to take the full two weeks.

She quickly typed in her response. *That's good?*

His reply pinged back. *That's good. For them. I preferred not to. Be at Dottie's in a bit. Need to shower.*

She slid her phone back into her jacket pocket. "He's taking a shower and then will be over."

Dottie nodded, rose, and collected the teacups. "I made some cinnamon rolls. Would you like one?"

"No. Thank you, though." Angela stood and called to Max. "Max, come in and have some cinnamon rolls."

"Yes!" He quickly swiped the toys to the side and piled them against the house. "Come on, Frolic. 'Ninnaman rolls are ready."

She held the door open as her rambunctious child stumbled over the threshold. A loud bang echoed across the air. Angela looked down at Scott's house. Debbie was hurrying to Scott's car, the hood of her raincoat pulled over her head. Scott struggled with the door a bit, slammed his shoulder into it, and then kicked it before finally letting the storm door close behind him. She shook her head at his irritation. His door must stick in the weather, too.

Angela let the door bump closed behind her and went into the dining room, where Dottie had placed her cup of tea. Steam drifted up. Bless that woman. She had poured fresh tea for her.

###

Scott followed Angela down the brightly lit hall. He hid his snarl. As a paramedic, he should relish the feel and sounds of a hospital. It was his calling. But now, it seemed to be his curse. Angela peered over her shoulder at him and gave him a wan smile.

He reached out and caressed her shoulder, pushing a wild strand of hair back. "Are you still nervous about telling Douglas?"

She nodded.

They paused outside Rochelle's room. Scott placed a hand on the handle but turned to her before opening it. "I trust him, Ang. Always have. He's one of y'all."

"One of us? You mean Christian, right?" Her voice had a hint of exasperation to it.

"Yes. Look, I may not be a believer, but I have found that Christians are the most trustworthy souls out there. So, yeah, I trust him because he's a Christian. But also, because he is my friend and partner."

Angela nodded. "Fine. When he gets here, we will tell him. But what can he do?"

Scott pushed open the door and stepped into the room lit only by the light from outside. "I have no idea."

Tom looked up as Scott gently closed the door. "Hey, you two. Still no change, but she did move a little. Doctor said it wouldn't be long before she woke up."

"Did they say how long she would have to stay?" Angela pulled the small chair to Rochelle's bedside and settled in to start her mother-hen worry session.

"Probably two or three days depending on how she is." Tom cleared his throat and seemed to sink further into the hospital's vinyl chair.

Scott leaned against the windowsill, glancing down at the action below him. "Don't worry, Tom. Ro is pretty tough. She'll do fine, and she will be zipping through the roads on that moped of hers in no time flat."

Tom chuckled. "No moped. I'm selling that thing and getting her a little compact. Those have doors that lock."

Scott turned at Angela's chuckle. "She will probably ask for a bright red one, you know."

"Oh, that's fine." He unlocked his phone and pulled up a website. "Check this out. Found it on a used-lot website. It's not too old. The right size. And it's not too expensive."

Scott took the phone and smiled at the Ford Fiesta on the screen. "I think she'll like that. Actually, looks like something she would drive." He passed the phone to Angela.

She smiled at the image before giving it back to Tom. "Looks perfect for our girl."

The door creaked open, and Douglas entered, casting a glance over his shoulder as he did so. "Hey, guys. How's she doing?"

Tom gave Douglas an abbreviated update. Scott watched his friend as he stuck his hands in his pockets, pulled them out, and slid them into the back pockets, before repeating the gesture again. His gaze traveled from Tom to Rochelle to Angela, and he wasn't able to hide the fearful look.

"I'm sure she'll wake up soon, though." Tom stood and stretched. "Do you mind watching her? I need some more coffee."

"We don't mind, Tom." Scott pushed off the window and laid his hand on Angela's shoulder. "Why don't you go with him and grab us some."

She frowned at him. He tilted his head slightly toward Douglas, hoping she would catch his drift. Her eyes widened slightly.

"Sure. Douglas, do you need any?" She rose from the chair, and a small smile played across her lips.

"No thanks, Angela. I'm good." He stood at the end of Rochelle's bed, oblivious to what transpired, it seemed.

Angela and Tom eased through the door. Once the door clicked, Scott stood in front of Douglas, waiting.

Douglas watched him for a few seconds before narrowing his eyes. "What gives? You sent Angela out for a reason? What's on your mind?" He started to round the foot of the bed, but Scott blocked his way. "Look, dude, I already told you I'm here only as a friend to Rochelle. I'm not planning on making any moves on her."

"Oh, that's not what I want to know." Scott grabbed his arm and pulled him to the corner in front of the bathroom. "I saw your look as you came in, Douglas. You were looking out for something. What is it?"

Douglas briefly closed his eyes, his muscles tensed under his shirt. "Let it slide, man."

"I can't. Rochelle was assaulted for a reason. And we all know that reason is because she found something that related to Angela's article. And we all know that our homes had been searched. These people are wanting something. What do you know?"

With each sentence, Scott stepped closer to his partner until he was practically nose-to-nose with the man.

Douglas took a half-step back and met the wall. He shook his head. "Seriously, man. It is better that you and Angela stop. I tried to warn her."

"You know what's going on?" Scott lashed out and grabbed a handful of Douglas' shirt, twisting it in rage. His words growled between teeth. "Tell me, or by all that is holy, this hospital will have another patient."

Anger flared in Douglas' eyes. His hands squeezed Scott's as he tried to unlatch him. "Chill, dude. Look, I can't tell you everything. But—seriously! Let go of me, and I'll tell you what I can. I really don't want to have to lay you out, Scott."

Seconds ticked by. Scott tamped down his anger and slowly released Douglas. He took a step back. "I'm not kidding, Douglas. I don't want anything to happen to Angela and Max because of something you could have told us. Did you not think it would seem odd to me that you would show up here after Rochelle was hurt? Do you not think I would see it as strange that you want to be here during your time off? You're protecting Rochelle from something. What is it?"

"Garrettville."

Douglas seemed to sag slightly against the wall. He held up a hand to stop Scott's question. "It started a few years back. I was approached by a couple of fed agents. You know my dad worked in the State Bureau, right? They thought I would be a good informant about some things that were happening between the hospital and city hall."

"So, Angela was right?" He ran a hand over his face and walked over to the couch. The cushions sank with him as he sat down.

"Partly. Donald Pierce was working with them, too. Collecting evidence—or as much as possible. When his son was hurt in that accident, he spooked. He told the feds he was pulling out. His son's life was more important." Douglas grabbed the chair Angela had sat in and straddled it. "Look, it goes a lot deeper. Donald was bringing one last bit of evidence to Agent Williams. But he died before then."

Douglas sighed and steepled his fingers. "I knew that if Rochelle was attacked, then she must have come across something. Something that when pieced together with others would have been incriminating."

A pounding increased in Scott's head. It was more than that. More than dirty dealings. The medicine. Melbourne. The hospital. How much evil and greed permeated his town?

"Still with me, man?" Douglas' voice dripped with concern.

Scott ran a hand over his face and grimaced. "Yeah. You said to trust you the other day. So, I'm trusting you." He fished around in his pocket and pulled out the bottle of medicine. It rattled as he chunked it to his friend. "Here's another piece of the puzzle."

Douglas opened it, dumped a few onto his palm, and frowned. "What is this? Ecstasy?"

"You know, man, I don't even want to know how you know what Ecstasy looks like." Scott crossed an ankle over his knee. "No. It's some sort of drug. Mrs. J. was taking it. I thought it was something else when I swiped it."

"Swiped?" Douglas raised a blond brow before dumping the pills back into the bottle and recapping it. He read the label. "Melbourne, huh? Well, that's interesting."

"Has something to do with the rest of the stuff?"

"Yes."

Scott stared at his friend. "Why didn't you tell me, Douglas? Or at least let me know that something was going on."

Douglas sighed. "You were reeling from Julie's death. And even though I trust you, I didn't know how far I could trust you. It is complicated."

"Always is." Scott lowered his foot and stood. He held out his hand to Douglas. "We're friends, Douglas. I will trust you with Rochelle's life, but you have to trust me with Angela's. Deal?"

Douglas grasped his hand. "Deal. I'll give them a call and turn these in." He slipped the bottle into his right cargo pocket.

"One more thing—" They looked up as Angela and Tom entered the room. Angela looked from one man to the other, a frown creasing her face. She set two cups of coffee on the tray by the wall.

Tom paused and then took a sip from his own cup. "You know what makes me a great journalist and teacher, boys? A knack at knowing when something is happening, like right now. Two men, facing off, in my granddaughter's hospital room reeks of a story. But I'm too old, too tired to put up with any nonsense." He took another sip of coffee before placing it down beside the others. "Now. Which one of you is going to tell me the truth, or which one of you will be the first to pick himself up off the floor?"

Tom's stance went from jovial teacher to enraged grandfather. Scott didn't know what to say. This was a side of Tom he had never seen before. He glanced at Angela, but she stood there wide-eyed, watching from Tom to them, waiting.

He opened his mouth, but Douglas spoke first. "I was sent here to protect you and Rochelle, Tom. No one would question me being here because they are watching."

His words spilled out, telling Tom about the federal agents and how he had been an informant for the last two years. Tom settled into the lounge chair and listened patiently. Scott eased over to Angela's side, but halted when Tom's gaze pierced him when the story about the pills were told.

Shame ate through Scott. He didn't need Tom to know that part, but Douglas wasn't through. Angela slid the coffee into his hands as Douglas finished informing Tom about Donald Pierce.

"And we are waiting on Rochelle. To see if she can identify her attackers. But Tom, it is personal for me. I've been watching Rochelle for a long time. And I do care about her."

"No one is questioning how you feel, son." Tom sighed and pointed to the couch. Douglas sat down and tried to get comfortable. "Scott."

It was like grade school relived. Scott walked over and sat on the edge of the couch beside Douglas. Tom's stare bit into them. Angela resumed her station by Rochelle's side.

"Did you know about any of this, Angela?"

She shook her head. "Only about the pills. And the print-outs. And what I've already shown you about my research."

Tom nodded. "Look, boys, this isn't a game—"

"I know that, Tom." Tom's angry glance sliced into him, but Scott couldn't stay quiet. "I know that things are dangerous, and even more so now."

"How?" Douglas leaned forward, glancing from Scott to Tom.

Angela dug into her purse and pulled out the flash drive. At Tom's nod, she passed it to Douglas. "This was with Donald when he died."

"This was the 'one more thing'?"

Scott nodded.

Douglas rolled it around between his fingers and looked back at Scott. "You found it, didn't you? When you cleaned the van."

Scott could only nod. Again.

His friend sighed and pulled the pill bottle out of his cargo pocket. He held the two side by side. "Y'all have really gotten yourselves in one devil of a storm. Here, Scott, keep this with you. I'm being watched. They won't know you have it." He passed the flash drive back to him.

"Let me deal with this medicine issue first. The flash drive—what does it contain?"

Angela's voice was soft as she spoke. "Missing budget, missing minutes, memos, and other stuff. A few extortion emails."

Douglas nodded. "That's what Donald had said he was bringing in. He was supposed to pass it along to me. And then I would pass it up the chain."

Scott frowned. "You didn't work alone?"

"No, man. There is another, but I can't tell you. Not because I don't trust you, but because this person is so well-entrenched, I can't take the chance that something would slip out by accident, if you know what I mean."

Scott and Angela nodded.

Tom cleared his throat and looked at them. "There's something no one is thinking about."

"What's that?" Scott shifted on the couch.

"Your families. They didn't hesitate to hurt Rochelle. Can we be certain that they will leave your nana alone, Scott? Or not go after your son or Dottie, Angela? Dottie is like a grandmother to you, right?"

Fear flooded her eyes, and she fumbled for her phone. Scott couldn't let her act prematurely. By the way her lips and hands trembled, her emotions were getting in the way. Her imagination probably had her envisioning horrid accidents or attacks.

Scott jumped up and stilled her hands. He knelt before her. "Stop. They are okay right now. The Double Ds are having a grand time with Max, and they are together. And they will stay together until we get home. Don't worry them needlessly, okay?"

She pressed her lips together before speaking. Her sweet voice cracked. "But Max. I can't let anything happen to him. He's all I have."

"Shh. Where's my brave reporter, huh?" An angry glance was his answer. He smiled at her and clasped her hands in his. "Look. When we get home, we will send them somewhere. To Florence, to the habitat. I'll make reservations for a nice hotel there. One with an indoor swimming pool. The gals can take Max on an adventure. We will work with Douglas, get this all taken care of, and be safe once again. Deal?"

Angela took a deep breath and glanced at Rochelle.

"I'm helping Tom keep an eye on her, Angela. She's going to be okay." Douglas nodded at her, giving emphasis to his words.

Scott brought her hands to his lips and kissed her knuckles. "I will keep you safe, Angela. That I promise."

She broke away from his hands and touched his whispered cheek. "You may not be able to keep that promise, Scott." Her finger trailed a small line down his jaw, causing his gut to clench. "And it doesn't let you off the hook about Sunday."

Scott chuckled. "That's my girl."

Max bounded on the bed, rocking the small, overstuffed suitcase. "Am I really going to see the elephants?"

"No. Not elephants. They may take you north to see the elephants, but only if you are extremely good and don't give them a hard time. Now, where is your tiger?" Angela slid an extra pair of socks in the case.

Max brandished his stuffed and tattered tiger from behind his back. "Why can't I keep him with me? He won't be able to breathe in there." He hugged the tiger to his chest. "What am I going to see if not the elephants?"

"Lions. Two beautiful lions." Angela zipped the suitcase and collected his coat from the bed. "You don't think you will forget Tiger if you don't pack him?"

"Uh-uh. I won't forget him." Max jumped off the bed and grabbed his suitcase. "I'll carry it, Mom. This is like an adventure. Do you think Miss Dottie will get too tired? What if Nana can't do all the things like me and Miss Dottie?"

"Nana?" Angela slipped into her coat and motioned for Max to do the same with his. "You call her Nana?"

"I do now. She said the other night that Miss Debbie makes her sound like a snack. And she might be sweet, but she didn't want to be like a snack. She said I could call her Nana." Max fumbled with his zipper. She reached down to help him, but he shrugged her away.

Angela smiled. Her little man was becoming more independent every day. He smiled as the zipper caught and he was able to fasten his coat.

"Well, that's good that she gave you permission. She really is a sweet lady, huh?"

Max nodded his head so hard, his little locks danced about. "Oh, yeah. And they said they were going to spoil me. What's that mean?"

Angela laughed. Max picked up his suitcase but struggled with his stuffed tiger.

"Here, let me hold Tiger for you."

He handed her the animal and followed her out the door. She turned and pulled the door closed. "That means that they plan to give you just about anything you want, do anything you want, and make you very, very happy."

His eyes brightened. "Oh, wow."

"Oh, wow, is right." She stopped at the sidewalk and motioned for him to do the honors.

He looked both ways, then to his left once more, before nodding to her. "We can cross."

Angela reached down and grabbed his hand. As they crossed the street, Max's suitcase periodically thumping against the asphalt, she reminded him to be on his best behavior. The gate squeaked as she unlatched it and Dottie met her on the porch.

"Come on in, you two. Debbie called. They will be here in just a bit. I made some dinner. Nothing fancy, just something quick."

Angela laughed. "Dottie, you never make something quick." She slipped off her coat and hung it on the rack. Max struggled with his coat and for once allowed her to tackle the zipper. It stuck midway and almost ripped the fabric when it released. She definitely needed to get him another coat pretty soon. And this time, a new one and not a thrift store one.

He shrugged out of the coat, grabbed the tiger from her, and hightailed it to the dining room. Angela hung his coat next to hers as the front door opened. Debbie greeted her with a smile.

"Angela, dear, how are you?" She enveloped her into a hug and then leaned back to study her. "You look too tired. Get some sleep tonight. Max is in good hands with us."

Angela smiled and offered to hang Debbie's coat for her. "Oh, I am sure you will spoil him rotten. Scott have everything set up?"

"Does he ever. That dear boy made reservations at the Marriott Shoals. And he even said he made arrangements for the 360 Grille. Then he printed me a map to the lion habitat and directions to the zoo in Nashville—'just in case,' he said."

"I guess he found an excuse to splurge?"

Angela followed her into the dining room as she spoke. Dottie wasn't kidding about a quick dinner, but it was more than just sandwiches. She had made an array of salads, veggies and fruits, and finger sandwiches along her dining room table.

"Scott is like that. Won't spend much money on himself, but give him a reason, and he will go all out for someone else. Max will have the time of his life." She turned to Angela with a worried look on her face. "But please, you two be careful. While we might be having fun, you and he will still be in danger."

Angela reached out and gripped the older woman's hands. "I promise, we will be careful. We don't want anything to happen to you or Dottie, and especially Max."

Debbie caressed Angela's cheek. "I know. And will you make sure Scott takes care of himself? He worries too much. He hasn't learned that he can't save the entire world, much less Garrettville, Alabama."

A shadow passed the window as Debbie settled down next to Max and Dottie and allowed the boy to serve her. He piled a stack of small sandwiches and strawberries on her plate. Debbie laughed and encouraged him, piling the same on his.

A blast of cold air reached her as Scott opened the door. He spotted her and approached. His cold fingers brushed at her cheek and then cupped her face. Scott took a closer step, his face mere inches from hers.

His eyes seem to speak a million emotions at once before dimming. "Are you okay?"

His voice was just a whisper.

She nodded.

Dottie looked up from the table. "Scott, hang up your coat and come eat."

He shook his head, not turning away from Angela. His eyes never left her face as they searched her. "I need to load your suitcases, Miss Dottie. Nana Debbie will use my car for the trip."

Angela broke away from his stare. She couldn't go down that road with him. His eyes were promising so much and yet were holding so many other things at bay. "You can do that in a minute . . . after you eat something. They have plenty of time to make it to Florence."

She stepped back, and his touch fell away. But the distance did nothing to diminish the heat that seemed to connect them. Friends only. That was their agreement.

Scott inhaled sharply. He stood a little straighter and gave his mega-watt smile. "Tell me you have those pimento cheese sandwiches."

Dottie chuckled. "You know I do."

Angela settled into her customary seat as Scott hung his coat next to his grandmother's before he entered the dining room. He pulled out the chair next to her and sat down. His knee skimmed hers for an instant, and then he readjusted the chair. It was enough space between them to stay close, and yet still a respectable distance that "friends only" should maintain.

As he bickered with Max over which sandwich was the best—the man did have a way with children—she couldn't help but wish that his touch could have lingered a little bit more.

Angela mentally shook herself. No time for all that. There was too much danger around them for sappy feelings. But still . . .

Scott glanced at her, his smile bright, but his eyes dull. Too much worry and pain lingered in those depths.

CHAPTER NINETEEN

Scott vaulted the gate to Angela's yard. He turned and twisted the catch on the latch. It barely gave way. He looked at Angela. "How partial are you to this gate?"

Angela shook her head, hunching her shoulders inside her coat as the wind picked up in intensity. "Not very. More annoyed at it than anything. What do you plan to do with it?"

"Take it off." He pulled the Swiss Army knife from his cargo pocket and flipped out the Phillips head screwdriver. With quick movements and a few curse words in his head, he removed the hinges and then the latch. Closing the knife, he slid it back home into his cargo pants.

Angela smiled when he lifted the gate and set it to the side. Frolic, who'd followed them from Dottie's house, bounded into the small front yard; his ears flapped as he ran in circles and scooted across the stone steps.

"Thank you! I truly hated that gate."

Scott bowed, sweeping his arm to the side. "Milady."

Her small laugh was whisked away by the wind. "At least that is one thing removed from my miles-long to-do list."

Scott fell into step beside her as they walked up the porch steps. "That many items?"

"Seems like it's never-ending." She plucked the key from under her robin and opened the door. Scott followed her, giving slight room for Frolic to push his way inside.

She stood in the middle of the small foyer, her hands at her mouth. "Ang?"

Angela turned. Tears highlighted the blue of her eyes. "Sorry. It just hit me suddenly. Without Max here, it's so quiet. Knowing that they are still out there, spying on us, watching us . . . How do I know that they aren't watching us now?"

Scott reached out to her, but she shook her head and ventured into the kitchen. Frolic's nails clicked against her worn, hardwood floors as he followed. Scott sighed.

She was right. How could they know? Could he live with himself if something happened to her? They already proved that her house wasn't that secure against intruders. He walked into her kitchen and leaned back against the counter, crossing his ankles.

"Come stay with me."

Angela paused in pouring a glass of milk. "What?"

"Stay with me. I mean, stay at our house tonight. You can sleep in Nana's room. That way, you won't be alone. And you'll be safe."

She turned from him and recapped the jug of milk before sliding it back into the refrigerator. Her red curls bounced as she shook her head. "I don't want you to feel responsible for me. I can take care of myself."

She kept her back to him as she sipped her milk. Scott pushed away from the counter and stepped closer to her. Her shoulders tensed slightly as he placed his hands on them. Small trembles shook her body. Hiding her cries. She was too strong-willed to cry in front of him.

Scott stepped even closer and wrapped his arms around her, pulling her against his chest and resting his chin against her head. "It will be okay, Angela. I know you can take care of yourself. We will let Dottie and Nana know that you will stay with me. They will be less worried knowing that we are sticking together."

Her shoulders relaxed little by little as they stood in her kitchen with the refrigerator humming quietly and the lights overhead buzzing softly. He turned her around and looked into her eyes. They held a trust that he never knew he desired. But trust in whom? Him? Or the God she prayed to everyday?

His gaze settled on her lips, and he laughed. "You, uh . . . " He motioned at his mouth. " . . . you have a slight mustache, my fearless reporter."

A red blush crept up her cheeks, and she tried to wipe away the milk from her lips. Scott stopped her and wiped it away himself, rubbing his thumbs over her mouth. And then he paused with his hands cupping her face. His breath hitched. When had he fallen for her? This sassy redhead who forged head-on into any situation.

His mind warred with him as seconds ticked by. She had said, "friends only." But how could it be "friends only" when she looked back at him with the same expression she was probably seeing on his face? He closed the gap between them. Her fingers tightened around his, and her shoulders tensed. He kept his fingers from curling into her hair and fought down his impulsiveness.

He couldn't do this. She had to be the one to decide. Scott dropped a small kiss on that little freckle above her eyebrow, and then pulled her into an embrace, cradling her head against his chest. Surely, she could hear his heart thumping loudly in there.

"Get your things. We have church tomorrow, right?"

She nodded and then gently pulled away from him. Her eyes held relief, but also a deeper trust. Did he pass some sort of unspoken test? He felt as though he did. She walked away, gripping his hand until the last possible moment. As their fingers let go and Angela disappeared around the corner, Scott let his arm stay suspended in the air for a moment.

His heart hammered against him. Peaches and roses drifted slowly around him as he let his arm drop back to his side. He would give his life to keep her safe.

Nana Debbie's voice spoke in his head, "Greater love has no one than this, than to lay down one's life for his friends."

Angela was more than his friend. At least to him. He shoved his hands into his pockets as his mind replayed the rest of Nana's comment. *Jesus loves us, Scott. He considers us more than friends, and He laid His life down for all of us.*

"Scott?"

He cast Nana Debbie's voice away and took a deep breath before meeting Angela at the door. She stood at her small table, staring at Max's "parry-medic" drawing.

"They will be okay." He refrained from touching her this time.

She nodded and reached for the drawing but pulled back. With a deep breath, she straightened her shoulders and turned to him. "I have what I need and my laptop. Let's go. Are you sure Frolic isn't going to upset your pets?"

"Phftt. They would probably enjoy his company." He ushered her out the door and closed it behind him. "Keep the key with you after you lock it."

With a click, the lock turned, and Angela dropped the key into her oversized bag. "Let's go, then. You know I probably won't be able to sleep, though."

"Same here." He led her through the de-gated fence and down three houses. "But Nana has an extensive DVD collection. I'm sure we should be able to binge-watch something."

Angela smiled at him. "What about you? What kind of shows do you have?"

"Well . . . " Scott grinned back at her. "I'm more of a musical-type man. I have older musicals like *The King and I* and *Seven Brides for Seven Brothers*. Or we could watch *Phantom of the Opera*, my favorite. Plus, I'm a big John Wayne fan."

"I never would have thought it, but it makes sense. The more I get to know you, the more everything becomes clear about you."

He led her up the steps and mulled over her comments as he unlocked the door. So, she tried to understand him, which meant she wanted to get to know him.

He pushed open the door and allowed Frolic to trot inside. Judas and Dixie waited inside the dining room entrance, until Judas saw Frolic. With a hiss, she took off; Dixie howled; and Frolic followed suit as they chased the cat down the hall.

"Well, looks like Frolic made himself right at home."

Angela laughed and eased past him. She glanced around the home. "Which room is Nana's?"

"On the left. I'll call Nana and let her know that you are staying in her room tonight." He pointed down the hall. "Want a glass of tea?"

"Sure." She paused outside the bedroom and looked back at him. "And choose a good John Wayne movie. I love The Duke, too."

He couldn't stop the smile that grew across his face as he dialed Nana's number. The woman liked The Duke, too? Why did that not surprise him?

###

Scott wiggled on the hard pew. They needed cushions. Then maybe people would stay awake. He brought his finger up to hide his smile as the snore behind him snuffled. Angela elbowed him.

He pursed his lips to kill the smile. It was hard to sit here and watch the people of the congregation. Already, he had sneezed twice from cigarette smoke that clung to clothes. He still couldn't quite pinpoint who had the irritant stuck to them, but they had to be somewhere nearby. Every time they stood for a hymn his violent sneeze would attack the air. There was no way his handkerchief could handle another contribution.

Thankfully, the preacher was winding down. And he had survived. Although he had to admit that the man had made some interesting points for him to consider, and he had been doing a lot of considering of late.

"We all heard that God is love. But let us not forget that God is also wrath. How can that be? He becomes angry over the persecution of His children. He becomes angry over the slaughter of the innocents. When we approach God with love, we receive love in return. And to approach in love is to live for Him and to follow Him in spirit and action.

"Read in Matthew five. Read the Beatitudes, but I'll leave you with this: 'Blessed *are* those who are persecuted for righteousness' sake, For theirs is the kingdom of heaven."

The preacher closed his Bible and rounded the podium. "Before next Sunday, I ask this: read Psalm fifty-nine. See what God's Word has to say to you." He motioned toward the pianist, a lady in a bright blue, long dress. "Miss Bobbi? Give us a really good one this time."

Angela leaned toward him. "One more song, and you're free." She stood, and Scott followed suit.

Her elbow brushed against his side and sent a shiver through him. Two layers and he could still feel her touch. He angled his body and helped steady the hymnal as those around him sang the invitational.

Miss Bobbi's fingers slid across the keys, and the melodic sounds swarmed the sanctuary. Scott's breath hitched as Angela's soft voice lifted in praise.

"Just as I am, without one plea, But that Thy blood was shed for me, And that Thou bidd'st me come to Thee . . . "

Scott gripped the book until his knuckles whitened. Come to Him? Why did that phrase pull at him?

" . . . tho' tossed about, With many a conflict, many a doubt, Fightings within and fears without, O Lamb of God, I come! I come!"

He let go of the book and gripped the back of the pew in front of him. At the front of the church, the pastor sang with the congregation, patiently waiting. For a brief moment, their eyes met. A smile creased the pastor's face, and a light shone from his eyes. The urge to follow the aisle to the altar called to Scott, tugging his heart.

Scott dropped his gaze and shook his head. No. No. No.

Angela's voice faltered and then stopped. She nudged him aside and slid past him. She walked up to the pastor, who bowed his head, listening to what she was saying. He nodded, placed his hands on her shoulders, and with heads touching, seemed to be praying. Miss Bobbi looked up and then continued, her fingers nimbly plucking the soft tune from the keys.

Scott glanced down at the hymnal Angela left lying on the pew. He picked it up and found the congregation's place. A six-stanza song. And they were on the fourth. "Yea, all I need in Thee to find"? Scott frowned at the line. Could it really be that simple?

A slight bump against his side caused him to look up. Angela had returned. She slid back into her place and smiled at him. There was a peacefulness resting not only in her eyes, but also on her face.

The song wound down. Scott gave the book back to Angela and returned his gaze to the front. But his mind slipped back to his past. That song was sung the day Julie walked the aisle. The next Sunday, she was baptized. A strange sort of guilt permeated his soul. He followed her lead the next week because he didn't want to be left out; he didn't want Julie to leave him behind. Was there actually more to it?

Stanzas of songs filtered through his head. Passages from sermons and Nana Debbie's voice. He swallowed against them. His life was simpler without all that.

Wasn't it?

He frowned at the unwanted intrusion in his thoughts. "Fightings within and fears without." The line, that had been sung in Angela's voice, bounced through his mind and haunted him.

"Scott?" Her voice broke through his jumbled thoughts.

He shook his head, breaking the spell, and smiled down at her. "Ready to go?"

"Yup." She frowned and leaned closer. "I've noticed that guy in the tweed these last few Sundays has been watching me. I keep thinking it's my imagination, but do you know him?"

Scott slowly twisted around, picking up his jacket from the back of the pew, and glanced up. The man in the tweed . . . Dan.

Scott shrugged into his jacket and let Angela lead the way out through the side door.

He leaned down and whispered. "That's Dan. Police officer who is the bane of my existence. I have about four parking tickets because of him."

Angela nodded and pushed open the door. The wet, cold air hit them full force. "He's been here, reeking of tobacco and mothballs, for the last several weeks. Debbie said she didn't know him and that he wasn't a member of the church." She glanced at the sky.

"Don't worry about it. Maybe he's trying to change. Dan has always been an —" He clamped his mouth shut. Not here. Couldn't say that at church. "An irritating fool."

"That's not what you were about to say." Her eyes twinkled at him.

"No. But I'm at church. I don't think your God would approve of what I was about to say."

"Our God would not approve of it, no matter where you were." Her little freckle rose with her brow, and Scott smiled at her glare.

"You are so cute when you glare."

The punch in the arm was worth the snort she gave him. "Come on. Let's go grab some lunch before we head to the hospital. Hopefully, Rochelle will be awake."

He opened the door to her Grand Am and paused when she held out the keys.

"Mind driving? I really don't want to." Her voice held a plea. And he couldn't resist.

Scott took the keys from her hand, rounded the car, and opened the passenger side door. "In you go. I think—"

Sirens blared as a fire engine roared around the corner and down the street. Another tanker truck followed, along with two police cruisers. Scott frowned as the convoy turned left. The sirens faded as they raced down the road.

Angela had paused to watch with him. She glanced at him as she slid into the seat. "I hope that isn't anyone we know. They are heading in our direction."

Scott closed her door and hurried to the driver's side. Call it premonition. Call it a feeling. Call it whatever, but he felt that it wasn't just someone they knew. It was something more than that.

He cranked the car, listening to Angela as she rehashed what her adult Bible class had talked about that morning. Cars slowly pulled out of the parking lot, and Scott followed them. His heart hammered in his chest. Couldn't these cars hurry up?

It had to be all those years of working EMS. Hear a siren, and he had the itch to go.

Finally! He pulled onto the road and drove to the intersection. The turn lane was full, and the light was short.

"Anyway, I told Tina that the references she had were pretty impressive. Told her to come by the—whoa! That plume of smoke is huge!" She sat forward in her seat and gazed up at the dark smoke that rose above the houses and buildings.

Scott peered past the sun visor. "Wonder what's going on."

The light turned green, and his line of cars surged forward, but right before he made the turn, the light turned yellow. Scott glanced behind him and took the turn anyway. Hopefully, Dan was off duty.

Angela's hand gripped his arm as they turned at the second right and onto the last stretch before their street. The dark smoke loomed larger and darker. The sirens grew louder.

Scott sped down the street and stopped at the intersection. To his right, further down the street, the convoy of rescue vehicles surrounded Angela's house. She scrambled for her seat belt, but Scott grabbed her hands.

"Stop. I'll get us as close as I can. Looks like we can park at my house." He turned down the street, one hand still gripping Angela's to refrain her frantic flight, and then pulled into his driveway. Her seat belt was unhooked and the door opening before he could slam the Grand Am into park.

"Angela!" Scott cursed as she bolted past the front of the car and ran down the sidewalk toward her house. He fought with the keys, the seat belt, and unfolding himself from the low car before he could chase her down.

His legs ate up the concrete. She had reached the edge of her yard before a firefighter stopped her. Scott almost collided into her.

"Tim, when was the call made?" He wrapped his arms around Angela as she looked with horror at the burning house. Her weight pressed against him, and her body shook.

The firefighter pushed his helmet off his head. Sweat dripped from him and pooled around the collar of his turnout coat. "Probably about five minutes ago. By the time we arrived, the house was fully involved. I'm sorry." He looked at Angela for a moment and then returned his gaze to Scott. "I can't let you any closer."

Chief Jerald Downey approached. "Scott, you know whose house this is?"

"It's mine." Angela stared at the flames that devoured her home. She pushed away from him and took a half-step forward. "What can you tell me? What happened?"

The Chief shook his head. "We won't know until the flames are put out and the fire marshal has a look."

"Fire marshal?" Her hands gripped Scott's arms, and she fell back into him. "Arson?"

"We won't know. It's standard procedure." Jerald looked at Scott. "We are doing everything we can to save the home, but I fear it won't be enough. At this stage, it's more keeping it from spreading to other homes." His gaze dropped back to Angela. "I'm truly sorry."

Angela said nothing.

Scott reached out and shook Jerald's hand. "I'm taking her to my house. Let me know when the marshal arrives, okay?" A couple of officers headed their way. "And if you find anything else."

"Oh, there is one thing. Tim found it lying on the porch after we rolled up. I'll have him bring it to you." He walked away and was replaced by the officers. Thankfully, not Dan.

"Scott. Miss Mabry." Officer Donaldson reached out and shook their hands. "There isn't much to say. We received the call about twelve-oh-five. Neighbor said black smoke was billowing from the kitchen. Where were y'all at the time?"

"Church. Fellowship Community down the road." Scott glared at the other officer's snort. "No joke, Bill. I was at church."

Angela smiled. "It was part of an agreement he made with me."

Officer Heightmeyer shook his head. "That would be the only way Scott would attend. I'm really sorry about your home. Do you have some place to go?"

"She can stay with me and Nana Debbie. That's where we will be."

Officer Donaldson nodded. "If we have any further information, we will let you know." They walked away and to their cars to wait for the fire crews to finish.

"Come on, Angela. No sense in standing here." He gently led her back down the sidewalk. Her shoulders trembled, but she managed to stay strong and hold back her tears, although they glistened in her eyes. They had reached his driveway when he heard his name called.

Tim approached with a broken and charred frame in his gloved hand. "I found this on the steps. I'm guessing it was blown out by the fire. I'm so truly sorry. Nothing else seems to have survived."

Scott accepted the blue frame, and an invisible hand clutched his heart. Max's "parry-medic" drawing. He nodded at Tim, who gave Angela one last sorrowful look and hurried away.

Angela reached out and took the drawing from him, her finger tracing Max's version of him in uniform.

She looked up at him. "My grandmother's quilts. They're all gone. My photos. Max's baby book. Everything."

Scott led her to the porch and sat down on the steps with her. Her faraway gaze watched the water drown the fire and smoke. It would be a few hours yet before they could see if anything could be salvaged.

"Maybe something survived. We will have to wait to see."

"And pray."

Pray. Scott sighed and pulled her close. She could do the praying. He wasn't ready to do all that yet. But maybe her God would look favorably upon her.

He hid his scowl behind Angela's wild curls. This fire couldn't have been an accident. Her house was old, but not decrepit. It had all the updates. It had been restored. Old, but modern updates. Old, but new electrical wiring and plumbing. Jake had made those updates. Correction: Jake had paid for those updates.

"Angela . . ."

"I know. I've already put two and two together."

Once a reporter, always a reporter. Of course, his Angela would be churning those thoughts through her head.

"I'm calling Douglas, okay?"

"Please. If they are willing to destroy my home, what else are they willing to do?" She leaned away from him and climbed to her feet. "I need to use the bathroom. Where's the key?"

Scott stood and dug the key from his pocket. As she unlocked the door and disappeared in, he fished his phone from his jacket pocket and dialed Douglas. Hopefully, the man wasn't on a call at the moment.

"Dude! What's up? Thought you would be heading to the hospital right now."

"I'm going to talk quickly, Douglas. Angela's house was burned down. We think whoever is after the flash drive and medicine did it. Nothing to prove, but it makes sense. We already knew they had entered our homes. I need you to stay with Rochelle. Keep her and Tom safe." Scott leaned against the porch railing and kept an eye on the activity down the road.

"Man." Douglas' harsh sigh reverberated through the phone. "I'm still at work. But I'll head over as soon as I'm off. Hold on."

A lot of rustling sounds echoed through. A bang. A pressurized hiss. Then another bang. Douglas' voice came back online. "Look, my parents own a cabin outside of Waterloo, close to Pick Wick. Go there. I'll text the address and where the key is. If they went after Angela's home, then they may do the same with yours. I can let Gr—I can let them know. They can't spare someone to watch your home, but Officer Donaldson can."

"Can we trust him? What if they are part of it all?"

"Not Chase. He's another one involved with the investigation."

A curse burst forth from Scott's mouth. "How many of you are a part of this?"

"Language, dude." Douglas sighed. "Not many, but enough. Look, head to my parents' cabin. Stay there until I call. You'll be safe there."

Scott took a deep breath. "Fine. But you stay with Rochelle."

"I will, man, I will. Gotta go."

"Thanks, Douglas. Pray for us?"

Silence reigned for a couple of seconds. Did Douglas think he was mocking him?

There was a strange catch to Douglas' voice when he replied. "Will do. Stay safe."

The call ended.

Scott slid the phone into his pocket. He watched the firefighters. Some were disconnecting hoses. Some were poking around the house. Some were still dousing hot spots in the home. He glanced at the sky. The darkening clouds hinted at rain. Maybe that would help put out any missed hot spots. He shook his head. Weatherman had said clear skies.

He took a deep breath of the cold air. Time to tell Angela the plan. But they couldn't leave until later. Dusk would be better. It would take only about thirty or so minutes to get there. The Beach Boys' "Kokomo" sounded from his pocket. Douglas' text message.

He opened his door. Time to plan. And time to call Nana Debbie.

###

It was quiet. At first. Small sounds trickled into Rochelle's mind. A scrape of what sounded like a chair. That was to her right. The low volume of the television somewhere across from her. Her grandfather's cough and then a quick clearing of his throat.

And the smells. Astringent. Starchy.

She blinked her eyes opened. Pops, backlit from the window, sat sipping from a Styrofoam cup. Her gaze roamed over the bland walls, the lines leading away from her, and the crisp linen covering her.

"Pops?" Was that her voice? It croaked more than spoke.

Her grandfather whipped his head around and smiled gently at her. With quick movements, he rose and leaned over her. "Ro? Thank goodness you woke up." His hand stroked across her head. "The doctor assured me you would wake up soon."

"Doctor?" She squinted her eyes against the overhead wall light. "I'm in a hospital?"

He nodded. "Can you remember what happened?"

She frowned. Could she remember? She left the office. The road was dark. A truck. Her mind tried to find the memory. It was there. It had to be there. The truck stopped her. But what else? Tears trickled down her face.

"I can't remember, Pops. I left the office. Was driving to Angela's. Took Turnbill Street. I wanted to reach Angela's house as soon as I could."

Her throat closed. Rochelle coughed against the tightness. Pops reached over and held a plastic cup with a straw to her lips. Cool water slid down her throat and relieved some of the grittiness.

"I know I found something, Pops. There was this truck. It stopped behind me? No. It was coming in toward me? I can't remember." She shook her head and gasped at the pounding that ricocheted in it. The pain wouldn't subside. Rochelle reached up, but pain ripped through her shoulder.

"Rochelle?" Pops hovered over her. "You need to lay back and rest. You're pretty beat up, girl."

"My shoulder. They did something to my arm. I remember that. They twisted it? I think." She allowed her grandfather to ease the pillow behind her, and a bit of the pain receded.

"I'll notify the nurse. They knew they would reassess your injuries once you awoke." He pressed the call button. A nurse spoke a couple of seconds later. "She's awake. And she's complaining of her shoulder. Said they had twisted it."

The disembodied voice replied. "I'll let the doctor know, and I'll be right there."

Pops pulled his chair closer to the bed and continued holding her hand. "You took ten years off my life. I have no idea what I would do without you."

"Me neither, Pops. I'm just glad they didn't kill me." She paused, and then sniffed as tears coursed down her face. "I want to remember. I have to remember why they did this to me. Do you think I found something?"

Angela. Scott. She gasped and gripped her grandfather's hand. "Angela and Scott? Max? Nothing happened to them, did it?"

"Shh, shh, shh." He patted her hand and then brought it to his cheek. The rough whiskers scraped against her skin. "They are fine. They've been here practically every day helping me keep an eye on you."

She sighed in relief. A knock sounded at the door, and a nurse peeked in.

"Hello, Rochelle. I'm Karen." Her crisp attitude was softened by her smile. She logged into the computer on a rolling stand near Rochelle's bed. "Let me take your vitals, and then you can tell me what hurts, okay?"

Rochelle nodded. The nurse stuck a thermometer in Rochelle's mouth and checked her pulse. The thermometer beeped.

"Good, good," the nurse mumbled. With quick movements, the blood pressure cuff was readjusted on her arm and activated. The painful squeeze lasted only a few seconds before deflating. Karen noted the results into the chart. She turned to Rochelle. "Where does it hurt the worst?"

Rochelle used her left hand and pointed to her right shoulder. "Right back there. I can't move it without it hurting. And here." She placed her hand on the top of her head. "The lights bother me a little bit, too."

Karen dimmed the wall light. "From a scale of one to ten—ten being the worst you've ever felt—how do you rate your shoulder pain?"

"About an eight when I move it."

"Okay." Karen typed it into the chart, and then moved to the foot of the bed. She raised the sheets. "I want you to move your feet."

Rochelle exhaled through clenched teeth as pain shot through her legs. Karen pressed around the ankles. Rochelle cast the thoughts of kicking her out of her mind. If she did that, the pain would only increase. After the grueling torture, Karen recovered her feet and smiled.

"The doctor will be in soon." She rounded the bed and readjusted the pillow. "I'll be back in just a few moments."

Then she left. Rochelle tried to grin at her Pops. "I really hate hospitals."

He chuckled. "I do, too."

She started to reply, but the doctor walked in as a dark haze of fatigue claimed her. Despite the veil threatening to close down around her, the doctor poked and prodded and then pummeled her with questions.

No, that didn't hurt. Yes, that hurt. She vaguely remembered a "yes, I can move that" and a "going to sock you one if you do that again." Then nothing.

Something beeped. Then a voice spoke.

Rochelle opened her eyes, ready to mouth off at the doctor again. But it wasn't the doctor who spoke. She turned her gaze to the window. Pops sat with someone on the couch.

"Pops?" The light outside was darker than before.

Her grandfather stood and approached her bed. "Hey, my girl. Awake again, I see."

"What happened? Did I pass out?"

He chuckled a bit. "You were still groggy. Fell asleep after practically calling the doctor a horse's rear end."

Heat flooded her face from chin to hairline. "Seriously?"

"Don't worry about it. The doctor laughed. Said it was the pain talking." He sat in the chair by her bed. "They ran some x-rays on you. Nothing broken. You have a severe sprain in your ankles and a torn muscle in your shoulder."

"That's good, right? Better that than broken bones."

"Depends." The man on the couch spoke. "You will probably feel the aches from the shoulder on cold days for the rest of your life."

Rochelle tried to lean forward and squint at who it was. He stood and approached. She frowned at him. Douglas. What was he doing here? Better yet, why?

"Before you start hammering questions at him, let me explain." Pops patted her leg. "He's here to protect us. Keep us safe."

She shook her head. "I don't understand. What's happening?"

She thought back. The truck. There was a voice. They wanted the flash drive. And papers? No. They had the papers, but she could print that out again. But why did they think she had a flash drive? What was so important about one flash drive?

Douglas bit his lip and shoved his hands in his pockets. "Long story or short?"

"Uh, I guess short." She closed her eyes. "Can you turn the lights down a bit, Pops?"

Her grandfather reached up and switched the overhead off. He stood and walked to the sink and turned on its light. "Is that better?"

She nodded and turned her gaze back to Douglas. "Tell me the shortened version. You can fill in details later. I am sleepy again."

Douglas looked askance at Pops, who nodded. He sat down in the chair and looked Rochelle straight in the eyes. "The people who were after you wanted something that Scott had found. A flash drive that belonged to Donald Pierce. You and Angela found articles that if tied with the flash drive would destroy what they were doing. There's more to it, but it doesn't concern you at the moment. Right now, we have to keep you safe. They already burned down Angela's house. I sent Scott and Angela to my parents' cabin for safety."

"Wait!" She focused her gaze on Douglas' blue eyes. "Burned her house? Safety? What do you have to do with all this?"

"I'm an informant for the DEA." He held up a hand to stop her from talking. "Let me give you the long version. I knew I should have started with that."

She tried to hang onto his words as he spoke about memos, flash drives, hospital drug trials, and how Scott and Angela stumbled upon the scheme. Rochelle raised her eyebrows about Scott's stolen medicine. She always thought Scott was perfect. Guess perfect people can fall off pedestals, too. Tears pricked her eyes when he related about what happened to Angela's house. At least, they would be safe at the cabin. And Max was safe out of town with Debbie and Dottie.

Pops held a glass of water and helped her sip from the straw. "At least they are safe, Ro. And soon, this will all be over with."

Douglas smiled. "It all seems to be centered only around Melbourne—"

"Stop! Melbourne. Brent said he worked for Melbourne—" Rochelle clenched her eyes shut, bolted upright, and grabbed at her head. "Pops!"

"What is it?" Her grandfather immediately gripped her hands and brought them down. Douglas held the pillow as she was forced to lie back.

"I remember! Brent. It was his voice. He was saying something about papers and flash drive . . . a name!" She fumbled for Douglas' hand and pulled him near. "He said a name before he dragged me into the ditch. Dan. Who's Dan?"

Her grandfather and Douglas' faces paled. She never understood the meaning of the saying "whiter than a ghost" until now.

Douglas looked at her grandfather. "Dan was at Donald Pierce's accident."

Pops nodded. "It was Dan the mayor mentioned when he wanted me to drop the story. Dan Pritcher was one of the officers who arrived to see if you were awake and to question you."

Douglas pulled out his phone. "Hold on. Let me ask Scott something."

His thumbs flew across the surface of his phone. Within seconds, it dinged with a reply. "Well, after a few choice words, the edited version is Scott said Dan was at the church, and he was sure he followed them to the house but hasn't seen him since then."

"It could be some other Dan."

"Is there any other Dan who hangs out with Melbourne?" Douglas shook his head. "No. It has to be Officer Dan."

"Officer? You mean the guy who hurt me was a cop?" Rochelle sank further into her pillow and pulled at the covers. "Is the police department involved?"

Douglas shook his head. "No. Just a couple of them. I know a couple of them who are above-board and trustworthy."

Her grandfather stood, reached across her, and collected his phone from the side table. "Give me their numbers. Since Rochelle can remember now, I want them to take the statement."

Rochelle glanced up at the ceiling as Pops made the call. A tear traced down her face, but she was too tired to worry about that. One stupid article. And look where it got them. Why did she and Pops even stay in such a rinky-dink town? Please, Lord, keep Angela and Scott safe.

A soft touch from a rough and callused finger wiped the tears that coursed down her face. She turned to Douglas. So much compassion flooded his gaze.

"It'll turn out okay, Rochelle. I promise."

For some reason, unlike Brent, Douglas brought a feeling of peace to her. "Do you pray?" Why would she ask that? Regardless, she did, and now she couldn't take it back.

He nodded. "I do. Every day." He held his hand out to her. "Want to pray now?"

She slid her hand into his. He clasped it with both of his and bowed his head over their joined hands. It was a simple prayer, but heartfelt. Asking for guidance, strength, and protection. And that's all she could ask for, anyway. Everything else was out of her hands.

She could only trust the Lord with Angela and Scott's life. "Douglas?"

"Hmm?"

"Is Scott a believer?"

A look of sadness traveled briefly over his face. "No."

"Let's pray for his salvation. Just in case."

Douglas looked at her. His expression held a hope and a smile. "Pray with me."

And she did. As Pops' voice talked with the police, hers and Douglas' whispers lifted Scott in prayer.

CHAPTER TWENTY

Scott pushed the door open and peered in. The gloomy, cold interior of the cabin stared back. He stepped past the threshold and pulled Angela along. He squinted into the darkness. To the left was the kitchen, a dark hulk in the shadows. To his right was the den and its fireplace, a cramped space with only one couch piled with cushions.

"Shut the door." He flicked the light switch. Nothing. "I'll see if there's any candles or a flashlight. Stay there."

Angela nodded and tucked her hands under her arm, bouncing slightly on her toes. "Oh, it's freezing in here."

"I know." He shuffled through the small foyer and into the kitchen. Pain shot through his knee as it met the low table. He bit off his curse. "Douglas said his parents don't visit that often, but there has to be something left behind."

He gritted his teeth against the cold of the cabinet handle as he pulled it open. Buttery crackers. Canned potted meat. He pulled a box down and read it. "We've got some dry cereal, generic frosted flakes. Let me see if there's anything to drink."

He held up his hand when Angela ventured further into the cabin. "Stay there." The box fell to its side when he replaced it in the cabinet. He righted it, and then closed the cabinet and turned to the counter.

The silverware rattled as he pulled open a drawer. No candles. No flashlight. He opened the next one. A cheap, yellow flashlight rolled forward. Scott lifted it and pressed the button. A weak beam sliced through the frosty air.

"Let me have that, and I can check out the back rooms. See if there's anything back there for us." Angela's shoes scuffed against the wooden floor. She held out her hand.

"There's only two bedrooms and a bath." He turned on the faucet. Water swirled down the drain. "At least we have water."

"Hot?" She came up beside him and wrapped her arms tighter around her waist.

Scott twisted the hot water, one full turn. His fingers grew numb as he held them under the running water. "No. Water heater must be electric. Bet the heat is electric, too."

"Well, we can use the fireplace. Surely, there's firewood outside?"

Scott turned off the water and nodded. "I'll check." He turned and spied the back door across the kitchen by the oven.

Angela hurried down the hallway, her beam bouncing up and down the walls.

A blast of frigid air hit him in the face when he opened the back door. So much for the weatherman being accurate. He huffed and hunched his shoulders and let the door close behind him. A small pile of wood lay stacked in the typical pyramid near the grill. Scott crossed the small, wooden patio, dodging the rotten portions of the deck.

Pieces of bark fell as he lifted the logs. He balanced five in his arms and trundled back to the door. It opened. Angela stood there, arms outstretched.

"Give me those and grab more. Let's get as much as we need inside."

"Good idea. Here." He helped her dump the logs inside the kitchen. "I'll grab five more. That should be enough. Is there something to start the—"

"Ahead of you there, big boy." She held up a red grill lighter. "Found it under the sink. Checked the stove. Electric."

Scott pursed his lips and squinted. That would be a problem. He motioned to the logs. "Take those to the fireplace." A cold drop hit his face. He looked up at the gray, dusky sky and frowned. "Storm's almost here."

"Then hurry." She pushed him away from the door, and then twirled and scooped up a couple of the logs before disappearing inside.

Scott hurried across the deck and grabbed another armful. Misting rain coated him. He loaded the last log and arched his back as the logs teetered in his arms.

"Scott!"

He turned, narrowly missing the rotten hole in the deck, and staggered back to the cabin. The misty rain let loose and slammed down. Angela's hands pulled the top two logs off the pile and ushered him inside. His coat and pants dripped water onto the floor.

He waved her off and pointed to the lower cabinets. "Look in the cabinets and see if there is a pot or something that we can set on the fire." She knelt at the bottom cabinets near the stove and half-buried herself inside the opening.

He pulled at his coat as he passed her, and then spread the heavy, wet garment across the table. His fleece hoodie underneath didn't survive the onslaught either. Stupid man. He should have buttoned his coat.

"I found a cast iron skillet." Angela rushed past him and into the den. "It'll work."

Scott hung his hoodie over a chair and followed Angela. Damp spots covered his thin, long-sleeve shirt. His skin underneath prickled with goosebumps. His pants clung to him, and his body shook as he sank beside the fireplace with Angela. "Where's the kindling?"

"I already have it in there." She passed him the lighter. "Get it going while I get us an area fixed. Oh, wait. I found something in a bedroom that will help you." She disappeared down the hall with the flashlight.

His hands shook as he held out the lighter and flicked it. Come on, come on. He needed to get warm. He would be no good to Angela if he died from hypothermia. The fire caught and slowly ate its way to the seasoned wood. Angela bounded back into the den.

"Take those pants off. I found a pair of jammies in the back room." She held out flannel lounge pants to him. "Should fit your skinny frame."

He tried to nod as he pulled the pajamas from her hands. His teeth chattered and threatened to rattle his brain apart. "Bring a pitcher of water. We can m-make some t-t-tea in here."

"You're not going to make anything if you keep standing there in wet pants." She smiled and turned her back. "I found all the blankets and quilts I could find. That should help us stay warm through the night."

"It s-shouldn't take long f-for the f-fire to start putting out heat." Scott kicked off his boots. He peeled off his pants, biting back a curse as the garment hung up on his feet. The soaked denim hit the floor with a thump, and he quickly slid on the pajamas. "Okay."

She turned back around, grabbed the pants off the floor, pulled a chair to the fire, and hung them over the back. "It'll take a while, but it'll dry faster near the fire."

Scott pulled at the strings on the pants. He slumped. Why did he have to be so skinny? "Is there a pin or something somewhere?"

Angela stepped closer and laughed. "Here, let me help." She grabbed the strings and yanked. Scott stumbled a little toward her before righting himself. "Put your finger here in the middle and hold it tight."

He grimaced as the knot she tied squeezed his finger. It caught slightly as he pulled it free. She let go. The pants drooped to his hips and stopped. He pulled his shirt down as far as it would go. "Feels like they are about to fall off."

"They look like they will." She hurried from the living room, calling over her shoulder. "Be right back."

He forced his shoulders to relax. Now that they were finally safe somewhere, he could think. No more just reacting. He could plan now; but first, he needed to fix up their little area for the night.

He pulled the couch a little closer and draped a blanket over it. Angela had found three quilts and had flung them across the floor. He straightened one on the floor and dropped the other two at the foot of the couch. They could cover up with those.

Thick socks or not, his feet were freezing. He reached and pulled his boots back on. Her soft-soled shoes scuffed against the floor as she padded back to him. He looked up and smiled at the laundry basket full of food and drinks.

"I found some can cokes in the pantry. Only three. Grabbed the crackers, potted meat, and cereal. Plus, looky here." She held up three

Little Debbie cakes. He stood and grabbed the basket from her. "Don't know if they're stale or not, but at this rate, who cares?"

"Not me, that's for sure." He set the basket down and knelt in front of the fire. The fireplace had no room to set the skillet nor a rack, so he poked at the logs until he cleared a small area near the corner. The iron pan thudded against the brick inset as he set it down. "Some ash may get in the water, but it can heat up a little for some hot drinks. You found tea, didn't you?"

"Yeah. Small box of English Breakfast." She pulled it out and set it down next to some mugs. "You need to cover up."

He shook his head. "I will soon. Let me get things set up first."

Her cold hand settled over his. "Scott, you're freezing." He turned to her. Her worried gaze stared at him. She scooted closer and reached past him for the quilt. "Get warmed up first."

It settled over his shoulders, and she pulled it tight around him. Her rose-and-peach scent drifted up to him. He breathed in deep. This was not how he pictured a fireside dinner. "Thank you."

She smiled. "You're welcome. Care for some dinner now?"

"Not yet." He captured her hand in his and pulled her closer. Confusion drifted across her face as he lowered his head until their foreheads touched. "I don't know how we are going to get out of this, but I'll think of something. I'll keep you safe, Angela."

The stubble on his face rasped against her hand as she caressed his cheek. "I know you will, Scott. I trust you."

He sighed. It had been a long time since someone trusted him. He brushed his lips across her hair. As soft as rain. Her arms circled around his chest as he cupped the back of her head, tangling his fingers in her hair, clutching her close to him. A drumming echoed in his head, and heat flooded through his body. He released her.

Words beat around in his head. Words that needed saying, but how?

She pulled away and patted his chest. Her slender fingers cupped his face. "Shh. It's okay."

She always knew before he did. His Angela. "Yeah." He set his chin on the top of her head. Strands poked and tickled his nose. "Guess we should eat, huh?" His stomach rumbled as they knelt there in front of the fire, the quilt around them, and holding on to each other.

"Especially you, Mr. Skinny Man." She tightened her arms around him. "But let's stay like this for just a while longer."

Scott sank back against the couch and pulled her with him. As she snuggled closer, he snagged the extra quilt and draped it over them. They could do with some rest. She dropped her head down to his chest. Her arms tightened around him some more.

"It's going to be all right." He reached under the quilt and rubbed her back. "Somehow, we'll make it through." Somehow. Somehow, he would keep his woman safe. He smiled. When and how he had managed it, he didn't know; but somewhere along the line, he started loving her. His bossy, nosy reporter.

The fire crackled and popped in the small space. Warmth slowly reached out to them. He sighed and leaned his head back against the couch cushions. Just a little while. He would rest his eyes for just a little while.

Angela ran her hand over the cool feel of the quilt beside her. Stitches and flannel fabric greeted her inquiring fingers. She opened her eyes and peered at the bundle of covers that lay as cast-offs. Soft sunlight caressed the fabric and highlighted the intricate patterns of the stitching. She ran a fingernail over the feathered pattern. Nice work. Looked a lot like her grandmother's quilts.

A slight pang of regret hit her. Barely twenty-four hours had passed since the fire. After all this was over, insurance and paperwork were going to be a killer. But no amount of insurance payments would ever replace those beautiful and beloved quilts.

A yawn escaped her. Angela rolled over, groaned at the hard surface beneath her. She knew she should have opted for the short couch; but it was much warmer on the floor near the fire, so she had demanded that Scott take the lumpy couch. She looked around for the man.

His voice carried from the opened door of the cabin and into the living room. "Are you serious, Douglas?" If a voice could boom louder than the thunder from last night, his was in the front of the race. "When did he find out?"

Angela threw off the quilt and grimaced at her full bladder. That could wait for a moment longer. Whatever Scott was thundering about was more important.

She stumbled over the wadded covers, caught herself on the side table by the couch, and hurried to the front door. Her socked feet slid slightly on the polished hardwood.

The screen door caught on a small rock. Angela flicked it away with her toe and frowned. It was warm out. Southern weather struck again. Today would be a burner for November. "Scott?"

He held up a hand, nodding at whatever Douglas was saying on the other side. "Gotcha. We'll take the Natchez, then cut across Two, then down the Thirteen to Seventeen down to Hamilton. We can meet you there. How's Rochelle?"

A few more head nods before he ended the call. His face darkened even more with worry when he turned to her. "Douglas said Jonathan was standing right outside the door when Douglas told us about the cabin. He didn't know until this morning when the DEA showed up at the hospital looking for Jonathan and Melbourne that Jonathan was in on everything that has been happening." Scott sighed and pushed past her into the living room.

He still wore the pajamas, and his hand held one side to keep them from falling past his hips. "I need to dress, and we need to get out of here. He doesn't know how, when, or whether they are showing up or not, but we can't take the chance."

Angela grabbed his pants from the chair. "Scott." He piled the quilts on the couch one at a time. "Scott." A little louder this time. But the man continued to push aside pillows, searching. "Scott!"

He whipped his head around. "Where are my boots?"

She nodded at the far side of the fireplace. "There. And here, you need your pants." She held them out to him. "How would they know about this cabin here in Waterloo?" He approached her, but she held onto the pants. "Tell me what is going on. You can't talk to Douglas, and then start issuing orders without me knowing what is happening."

Scott reached up and brushed away a curl that clung to her cheek. "Douglas said that Grace is in Hamilton with the FBI. She was the informant that Douglas reported to. And to think I worked with those two and never even suspected a thing about them." He pulled the pants from her hand and started untying his pajamas. "Douglas had invited us up here one summer for a cookout. I couldn't come. Jonathan wasn't EMS then, but he came with a nurse we knew."

He twirled his finger. "Mind turning? I'm not that modest, but you are."

Heat flamed her face. She turned away from him, grabbed her bag from the floor, and started stuffing the remaining crackers, cakes, and the last can of soda into it. "What's the news on Rochelle?"

"She's being released. Tom and Douglas are sticking by her side." The sound of a zipper closing followed his words. "You can turn."

Angela faced him. "Do they know that we have the flash drive then? Or that Douglas has the medicine?"

It was too surreal. How did her life end up being a live enactment of a Terri Blackstock suspense novel? This was not what she was asking for in her prayers last night when she asked the Lord to show them the way. Maybe she needed to rethink her words spoken during prayer.

"Douglas had already turned the medicine in. Reason why DEA arrived. He said there was a lot going on. The hospital is being shut down, and patients are being transported. It's a mess. He doesn't know much right now. And yeah, they know we have it." Scott's hands settled on her shoulders.

His spicy cologne had worn off throughout the night. In its wake was the strong, heated scent of his own skin. Dark and almost woodsy in a way. Angela caressed her cheek against his knuckles.

Scott's hands moved from her shoulders to her face. Strong fingers, callused and tough, cupped her cheeks. He leaned down and kissed her brow. Why did he always kiss the left one?

"Everything will turn out okay. It will. Trust me." He ran a hand through her curls, snagged a tangle, and worked it out with gentle fingers. "We will head to Hamilton, turn the flash drive in to the FBI, and then be safe to go to Florence. Collect Max, Debbie, and Dottie, and go home. Yeah?"

Home? What home? Despite the feeling of loss over her house and possessions, Angela nodded. It sounded perfect. But what in life went according to plan? Even with Scott's dedication to order, life hadn't listened to him neither.

"Grab your jacket. Though I doubt you will need it today. Seems like another seventy-degree day for us."

"Just another Southern day in Alabama, my dear." He trudged to the dining area for his hoodie. His voice was muffled by the pullover as he slipped it over his head. "At least the coat and pullover are dry."

"That's a plus. I'm using the bathroom, and then we'll leave." She hurried down the hall and entered the small, tiled bathroom. It didn't take long, and soon she stood at the sink staring at her reflection in the mirror. Her hair stood out like a red Medusa. No time to tame it, though.

Angela turned the knob and ducked her face down into the sink bowl. A few splashes of cold water revived her enough to make her feel fresh and clean. Two swishes of water in her mouth cleansed it enough. At least she could smile at Scott without wondering if she was growing a moss garden in there.

Her mind drifted to his eyes. The man had such captivating, coffee-colored eyes. The sparkle that came to them when he smiled. And the way he smiled. Such a brightness to it. She ran a finger over her brow. His lips were always so cool when he kissed her there. She dropped her finger to her lips. How would they feel there?

Snap out of it!

She shook her head and turned off the water. Friends only. Only now she wished she could take those words back.

"Angela!" Scott's yell seemed to echo down the hallway.

They were in a hurry, and here she was lollygagging and thinking of romance. Typical for a romance heroine, but not real life.

Angela pulled open the door and hurried to the living room. She skidded to a stop, her socked feet sliding her further into the room. Two men, one brown-haired and the other balding, tussled with Scott by the window near the door. Brown-head had arms wrapped around Scott's chest, while the other fought to gain control of his legs that pushed and kicked out.

Her breath caught in her throat. No time to think!

She raced to the fireplace and grabbed the poker. The balding man trying to keep a hold on Scott's legs turned. He saw her and lunged. She didn't know him, but he came to know the business side of the poker.

Angela whacked him across the face with a resounding thud. Vibrations rattled her arms. The man rolled with the blow. She toppled to the side with the momentum of the hit and landed on the floor in a teeth-clacking heap.

Out of the corner of her eye, she saw Scott squirm away from the guy holding him—a man about Rochelle's age—and then turn to deliver a fist into the man's face.

That was all she saw.

The bald man had turned his attention back to her. She scrambled around the couch and away from the man beside her. Next time, she'd have to remember to check her swing. Treat him like a baseball she planned to bunt.

The floor seemed slippery as she tried to gain her feet. A hand latched on to her ankle. She turned and whacked it with the poker. It wouldn't let go. Angela kicked with her other foot and met a spongy nose.

With a hard curse, Mr. Baldy let go. Angela gained her footing and scampered to stand with the poker held like a baseball bat. She risked a glance at Scott. He was trading blows. A sickening punch landed in his gut, and he went down to his knees. Then Mr. Baldy rushed her.

His meaty hand grabbed the poker on her downswing.

Stupid woman! She wasn't supposed to swing during close quarters. She was supposed to thrust. That was what the instructor taught in Mobile. Perfect time to forget.

He wrenched the metal rod from her hand and threw it behind him onto the floor. She barely had time to react as the other hand landed across her cheek and sent her reeling. Ash-covered hardwood met her face. She whimpered once before rage set in.

No way was the man getting another strike in. Her glance landed on the glowing embers from last night's fire. She flipped over and kicked at him, her foot meeting hard fat resistance. But it did knock him back a few inches.

Angela snatched the shovel off the stand beside her head and scrambled to her knees. The man only grinned.

She shook her head. He probably thought she planned to swing it at him. In quick movements, she shoveled, turned, and flung hot ash into his face.

His howls filled the room. Large hands grabbed his face, probably pushing the embers deeper into his skin and eyes. Who cared? She leapt up, jumped onto the couch, and brought the flat side of the shovel down on Mr. Brown-head. Like a bull, he shook his head once and collapsed like a marionette whose strings had been cut.

Scott lowered his fists and stared at her in wide-eyed astonishment before he grinned. "That's my girl!"

He grabbed her hand and pulled. Angela fell into his arms. "We've gotta go!"

"I know. Grab your bag. I have your shoes." Scott scooped her shoes from the floor by the couch and rushed her out the door as she dug in her bag and ran. "Keys!"

"I'm getting them!" Her fingers closed over the cold metal and pulled them out. Wet grass quickly soaked her socks as she ran to the car.

If she cussed, she would be cussing out those men right now. Wet socks were the limit. If they followed her now, she'd put whatever she could find through their brains.

The passenger door stuck for a moment when she tried to open it. Scott had already slid inside. He reached across and pushed it open. Angela fell into the seat and jabbed the key into the ignition. "Please, Lord, let it start!"

The prayer worked. The motor belched. Angela slammed her door shut and caught herself against the dashboard as Scott backed up the car. He slid the gear into drive and drove away like a NASCAR racer, swerving once to avoid a pothole in the driveway before he pulled out onto the road.

Bumps and ridges along the gravel road clicked her teeth together and bounced her in the seat. But she would endure whatever it took to get them away from those guys.

Silence reigned for terse minutes as Scott wove his way off the gravel roads and onto the scenic highway. He gripped the steering wheel, his arms tight cables that linked him to the car. His nostril flared periodically. Angela twisted in her seat and looked behind them.

"I don't think they are following, Scott. I doubt Mr. Baldy can see. And I walloped the young one pretty good, didn't I?"

Scott nodded. "At least a concussion." He eased the car to a stop at the sign and glanced both ways.

Nothing came. He pulled onto the road and began to relax.

Angela shifted in her seat and grabbed the seatbelt. It clicked into place. She then reached down and peeled her wet, clingy socks off her feet. Yuck.

"Shoes are in the back seat. Here." He reached back with his right arm and then handed her the shoes.

Angela took them but placed them on the floorboard. "I need to let my feet dry for a moment." She placed her hand on his arm. "Scott, are you okay? Please tell me that it looks worse than it is."

"What looks worse?"

She would have laughed at his expression if the situation had not been so dire. Instead, she pointed to his cheek and then his eyebrow. "There's quite a bit of blood on you. And . . . " She ran a finger over his knuckles. "These are pretty red."

"Not as red as the guy who got a face full of ash." He opened and closed his hand a couple of times. "Nah. It's fine. Might be a little bruised. I'm tougher than I look."

"I've noticed." She reached into her bag and pulled out her small tissue package. "Here. Let me." The blood had dried some, but most of it came off as she dabbed at his face.

He turned slightly toward her, his eyes still on the road, as she scrubbed at the small gashes. Bits of tissue snagged on his whiskers. Angela used her fingernails to scrape it out of his half-grown beard.

Scott's hands captured hers. "Please, don't do that." A small fire lit his eyes when he glanced at her.

"But tissue's stuck in your whiskers, though." She pointed at his jaw.

His fingers scratched at it, and the bits fell away. "Did I get it?"

"Yeah." She settled back into her seat, and then pulled down the visor. "Oh, I am a mess!"

Black soot marred her face along her cheeks and chin. She wiped at the soot. It only smeared.

"Spit in it."

"Ew. No way." She reached into her bag and pulled out the can of soda. The pop-hiss filled the car. Angela wet the tissue with the soda and scrubbed at the soot spots. It wiped off in no time. "Well, now I will smell like soda."

Scott smiled. "I won't complain." He reached for the can. "Spare a little for this thirsty man?"

She handed him the can after downing a swig herself. "I'm going to call Douglas and let him know we are on our way, but that we also ran into trouble."

Scott slid the can into the cup holder as she dug in her bag. Seriously? She pushed aside the crackers and cakes. A notebook. Her checkbook. Wallet. Pens. Pack of gum. But no phone.

"I can't find the phone. Wait. I left it on the table after calling Dottie last night." She threw her bag onto the back seat. "Where's yours?"

Scott reached into his back pocket. And frowned. "Wait." He switched hands and repeated the movement. The frown deepened. "I don't have it. It must have fallen out."

Angela buried her head in her hands and leaned forward. "Now what?" So, this is what turmoil felt like.

"We stick to what we planned. Head to Hamilton." His hand caressed hot paths down her back. "We can grab a disposable phone at a gas station, okay?"

"I deleted my texts and calls last night. So, they can't figure out what we were planning by reading anything. What about you?"

"I have the lock screen password protected." He glanced at her.

Angela nodded and leaned her head back against the headrest. "Isn't this bothering you any? Running like we are in some action film? Bad guys chasing us. Trying to reach the good guys but being thwarted at every turn?"

Scott shrugged. "You are at my side, safe. That's all I worry about right now." His hand settled over hers and held on, his finger idly brushing across her knuckle.

He avoided her gaze, but she didn't mind. Apparently, he, too, was no longer thinking along the terms of "friends only." That was okay with her. She was tired of pretending that she wasn't falling for him, anyway. Amazing how much a fight can take out of a person. She was tired of fighting the bad guys. Tired of fighting against life. Tired of fighting against her attraction to Scott Weatherby Wilson.

She leaned against the console and tucked herself closer to his grasp and said a quick prayer to Heaven: O, Lord, please keep them all safe.

It seemed like a long drive. Angela drummed her fingers against the side of the door and waited. After using the restroom, Scott decided to grab a couple of drinks, some hot food, and a disposable phone.

She stifled a yawn. The convenience store was in the middle of nowhere. Smack dab in the highway, it seemed. And they still had a ways to go. Hopefully, they could reach Hamilton soon, and this nightmare would be over. She could see Rochelle. Make sure she was safe and sound. Had she been released yet? That was one thing she needed to find out once Scott activated the phone. And then she needed to call Dottie. Let her know that it was all over with . . . that is, if they could make it to Hamilton and meet with the federal agents.

Angela tapped a fingernail against her front teeth. Maybe she should change professions. Apparently, leaving Mobile and moving to Garrettville didn't guarantee a safer life. Who would have thought that her small, childhood hometown had become so corrupt? Maybe they were heading that way long ago. She nodded to herself. Yeah. That was one thing to check on. It had to begin somewhere.

The car door opened, and she jumped, banging her head against the window.

Scott smiled. "You seemed lost in thought. Did I startle you?"

She laughed. "Slightly. Was thinking about Garrettville."

"What about it? Here." He handed her a cold bottle of peach soda and a hot dog. "Probably give you indigestion, but we needed to eat."

She looked at his hands and frowned. He only had a root beer and his own hot dog. "Phone?"

"They didn't have any. We can stop somewhere and hopefully use their phone. Maybe stop at a Walmart." He took a bite of his hot dog and seemed to melt into his seat. "Junk food. There's nothing like it when you're hungry."

She nibbled at hers before taking a bite. The saltiness bit at her tongue, and the greasiness seemed to coat the inside of her mouth.

But she had to agree. It was better than nothing. They ate in silence for a while. Cars sped past them. Men in overalls and women with children came and went. One of the workers carried a bag of trash to the dumpster. Angela watched him as she chewed the last of her hot dog and washed it down.

Scott crumpled his wrapper and shoved it into the plastic bag. He held his hand out for hers. After draining the last of his root beer, he added the empty bottle to the bag. She shook her head when he pointed to hers.

"I'm not through with it."

She sipped it as he opened the door, unfolded his lanky frame from the car, and threw the bag in the trash receptacle. He paused by the door and looked over his shoulder before sliding back into the car.

"Did you see something?"

"I'm not sure. Thought for a moment it was Dan, but I couldn't tell." He started the car and pulled out of the parking lot. "You didn't answer me."

"About what?"

"About Garrettville. What you were thinking?" He turned onto the highway and headed south. The car sputtered and then sped up.

"I was wondering when the town became so corrupt. I was thinking about what to search for to see if I could pinpoint the turning point of the town."

"No." Scott shook his head. "Oh, no. Your investigation got us into this. We don't need a repeat."

"My investigation? It wasn't only me. You stole the meds that uncovered illegal drug trials. So, it wasn't just me, buster." She smiled at him to soften her words. "Anyway, it was just a thought."

"Let it go. Let Garrettville's past be just that—the past." He glanced at her before turning back to the road. "Who knows? This might actually turn the town around."

"Maybe."

He started to speak, but the car sputtered again.

"Is it out of gas?"

"No. It still has half a tank." He pressed the accelerator. The car barely surged forward. A knock vibrated through the chassis of the car, and it slowed. Scott muttered a horrible curse and stomped the pedal again. Nothing happened.

Why now? She wanted to cry. This wasn't the time for her car to do this. How many prayers were answered to keep it going?

The car gave a final shudder. Scott steered it to the side of the road amid the tall grass and practically into a ditch. He shoved it into park, dropped his head to the steering wheel, and heaved a deep sigh that ended on another curse that he repeated three times in a row.

Angela sat still and waited. Maybe they could hitch a ride. She looked around. It was quiet. They were on a lone highway in the middle of northern Alabama between towns. Surely, someone would drive by soon, though.

She glanced to her right and squinted at a sign in the distance. It stood near a gravel road. "What does that say?"

Scott raised his head. "Dismals Canyon. I can't read the distance, but there's an arrow pointed down the road." He looked at her, his dark eyes questioning. "Up for a hike?"

"Why not? I have shoes, no socks. It's seventy degrees outside. A pretty day. We have half a peach soda between us, and I still have a Little Debbie cake in my purse." She shoved open the door and climbed out of her dead car. The gravel on the side crunched under-foot. She slung her bag over her head and across her shoulder, and then straightened her back.

Scott rounded the car and held out his hand. "Well, let's get to it. Maybe we can use their phone. I'll tell them mine died, and we need to let a friend know we are waiting for them."

Angela smiled and slipped her hand into his. "You could just tell the truth and say that you lost your phone. And that I forgot mine."

He shrugged. "I guess I could. We'll see how the wind blows when we get there." He puffed out his cheeks and then released it. "I hate hiking."

Angela laughed. "It's not so bad. Come on." She pulled him, and off they went down an old Alabama gravel road. She smiled again.

"What are you smiling about?"

"Just thinking of a song I heard once. It isn't an old dirt road but walking down it with you made me think of it."

"Let me guess . . . 'The Valley Road.' I was thinking the same thing." He chuckled. His rich, baritone voice melded well with the birds chirping and the tree frogs croaking. It gave the perfect ambience to the lines.

He continued singing as they walked. That one line replayed in her head: would he go where she wanted him to go? She peeked a glance at him as the song wound down to a close. Wonder how he would sound singing the hymns at church? He let the last words die on his lips and fell silent. She wasn't ready to give up on him yet. The Lord was at work on him. She could see that, even if he did let a foul word slip out every now and then. She couldn't blame him. With all that was happening, it made her want to cuss, too.

"Know any other songs?" Her voice seemed to rip the air, damaging the country silence.

"Plenty. Not sure what you would want to hear, though." He pulled her slightly closer and gripped her hand a little tighter. "I do know a song you may like. Heard it one night. Reminded me of my parents. I don't really believe in it, but I do enjoy the melody."

"What is it?"

He cleared his throat, and then took a deep breath. At the sound of his voice, the world seemed to drop away. It was only her, Scott, and the gravel road. Even the birds seemed to stop and marvel at the song that poured from his lips.

"'Tis so sweet to trust in Jesus, Just to take Him at His word; Just to rest upon His promise, Just to know 'Thus saith the Lord.'"

She joined in the chorus, her voice wrapping around his until they blended. "Jesus, Jesus, how I trust Him! How I've proved Him o'er and o'er!"

Across the barren fields, through the treetops, and into the sky, their voices carried as they sang. Surely, God was protecting them as He listened to their song.

CHAPTER TWENTY-ONE

Rochelle waited until Douglas set his phone on the table beside her. His worried expression began to concern her. "No answer?"

"None. I have no idea what is happening." He sat beside her on the hospital bed.

It wasn't an uncomfortable silence. Each lost in thought while waiting on Pops to show up with the nurse and wheelchair. She could walk out on her own—well, hobble—but, apparently, hospitals didn't like that. So now she had to be wheeled out the front door and deposited into her grandfather's car like an invalid or some century-old person.

"What about Angela's number?" She looked over at Douglas.

"I don't know her number. Do you?"

Rochelle held her hand out for his phone. He dropped it onto her palm. "Make a backward seven to unlock it."

The screen lit up with nine icons, awaiting the swipe of her finger. Rochelle stared at the phone a moment. Wonder if it would be called a "pass swipe" instead of a password? She traced her finger across the screen in the proper code and almost laughed at the wallpaper used on his phone. A Golden Retriever on a jet ski.

"Pick Wick?"

Douglas smiled at her. "One of my wishful luxuries. Always wanted to jet ski on the river."

She dialed Angela's number. "Maybe you can soon, since the hospital is shutting down. Looks like you'll have a little vacation time."

"Yeah, but not in this weather. I want it hot and sunny."

It rang on the other end. Over and over. She was about to hang up when it was answered, but no one said a thing. Quiet hung over the digital waves.

"Angela?"

No answer. Then a click. Rochelle looked at the phone. It was still connected; it had sounded like someone placed the phone on a hard surface.

"Angela?"

Rochelle handed the phone to Douglas. He listened for a while before disconnecting.

"I heard a door slam and then nothing else." He pocketed the phone. "It couldn't have been them."

Again, each were lost in thought. She sneaked a peek from under her lashes at the man beside her. Why did he want to help? What was so special about her that he decided to hang about? Not that she could complain. He was generous and thoughtful. Compassion shown in his eyes; but more than that, he shone with a love for Christ that she hadn't seen in many men. Her Pops, the deacons, and her pastor, to name a few.

Thinking of Pops caused him to materialize. He arrived with the wheelchair.

"Told the aide that I would wheel you out. You're still looking a little green, so I didn't want to chance that the aide would be a NASCAR wannabe." He stopped and looked at them sitting side by side on the bed. "What's up?"

"Angela and Scott aren't answering their phones." Douglas stood. "I need to make a call. Let them know. Something had to have happened."

Pops nodded, and Douglas walked out into the hall. She rose from the bed and lowered herself into the wheelchair. Her grandfather spread the red fuzzy blanket he bought at the gift shop across the scrub pants she had been given to wear. Rochelle tucked it around her. Despite her thermal shirt that Pops had bought her, she was still cold.

She almost smiled. The red blanket clashed with her dull green scrubs. "Do you think they will be okay, Pops?"

"I am sure they will."

Karen walked in and smiled at her. "You do look better this morning. Here's your discharge papers . . . "

Rochelle listened with half an ear as the nurse went over what to do and what not to do, what to look for and what to expect. Pops nodded and commented; then the papers were shoved into a bag where it nestled beside her tattered clothes, jacket, and bag.

"Will the officers be with us?"

Pops shook his head as Karen patted her shoulder one last time and left the room. "No. You already gave your statement to them. Douglas said we will head to Hamilton and meet with Scott. They are looking for Brent. But we need to stay close to Douglas."

"Do you think we could grab a Sprite before we leave?"

"Feeling sick?"

"Slightly." She closed her eyes as Pops gently and slowly wheeled her out of the room. Maybe she should be grateful for the wheelchair. Getting knocked on the head surely messed with the equilibrium.

"Well, you won't believe what happened." Douglas' hushed whisper forced her eyes opened.

He waited with them by the elevator. When it dinged open, they piled in. Douglas hit the "close door" button before anyone could decide to hop on with them.

Once the doors closed, he turned to them. "Just got a call from Scott. They are at Dismals Canyon. Apparently, two guys arrived at the cabin. Scott and Angela were able to get away, but they left their phones behind. Couldn't find a disposable, and before they could make it to a store that had one, Angela's car quit on them. They were only a few miles from Dismals Canyon, so they hiked there, and the manager at the country store let him use the phone to call me."

Rochelle gripped her blanket tighter around her. "So, we are going to Dismals? Will they be okay?"

Douglas looked at Pops. "What do you think? I'll head to Dismals Canyon, but I don't know if Rochelle can handle the ride there."

She shook her head slightly. "I might barf on you, but I can handle it. Please don't leave us. What if they are still after me? Or are following us?"

The elevator opened, and she was wheeled out into the bright lobby. Pops followed Douglas outside before answering her question. "We will be okay in Hamilton. Our statements will be taken there, and then we can go home."

Douglas knelt before her and held her hand. "Your grandfather knows what to do, Rochelle. It will be fine. But I have to go and help my friend. Scott's the best friend and partner I've ever had, and I owe it to him." He clasped both of her hands in his and lifted them to his lips. A soft kiss grazed her knuckles. "My dad is down there with the agents. He knows you're coming, and you'll be safe with them. And soon, all the people involved will be arrested, and you will be able to go home, okay?"

"Will you be safe?" Heat crept up her neck. She didn't need him to get the wrong impression; but for some reason, she really was concerned about him.

"The Lord will watch out for me." He gave her hands a gentle squeeze. "Pray for us?"

Rochelle gazed back into his ocean-blue eyes. "I will."

Her whisper seemed to give him strength. He breathed deeply and looked deep into her eyes before standing. He shook hands with her grandfather, and then left them on the curb.

Pops' hand fell softly onto her shoulder and squeezed. "He's a fine young man."

"Yes, I know." She leaned her cheek against his hand. "Can we get my Sprite now and get going? I really don't like sitting on the curb like this."

Pops dropped a kiss on her head and chuckled. "Absolutely, my girl!"

Angela waited near the door for Scott. His deep voice drifted over to her as he spoke to Douglas. He played it off as though he was waiting on him to arrive and that they had arrived earlier than he thought. She smiled. He didn't have to be so cryptic; but with all that had happened, who could blame him?

A few cars pulled into the parking lot. People exited the vehicles, but she couldn't see much past the wooden archway. Scott thanked the manager and came to stand beside her.

"See anything interesting?"

"Just people arriving. So, what's the word?" She glanced up at him.

"He's on his way—" He bit off his sentence with a harsh curse. "That's Dan."

"What?" She tried to look out the door, but Scott grabbed her arm and pulled her toward the counter, where he asked about the price of walking the canyon. He pulled out his last bills and handed them to the clerk. Then he pulled her out the door and onto the back deck. The temperature had warmed. It was easily a seventy- or seventy-five-degree day.

She glanced around. The beauty of the place would have been astounding had she had the chance to admire it. Instead, she was being yanked and pulled down the stairs, across the concrete pad, and onto a sandy trail.

She glanced back; and at the edge of the creek branch, beyond the fencing, and by the corner of the store stood two men, shading their eyes and staring in their direction. They were too far away for her to see them clearly, and then not at all as they passed a place called Rainbow Falls and rounded a bend.

Her hair bounced into her face, and she pulled Scott into a stop. "There were two men at the corner of the store. Do you think they saw us?"

Scott reached out and held a curl between his fingers. "There's no mistaking this. They will be right behind us. I've been here before, so we can keep heading down the trail; cut across at the end;

and instead of following the trail around, we can go up through the woods and rest on top of one of the cliffs."

He urged her forward until they came to a narrow opening between two stone cliffs. The plaque read *Phantom Falls*.

"We can go in. Usually, there are timber rattlers hanging out under the ledge; but with the temps today, they are probably still hibernating."

Angela stopped him before he entered. "Can't we just go around?"

"It will take longer."

She pointed behind him. "Then we move fast because I don't want to risk falling in there. It's rocky and narrow."

Scott grabbed her hand and propelled her down the sandy path. "Fine. But move fast."

Her shoes squished and pushed at the soft flooring of the canyon until they came to an open area under an overhang. Water dripped from the walls and into shallow pools in the large rock floor. She glanced around as she followed Scott across the boardwalk. Whenever this was all over, she would have to bring Max here. Never had she seen anything so gorgeous before.

"It's called the Grotto." His voice reverberated off the stone walls. "The Chickasaws and Cherokees used this area, usually to hide from their enemies or to live. Before the Trail of Tears."

"I'm not surprised that you know the history of this place." They slipped past the Grotto exit, and she looked back at the narrow passage between the walls. On the other side was the brown-haired young man from the cabin.

A sneer warped his face, and he began to side-walk his way through the passage. Scott grabbed her hand again and started pulling at her when the boy's scream echoed off all the rock walls and trees. He'd stumbled, face-planted in the sandy soil, flailed about, and was scooting through the passageway.

Tears streaked his face as he rolled away from the opening. He ignored them as he pulled himself along the rocky and leaf-covered ground. His gaze turned to Scott. "Help me, please."

She glanced back at Scott. Indecision warred on his face. With a curse issued through gritted teeth, he trudged to the fallen man. Angela followed, keeping herself hidden behind his skinny frame.

"My leg. I can't move it."

Scott knelt and pushed the boy back onto the ground. "Shut up, and quiet down." He probed the leg and ankle. "I have to remove your boot, and it will hurt."

Scott untied the boot and pulled it off. The boy's groans turned to whimpers as Scott examined his leg. "You have a phone?"

The young man nodded. "Pocket."

Scott fished it from his jeans and put it in the boy's hand. "Dial nine-one-one. Tell them you are at Dismals Canyon just behind Phantom Falls. You have a broken tibia. Feels like two places. I need your jacket." Mr. Brown-head allowed the jacket to be stripped from him. Scott rolled it and placed it under his leg. "This will help slow the swelling. Now make the call."

He grabbed Scott's wrist as Scott stood. "Why? Why help me?"

"Because that is what I do." Scott looked at him with contempt and then turned away, grabbing her hand and leading her away.

Would the guy call nine-one-one? She hoped so. Despite what he had done, she lifted a silent prayer for him. Maybe he could find his way away from the lost path he took.

Wet foliage coated their shoes and pants. She read the signs as they ran by: *Kitchen, Indian Head Rock*. Yup. It looked like a Native American warrior. Then there was Temple Cave. She smiled at the beauty of the ferns that grew all around them. The crystal-clear waters. But she really wished Scott would slow down. Her breath hitched in her chest, and her heart pounded.

She pulled her hand out of his grip, stopped, and leaned on her knees, her chest heaving. "Gotta stop . . . for just . . . a moment. Please."

Scott frowned, but leaned against a boulder. His gaze wandered over the landscape. Around them, the forest had thickened. Trees practically blotted out the sun. Only small trails of light trickled their way down to wash this hidden wonder in a soft glow.

"It is beautiful." She nodded to him, and they started walking. "You said Native Americans used this?"

"Yes. The records show that arrowheads dating back ten thousand years have been found here. I've always wondered about it. Did they use the Kitchen as a communal place to eat? Did they use Pulpit Rock, which was above the Falls, for their worship? And wait until you see Weeping Bluff. The walls cry streams of tears."

Angela smiled. "Streams of tears?"

"Yes." His brown eyes crinkled. "It's water from the land at the top of the bluff that empties over the edge. Looks like it's crying. And the sound it makes. Purer than crystal."

Loud voices drifted their way down the path. Scott scowled and looked at her. "Just when we thought we could have a breather. Come on. Just a little further, and then we can cross the bridge and head up into the woods."

Angela allowed him to grab her hand and pull her along again. Sweat pricked her scalp and ran down her back. Water from the plants, rocks, and mudholes soaked through her shoes, her clothes, and her hair. The curls would be kinky by now. Probably a wild riot of frizzy strands.

Scott's hair glistened from sweat and water. His hoodie sported wet patches along his back and under his arms. No telling how soaked his shoes were. She couldn't stop the grin across her face as they rounded another bend in the trail. It was no telling how bad they smelled.

"Up there." Scott pointed to a low bridge ahead of them.

A surge of energy propelled her forward. Hopefully, they could rest at the bluff. And hopefully, this would soon be over.

CHAPTER TWENTY-TWO

"How long do you think they plan to remain down there?" Fallen and damp leaves muffled Angela's voice as they peered over the edge.

Scott eased away from the edge and rolled over onto his back. Water soaked through, but it was better than sitting up and being seen from the other side across the creek. Although the trees were thick, there were still enough breaks that anyone could see through them. Hooray for autumn.

Angela scooted back and flipped onto her back beside him. She gazed up at the sky, her fingers quietly drumming against her stomach.

"They will probably be there for a bit. I want to stay and listen to see where they plan to go next." He ran his hands over his face. Whiskers rasped against his palms. Weariness had started leeching into his bones. Pretty sure he was beginning to become ill. Of course, what did he expect? He'd been on the run for a while with hardly anything to eat; his sugar was bottoming out; and it seemed as though this horror wasn't planning on ending anytime soon.

Angela's elbow nudged him. "Can you hear them?"

He eased to his side and peeked over a rock. Voices floated up to them, muted by the gentle fall of the water.

"They couldn't have gone far. Did they double back?"

"Jerry would have seen them."

"How about up?"

"They couldn't climb the rocks!"

"Not that. Up around the cliff. Into the woods. Scott's smart. He probably took the first chance he had to get off the trail . . . "

Scott scooted back through the dead leaves. Guess there was no time to rest at this moment. He climbed to his feet and helped Angela to hers. "Time to go. I swear—"

"Yes, you do."

At her playful interruption, Scott's sentence faltered to a stop. He smiled as they wove their way through the trees. "I seemed to have developed that habit recently. Sorry about that."

She ducked under a branch and gave him a small smile. "I can understand it. But don't do it around Max."

There was no ultimatum in her tone. Scott pushed a wet branch to the side and allowed Angela to pass. He wouldn't argue about her demand. Running through the events of the last month, he replayed all his actions and thoughts. His reactions and speech. All the way back to Julie's death.

Grief almost hammered his breath from his chest. But that was the turning point. Billy's death. He had cursed then. He vaguely remembered cursing God. Scott paused with his hand on a tree trunk. Angela walked a few more feet before stopping.

"Scott?"

God. When did he start thinking about Him? When did he stop? Before Julie and Billy, he listened. He talked about God. He read about God. But he never accepted God. And after their deaths, he refused to even consider it.

Angela's hand settled on his chest, breaking his reverie. He raised his head and looked into her eyes. They sparkled so bright. Her smooth, pink lips parted slightly, forming a question. He blinked and forced the tears back inside.

"I'm okay. Just that I remembered when I started cursing and why. It kind of just hit me suddenly." He pushed off the tree and urged her forward. "Keep walking straight. We can make it to the Secret Falls and climb down from there. A little dangerous, but doable. Even if the rocks are slippery."

The wet, brown leaves softened their footfalls. Their labored breathing created a kind of cadence to their hurried strides. The undergrowth rustled as they passed through. Drops of water fell onto them from the overhead branches. Angela gasped as a low branch caught its twigs in her hair. Scott freed the red mass from its captor and urged her forward. Her red hair struck a sharp contrast to the surrounding woods.

His Celtic spitfire. She looked like she was at home in the woods, in her element. But looks were deceiving. She muttered angrily as some thorn bushes grabbed at her pants. Not that he could blame her. His own pants sported the prickly hitchhikers. And he was sure little red rivers ran across his legs by now.

He glanced up ahead and almost sighed with relief. They had made it.

Scott knelt at the edge and peered over. A small ledge, right near the waterfall and by a boulder, wasn't too far down from them. He eased down onto his belly and dangled his legs over the edge. With a last glance to judge his distance, he dropped. His teeth rattled when he landed.

"Okay." His whisper sliced through the air. "Just do like I did, and I will catch you."

He read in so many novels where the heroine would balk or whine about being afraid or not trusting the hero. But not his Angela. She squirmed her way over the edge, looked down, and let go at his nod. His hands caught her around the waist and helped slow her descent.

"Thank you for trusting me."

She looked back at him as he helped steady her on her feet. "Always, Scott."

Her statement warmed him inside, seeming to bloom in his chest. It shouldn't have. But it did. He tugged at her and nodded toward the small path leading down to some stepping-stones. "We will head that way."

She followed him without a word. Once across the stones, and then back on the trail, Scott quickened his pace. Angela dogged his heels.

"You know, this would be a nice vacation to come see all the wonders this place holds."

"I loved it when I was younger. Julie and I used to come a lot. We introduced Jake to it."

"You hardly talk about Julie."

Scott cast a glance back at her. "The same could be said about you when it comes to Mike."

Angela mulled over his words and then nodded. "I guess. It's not so painful to me now. But I've had a few more years of healing than you have. Do know that I understand what you are going through."

"I know." He paused outside a crevice in the rock wall. "I know you do."

He bent down and moved a few stones around, scuffed the sandy dirt from the opening to approximately three feet into the crevice. Then he searched the ground for some twigs, located two dead ones, and broke them in half with a stomp.

"Let me guess, John Wayne, you're creating a false trail?"

"My brilliantly deductive reporter." He tweaked her nose with a dirt smudged fingertip. She laughed gently and then grabbed his hand as they jogged even further down the path.

"How close do you think they are?"

"Probably close enough." They reached an area of the path that meandered into a darkened cavern.

Angela paused at the sign. "Witch's Cavern. So, witches used this?"

"Nope." She followed him into the dark labyrinth. Moss covered the walls, boulders, and stones, while ferns peppered every little nook and cranny. He pointed deep into the shadows to a glowing spot on the wall. "Dismalites."

"Dismalites?"

"Similar to glowworms. Larvae stage of an insect related to the fungus gnat. North American Orfelia fultoni."

Her snicker bounced off the walls. "I didn't take you for an entomologist."

Scott slowed his walk to ease around a bend. His chest brushed against the moss, which left a green smear across his hoodie. "Confession: I'm not. I studied up on some of the history before we brought Jake down. Wanted to one up him, you know. I was a little jealous of him stealing Julie away from me."

"So, what happened?" She held out her hand and followed him out of the cavern and back onto the dirt trail.

"Julie had warned him, and he learned some of the history, too. So, our day was spent seeing who retained the most knowledge about the canyon." He gave her a small smile. "Want to take a gander at who won?"

"No. I already know." She suddenly stopped.

Scott cocked his head and listened. Voices drifted closer. He bit his curse back. So much for not constantly running. His legs couldn't take anymore. And Angela's face was already flushed red and splotchy. She hadn't complained; but if his throat was becoming parched, no telling how bad hers was. He cast a quick look around. They were almost to the swing bridge and back at the beginning, but they would never make it in time before the men saw them.

He urged her forward. "There's a spot up ahead. We can hide. If Aaron Burr could do it over two hundred years ago, then we can do it."

Angela shook her head but allowed him to pull her along. Within moments, they arrived at the split trail. One went right to the Burr's Hideout, the other left, back to the trail leading to Phantom Falls. The voices became louder.

There was no time. A group of rocks right behind the larger boulder offered some protection. It would have to do. The voices grew ever closer. Scott recognized Jonathan's voice.

"Quick!" Scott pushed her up onto the large, moss-covered boulder. "Go to the other side."

She knelt and slid her feet over the edge. "Are you sure? There's not much room here."

He lowered himself over the slick edge and propelled her downward. "It'll have to do. The depression there should be enough for us."

Smaller boulders, flat pieces of slate, and large rocks created a jumble around them. One of the green boulders rocked dangerously as he knelt on it. Moisture slicked the lichen that grew on the rocks.

Angela looked back at him as she slid a few inches further down the rock, her foot stretched out on a protruding stone for balance. "I'm not so sure about this. Looks too dangerous."

He pointed to a spot near them. "Right there. Lay down in it." Voices drifted his way, still indistinct but loud. "Just do it, Ang. They're right behind us."

She plopped down on her back in the slight depression between the jutting rocks and boulder. Angela grimaced and squirmed. She pressed herself closer to the side of the boulder. Her hair gleamed in striking contrast next to the gray rock.

Scott peered around him. Nothing else would do. Going further into the mass of rocks and boulders would be their death warrant. One slip, one fall, and other rocks would either cascade on top of them, or they would fall between those pointing up, breaking a neck or worse.

He would have to figure out a way to hide her hair.

Scott pulled at his hoodie, slipping the hood over his head. His favorite black shirt ripped as he pulled it from his waistband and stretched it low over his hips. It had to blend in.

It was the only way.

The depression barely allowed enough room for both.

"Sorry about this." He lowered himself beside her, teetering on the very edge of the rock. "Scoot farther in." She squeezed closer to the boulder's side. Scott rolled partially on top of her and pressed his cheek against hers, pulling the hood over her head to hide her hair. Water from the rock seeped through his sweatshirt at his elbows. "It's the only way to hide your hair."

Her breath tickled his ear as she whispered. "Are you sure they won't see us?"

No, he was never sure about anything. Not anymore.

"I don't know. Not unless they climb on top of the rock. Be still." Her body stilled underneath his. Her hands tightened on his sides. He strained to keep his weight off her.

She pulled him tighter to her. "If you keep holding yourself up, they'll see you. You're not that heavy, Scott. I can hold your weight."

Scott sighed. No choice really. He buried his hands under the hood and relaxed. She grunted once as he settled his body half on the rock, half on top of her.

Scott ducked his head further down until his lips met her neck. Her rosy-peachy scent flooded his senses. If this was any other time . . .

A scuffle of boots across the path, followed by a voice, bounced off the rocky overhang. "There's the swing bridge. They could have doubled back through Phantom Falls or the Grotto."

"Where's the map?" Scott tensed as Jonathan's voice drew nearer. "Where're we at?"

"There's the sign. Up ahead is Burr's Hideout. Think they went there?"

"No, too dangerous. Look at those rocks. Call Dan. See if they turned back at the bluff and crossed back. Scott's skinny enough to go through Fat Man's Misery. Looked like he might have gone that way. They could be hiding in there. Jerry, tell Dan to check it out."

Scott's muscles ached from tension as Jerry made the call, and he flinched as the sound of rough fabric scraped against the boulder. The vibration of the sound skittered through him.

Angela's hands tightened, and a small moan rattled her chest. Scott pressed his face closer to hers. His lips grazed her ear. "Shh."

His lungs ached at controlling the volume of his voice. Fear fluttered next to him. If whoever sat on the rock just turned around and peered over the top of the boulder, he and Angela wouldn't stand a prayer.

Prayer.

A small, flutter of movement, like the beating of a captured butterfly's wings, grazed his neck. Something wet slid between their pressed faces.

His body trembled inside. The temptation to move and run overwhelmed him.

He squeezed his eyes shut. Let him stay strong. He had to stay still.

Angela's fingernails dug into his side, spikes of fear.

What was she saying? Silent prayer was what Nana Debbie called it. Would it work?

Another rasp against the boulder and a dull *thunk* traveled through the stone. Scott held his breath. Surely, they could feel his heartbeat through the rock. Every movement they made as they waited for their friends reverberated through the boulder and into him.

Angela's lips still moved against his skin.

Pray.

He opened his eyes. Surely, everyone heard that loud voice.

The trill of a phone broke the silence. "Yeah? . . . Okay, I'll tell him. Meet us up here at the swing bridge . . . Dan said no one's at Fat Man's Misery."

Another scrape against the boulder. "Good. They had to have crossed and made it to the Falls. Did anyone check Pulpit Rock?"

"No. Don't think so. After Brent fell at the Falls and was helped back to the store, everyone either took off down to the Kitchen or across to the Dance Hall."

"Go check it out then. I'll wait for Dan."

Heavy footsteps tapped across the wooden bridge. A rasping sound pierced the quiet, and then the first wisps of cigarette smoke floated across the boulder.

Please, no! A tickle formed in his throat. Please, not this! He had to keep Angela safe.

Pray.

He fought the urge to shake his head. Praying was a joke. He didn't know how, anyway.

Nana Debbie's voice sang in his head. "It's easy, Scott. It's like talking to a friend. You have a sharp mind. You remember everything you hear, dear boy, so I know that you can remember things I've read to you . . . "

Pray.

His ear rang from the loud and insistent voice. The Book of Isaiah popped into his mind. He moved his lips. His voice, a bare breath's whisper of sound, stirred strands of Angela's hair, sending the wisps curling around his mouth.

"When you pass through the waters, I *will be* with you; And through the rivers, they shall not overflow you. When you walk through the fire, you shall not be burned. Nor shall the flame scorch you . . . "

Angela's lips stopped moving against him. Scott squeezed his eyes shut. A small drop traveled down his nose. Please, don't let them hear. The insistent urge to speak returned, battering against his head. Psalm forty-two ran through his mind. He swallowed and continued, his voice softer than a dove's touch. "For You *are* the God of my strength." Angela moved slightly and pressed her cheek to his neck. "Why do you cast me off? Why do I go mourning because of the oppression of the enemy? Oh, send out Your Light and Your truth! Let them lead me; Let them bring me to Your holy hill and to Your tabernacle."

Another tickle in his throat threatened to rip a cough from him. "Please, my Lord. I do not deserve Your compassion nor Your love. I don't deserve Your forgiveness, which is why I ran from You. Why would You love me, a filthy drug addict? Why would You love me, who fought against You, who denied You for so long? Why would You care about me when You took away my best friend? Why would You allow Rochelle to be assaulted? Just as I ask those questions, I know the answer. To bring us closer to You. Julie loved You. Rochelle loves You. Even my dear Angela loves You. I want to know that love, too."

A sharp, cold wind blew against them. The tickle in his throat subsided. "I know Who You are. You are the Son of God. I deny You no longer. Please, forgive me. Oh, Lord, please forgive me. I ask for Your protecting arms to hold us . . . "

His body melted. Muscles and bones became butter, draping along the rock's surface.

Tears fell from his eyes when he blinked. The insistent banging in his head left. In its place, a light, pillow-like comfort rested upon him.

Heavy thuds on the wooden swing bridge echoed away from them. Angela pushed at him.

"They're gone. Dan just came, and they left."

Scott levered himself up on his hands and stared down at her. Tears caked her cheeks. Wet strands of her hair plastered the side of her head. Her vivid gaze was soft as she stared back at him. Angela reached up and caressed his stubbly cheek. Cool fingers wiped away hot tears.

Her lips parted, and then closed. Silence reigned.

The wind picked up some more and whipped leaves around the rocks. He pushed away and grunted as he pulled himself up on top of the rock. His hands slipped against the surface, and his pants rasped as he slid back until his back pressed against the rock wall.

Nothing. He could think of nothing. So surreal was his surroundings. The wind played with the leaves. The trickling creek sang as it rushed underneath the bridge. Birds flitted from limb to limb. He stared at the sky.

A layer of gray clouds gently rolled across the sky.

It was beautiful. He never noticed these things before.

Angela slid across the wet rock and grabbed his hands. "Scott?"

He swallowed and brought his gaze down to hers. His heart thudded against his ribcage. "Was I speaking?"

She nodded. Heat flowed across his face.

"We were protected. Jonathan sat on the rock. I'm sure of it. I heard him scraping against the surface, but he didn't see us." She cupped his face and brought her face closer to his. "Scott?"

Scott closed his eyes and drew in a ragged breath. "Is it always like this? So emotional? I may not like it, you know."

Angela laughed quietly. His eyes nearly popped out of his head when her lips pressed against his in a small kiss. She pressed another kiss to his forehead. "You'll like it. You and Jesus will get along just fine." She slid off the rock. "Come on. I heard them say they were headed to Pulpit Rock. We can shoot up to the caretaker's cabin; and they won't see us, but we have to hightail it now."

He nodded. Everything that just happened could be catalogued later. Much later. Maybe. Depending on if he could figure out what just happened. Nana Debbie should have warned him about the side effects.

He landed on the soft path beside Angela and followed her to the swing bridge. It oscillated under their footsteps. He stumbled a little as his foot hit the sandy patch on the other side. If prayer worked to keep them safe last time, then maybe it'd work again.

Scott smiled. And it wouldn't take that sharp voice in his head three times to tell him.

He sped up, grabbed Angela's hand, and pulled her along behind him. Their feet ate up the path as he recited under his ragged breath another of Nana Debbie's reading—Isaiah again, "But those who wait on the LORD shall renew *their* strength; They shall mount up with wings like eagles—"

Angela's lilting voice joined his as they passed Rainbow Falls and reached the canyon's entrance. "They shall run and not be weary . . . "

Angela's breath caught at the hitch in her side. Her heart pounded, but they were almost there. She couldn't keep up with Scott's litany of verses. Salvation came for the man, and now he couldn't stop his reciting.

The caretaker's cabin loomed in the distance. Not too far. They had scrambled past the pool and past the country store. At the top of the hill, flashing blue and red lights highlighted the area. Guess the boy called nine-one-one after all. Angela scowled.

She had mixed feeling about Brent. Now that she had heard his name, she remembered that he was the one whom Rochelle had dated . . . and the one who tried to force himself onto her. She didn't wish him death, but she did wish him harm—Lord, forgive her for such a thought.

Angela stumbled. Scott's arm immediately wrapped around her and pulled her to her feet.

An angry yell penetrated the air. Behind them, Jonathan and Dan raced their way. Fear etched itself across Scott's face as he helped her claw her way up the hill. Her foot slipped, sending her and Scott crashing onto the wet ground at the edge of the parking lot. He groaned and tried to rise, but his arms gave out from underneath him.

The yells drew closer, as well as shouts from above. Angela grabbed Scott underneath the arms and tugged. "Come on. We are almost there."

Scott rose on shaky arms as he looked across the parking lot. Another shout echoed. "Scott!"

Douglas hurried toward them, his legs pumping against the pavement. Two other men followed him, while three others veered off toward Jonathan and Dan. Angela looked down at the men who caused their misery for so long. They skidded to a stop, started to run, but must have decided against it. Instead they held up their hands and waited.

Angela sagged against the ground in relief.

"It's finished. Thank you, God, for keeping us safe." Scott plopped down onto his back and hid his eyes behind his hands.

When Douglas arrived, Scott reached into his pocket, pulled out the flash drive, and held it up like a long, sought-after treasure. "Take this cursed item. I want nothing more to do with it. I want something to drink. Food. And a shower. And in that order."

Douglas laughed and took the flash drive from Scott's fingers. "I can smell you from here, man."

"Douglas, if I wasn't a recently saved man, I would show you what I think about that statement."

Angela smiled at Douglas' surprised expression. And then she almost laughed when Scott returned to hiding his eyes behind his hand and Douglas did a victory fist pump in the air. He held out his hand and she allowed him to help her to her feet.

"Rochelle?"

"Safe. In Hamilton." He dropped the flash drive into an evidence bag one of the men held open. "There's a car waiting for you. It'll take you to Hamilton, where they will take your statements, put you in a hotel for the night, and then take you home. Oh, we found your car. I called a towing company to haul it back to Garrettville. On Scott's dime, of course."

"Douglas, I swear, man, you are pushing the limits of this newbie Christian. Don't make me revert to my old ways." Scott rose to a sitting position and craned his neck to glare at his friend.

"And I suppose you are going to use that excuse for all it's worth?"

"Don't you know it." Scott stood, and Angela slipped her hand into his. "Take me to the air-conditioned car."

Douglas led the way. "So, tell me. What made you finally come to a decision?"

Angela leaned against Scott's side and tried to hide her smile when Scott replied.

"I thought I was running from the bad guys. Instead, I discovered that Jesus was chasing down a bad guy—me."

If he only knew how much prayer was said on his behalf. The banter between Scott and Douglas carried her across the pavement and into the car. Scott gripped Douglas' hand in a handshake before they embraced in a brotherly hug.

She scooted closer to him as he settled in the seat and laid her head against his chest, listening to his heart beat against her ear. "I'm glad it's finally over."

Scott's arm wrapped around her and held her close. "Me, too."

Before long, his even breathing started lulling her to sleep. She could rest. Finally feel safe. And finally know that Scott was the one for her. His arms tightened around her as she snuggled closer.

The driver door opened, and Scott snapped awake, fear dilating his pupils.

A man in a dark suit carrying a bag slid into the seat. "Ready to go?" He passed the bag over the seat toward them. "Food and drinks."

Scott relaxed against her and tore into the bag. "Thank you!" He passed a wrapped sandwich and a cold bottle of water to her. Then he grabbed some for himself.

Angela screwed the top off and took a long sip. If this water cooled her thirst, she could only imagine what Scott was feeling now. He had more than just cool water. He now had the Living Water inside him.

The car backed up and then pulled out of the parking lot. She eased back against the seat and into Scott's side again. She had no words for how she was feeling. She went from a hungry reporter, to a homeless, single mother, to a woman loved, gaining a new beginning and a new life along the way.

Her gaze traveled over Scott's grimy and heavily whiskered face as he devoured his sandwich and drink. On his face was relief and contentment. Gone was the haunted look. In its place was a brightness—a peacefulness.

And to think, Scott's new life started with one long, gravel road on an Alabama day . . .

EPILOGUE

Angela held up the white outfit. "Well, what do you think?"

She stood in the middle of Scott's living room. Tonight was the night before the Christmas pageant, and they needed to make sure the costume fitted her son.

She waited. And then cleared her throat. "Well?"

Max looked up from Scott's lap, letting the book they were reading together fall to the floor. He stared at the angel costume, turned to Scott, and then squinted back at her. "Are you sure? Girls are the only ones who are angels."

Scott laughed, moved the boy off his lap, and retrieved the book from the floor. "Says who?"

"Well, you know. They always give that part to the girls. I ain't a girl." Max crossed his arms and leaned against the back of the sofa.

Angela sighed and placed the outfit on the easy chair by the Christmas tree. "We know you aren't a girl, Max. But angels are not females. They are males."

"I don't care."

Scott shook his head at her, stood, and walked to the fireplace to stoke the fire. "Do you remember what I read to you last night, Max?"

"Yeah." Her obstinate son looked away from them, his arms still crossed defiantly.

"What did I say?"

No answer came from the sofa. Scott strode to the coffee table and picked up the Bible. "Well, I guess I have to read it, huh? Let's see. Yes . . . here we go. Luke chapter two, verse nine is the beginning of your lines. 'And behold, an angel of the Lord stood before them, and the glory of the Lord shone around them, and they were greatly afraid. Then the angel said to them—'"

"Do not be afraid, for behold, I bring you good tidings of great joy which will be to all people. For there is born to you this day in the city of David a Savior, who is Christ the Lord." Max climbed from the sofa and touched the costume. "But won't people laugh because I'm an angel?"

Scott knelt on his level. "Definitely not. It's a great honor to play the angel. He was a great messenger of God. And what did he tell the shepherds?"

"That they would find the baby wrapped in swaddling clothes."

"Exactly. Now, let your mom help you with your costume. And then we can practice your lines, yeah?"

Max sighed. "Okay. But will it be a dress? I don't want to be an angel in a dress."

Angela smiled and shook her head. "It is a robe. Nana made you some white pants for it and this . . . " She picked up the costume and held it out. "This is a robe and sash. Just like they wore back then."

At Scott's urging, Max slipped on the pants and allowed the robe to be draped and sashed to him. "What about a halo?"

"Miss Bobbi has something for you. She said she made it out of glow bracelets. How cool is that?"

Max's grin showed off his missing front teeth. "It's going to be white?"

"As white as the Christmas star."

"Scott, did you hear that? As white as the Christmas star!" He whooped and took off down the hallway. "Nana, Mom said Miss Bobbi made me a halo as white as the Christmas star!"

Debbie's voice mingled with Max's as she "oohed" and "ahhed" over his costume. Angela leaned against Scott's side and wrapped her arms around his waist. "Well, that didn't take much coaxing."

Scott chuckled. "It never does with him. Coffee?"

"Oh, my goodness, yes." She followed him to the kitchen and opened the cabinet as he pulled out two single serve cups from the drawer. "I can't believe you splurged on such an expensive coffee-maker. Your money won't last long if you keep spending it."

A mischievous smile spread across his face, causing his eyes to sparkle. "Well, I bought it as a celebration." He took a mug from her, slid it on the plate, and hit the brew button.

"Celebration?" Angela clasped her hands together. The rascal was withholding information from her. And she bet she knew what it was. "You didn't? They did?"

Scott nodded. "They did. Jerald said that they could use not only a medic but also a certified instructor."

Angela squealed and then jumped into his arms, wrapping him into a hard hug. "That's great!"

He dropped his forehead down to hers. "I didn't think he would give me the job. Especially since it was released about how I found out about the medicine. But Dr. Morrison put in a good word for me. And basically, well, Jerald is a friend. He said he wanted someone he could trust."

When he lowered her back onto the floor, she caressed his cheek. "I've been praying that you would find a job. You were driving Dottie and Nana absolutely crazy. Pacing like a caged tiger."

His deep laugh rumbled in his chest. "And the Double D's were driving me crazy with their endless chores."

She pulled away from him and finished preparing their coffee. "Did you hear if they were going to call us in to testify?"

"No. With Melbourne and Jonathan taking the plea deal, it will probably be enough against the others that they don't need us. Our sworn affidavits should be plenty." Scott accepted his coffee and waited while she sugared hers up. "Besides, does it matter? If they call, they call. If not, no worries."

Angela smiled and followed him back into the living room. "Rochelle called today. She said she and Tom found a place in Florence."

"It's going to be different not having her around. And Douglas."

"He only took that job in Florence to be around Rochelle."

Scott winked at her and settled into the easy chair. "Of course." He set his cup on the side table. "If I went to a different town, would you follow to be with me?"

Angela gave him a devilish grin, set her coffee mug beside his, and leaned down using the chair arms for support. "Maybe."

His brows rose. "Maybe?" He grabbed her and yanked her into his lap, his finger tickling her sides. "Maybe?"

She gasped and laughed at the same time. "Okay, okay. Yes. I would." His fingers stilled, and he held her in his lap. "What about you? Would you do the same for me?"

"No doubt." There was no hesitation in his voice. His eyes darkened as he cupped the back of her head. "To the ends of the Earth."

His lips claimed hers in a soft kiss. The fire in the fireplace crackled as a log fell. Outside, the wind howled around the porch. And Max's voice drew closer. Scott ended the kiss and touched his forehead to hers.

"You know I want to spend the rest of my life with you, yes?"

Angela smiled. His arms wrapped even tighter around her. "I do."

"So . . . how's April sound?"

"I like March better."

"Then, how does March sound?"

"It sounds perfect, Mr. Wilson."

His so-very-white teeth gleamed in the firelight. "Then March it is, soon-to-be Mrs. Wilson. And then you will officially move out of Dottie's and in here with me."

"What about Nana?"

"Well, I already talked to her. Told her I wanted to marry you. She gave me a lecture. Her blessing on top of another lecture. And then said she and Dottie knew I was going to ask you. So, they came up with the idea that Nana would live with Dottie. I told her she didn't have to."

"You haven't asked me yet, Scott Weath—"

"Uh, uh." He tweaked her nose. "No using the middle name." His eyes grew serious. "Please marry me?" A small smile played at the corners of his mouth. "If not, I might have to just kidnap you and live in sin."

She giggled. Just like the man to make light of a serious moment. "You are something else, Scott Wilson." She planted a small kiss on the corner of his mouth. "And yes. I will. I can't be the cause of you falling into sin now, can I?"

Max bounded into the room and ran to them. He piled into Angela's lap, driving her weight further into Scott, who groaned.

"Oh, Max! You are getting heavy."

Her son wrapped his skinny arms around them both and gave them a hug. "I love you."

She kissed his head. "We love you, too."

Scott reached a hand around her and ruffled the boy's hair. "How about standing in front of the tree and trying out your lines?"

Max hopped off the chair. He moved a few presents out of the way and then stood tall.

Angela rested her head against Scott's chest as they listened to Max recite from the Gospel of Luke. Never mind that he misquoted a few things. It really didn't matter. With the red lights from the Christmas tree highlighting his robe, Max really was an angel of the Lord.

She peered up into Scott's face. A deep love shone in his eyes as he listened. No more ghosts lived there. No more sadness. No more pain.

An inner light shone from his face and eyes as he praised Max for a job well done.

She smiled. God surely had a way of healing a heart. Sometimes, He had to break it in order to mend it. But He never let anyone down.

Scott turned his gaze to her. "What?"

"I was thinking, I am really looking forward to our new beginning."

"Me, too, my fearless reporter. Me, too."

AUTHOR'S NOTE

While Garrettville is a fictional town that I decided to situate near Florence and Sheffield (two lovely cities) in Northern Alabama, Dismals Canyon is a real place. I took a bit of artistic liberty with the portrayal of some of the landmarks and descriptions in the book about Dismals Canyon; but the beauty of the park is astounding, and its history is extensive.

You can find more about it at www.dismalscanyon.com.

ALSO IN DAPHNE SELF'S
SOUTHERN SAGA SERIES:

A SOUTHERN SAGA

MISSISSIPPI
N I G H T S

D. M. WEBB

PROLOGUE

The squad car radio blared its announcement and caused Sergeant Jeremy Boyette to dribble coffee down the front of his uniform. Nine o'clock at night with four more hours to his shift, Jeremy needed the extra caffeine kick to stay awake. He swiped at the wet spots and scowled.

The radio blared again, asking for J forty-three to contact dispatch. Jeremy reached over to turn it down. Same-o, same-o. A quiet May night. The flickering neon light from the movie theater's sign beat a tempo against the hood of his car. He had parked his Jasper City squad car by the building and decided to enjoy his rare Jack's Express coffee, taking a much deserved break. His only battle was the one he waged against the jumbo jet mosquitoes.

His phone belted out Journey's *Don't Stop Believin'*. "Yo, little brother."

"You sleeping in the squad car again?"

Jeremy grinned at his brother's teasing. "Naw, just taking a break. It's quiet tonight. Where are you?"

"Fire Station Three."

"Thought you were off tonight."

"I am. Figured I would play a hand with Sam and Toby before heading home. Oh, Rebecca wanted me to give you a message."

Jeremy leaned against the headrest. "And that would be?"

"She doesn't care if you are on duty or not. You cannot weasel your way out of a fitting." David's laughter boomed across the phone. "She said you better show up at Mike's for the final fitting tomorrow because she will not have an ill-fitted best man at her wedding. Her words."

"You told her I was working?"

"Yup. But she said, and I quote, 'I don't care. It only takes five minutes, and if he wants my cheesecake on Sunday, then he'd better show up tomorrow.' End quote."

Jeremy laughed. "Okay, I'll go. I'll go."

"I know you will. Sarah said she would drag you in there by your nonexistent hair."

"Hey, hey. Low blow." Jeremy removed his cap and ran his hand over the stubble. "I didn't mean to lose the bet."

"Yeah. I told Rebecca that I would probably need to shave my head so you wouldn't feel like a total fool."

"I bet she liked that."

A crash sounded in the background. "Hey, the boys got the table down from the attic. I'll call you later."

"Later." Jeremy closed his phone and slipped it back into the holster on his belt. "Yup. A quiet night."

Another announcement squawked. "All units, a report of a two-vehicle accident at intersection of Fifth and Terrence Drive. All units respond."

Jeremy cast the dregs of his coffee out the window and threw the empty cup to the floorboard. He grabbed his mike. "Dispatch, show four nine responding."

He hit his lights.

The blue strobes battled with the flickering neon sign as he pulled away from the sidewalk.

"Forty-nine, be advised there is entrapment. Fire and Rescue are responding."

"Copy that, dispatch."

Jeremy peeled around the corner and zoomed past the brightly lit strip malls. A couple of blasts from his siren edged vehicles out of the way. Up ahead, a thin line of smoke climbed into the air. Not good.

Jeremy raced down Terrence Drive. His tires squealed as he jammed the brakes. He jumped out of the car, leaving the engine running. Onlookers stood on the sidewalks and gazed in morbid fascination as he ran to the scene. A man sat doubled over on the opposite curb. Blood at his feet.

The twisted remains of a Chevy Silverado meshed into a silver Ford Taurus greeted him. Oh, no. Rebecca's car.

Jeremy hurried to the side of the car and peered in. Her head lolled against the headrest. Her hands still gripped the steering wheel. Blood flowed from a deep laceration to her forehead.

"Rebecca? Can you hear me?" Jeremy reached through the smashed window. He detected a faint and thready pulse through the sticky warmth of blood.

Damage assessment. The truck had wedged the steering column against her legs. He tried the door, but it was crushed in at all angles like an empty beer can.

He hit his mike. "Dispatch, one victim. Single, white female. Trauma to head and legs. ETA on Rescue?"

"ETA three minutes."

Jeremy leaned in as far as he could and gripped her hand. The edge of the door pressed against his mike. "Rebecca? Listen to me. You will be fine. Stay with me now. You have a wedding next week."

Dispatch came back. "All units mike check. Open mike on the channel."

Jeremy cursed under his breath. Maybe David wasn't listening to the radio chatter. He removed his mike from the vest and attached it at his collar. Then, he sniffed.

The ozone stench of an electrical burn wafted through the car. Panic beat at his chest. Rescue needed to hurry.

"Rebecca, you hang in there."

More squad cars arrived. Two officers leapt from a car and cordoned off the area. Two men from the other cars rushed to him. Jeremy released Rebecca's clammy hand.

"Markston, the other driver is over there on the curb. I want his statement. Baers, with me. We got to find a way to get her out."

They tugged at the passenger door. It refused to budge.

Jeremy crawled onto the hood. Heat emanated from under the buckled metal. He took the glass punch from Baers and attacked the windshield. It spider-webbed from the impact. He and Baers folded it away from the dashboard.

Head first, he climbed into the car. Sirens wailed in the distance.

"Rescue Two en route."

Jeremy wormed his way over the steering wheel, keeping his right hand on the dashboard for balance. Smoke burned his nose and eyes. Heat seared his hands.

Her eyes fluttered opened. Thick clouds billowed up from the dashboard and choked him.

Baers tugged at his uniform's vest. "Boyette, get off! Engine's on fire!"

Jeremy stretched further. His fingers fumbled at the belt's catch. "I almost got her."

"Get off!"

Rebecca's eyes, cloudy and vibrant blue, gazed into his, but then he slid away. Jeremy struggled as Baers dragged him off the hood.

Baers spoke into his mike as he pushed him away from the car. "Dispatch, we can't reach her!"

"All units, stand down and await Fire and Rescue." The calm voice contrasted against the chaos of the scene.

Orange flames licked out from underneath the hood. Oh, please, no! No! Rescue wouldn't arrive fast enough. Baers latched on to his vest and pulled him away from the car.

Jeremy grabbed his mike. "Dispatch, please advise! Victim is still trapped! Car is fully involved."

Seconds ticked by. "All units are commanded to stand down."

Jeremy cursed. Orders were orders, but not this time. He strained against Baers. "I have to get her, Thad!"

Baers' arm wrapped around his neck. "Stop, Boyette. You can't get to her! Chief ordered us to stand down."

Jeremy bucked against his friend. His vision reddened as Baers tightened his hold.

"Jeremy, you can't reach her, man! Stop."

The fire truck arrived. Firefighters vaulted to the pavement and pulled hoses. A smaller truck barreled onto the scene. A man heaved a large, heavy tool out of the truck's side panel. The jaws of life, made to rip apart doors.

A black '65 Mustang slid to a stop behind the fire trucks.

David didn't need to be here. Jeremy strained against Baers' hold. "David's here. Let me go!"

Baers released him, and he hurried to his brother's side.

David's terror-widened eyes absorbed the scene. He plowed past the officer at the yellow tape. "That's Rebecca."

Jeremy pressed his hands against his brother's chest. Veins popped up along his arms as he strained to hold him at bay. "They're getting her."

David pushed past him. His long legs ate up the pavement as he raced to the fire. "You left her there? You left her!"

"David! Stop!" Jeremy caught his arm and spun him around. "We were ordered to stand down until Rescue puts out the fire."

Wild, unbridled anger lanced from David's face, and his voice broke. "You left her?"

His hands slammed into Jeremy's chest. Jeremy stumbled, then righted himself and dove after his brother as David whirled around.

Jeremy grabbed a fistful of David's shirt. Fabric ripped out of his hands. "Baers! Stop him."

His mind catalogued every action like frames of a film. He tackled his brother around the waist, halting David's flight and bringing him to his knees. Firemen ducked back as orange flames shot into the night sky. He heard a strangled scream beside him.

The heat from the blast seared into him. The weight of the impact pushed at his chest. He fought and struggled to contain his brother's crazed flight.

David's arms and legs clawed and crawled across the pavement, dragging them both closer to the inferno. The fire's deafening roar filled his ears. Heat radiated against his face.

A fist pummeled into him.

Pain exploded inside his head.

Other hands came to his aid. Markston and Baers hauled David to the curb. His brother fell to his knees. Sobs racked his body. Jeremy staggered and knelt beside David. Pain from his brother's eyes bored into him. Tears streaked both of their faces.

In the distance, men shouted. Water sizzled as it fell down onto the burning car.

But nothing would ever erase the scream, erase the howl, that poured forth from his little brother's soul.

For more information about
Daphne Self
and
Alabama Days
please connect at:

www.authordaphneself.blogspot.com
www.facebook.com/authordaphneself

@AuthorDaphneS
www.instagram.com/authordaphneself
www.goodreads.com/authordaphneself
www.bookbub.com/authors/daphne-self

For more information about
AMBASSADOR INTERNATIONAL
please connect at:

www.ambassador-international.com
@AmbassadorIntl
www.facebook.com/AmbassadorIntl

*If you enjoyed this book, please consider leaving us a review on
Amazon, Goodreads, or our website.*

www.ingramcontent.com/pod-product-compliance
Lightning Source LLC
Chambersburg PA
CBHW071525260626
47170CB00002B/514